THE FALL OF SKULLKEEP

HISTORIES OF DRAKMOOR
BOOK 5

ROBERT M. KERNS

K F P

* * *

Published by Knightsfall Press
PO Box 280
Mineral Wells, WV 26150

ABOUT THIS BOOK

Skullkeep is an ancient fortress built to defend Hope's Pass. Now a bastion of a massive undead horde and controlled by a necromancer of terrible power.

A necromancer who has already defeated Gavin once.

Gavin must rally the old alliance and lead the largest military campaign since the Godswar, and the fate of Drakmoor hangs in the balance.

The Necromancer of Skullkeep versus Gavin Cross, Archmagister of Tel and Head of House Kirloth. Only one will emerge victorious.

Get your copy today!

To Judy Kerns:
You'll always be my first reader.

CHAPTER 1

Wind whipped across the terrace and billowed Gavin's robe. This high up, he couldn't smell anything on the wind as he leaned against the waist-high parapet and looked out over Tel Mivar. He didn't like how the Citadel floated so high above the countryside; it made him feel like he was supposed to believe he was far too good to live among the people he governed. The question of why the Citadel floated so high above Tel Mivar was a persistent thought that had poked him like a thorn since shortly after he'd returned from Vushaar.

Kirloth and his Apprentices created the Citadel during the Founding, the period of time when the world rebuilt in the aftermath of the Godswar. The man Gavin knew as Marcus—who had trained Gavin in the Art—was in fact *the* Kirloth of legend. He dueled Milthas for supremacy in Arundel, trained the God of Magic, and founded the Kingdom of Tel. Still, given everything he knew about Marcus, Gavin couldn't picture him thinking he was better than other people. A more proficient arcanist, certainly. Marcus's proficiency was almost a forgone conclusion, but he had never exhibited the kind of unthinking, ingrained arrogance that typified the 'better than you' mentality.

"Gavin?" Kiri's voice pulled his attention away from his musings, and he turned to face her.

She stood just outside the door to the balcony, wearing a simple dress in a deep sapphire trimmed with emerald green. The dress accentuated her form in a manner Gavin appreciated, and he wanted nothing more than to hold her close and never let her go. After considering that for another moment, he decided to put action to desire.

He smiled as he crossed the terrace and pulled her into his arms, kissing her deeply before saying, "I missed you. Are you here for the war council?"

"Yes. I brought Roth with me, too. Everyone else is waiting for you in the Conclave room."

Gavin released his wife with great reluctance. Married less than three months, Gavin felt he had far too many demands on his time keeping him from being the kind of husband he wanted to be. Especially now that he remembered Emily, his first wife and Jennifer's mother.

"We'd better go, then," he said, almost sighing the words, and allowed Kiri to lead him from the terrace.

Mere minutes saw them standing outside the room for Conclave meetings in the Citadel, and laying his hand on the doorknob, Gavin took a deep breath and exhaled before opening the doors and entering.

The moment he crossed the doorway's threshold, everyone in the room stood. Not only was the Archmagister of Tel—the last of the Divine Emissaries—entering the room, but the Crown Princess of Vushaar also walked at his side. Gavin escorted Kiri to her seat, assisting her with the chair out of respect and love, before making his way to his seat at the opposite end of the table.

"Please, be seated," Gavin said as he did so, himself. "I want to thank you for coming to this first meeting of the war council. As you all know, I believe the time has come to remove the threat to our peoples posed by the Necromancer and his various plots. This will not be easy, in any sense of the word, but the most worthwhile goals rarely are."

Gavin paused for a breath and met each person's eyes with his own. Down the right side of the table from his perspective sat the Conclave of the Great Houses and their heirs: Torval Mivar, Lillian, Sypara Wygoth, Braden, Carth Roshan, Wynn, Lyssa Cothos, and Mariana. Down the left side of the table sat the foreign representatives: Telanna of the High Forest, member of Sylvan Synod and also Ambassador to Vushaar as needed; Xythe, his former apprentice and now Ambassador to Tel from the dracons; King Gildar of Stonehearth and Hakamri, Gildar's Ambassador to Tel; the former Chieftain of the Giants, now Ambassador to Tel; Othron; Ovir Thatcherson, representing the clergy of Valthon; and Roth Thatcherson, Vushaari Cavalier. Declan sat in a chair off to one side; a sheaf of parchment, a pot of ink, and a stylus or two on the small desk before him proclaimed his readiness to record his notes and thoughts on this piece of history as it unfolded before him.

"The primary issue as I see it," Gildar said, "is our lack of current and reliable information. How are we supposed to plan for an assault, when all of our documentation of the fortress is centuries old?"

Gavin nodded his agreement. "You raise an excellent point. To that end, I will dispatch several intelligence operations against Skullkeep after this meeting. I hope that we will receive actionable information well before we mobilize to move against the Necromancer."

"Is that so?" Gildar asked. "And just what operations might these be?"

Gavin's lips curled in a friendly partial smile. "I'm afraid I can't speak as to the nature of the operations or the operators, but trust that they have never failed me. Not even when my life or the life of someone I care about has depended upon them."

Gildar held Gavin's gaze with his own for several moments before he gave a firm nod. "Aye, and fair enough. I probably owe ye an apology while I'm at it; there's some who'd say asking about yer spies and such is very bad form."

Now, Gavin did smile and added a dismissive wave. "Don't worry about it. I'm new, both in this role and in your experience. A certain amount of skepticism that I can deliver is healthy."

"Yer very generous for sayin' so, but if Bellos trusts ye to be the Archmagister, that should be good enough for me or anyone else."

The meeting continued for a couple hours, wherein everyone discussed mobilization and precise timeframes for actions. Once the entire agenda for that meeting had been discussed, including scheduling the next meeting and specific milestones for their preparations to assault Skullkeep, it was time to close things down. Gavin thanked everyone once again for coming. The Conclave saw to their own transport, and their heirs provided gateways for those who could not teleport themselves. Soon, only two guests remained: Othron and Torval Mivar.

"I take it you both have matters you wish to discuss with me?" Gavin asked.

"Yes," Torval replied.

Othron nodded, his voice accented by the eerie clacking of teeth. "If you have time."

Gavin looked between the two, asking, "Who wants to go first? Or is either matter time-sensitive?"

"I'm happy to wait for Othron to have his say," Torval replied. "Is there somewhere I can wait?"

"Hartley!" Gavin called out.

The spectral majordomo of the Citadel formed mere inches off Torval's shoulder, saying, "You called, Milord?"

Torval jumped. Gavin exerted considerable willpower to keep from laughing.

"Yes, Hartley. Would you please conduct Torval to the sitting room and offer him refreshments? He wants to wait for me to discuss something with Othron."

The specter nodded once. "Of course, Milord. Sir, if you would please follow me?"

Without waiting for a reply, Hartley pivoted and 'walked' straight through the room's closed door. Torval opened the door to follow and closed it behind him.

Now that they were alone, Gavin pointed to one of the chairs along the table and pulled another out for his own use. He didn't sit so much as flopped and leaned back against the chair. "So, what's on your mind, Othron?"

"I..." At another gesture from Gavin, Othron pulled the seat back from the table and sat. "I have a confession to make. The Necromancer of Skullkeep is my fault. From the proper point of view, you might even say he is my grandson."

Gavin blinked. "Come again? How can the Necromancer be your grandson? Not to put too fine a point on it, but you're rather desiccated. Is he from before you developed the path to lichdom?"

It felt like Othron would've winced if he still possessed muscles and living flesh. "Not as such, no. There was a time in the early days of my new existence that I fell into despair at the depth of the loneliness I faced. Your mentor did what he could, but you have no concept of what it's like to watch your comrades—those people you fought with and sacrificed with and risked it all for—grow old and die. In what seemed like the blink of an eye, I was all alone. So, I sought out apprentices. I felt that, if I helped others advance in their understanding of the Art, I might develop new friendships and connections. To an extent, I did, but these too passed on with time. I considered offering the secrets of lichdom to my most promising students, and in the end, I decided there might be one with the understanding and mastery necessary to survive the process. You may have heard of Emperor Xartham, who rules the arid plains east of Vushaar in the southern foothills of the Godswall Mountains?"

Gavin fought the urge to gape. "Emperor Xartham is a lich?"

"Oh, yes, and a very accomplished arcanist as well. I would not rate him at your level in terms of sheer power, but he's been around long enough to have learned and mastered quite a bit. It was Xartham, you see, who was a bit less... selective, you might say... than I was. I lost count of the number of his so-called 'students' who sacrificed their lives in pursuit of lichdom. I even heard rumors suggesting he modified the ritual somehow to drain their power and life to strengthen his. I have no proof of that, mind you, but I did hear it from more than one source. In the end, only one of Xartham's students ever succeeded at becoming a lich, and that student is the creature now in control of Skullkeep."

"Yes, I see," Gavin remarked, a partial chuckle escaping his lips. "The Necromancer would indeed be your grandson, from the proper point of view. Do you know any more about him?"

"I do. He was a young and hungry arcanist, always seeking more power and knowledge. In truth, he approached me for tutelage, prior to approaching Xartham, but there was an almost feral aspect to the man I didn't like. He came across as too hungry for power, too intent on advancing his mastery. His name is Drannos Muldannin."

Gavin felt his jaw drop but couldn't stop it. For several heartbeats, all he could do was gape at Othron, and when he could respond, only one word escaped his shock. "Bullshit!"

"I assure you it is not. The third lich—Xartham's successful student—is Drannos Muldannin."

"You mean to tell me that the Magister of Thaumaturgy is the Necromancer of Skullkeep?"

Othron lifted his hands in a gesture of uncertainty. "I cannot say that for certain as I have never met your Magister of Thaumaturgy, but I am very certain that the Necromancer of Skullkeep bore the name Drannos Muldannin during his mortal years."

"Hartley!"

The specter re-entered the room by walking through the door. "You bellowed, Milord?"

"Send word to the Grand Inquisitor at once. I want a full report of the whereabouts and associations of the Magister of Thaumaturgy, and I want it last week. This is the utmost priority for her as of this moment. All other ongoing operations pale in comparison to the importance of this task. Understood?"

"Yes, Milord. I shall inform Grand Inquisitor Reyna myself."

"Thank you, Hartley." The spectral majordomo faded back through the door, and Gavin regarded Othron.

At last, Othron broke the silence. "I understand if you feel this constitutes a conflict of interest for me. I assure you it does not, but—"

Gavin waved away that topic. "No. Don't even go there, but I totally understand why you wanted to speak to me in private. Not everyone has the same history with you that I do, so it would be almost unavoidable to question your motives. Knowing this, are there any secret weaknesses you would trust me and the Wraiths with?"

"The Wraiths?" Now, Othron sounded shocked. "What does my old friend's irregular military unit from the Godswar have to do with this?"

"He never disbanded them."

"Oh. Oh, my. You are far more formidable than meets the eye. Very well. Yes, there is one crucial weakness to creatures of my kind... the soul jar. We all have one, and we tend to be very protective of it. If the soul jar is destroyed, we are trapped in our current forms until we can craft a new one, which is a painstaking, laborious process in itself. The only way to ensure that a lich is truly dead, never to re-form, is to destroy the soul jar first and then the lich."

Gavin nodded. "Thank you. That's very good to know, and I promise I will only speak of it to the Wraith I send to infiltrate Skullkeep."

"I appreciate that. I don't feel like I am in any danger, but that information leaking into the world would be worrisome."

"So," Gavin began, as he leaned back against his seat once more, "is there anything else, or was that little bomb you dropped on me the extent of your topics?"

"I think we've kept Torval waiting long enough," Othron answered, "and I'm grateful you'd take the time to hear me out."

Gavin stood, prompting Othron to follow suit. "You're welcome, my friend. If you ever need my help, you need only ask."

"Of course, and I appreciate it." Othron stepped back and formed a gateway by invoking a Word of Transmutation. The moment the gateway was complete, he stepped through it and was gone.

Now alone, Gavin sagged back into the chair and contemplated this new information. It was little surprise the Necromancer had always been one step ahead of the Council, if it were true; with that kind of advantage, only an utter idiot would fail.

"Yeah," Gavin muttered to himself, "I'm gonna need a minute to process this before I see what Torval wanted."

* * *

GAVIN FOUND Torval waiting for him in the sitting room that he had used so often prior to his sojourn to Earth. Lillian's grandfather stood when he entered, but Gavin was quick to wave him back to his seat.

"I'm sorry to keep you waiting so long," Gavin said, as he himself eased into a seat. "To be honest, Othron dropped a bomb or two on me, and I had to take a moment to process it. I wasn't expecting that conversation... *at all*. But I digress. What did you want to discuss?"

Torval gave Gavin the indulgent smile that Gavin remembered his own grandparents giving him, years back. He settled himself in the chair and interlaced his fingers in front of him. "During the year you and Kiri were gone, the Conclave went through some changes, and I wanted you to be aware of them. The most significant of these is that the heirs are now heirs pretty much only in name. We weren't too long into your disappearance when Lillian stepped up and took over liaising with Nathrac on matters of governance and policy, working to answer the question of what you would've wanted done. As months unfolded, she drew the others deeper into administrative roles of one kind or another to the point that we—that is, the traditional Conclave —stepped back, considered the new situation, and made the decision that the heirs should step into the foreground officially and transition into the leadership roles that have always been theirs. Lyssa, Sypara, Carth, and I now serve as just advisors and a kind of living history... answering questions about why certain decisions were made or why actions were taken."

Gavin nodded. "I see. I'm rather glad to hear that. Not that you've stepped back as such; I see no reason that any of you should step back until it is *your* choice to do so. No... what I mean is that I'm glad Lillian and the others stepped up. I'll make sure to speak with them

—both collectively and individually—to thank them for all the work they've done."

"I appreciate that," Torval replied. "They certainly worked themselves hard to keep the wheels on the wagon. The day you both returned, we discussed the very real fear that Tel would soon face some level of significant unrest... which your return has ended. As far as I know, we never tracked the simmering unrest to any specific actors, but if there were, they quickly vanished back into the woodwork."

"Amazing how fast that happens when Kirloth is close by," Gavin remarked in a dry, sardonic tone as he tapped his medallion to indicate his House's glyph.

Torval laughed. "No doubt."

Silence descended on the sitting room for several moments. Then, Torval said, "I don't know that Lillian will say anything, but we are all relieved and happy that you came back. That year you were gone aged all of us who care about Tel and our responsibilities."

Gavin nodded his understanding. "I appreciate that. There was never a question of wanting to return. The difficulty was figuring out how to achieve cross-planar scrying and teleportation. That... well... it was an adventure."

"You'll have to tell us all about it sometime," Torval replied as he pushed himself to stand.

"Declan has already badgered me for the story." Gavin joined Torval in standing and walked with him as he moved to leave. "We've discussed some of it, and we dig into a little bit more each week as I have time. He promised me to get an accurate idea of the story before writing any of it."

Now, it was Torval's turn to express his understanding with a nod. "I shall keep a look-out for it. Thank you for taking the time to speak with me, Gavin. I'm sure you have all sorts of concerns vying for your time and attention."

Gavin clapped Torval on the shoulder and gave the man his warmest, most welcoming smile. "Think nothing of it, Torval. You are always welcome to discuss anything you need with me."

Hartley faded into existence as Torval opened the sitting room's door. "Ah, Master Mivar... shall I escort you to the portal?"

"Thank you, Hartley."

Gavin watched the man and specter move down the hallway before slipping back into the sitting room. The conversation with Torval gave him several ideas, and he chuckled at how history would once again repeat itself if he had his way.

But first... Skullkeep. It was long past time to end the Necromancer's influence in the world.

CHAPTER 2

When Gavin emerged from his thoughts and sought Declan, the bard was already somewhere else. Fortunately, Gavin knew just where to look. A simple matter of a Word of Transmutation opened a gateway to the first room of the chapterhouse for the Wraiths in Tel Mivar, and Gavin retraced the path he had followed with Declan what seemed so long ago now... but wasn't more than three years at the most.

Fifty or more Wraiths shot to their feet as Gavin entered the underground common room, and Gavin smiled at seeing Declan leaning against the large table, an ale cup in one hand.

"Stand easy, everyone," Gavin said, adding a dismissive gesture as he crossed to the person of his search. "You disappeared from the Citadel rather fast."

Declan shrugged. "No one told me to stay, and besides, I had important business here."

"I see that," Gavin replied, adding a meaningful look at the ale cup.

"Shush," Declan shot back and waved the ale cup. "This wasn't my important business. Making sure *she* was waiting for you was."

Gavin looked in the direction of Declan's exaggerated head nod and saw a young woman wending her way through the crowd. His mind immediately told him she was familiar but went no further than that. He watched her approach as his mind parsed everything, and recognition bloomed.

"Hello, Cyn," Gavin said. "How have you been since Vushaar?"

The young woman beamed at Gavin remembering her, and a slow blush crept up her cheeks. "I've been well, Milord. I am a full-time Wraith now; my mentor, Master Declan, signed off on my advancement while you were away."

"Well, in that case... belated congratulations," Gavin replied. "Have you learned what the reward for work well done is?"

Cyn blinked. "Uhm... I'm not sure, Milord."

Gavin grinned. "More work, of course. You're to infiltrate Skullkeep and serve as our stealth asset inside the fortress prior to our assault. Your primary mission is to locate the Necromancer's soul jar, and that will be the most difficult assignment you've had thus far. Your little jaunt to capture Ivarson in Vushaar will seem like a picnic compared to this one. I have it on very good authority that liches hide and guard their soul jars more than a miser guards his coins. We'll send you with all the information on the fortress we can, but even the most recent information is something like six hundred-odd years old."

Cyn's eyes slowly widened as she processed the enormity of the task. "That... that's a lot of responsibility, Milord. Are you certain I'm best suited for it?"

"Declan thinks you are," Gavin replied, "and I trust him. I personally think this is a good move for you, but if you honestly and genuinely would prefer the close protection job for my daughter, I'm sure we can arrange that."

Silence descended on the trio. It was apparent that Cyn weighed the career choice facing her, and after a few moments, she lifted her head to meet Gavin's eyes once more and squared her shoulders.

"No, Milord, I will infiltrate Skullkeep," she answered. "Thank you for this opportunity and believing in me."

Gavin smiled, replying, "You're welcome, Cyn, and you've earned it. Prepare for your journey. Declan and I need to handle the matter of a Wraith for my daughter, and after that, he will bring you all the documentation we have for you to study."

Cyn nodded once, then pivoted on her heel and disappeared back into the crowd.

Declan finished off his ale and placed the mug on the table behind him, nodding toward the door. Gavin followed him out of the chapterhouse's common room, and they went back toward the stairs before turning into what looked like a combination bedroom and office, closing the door behind them. Declan sat on the bed, gesturing for Gavin to take the desk's chair.

"Cyn has a lot of potential, and I have no problems entrusting the Skullkeep mission to her," Declan began. "That being said, though, we would be utter fools to rely on only one person. We have four others selected and have gone some length to ensure none of the five know each other or will even recognize one another. There is always the chance that one or more will trip over the others, but given the sheer size of Skullkeep and the force the Necromancer is assembling, the leadership feels that five is a good number. Now, let's discuss the Wraith you want for your daughter."

"Okay, but I'm not all that certain what else there is to discuss. I'd prefer that whoever it is doesn't have family here in Drakmoor, but otherwise, everything is just as I outlined it in the common room."

Declan nodded his understanding. "None of the Wraiths have family. Well, not like spouses or children or anything like that. If one decides that is important, they transition to inactive reserve, and we set them up in the industry of their choice. You'd be surprised how many inns, general stores, or blacksmith shops have a 'former' Wraith as the owner."

"So, the Wraiths have a far wider reach than I originally thought. That's impressive." Gavin fell silent for a moment before he stood. "Anything else you need from me?"

"No, thank the gods. Get back to running the kingdom."

* * *

GAVIN DIDN'T SEE HIS PARENTS' vehicle when he stepped through the portal that connected the Kirloth Estate—formerly the Sivas Estate—to the front yard of his childhood home with Declan at his side. He did, however, see a blacked-out SUV with US Government plates sitting in the expanded parking area, which elicited a confused frown. Why hadn't Alexis just used a gateway?

Filing that question away for later, Gavin gestured toward the portal that would take them to the tower he'd raised deeper in the family land and headed off at a comfortable walk. He felt the tingling across his skin that signified passing through his ward on the property and saw two people in suits and sunglasses standing at the door to the keep. Their heads immediately swiveled toward Gavin and his associate, and Gavin noticed a couple people standing over by the fence that separated the training area he'd created for Kiri.

"State your name and business," one of the suits said as she lifted her hand in the classic 'stop' gesture.

Something about the woman's demeanor tickled Gavin's hackles, and he responded. "My name is Gavin Cross, and my business—especially on my family's ancestral land—is my own. It would be wise if you identified yourselves forthwith."

At the mention of his name, Gavin saw the two agents pale just a little bit, and the suit who had yet to speak actually twitched his hand toward a sidearm under his jacket.

Gavin made direct eye contact with the man, moving only his eyes. "If you are stupid enough to draw a weapon, you will spend the next month collecting a coating of bird shit as a living statue in the flower garden of Graham's roundabout."

"Baker... Hernandez... stand down," a woman said, and Gavin turned his head to see Gayle approaching from Kiri's exercise area. "He's cleared... and he wasn't joking about the bird shit. I know you've seen pictures of the FBI SWAT team."

"Hello, Gayle," Gavin said.

"I thought you went back to wherever it was."

Gavin gave the woman a smile that edged toward mirthless. "That's the wonderful thing about family, Gayle. They *want* you to visit. I'm guessing Alexis is visiting Jennifer?"

Gayle nodded. "We couldn't get away with the basic travel party this time. There have been some nut-jobs sending death threats that are a little more credible than the usual nonsense, so we're traveling with a full detail."

"That makes sense, but why did you drive all the way from D.C.? Alexis could've just opened a portal."

Gayle grimaced. "Yeah, I wish. They're refusing to update the travel protocols to include 'unverified phenomena' and insist that any trips away from protected sites use official, vetted transportation."

"Seriously?"

Gayle simply nodded.

Gavin snorted and shook his head. "Idiots. She's *safer* using a gateway."

"So, who's the guy at your shoulder?" Gayle asked.

"This gentleman is Declan deHavand, the guy who trained Kiri."

"He did?" Gayle's expression went blank. "He's the one Kiri described as Death walking when he needs to be?"

Declan snorted a laugh behind him, and Gavin nodded. "I have it on excellent authority that Declan is one of the most proficient we have... in addition to his other talents."

Gayle eyed Declan over Gavin's shoulder with a speculative expression. "I don't suppose I could convince you to have an exhibition bout while you're here, could I? Kiri said that what she knew wasn't hers to teach."

"I don't think it's wise... no," Declan replied. "I'm not certain it would be safe for whoever you would have me fight."

"Oh?" Gayle asked. "Why is that?"

"Well, not knowing what training you've had or its focus, there's an excellent chance of accidental death. It's one thing to have a sparring match with someone who has my background, but some random person is an altogether different prospect. I could slip into an evolution of strikes I'm used to my sparring partner easily countering and accidentally deliver grievous bodily harm, simply because your person doesn't know the counter to my moves."

Gayle eyed Declan in silence before her gaze washed over the ladies with him and Kiri before returning to him. "I would think a true master would be able to pull punches and whatnot. I know we do in our sparring."

Declan chuckled. "Even pulling a kill strike to make it non-lethal has the potential to break bones, so no. I will not spar with any of your people."

The woman who told Gavin to halt approached Gayle's elbow. "We'll need to do a full background and vet him."

Now, Gayle snorted a laugh. "Good luck. He's not from Earth, so you won't find him in any DMV database, and no, we have no authority to vet him. We're not technically on United States soil right now."

It was good she remembered that. Gavin didn't relish the thought of re-educating the federal government; he didn't have that kind of time.

"Now that we've established who's who and what's what," Gavin said, "we'll be going to see my daughter."

The woman eyed Gavin with a quasi-glare. "And if we say no, because you present a threat to our charge?"

"You have no authority to say yay or nay to anything as long as you stand on this property, and beyond that, I'm sure you'd look absolutely lovely wearing a month's worth of accumulated bird shit. Or... I suppose there's always Graham Lake. Do you swim, Agent?"

The thought of suddenly finding herself floating in Graham Lake did more to terrify the woman than the thought of bird shit in her hair, because she paled just enough for Gavin to notice and stepped aside. Gavin nodded once and strode toward the keep, where the other agent displayed excellent wisdom by choosing not to impede him.

* * *

GAVIN RETURNED to the Citadel at the end of what felt like a very long day. He chose to visit the library, desiring to read some of Marcus's journals as he wound down from his day, and found Lillian sitting in one of the chairs with a weighty tome resting on her thighs.

"Finally made it back, did you?" Lillian asked as she saw Gavin enter.

"Yeah. Say... I've been meaning to ask you something. Have you ever given any thought to being the Archmagister?"

Lillian gaped. "But... wouldn't that mean you'd be dead? I mean, the only way to become Archmagister is for the previous one to die, right?"

"Well, that's not the *only* way," Gavin replied. "There is historical precedent."

Lillian frowned as she searched her mind, and her eyes shot back to Gavin when she connected the dots. "You're thinking about stepping down? Like Marcus did? Well, he didn't really step down, more like faked his death, but still..."

Gavin sat in a plush armchair across from Lillian. "As long as I am Archmagister, I am constrained to this role, but being the Archmagister is not my only role. I am also Kirloth, and it is very difficult to be the specter in the shadows when I'm walking around in a gold robe. Beyond that, from what I've heard, I think you'd make an excellent Archmagister, and it's been a while since Mivar has had the honor."

"But what about Bellos? He always chooses the Archmagister."

"Lillian," Gavin began, almost sighing her name, "I am very grateful to be alive, but I wasn't consulted on *any* of this. Valthon—or Valthon and Bellos—plucked me out of the afterlife and dropped me in an alley in Tel Mivar for the sole reason that I am a wizard of House Kirloth, and then, Bellos went and named me Archmagister. Yes, I agreed, and yes, I feel it was the proper decision at the time. I honestly don't regret agreeing. But I cannot be effective as Kirloth as long as I am the Archmagister. As soon as we've ended the threat posed by the Necromancer, I plan to discuss the matter with Bellos. If you like the idea of being Archmagister, I'll toss your name in the ring while we're talking."

"I... I don't know. Can I think about it? I mean... it's a lot to drop on someone."

"Yeah, it is," Gavin agreed, adding a confirmatory nod. "Trust me; I know."

CHAPTER 3

Gavin entered the sitting room that he used for most of his informal meetings. Hakamri and Braden each occupied chairs sized to fit them, and he resisted the urge to smile at Hartley's thoughtfulness. Both of his guests moved to stand as he entered, and Gavin quickly waved that off. He didn't care for the pointless protocols that surrounded so many offices of state—whether here or back on Earth—and did his best to see that no one followed them too often.

He crossed the room in a few strides and sat in the open chair. It enfolded him as he surrendered his weight to it, taking a moment of relaxing peace. A whimsical part of him wished he could spend more time just enjoying the simple comforts of a well-crafted armchair, but he knew he had far too much to do and far too little time for it all.

"Thank you both for coming to meet with me," Gavin said as he focused on the meeting. "I have an idea for the coming mobilization that I think will appeal to both of you."

He let his words hang in the air for a moment, gauging his audience. Both of his guests displayed signs of eagerness—Braden more than Hakamri, for he had experience with Gavin's 'ideas.'

"I want to establish a weapons facility that will equip our troops with imbued gear. I want the equipment to be the most finely crafted in the known world, so I thought we'd start with dwarven crafters first before expanding as needed. Braden, we will be essentially creating artifacts en masse. The underlying effects won't be much of an issue, but I want to bind each set of equipment to the individual... and that means we'll need a sample of their blood at the time of outfitting. We'll need wizards in the facility, imbuing the items while they're made, but as long as we design the effect well, we can use mages to handle the blood drop when they're issued."

"What are you thinking for imbued effects?" Braden asked. "I can see several possibilities, but I'm curious where your mind is."

Gavin chuckled. "For the armor at least, my mind is on the camp wards from our first trip to Vushaar. I want increased protection against normal weapons, magical weapons, elemental effects, and undead. I want the equipment to adjust its size to create an optimal fit for whoever binds it."

"Lad," Hakrami said, "yer not talkin' artifacts. What yer discussin' is at least a level *above* what the world at large calls artifacts. There are whole racks of weapons and armor in the royal vaults back home that qualify as artifacts but only have one imbued effect, and those often are rather weak."

"So, you're saying we can't do it?" Gavin asked.

Hakamri chuckled and shook his head. "If we get to the buildin' stage, I can promise you a whole host of dwarven masters who will sign on, but where will the funding come from? Who will be paying for all this?"

A sly smile curled Gavin's lips. "I thought it would be an equal partnership between the dwarves, House Kirloth, and House Wygoth. The dwarves contribute crafters. House Wygoth contributes management and time, and House Kirloth will contribute funds. Once we have a few pieces to act as proofs of concept, I want to present them to the war council. We will outfit their troops, regardless, but if they wish to help with the development costs, we will happily accept their coin."

Hakamri leaned back in his chair, stroking his beard beneath a thoughtful expression.

Gavin turned to Braden. "You've been rather silent through all this. What are your thoughts?"

"I... well... I don't know," Braden rumbled. "It's an ambitious idea; I'll give you that. Do you have enough coin to cover the expenses? Paying the crafters... buying the materials... paying the wizards who'll imbue the effects... all of that will add up *fast*."

Gavin smiled; he couldn't resist it. "Braden, one of the many things I learned while we were in Vushaar was that House Kirloth— specifically, the man you knew as Marcus—was a founding sponsor of the Bank of Vushaar. Since coming back, I have had a few conversations with the Bank of Tel, also. Between those two accounts... well... suffice it to say that I won't run out of coin in my lifetime, and Jennifer has no reason to worry, either."

"Even with this idea? What if none of the other governments chip in to defray the costs?"

"I'll be okay," Gavin replied.

"What if House Mivar, Roshan, or Cothos want to get involved?" Braden asked.

Gavin pursed his lips, nodding. "That's an excellent point, Braden. I had not considered that. My mind went straight to you because of your interest in artifacts. How about this, then? Leave the dwarves with a third interest, and we'll split the remainder between whatever Houses want to throw in with us?"

"That's not a good deal for us," Hakamri said. "Sure... we'd be in for more coin, but more coin is not always the best. What happens if we go commercial after the fight with Skullkeep? I'll not have any situation that could lead to resentment between members of this enterprise. If each partner shoulders a fair share of the load, each partner will have an equal share."

"And let's face it, Gavin," Braden remarked. "You're more valuable to us than the coin you'll contribute. Yes, I can create permanent portals now, and yes, I understand *most* of what you've shared with us. But there is no doubt in my mind that you'll be central to developing the composite effect we will imbue in the equipment."

Gavin sighed. "I don't like being the indispensable man, Braden. I don't want this effort jeopardized if something happens to me or if I need to go back to Earth for a period of time."

"I completely understand your feelings, Gavin, but at the same time, *no one* understands or wields the Art like you do. Even *Othron* says you're a class unto yourself."

Gavin blinked. "Othron says that?"

Braden nodded. "Maybe it's something Marcus taught you without either of you realizing it, or maybe it has something to do with Earth being so saturated in raw power ever since Nesta forged the link between there and here. Regardless, you casually toss off workings of the Art that no one else alive today would even consider attempting. Like it or not, Gavin, you *are* the Kirloth of this age. I'm surprised more people aren't begging you to train them."

"Hmmm... I suppose there's always the chance that the gold robe intimidates them, and let's be honest. I don't really have time right now for any apprentices. I haven't since I agreed to this. Maybe once we've reclaimed Skullkeep and I step down, I might—"

"And you *what*...?" Braden gasped.

Hakamri's expression suggested a similar surprise, though he kept his silence.

Gavin chuckled. "Oh... yes. I haven't noised that about too much, so I'd appreciate you keeping it to yourself... well... yourselves. I imagine you'll tell King Gildar, Hakamri, but if you do, I ask that the both of you treat it as a state secret. I do not want word of this getting out until I myself announce it. I already have Bellos's agreement that I may step down from the position of Archmagister once we've settled the Skullkeep campaign. I've also told Him who I think should succeed me, but of course, that part is up to Him." Gavin chuckled and shook his head. "It's very difficult to think of Bellos as a god. When we're talking, He seems like nothing more than a fellow wizard, and the last time we spoke, he mentioned that He and I are brothers in a way. The very exclusive fraternity of arcanists trained by the man we knew as Marcus. As far as I know, he only had seven apprentices."

Hakamri shook his head. "I won't lie, lad. The fact the man who dueled Milthas trained ye in your Art is damned intimidating to those of us who know. Unlike you poor humans, we dwarves have— at best—half as many generations between us and the Godswar as ye do. And as such, it's a lot fresher in our minds. Kirloth—the man ye knew as Marcus—was a terrifying individual when he had his dander up, and he's the one who taught ye."

Braden grinned, then said, "Hakamri, you obviously haven't seen Gavin when he has... his dander up, as you put it."

The old dwarf merchant turned to Braden and squinted one eye. "Lad, I don't need to see him when he has his dander up. He fought the Necromancer of Skullkeep in the northeast plaza, and it was plain as the sun in the sky he was already half dead when that started, and he *still* damn-near beat the old bag of bones."

The longer that particular topic ran on, the more uncomfortable Gavin felt. He didn't... enjoy... being the center of attention, despite the number of times he'd had no other choice. And he wasn't all that fond of people he respected being afraid of him or intimidated by him. At this point, though, he wasn't sure what to do about it.

"Right, then," he said, entering the lull that had developed in the wake of Hakamri's response. "I think the best thing to do is speak to the other Great Houses and see if they want to be involved with this. Let's plan for another meeting... say... next week? That will give us time to sound out the other Houses and also for you, Hakamri, to start gathering crafters."

The dwarf nodded. "Aye, sounds good to me."

"Braden, I'll leave you the matter of arranging the meeting of your associates and elders. Let me know when everyone is ready to proceed."

"Consider it done, Gavin," Braden replied.

At that, both Braden and Hakamri stood, and Gavin followed suit, walking them out to the portal that would deliver them to the top of the Grand Stair.

As soon as he saw them off, he turned and went straight to his laboratory. His first thought—ritualizing a composite effect—did not seem viable. And, no... it wasn't because he didn't think he could do it. He'd already accomplished something Marcus never had—cross-planar portals—so he felt it was only a matter of time before he could follow in his mentor's footsteps in this task, as well. The reason he didn't like ritualizing a composite effect was that a ritual was something anyone with the proper training could do, and he didn't want the process to get out of the control of people he personally trusted. So, a ritual was right out.

But that meant wizards would be necessary to imbue the equipment. He *thought* he could arrange it so that only a mage was required for the final binding, but there was no way around the fact that the foundry... Gavin stopped his notes and leaned back in his seat.

"Huh. The Foundry. I kinda like the sound of that."

He swiveled his seat and grabbed a fresh piece of parchment, placing it off to the side of his main stack of notes. He scrawled a 'greater than' sign at the top and, next to it, wrote, 'Name the facility The Foundry.'

Then, he went back to brainstorming his thoughts on the *how* of creating the imbued equipment. He re-read the last few lines of his notes and nodded in satisfaction when the train of thought came back to him. Yes, the Foundry would have to employ wizards. There was no other option. The question, though, was how many.

Gavin leaned back in his seat once more and folded one arm across his torso, resting the other elbow on his wrist while he tapped his lips. No... the only way to work through it was to devise the composite effect first, then work on reducing it to manageable pieces *or* finding a way to make the power required manageable. After all, there weren't too many wizards wandering around who could go toe-to-toe with Gavin or any of his immediate friends. They were called the Great Houses of Tel for a reason...

* * *

THE NEXT DAY, Braden brought his friends and their elders to meet with Gavin. He hadn't told them the topic for discussion, just that he and Gavin had an idea that they might want to be a part of. In fact, he grinned like the cat who ate a canary as he led everyone into the meeting room in the Citadel, and Gavin felt the urge to sigh and shake his head.

Ah, well... everyone needed a little fun from time to time.

Everyone chose their seats, not even coming close to filling up the large table. Once everyone was comfortable, Sypara gave Gavin a slight glare. "All right. What's this idea my boy wouldn't discuss?"

"I went to him and Hakamri about creating a facility to craft imbued equipment for our troops," Gavin explained.

The number of gasps around the room might have created a small breeze.

"I went to them, because I expected the dwarves would be the best crafters to start with, and Braden has been interested in artifacts as long as I've known him, and make no mistake, these items will be artifacts under the classic definition."

Braden shook his head. "No, Gavin. Hakamri already discussed that. They'll be so far beyond artifacts that we don't have a name for them."

Every person turned from Braden to Gavin. Torval said, "Just what are you thinking of creating, Gavin?"

"Bladed weapons would have a keener edge, be more durable, and deliver extra damage to undead. Blunt weapons the same, except for the edge, but they'd hit harder. Armor... well... increased protection against normal and magical weapons, elemental effects, and undead. When I came up with the idea, my mind went to the camp wards we set up on our journey south to Vushaar."

Everyone who had direct experience with the camp wards gaped. Lillian said, "Gavin, if you manage to put all of that in a suit of armor or a shield, people would *kill* for that item four thousand years from now."

Now, Gavin grinned. "No, they won't. We will be binding the items to the person they're issued to, and if that person breaks his or her oath, the equipment will crumble. I'm not about to allow items of this much power out in the wild. Not at all."

Torval, Sypara, Carth, and Lyssa visibly relaxed at that.

Gavin met their eyes in turn and not quite smirked. "I may be reckless from time to time, but I'm not stupid."

"No one who has ever met you would think you're stupid," Lyssa remarked, "not even for an instant."

"Don't say that," Gavin replied. "You haven't met Jennifer's mother."

More than one person fought a snort or snicker.

"So," Gavin continued, "the main point of the gathering is to ask if any of you want to help get the Foundry off the ground and make it a going concern. Anyone who contributes an equal part of the load—in whatever capacity—will have an equal share of the enterprise."

Carth asked, "What would you expect from us?"

Gavin shrugged. "That all depends on how you're willing to help. I imagine Lillian, Wynn, and Mariana might enjoy working with me and Braden to develop and test the composite effects. Then, we'll need to refine them to permit mages to handle the final binding. I don't think we have enough wizards to go around, if they're required to see to the actual issuing and binding, too. We'll need ore and other materials. We'll need transportation. Pretty much every aspect of building an arms and equipment factory is up for grabs. Tell me what you want to do that you feel entitles you to a full and fair share."

BY THE TIME the meeting broke up and everyone left the Citadel, all the Great Houses of Tel were full partners in the Foundry Initiative. That pleased Gavin, no end. Until Braden mentioned that the rest of them might not appreciate being left out, the idea of including them hadn't occurred to him, especially since none of them had ever mentioned an interest in artifacts like Braden had. As Gavin returned to the laboratory, he made a mental note to thank Braden for speaking up during the first meeting.

CHAPTER 4

A few days later, Gavin stood on a grassy knoll south of the Tel Roshan road. The knoll was less than two hours' walk from Tel Mivar, and the capital dominated the westward view. A faint breeze carried hints of salt from the Inner Sea, not too far to the south, and Gavin wondered—not for the first time—just where along this coastline Kiri had washed ashore. He wasn't sure how having that information would make any difference to him, and it didn't feel important enough to ask his wife. The answer didn't matter that much, truth be told, but he wondered nonetheless.

The flare of his *skathos* announced the arrival of his friends several heartbeats before a handful of gateways rose out of the ground. Mariana, Braden, and Wynn stepped through a gateway each, but Lillian surprised him by bringing Kiri and a couple Cavaliers with her. The Cavaliers looked a little wild around the eyes, and they cast longing glances back through the gateway for the palace courtyard clearly in view.

Gavin smiled and crossed the distance to the new arrivals. When he reached arms' length, he pulled Kiri into a deep hug and kissed her cheek before he whispered in her ear, "I love you."

He stepped back and found Kiri looking up at him, a range of emotions swirling just below the surface of her expression, and she asked, "What was that about?"

"I hadn't told you today," he replied, adding a one-shoulder shrug. "There are all kinds of things in the world that you should justifiably doubt. That I love you more than anything should never be one of them."

Kiri's expression softened even more, and she gnawed at her lower lip with her teeth. Her eyes flicked to the other people around them, and for the briefest moment, she looked incredibly conflicted.

"Oh, kiss him already," Mariana said. "After a statement like that, he deserves it."

Kiri's cheeks flushed as she smiled and looked away, but she took the couple steps necessary to pull Gavin back into her arms and kissed him like she meant it. When she let him go, Kiri looked Gavin in his eyes and said, "I love you, too."

"So, what brings you here?" Gavin asked as he shifted to stand beside Kiri with one arm around her.

"Lillian was having lunch with me, when she realized she was going to be late. Why didn't you offer Vushaar a seat at your Foundry table?"

That struck Gavin as one of those 'Do these pants make me look fat?' questions. He wasn't sure if the women of this world trapped their men like some women of Earth, but he immediately saw several possible outcomes stretching out before him... and precious few of them were good. So, Gavin being Gavin, he told the truth.

"When you set out to create a place whose sole purpose is the crafting of arcane items that dwarven masters rate higher than the artifacts of old, I'm afraid Vushaar doesn't come to mind as a possible participant. I didn't mean for you or Terris to feel snubbed, but I just didn't see what or how you'd be able to contribute. Besides, you're already mobilizing an army larger than anything you've had since the Godswar."

Kiri held his gaze for several moments, her expression unreadable. Just as Gavin reached the edge of concern, she grinned. "We're not snubbed. Father even confessed a certain level of gratitude that you didn't invite Vushaar; he would've felt almost honor-bound to accept. You're quite correct that we do have our hands full right now. All of us do. He did ask me to find out what will happen to the gear once the campaign is over."

Gavin grinned. "Well, that's a bit of a complex question. You see, we'll be binding each set of equipment to a person, specifically that person's oath. They will be rather powerful items, and we don't want them out in the wild. So, the soldiers will be free to take them home. If their oaths terminate, so does the equipment. Otherwise, they'll have it for their lifetimes."

"Do you have any concept of the vast debt you'll be creating between the Great Houses of Tel and the other members of the Old Alliance? You will essentially be equipping all of our armies with artifact-grade equipment. Gavin, artifacts have sold for hundreds—if not thousands—of gold pieces. If you made the members sign notes, you could bankrupt us all if you ever called in those notes."

"Yeah... but I'm not asking anyone to sign notes. I'm not counting favors or any of that crap. We need to reclaim Skullkeep. Yes, I will face down the Necromancer, but beyond that, I need to contribute to the campaign somehow. So why not give our people the best chance possible?"

Kiri held his gaze for several moments, before her special smile broke through. She shook her head as she looked away. "Only you, Gavin. Only you. I cannot imagine any other sovereign in your position feeling like personally confronting the Necromancer of Skullkeep was not sufficiently doing your part and wanting to do *more*."

Gavin gave another one-shouldered shrug. "I'm not really sure what to say to that. I'm just me."

He scanned the faces of his friends and saw hints of pride sprinkled throughout their expressions as they regarded him and Kiri. He wasn't sure what else there was to say and turned to walk back to the road, pulling Kiri with him.

"Okay, folks. Let's gather at the edge of the road," he said, his arm still around Kiri. "This will be a rather large working of the Art, and there's no telling what side effects may accompany it."

His friends followed him, and when he reached what he felt was a safe distance, Gavin released Kiri with great reluctance and focused on the task at hand. He produced a rolled piece of parchment from inside his robe and unrolled it for everyone to see. Upon consulting with the scale in the bottom-right corner, he realized the Foundry would be almost as large as the former Sivas—that is, Kirloth—Estate. A number of crafting halls occupied three sides of a courtyard large enough to handle several freight wagons at once. Along the remaining side, a row of buildings would serve as armories, the store-houses of the completed items awaiting assignment. Behind the crafting halls, a single mess hall would stand and, beyond that, a row of bunkhouses for the smiths and arcanists crafting the equipment.

"This is the design of the Foundry we agreed on." He paused, then shrugged again. "Well, it's the design the dwarves wanted and we agreed to, because we're not the ones banging hot metal into submission. Let's start with marking stakes to lay out the perimeter, and we'll move on from there."

OVER THE NEXT COUPLE HOURS, they created and set marking stakes all around the perimeter, while Kiri and her Cavaliers watched. It was a boring, monotonous project except for the final stretch, but then again, so were most adventures. The marking stakes for the wall that would surround the complex all placed, Gavin and the others retreated to where Kiri stood with her two guards, who eyed the layout with a liberal amount of skepticism.

"Milord," one of the Cavaliers said, "if I may ask, how will you keep the items secure? There hasn't been a lock made yet that cannot be picked."

Gavin smiled. "There won't be any locks anywhere in the compound."

Confusion dominated the Cavaliers' expressions like cavalry battling swordsmen.

Kiri looked away so they wouldn't see her fighting the urge to grin.

"When we finish, only those people authorized to enter the compound will be able to enter the compound. No disguise or blackmail or coercion will allow anyone else to cross the gates' threshold," Gavin said.

"But what about the workers? How will you keep them from simply stealing and selling the equipment?" the other Cavalier asked.

Gavin's smile turned into a grin. "No unbound equipment will pass the wall—in any respect—and maintain its imbued effects. When the time comes to issue the equipment, each quartermaster tent in each mustering location will have a portal that will deliver the recruit here, where we will verify their oaths and blind their equipment to them with a drop of their own blood."

The Cavaliers frowned as they processed everything Gavin said. After a couple moments, one asked, "Then, how will you protect against a group of people rushing those portals? That would be a weakness, surely."

"The Foundry will be well fortified while we issue equipment, even though I personally don't see the necessity. And if the respective armies can't keep their own mustering fields secure, I'd say we have bigger problems."

At that point, Gavin turned to his friends, clearly indicating the time for questions had passed. He took the few steps necessary to join them and nodded once. "Okay. Let's do this just like we practiced. Remember... we want a solid stone wall. Let's worry about getting the structure right for now, and we'll circle back around for the protections later. Ready?"

Lillian, Mariana, Braden, and Wynn each signaled their readiness with a nod as they took deep, slow breaths. Through his *skathos*, Gavin sensed their work to saturate themselves with power drawn from the ambient. His view of the world took on a gold hue as he did likewise, and when he next spoke, his voice crackled with power.

"On three. One... two... three! *Rhyskaal!*"

Four voices joined his as they combined their will toward one massive invocation. The united strength of five of the most powerful arcanists in the world slammed into the ambient, creating a resonance that drove wizards to their knees as far as Tel Roshan to the west, Arundel to the north, and Birsha to the south. At first, nothing seemed to happen. For several heartbeats, not even birds serenaded them with song.

Then... they heard it. Moments after that, they *felt* it.

A faint rumbling, like the sound of a herd of horses running at a canter quite some distance away. By the time Gavin counted to sixty, the ground around them bucked and heaved worse than the sea during the fiercest storm.

"Lie down! Everyone, lie flat on the ground!" Gavin quickly heeded his own advice, though he positioned himself to see what happened.

Mere heartbeats after those around him hit the grass, a ridge— square but with a rectangular opening on the side closest the road —pushed up the field's topsoil. Then, stone broke through the sod and continued to rise toward the sky. As it rose, crenellations formed along the outside edge, and rounded towers complete with turrets and arrow slits formed at each corner. When the wall reached thirty feet in height, it stopped, and the ensuing silence felt eerie.

Gavin stood and rested his fists on his hips as he inspected their distant handiwork.

Braden jumped to his feet next, his expression alight with wonder. "By the gods, Gavin... I don't even feel winded. That should have put us flat on our backs."

"Marcus always said the Art was not as it was," Gavin remarked, not looking away from the new wall. "Kinda makes sense, now that we know it was slowly funneling to Earth all these years with no way back. You're getting a small taste of what it was like for me there *before* I created the portal to come home."

Lillian and the others joined him and Braden. Lillian asked, "And Earth didn't realize the Art exists?"

"No. The idea of magic and imbued items and all kinds of things like that is fiction to them."

Not for the first time, his friends shook their heads in a mixture of disbelief and wonder. Mariana said, "You must have been a god over there, Gavin. Why did you bother coming back?"

Gavin pinched some of the fabric of his gold robe between his thumb and finger and shook it. "I agreed to do a job, and as long as I was there, I wasn't here doing the job. Besides, as much as I liked being home and seeing my family again, it wasn't truly *home*. I never lost the feeling that I didn't belong there, no matter how welcome my parents made me. No matter how happy I was to see my daughter again. That's not my world anymore, and it isn't ready to handle the Art. That's why I only trained my daughter and her friend Alexis while I was there. Jennifer stumbled onto a Word of Power, and she was well on her way to dying from *skathos* cascade when Kiri and I found her. The same with Alexis, though I never did ask her how she did it. I probably ought to do that at some point, but I suppose it doesn't matter in the long run. But! Let's go inspect our new wall before we make the floor. I think the best thing to do is create the walls and floor before we embed the protections. That way, we can do all the protections at once and not have to worry about whether the different pieces would interfere with each other."

Gavin waved for Kiri and her Cavalier-shaped shadows to follow as he led his friends toward the solid-stone wall that had not existed mere minutes before. The first thing he did upon reaching the wall was reach out to touch it. It was rough stone. Somewhere between the texture of a hewn rock wall—like in a mine—and that of a rock cliff freshly exposed from a slip or similar event. As he envisioned, it was five feet thick, and what no one else would ever realize—maybe not even the dwarven smiths—was that the walls were unbroken stone all the way to the bedrock and fundament of the world. Gavin felt it very unlikely anyone would ever breach those walls.

While Kiri and the Cavaliers admired the new wall, Gavin stepped back and considered the opening that would become the gate. A band of stone already connected the two sides of the imminent gate, and it dislodged the topsoil like the rest of the wall. Part of Gavin wondered if they even needed to make the floor of the compound itself stone to match the walls. The people staffing the

Foundry might appreciate some greenery. As he took that thought further, the idea occurred that the Sylvan Synod might like to send some apprentice druids—or whatever they called their druids in training—to spruce up the place, Nature-wise. Some trees here... some flowerbeds over there... the more he examined that idea, the more he liked it.

"I have a question," he said, and the conversations around him faded as everyone turned to him. "What do you think about inviting the Sylvan Synod to send a group of student druids with a teacher or two to spruce up this place with trees and flowerbeds and stuff like that? Basically what their ancestors did for the College of the Arcane, but on a much smaller scale."

Braden and Wynn didn't react at all, Wynn even going so far as to shrug. The ladies, however, beamed at the thought.

"That would just be lovely," Lillian said. "What an excellent idea, Gavin."

Mariana nudged Kiri with her elbow. "You must be training him rather well for him to come up with that all on his own."

Kiri blushed as she fought to keep a straight face. Neither she nor Gavin wanted to mention that they spent almost as much time apart as they did together... nowhere close to the norm for newlyweds, but they each had considerable responsibilities.

"In that case," Gavin continued, "let's skip making the ground a stone floor and move on to the gate and gatehouse. From there, we'll embed the protections in what we've made so far... and... probably call it a day. We'll do the structures and footpaths tomorrow, and I'll contact the Sylvan Synod at that point."

Lillian, Mariana, Braden, and Wynn responded to the affirmative, each in their own way.

"Right, then. Let's go back a safe distance and make a gatehouse and gate."

BY THE TIME the sun neared the western horizon, they had completed their work for the day. An immense gatehouse enveloped the opening in the wall, and a pair of massive stone blocks on metal hinges formed the gate. The construction blazed in the wizards' *skathos*, the sheer mass of protections and effects embedded in the stone radiating power into the ambient.

Out of everything they accomplished that day, Gavin was most proud of the gate. To the casual observer, there should have been no way for the comparatively dainty hinges to support the incredible blocks of stone that would come together as the Foundry's gate, and if Gavin hadn't saturated both the hinges *and* the stone gate with powerful Transmutation effects, those hinges never would have. In the case of the hinges and their mounting brackets, Gavin embedded protection from the elements—all of them— exponentially increased the strength of the metal, and wrapped them in a silence effect; those hinges would never rust or otherwise decay, and they definitely would never squeak or squeal. As for the stone blocks that made up the gate itself, Gavin reduced the weight to such a degree that a toddler would be able to push the gate open.

The last thing Gavin wanted to do before calling it a day was to embed one final effect in the gate and gatehouse. He cleared his mind of everything but his intent, taking special care to ensure *only* his intent existed in his conscious mind. Then, he took a breath and invoked a composite effect, "*Rhyskaal-Sykhurhos-Rhyskaal.*"

The resonance of Gavin's invocation slammed into the ambient like a ten-ton boulder hitting a calm lake. Lillian and the others cried out when the resonance of their former mentor's power drove them to their knees as reality changed to meet his will. A few heartbeats passed before they regained sufficient composure to stand, and all four of them stared at Gavin.

"What did you just do?" Lillian asked.

Mariana still had her arms wrapped across her midriff. "That *hurt*, Gavin. What could possibly have required so much power?"

"Upon command, the gate will now close and fuse into solid stone that matches the rest of the wall, and the same command word will return it to a gate," Gavin said. "No silly wooden crossbeams for the

Foundry. If someone ever tries to drive a ram into this gate... well... that would not be the wisest idea."

Mariana's eyes flicked from Gavin to the gate and back again several times as a shrewd expression developed. "You didn't need us to help with this at all, did you, Gavin? You're *still* teaching us. Tell me I'm wrong."

Gavin stood silent for several heartbeats before a mischievous expression slipped through his control, and he replied with an exaggerated shrug. "Hmmm... could be."

CHAPTER 5

Gavin stepped through the gateway to arrive in the elven capital of Arundel. As with his first visit to the city, the crystalline construction of the structures inspired feelings of awe, curiosity, amazement... just to name a few. Not all of the crystals were the same hue, and the morning sun glinted off every surface in a rainbow of color, often favoring the color of the crystal itself, and despite the hustle and bustle of the elves going about their daily lives, he felt an underlying serenity to the city that simply did not exist in Tel Mivar. The pace of life was slower here. More reflective. More studied.

A slight breeze carried hints of the Great Forest that surrounded the city. He readily identified Pine, but that was only part of the bouquet floating along the current of air.

It was a beautiful city, and Gavin felt enriched for having seen it. But he didn't want to live there. It didn't feel like home to him, and what's more, it didn't feel like it could become home.

"Milord, may I help you?"

A soft tenor at his left shoulder drew Gavin out of his thoughts, and he turned to find a young elf standing a respectful distance away... or at least the elf *looked* young. They aged at such a different rate from humans that he could've seen a hundred summers and not looked any older than Gavin.

"Yes, thank you," Gavin replied. "Is the Sylvan Synod in session today? I realize it's short notice, but I was hoping to have a word."

Now, the elf did betray his youth in a nervous, uncertain expression as he glanced toward the massive tree that dominated the center of the city.

"I - I don't know, milord. I don't know that I've ever seen notices of when they hold sessions."

Footfalls and the rustle of garments drew Gavin's attention further to his left, and he smiled when he saw Telanna stop an equally respectful distance away from Gavin. The young elf at his side bowed deeply.

Telanna served as both a member of Synod and ambassador to Vushaar, when such was needed, and she was the elder sister of Elayna and Kantar, the Magister of Abjuration.

"The Archmagister is a friend," Telanna said, offering the young elf a soft smile. "I'll see to him, so you run along. I believe today's a school day, is it not?"

The young elf jerked a nod and dashed off.

Gavin smiled. "Now, Telanna... are you telling me that you never skipped school? Not even once?"

"Why, of course not, Gavin," she replied, a slight smile curling her lips. "One of my tutors was rather dreamy. Now, what brings you to Arundel?"

"I hoped to speak with the Sylvan Synod on a matter."

Telanna's right eyebrow quirked upward. "Oh? And just what is that matter, if I may ask?"

"The Great Houses of Tel and a number of dwarven clans are establishing an arms and equipment complex. We're calling it the Foundry, and the physical structures are already in place with arcane wards and such embedded as well. While my friends and I worked on that, the idea occurred to me that there might be some student or apprentice druids who would benefit from some practical experience. I don't want to imply that it's required in any form or way, but if the

Synod would like to send some students to the facility to give it more of a natural feel with flowers and trees and such, we would welcome them. Sort of like what the druids did for the College of the Arcane all those millennia ago, but on a much smaller scale and with no need of a hedge maze."

Telanna nodded. "Yes, I understand. Would you like to present this to the full Synod yourself, or would you entrust its presentation to me?"

"I have no problems leaving the matter in your capable hands, Telanna, especially since I'm pretty sure you're a member of the Synod yourself."

A slight smile crossed Telanna's expression. "Why, yes, so I am. I will discuss it with the Synod. How should I communicate the decision to you?"

Gavin took in the crowd growing around them as he considered that question. It seemed the Archmagister conversing with a senior druid of the Sylvan Synod on a street was worthy of gawkers. Gavin wasn't normally one to show off, but when the mood struck him, he put on a show with the best of them. And right then... the mood struck him.

He bent down and scooped up a small stone from the edge of the street and let it rest in the palm of his hand, presenting it as much to the gawkers as Telanna. Then, he concentrated his focus on the precise changes to the stone he wanted to create and invoked a composite effect of Divination and Transmutation, *"Klaepos-Rhyskaal."*

Wizards across Arundel felt the resonance of Gavin's power as the composite effect took hold, and it manifested as a cloud of kaleidoscopic lights that swirled around the small stone, faster and faster, until—all at once—the stone seemed to absorb them. In the wake of the composite effect, the stone resonated against Gavin's *skathos*, and through that resonance, he knew he had achieved his desired effect.

"Here," Gavin said, extending his hand to Telanna. "Speak the command word, and I shall hear whatever you say until you speak the command word again."

"And just what, may I ask, is the command word?"

As soon as Telanna took the stone from his hand, Gavin leaned closed and whispered, "Swordfish."

When Gavin withdrew to a respectful distance, he enjoyed the look of consternation that had claimed Telanna's expression. Her lips moved several times as if she started to speak, but she made no utterance. After several false starts, she said, "What kind of nonsense is a command word like that?"

Gavin grinned. "You won't have any problems remembering it, will you?"

"Certainly not." Now, it seemed Telanna noticed the crowd that had developed around them, and her expression became shrewd. "Never miss an opportunity to put on a show, do you?"

Gavin shrugged, maintaining his insouciant grin. "Oh, sure. I let all kinds of those opportunities pass, but maybe that's the problem. If I showed off more, I might not feel the urge to do so in such a grandiose fashion."

Telanna's eyes narrowed. It wasn't *quite* a glare, but it certainly wasn't a happy, carefree expression. "I think you've disrupted the day for long enough, you incorrigible cad. I shall contact you anon."

"I hope the day treats you well, Telanna," Gavin replied. He focused his intent once more and invoked a Word of Transmutation, "*Paedryx*."

He added a fingersnap at just the right moment to make it appear as though the snap was a crucial component of the invocation right before he vanished from Arundel.

* * *

GAVIN APPEARED in his quarters in the Citadel, high above Tel Mivar. He smiled and chuckled a bit over how he handled the gawkers back in Arundel and admitted to himself that maybe he should opt for a more dignified mien... especially while he was the Archmagister. But the more he thought about it, the more he decided that he should be himself in all things and moments. Sure... he could be serious if the occasion called for it, but by and large, he felt people took things too seriously.

A quick check of the clock standing in the corner informed him it was far too close to lunch to start any significant projects, and he decided he'd fill the short time between then and the midday meal by reading more of Marcus's journal. So he set off for the library.

A SHORT TIME LATER, Gavin sat in one of the library's plush armchairs, one of Marcus's journals splayed open in his lap. He *knew* he should be focused on the journal; it was the sole reason he sat in the Citadel's library while he waited for lunch. But it simply did not hold his attention. His mind swirled around the question of what came after eliminating the Necromancer and re-taking Skullkeep. As much as he sort of enjoyed being Archmagister and effecting his vision of what the Society of the Arcane should be, it wasn't what he wanted. Not anymore...

He and Kiri spent their days apart, and he nipped down to Vushaar as he could—usually on the 'weekends.' Still, though, the situation wasn't ideal. The downside was that he wasn't sure that stepping down from his position of Archmagister would help much. He still had responsibilities as Kirloth that would need his attention. And if he wasn't Archmagister, what else would he do? How would he spend his days?

Another reason he wanted to keep his professional distance from Vushaar was that he knew Kiri would come to him with arcanist questions or needs before she went to Fallon... if he were readily available. She wouldn't intend any slight toward Fallon at all, but she'd still naturally gravitate toward her husband.

Besides... even the most confident and mentally healthy mage would feel a little intimidated at having Kirloth so close at hand. He thought they had worked through all that before Bellos asked him to be the next Archmagister, but he wasn't sure it would be wise to poke at old wounds. That rarely went—or ended—well.

Then, there was the matter of what to do with all of Marcus's journals. As long as Kirloth was Archmagister—whether in the person of Gavin Cross or one of his descendants—those journals should reside in the Citadel's library, for ease of access if nothing else. But if he was successful in turning over the gold robe to Lillian? Did she or future Archmagisters have any right to them? It was a tricky subject, but considering some of the events Marcus chronicled, he didn't think so. It felt right to him that those journals remain with House Kirloth.

Gavin sighed, closing the book on his lap and placing it on the end table beside the chair. He would return to it when his mind was more settled, especially since he realized he hadn't even moved the bookmark.

The library door opened, and Gavin turned to see Bellos stride into the room. He crossed to the sitting area and gestured toward the chair facing Gavin.

"May I?"

Gavin smiled. "Of course. As far as I'm concerned, you're always welcome wherever I am."

"Thank you," Bellos replied. "You and I are brothers in a way, you know. You, Mivar, Roshan, my brother who inherited House Wygoth, Cothos, and I were all his apprentices. No one who hasn't experienced that could ever understand."

Gavin nodded. "I know what you mean. I have always felt that he and I barely had enough time together to scratch the surface of what he knew and understood about the Art. I would give a lot to have even another month with him."

"He would appreciate that," Bellos replied, adding a chuckle, "but he would pepper you with as many questions as you would seek to ask him. After all, *he* never completed a cross-planar portal."

Gavin leaned back against his seat and gave Bellos a speculative expression. "You know... about that... it wasn't especially difficult. Did he never complete it because he couldn't? Or did he simply get nudged to focus on other matters?"

Bellos maintained a non-expression for several moments before he broke out into a huge smile. "Damn... you found me out.

Balancing the connection between this plane and that of the refugee world was never supposed to be his task... not really. It wasn't something Valthon and I explicitly planned for you, either, but one must strike while the iron is hot. So, what's on your mind? I could tell you wanted to discuss something with me, but the particulars eluded me."

"As soon as we're stable after re-taking Skullkeep, I want to turn over the position of Archmagister to Lillian Mivar."

Bellos's eyebrows flicked toward his hairline for the briefest moment. "That... is rather unexpected. Will you explain your reasoning, please?"

"A few different reasons. First, I am also Kirloth now; I don't feel I can discharge the responsibilities of being Kirloth as long as I am also the Archmagister. Beyond that, I want to do other things with my life. I want to be a better husband to Kiri. I want to be able to visit my family on Earth without feeling like I'm ignoring significant responsibilities here. Bottom line... I don't really *want* this job."

"Do you have any idea how many people would wonder what's wrong with you if they heard you don't want to be Archmagister?" Bellos asked amid a hearty laugh. "And to give you a bit of insight, none of your predecessors wanted it, either. I have always been very careful to choose those who would see it as a duty and responsibility. Those are the types of people Tel and the Society deserve as Archmagister.

"Thank you, by the way, for sorting out the mess with the royal family succeeding to civil authority. I realize none of them were still alive after you ended slavery, but it's good that mechanism was removed from Tel's Constitution. Our mentor didn't want it in there in the first place, but it was a sop to the surviving nobility of the area —at that time—to reduce the number of matters vying for his attention."

Gavin chuckled and shook his head. "I always wondered how that slipped into the Constitution. Given what I knew of Marcus, I couldn't see him willingly adding that provision."

"Oh, no," Bellos agreed. "I spent the better part of a week talking him down from his preferred response to the nobility's demands."

"Molten rock and charred earth?" Gavin asked.

"Quite."

A silence descended on the pair for several moments before Bellos spoke again. "Have you discussed the matter with Young Mivar?"

"I have. She is not opposed to the idea, but she didn't jump to agree, either. I think the thought that I considered her appropriate to succeed me intimidated—or maybe overwhelmed—her."

Bellos snorted. "As well it should. You're not proposing she take over some small social club. I will think on the matter and consider what I know of Young Mivar. I may further explore her character and integrity, but from what I know of her right now, I am not opposed to the succession."

Gavin nodded. "Thank you. I appreciate that. If it should come to pass, I've pretty much decided to relocate our mentor's journals to the estate outside of Tel Mivar. After reading some of them, I don't think it's right that anyone outside House Kirloth ever read them."

"Hrmmm..." Bellos vocalized as he scratched at his VanDyke beard. "You're probably right about that. I haven't read them, myself, but I am aware of many events and actions that—while imminently necessary—are not for general knowledge, even restricted to the Archmagisters."

"So, what is tied to the Kirloth bloodline that you and Valthon needed me?" Gavin asked.

Bellos lifted his eyes to meet Gavin's gaze but otherwise gave no visible reaction. After several moments, he said, "Figured that out, did you?"

"Granted, I could easily be wrong, but sometimes, the simplest explanations are the best."

"Yes," Bellos remarked with a sigh, "I suppose they are. The truth of the matter is that I'm afraid this is another situation where you are far better off without that knowledge. Events are unfolding that may force the knowledge upon you, but for the moment, let's not kick that particular bear."

Gavin took a deep breath with a slow exhalation. "So, it's fairly major, then... whatever it is."

"I didn't say that."

"You didn't have to," Gavin countered, smiling. "The last time you used that particular answer, it involved me being dead for thirteen years—well, closer to eleven, at the time—before you and 'the old man' dropped me in that alley. If you stand me beside my daughter, I look young enough to be her *brother*. Not to put too fine a point on it, but that's a damn major revelation. So, yeah... if you don't want to talk about whatever it is, it's fairly major."

Bellos gave Gavin a mock glare. "Sometimes, you're too smart for your own good, but I'm still not talking about it. It's a matter of your possession of the knowledge changing how you respond to certain circumstances and events. It might change the decisions you make. So, no. We're not discussing it unless there's no other choice."

"Fair enough, and that actually makes a certain amount of sense. The more I consider it, I'm probably better off *not* knowing."

"Thank you," Bellos replied, offering a nod as replacement for a bow. "Now, if you'll excuse me, I'm afraid I have other matters that require my attention. Thank you for the welcome and the conversation."

Before Gavin could respond, the God of Magic vanished in a small flare of gold light.

* * *

LILLIAN LOOKED up from the notes in front of her when she caught movement in her peripheral vision and smiled when she saw Mariana standing at the edge of the table.

"Hi! When did you get back?" she asked the woman who had always felt like an older sister.

Mariana shrugged. "Not too long ago. I stopped by the family's suite here in the Tower and dropped off my kit. The druids are making great strides out at the Foundry. You'll have to visit sometime, especially since it's in your family's province and all. What are you working on?"

Lillian smiled. "I was talking with Braden the other day, and he got me thinking about creating a key for the manor gate that's tied to the bloodline. Father shouldn't have to ring the bell like some guest or courier to come home."

"Ah. How is it coming along?"

"I think I have most of it worked out," Lillian replied as Mariana sat in one of the chairs across from her. "Honestly, if Gavin coming back hadn't done whatever it did to the ambient magic levels, I probably wouldn't even consider attempting this. There's no way I would've been strong enough even as recently as a year-and-a-half ago."

Mariana chuckled and nodded for emphasis. "Tell me about it. He does more impossible things before breakfast than most people do throughout their entire lives. Say... have you talked to him about it?"

"Oh, no. He's much too busy for something like this, and besides, he'd probably just wave his hand and *do it*. I'd like to puzzle my way through it and learn something. Mari... do you have some time to discuss something that's been on my mind?"

Mariana nodded, her expression suggesting that Lillian shouldn't have felt the need to ask. "Of course. What is it?"

Lillian shook her head. "Not here. It's... well... it's pretty high-impact."

"Ah. Your place or mine?"

LILLIAN EASED into one of the armchairs near the hearth in her family's suite, just down the hall from the Kirloth suite where Gavin and Kiri had lived before the trip to Vushaar. Mariana occupied the other, and the notes on the gate key littered the top of the table behind them.

"All right," Mariana said. "This is far more private than the library, so what's on your mind?"

Lillian took a deep breath and released in a slow exhalation. "Gavin... well... the other day, he asked me what I thought about becoming the Archmagister."

"What?"

"I know! Here's the freaky part. Once our part of the world has stabilized after re-taking Skullkeep and ending the threat of the Necromancer, he wants to turn the position over to me. I... I don't know what to think about it."

Lillian watched Mariana stare into the inactive fireplace for several moments. "Well, part of me wonders how much of the smooth transition from the royal family's authority to having an Archmagister once again has been the simple fact that Gavin could scare a corpse if he put his mind to it. I mean... he's a true-born son of House Kirloth trained by the man who dueled Milthas and *founded* Tel. That's a serious amount of inherent intimidation, right there. But aside from all that, I think it's a great idea. I—"

"You do?"

Mariana nodded. "Of course, I do. The last six months or so before Gavin and Kiri came back, you pretty much ran things. Yes, Nathrac held the executive authority, but *you* consulted on everything. He never issued a directive or decision that didn't go through you first. Plus, you're the most level-headed of us. I love being a Battle-mage and don't want to quit until age forces me. Braden's head is so deep into the Foundry and everything that will be happening there that I'd be amazed if he's aware the rest of us exist, and then, there's Wynn..."

"Hey, now. That's not exactly fair. Taking over Gavin's apprentices worked wonders for him. He's even slowed down enough to get engaged."

"That poor woman has her work cut out for her," Mariana remarked with a sigh.

If she were being honest, Lillian couldn't deny that at all, but she felt like they ought to stick up for their childhood friend.

"But back to the matter at hand," Mariana continued. "The simple fact is that you've already demonstrated you can handle the responsibility of being Archmagister. That position was never about being the best or most powerful arcanist. It was totally about being the person Bellos decided was best suited to guide and lead both the Kingdom of Tel *and* the Society of the Arcane. Yes... for the moment, that person is Gavin. There were *a lot* of things to fix in the wake of the royal family's so-called stewardship, but there aren't as many as there were. And if Gavin passes the office to you, he'll still be around to act as a silent threat against anyone who might be a bad actor. So, yeah... I'm not really seeing a downside."

Lillian gnawed at her lower lip. "You're not jealous that Gavin asked me?"

"Gods no, girl! Do you think I *want* to be the Archmagister? I'd lose my cool in less than an hour. I don't see how you handled all the idiocy with the aplomb that you did, and don't even get me started on Gavin."

Lillian lost control of a snicker, and Mariana added her own. Amid the humor, Lillian replied, "There have been a few times Gavin's handling of a situation was... uhm... a bit expedient."

Mariana rolled her eyes. "Expedient? Really? I've thought more than once Gavin's default reaction was simple obliteration. 'Expedient' seems a bit understated."

"So, you're really okay with me telling Gavin that I'll do it? That I'll be Archmagister?"

"Of course, I am. If Bellos goes along with it, it means there's no chance he'll ask *me* to do it... and... I think you'd be perfect for the job, too."

Lillian gave her friend a mock glare. "It sounds to me like your support of me taking the job is just a bit self-serving."

Marianna beamed. "Well, of course it is. As long as you're the Archmagister, it means I'm free to stay with the Battle-mages, but in all seriousness, I can't think of anyone I'd rather have in the position. I know how much you care about the state of affairs in both Tel *and* the Society."

"Thanks, Mari," Lillian replied. "That means a lot."

"You're welcome," Marianna said, then clapped her hands. "Now that we've dealt with the weighty matters, have you eaten lately? I've felt like I'm starving since I arrived."

Lillian shrugged and stood. "Sure... I can eat. Dining hall? Or do you have some place specific in mind?"

"At this point, I'd eat a sickly horse," Mariana answered as she stood. "Let's see what the dining hall has, since it's closest."

As they left the Mivar suite, conversation moved on to the 'catching up' chatting between old friends.

CHAPTER 6

The horse clopped along the dusty road, the repetitive and consistent sound serving as a backdrop to the otherwise-pleasant morning. The sun wasn't above the peaks of the Godswall Mountains yet, but the hues and gradients of color in the sky suggested it wouldn't be long. Flowers dotted the landscape and provided a complex collection of scents that still carried hints of the morning dew.

Cyn rolled with the steady gait of her trusty mount, her mind more focused on the job than her surroundings. Trickster made good time as he carried her north on the east side of the Vischaene River. She might have preferred to head north on the opposite side of the river, but ferries became very few and far between for a considerable span anywhere close to the mouth of Hope's Pass. The few ferries that did exist 'enjoyed' rather impressive Army garrisons, especially in the wake of the Necromancer's attack on Tel a year or so ago. The small community across the river from Tel Mivar was now a military encampment, for all intents and purposes, and Cyn had used all her skills to get through the area without any undue notice.

How anyone could *not* know war with Skullkeep was coming escaped Cyn. Tel's army started a massive recruitment drive, which was just starting to gain traction. The other members of the Old Alliance quietly mobilized, some not so quietly. If a person threw a rock in any direction within leagues of Hope's Pass, it would hit three scouts watching the pass for any movement before landing on the ground.

Many people debated the question of whether Gavin would've pushed the Old Alliance into the build-up if the Necromancer had not attacked Tel Mivar, and from what Cyn could gather, the opinions seemed to run about sixty percent asserting that war became inevitable the moment Bellos chose a new Archmagister. Especially as more and more information became publicized about just how thoroughly the Necromancer had controlled the royal family prior to its demise. Given her status as a Wraith, she had access to far more of the information than what Gavin had ordered released so far, and the depth of Leuwyn's betrayal was... well... 'staggering' was insufficient do describe how she felt when she stepped back and considered it all.

The sound of approaching horses pulled Cyn out of her thoughts, and she lifted her eyes. The road—more like a grassy track—wound around a thick copse of trees maybe twenty-five yards ahead, and while she could *hear* the horses, she couldn't see them yet. In a split-second decision, she nudged Trickster with her right knee and applied just a little pull on the left rein. He obliged by turning off the road and disappearing into the brush. She stopped him and dismounted, dashing back out with a branch to brush out fifty feet or so. Since the road was more grass than dirt, there weren't too many actual tracks, but she didn't want whoever was coming to see immediate signs of her passage. Then, she ducked back into the underbrush to return to Trickster.

She led him deeper into the forest, picking the deepest shadows while keeping him calm and quiet. Part of her wanted to know who it was. She was—at most—a day south of Hope's Pass; she passed the last outer ring of army sentries a couple of days ago and hadn't seen any true patrols for the better part of two days before that. Her gut told her it was a group from Skullkeep... or one of the less-savory mercenary groups. To hear them and have enough time to mask the trail a little bit and disappear into the forest meant there was decent number of them, and even as good as she was, any confrontation with them would not go well for her. Far better to disappear into the shadowy woods and do her best to keep them from ever realizing she passed them.

As she put more and more distance and trees between her and the road, the sound of the large group of horses faded, and she angled Trickster back toward her destination. She wasn't sure if the forest ran past the plain where Hope's Pass opened into Mivar Province, but she didn't want to miss it and have to backtrack. She hated backtracking... either literally or figuratively.

* * *

GAVIN LEANED back against his seat as he stared at the notes and diagrams arrayed on the table in front of him. The Wraiths had never let him or Marcus down—at least, that he knew—but at the same time, he felt uneasy at relying on them to ensure the destruction of the Necromancer's soul jar. There were too many variables, too many ways that mission could go horribly wrong. After all, they were supposed to collect general intelligence on Skullkeep and its forces *while* searching for the soul jar. If they were discovered without completing the necessary directive, then the Old Alliance needed a contingency.

Gavin's mind flitted to the Middle East village he had encountered during his time back on Earth. He did not like the idea of introducing nuclear weapons to Drakmoor. People feared wizards—the world's true arcanists—far too much for his liking, and he didn't want to add to any fuel to that fire.

No... the Old Alliance needed a *viable* contingency.

Gavin heaved a sigh. There was nothing for it. He needed to visit an old friend of the family.

"Hartley!"

The Citadel's spectral majordomo faded into existence at his elbow, saying, "You bellowed, Milord?"

"If anyone comes looking for me, I'm going to visit an old friend, and once I finish there, I'll probably nip over to Vushaar to visit Kiri."

Hartley nodded his translucent head once. "Of course, Milord. I shall tell anyone who asks that you have fled the Citadel for more congenial territory."

Gavin responded with a chuckle. "You're incorrigible, Hartley. Has anyone ever told you that?"

"I am getting on in centuries, Milord. I'm sure I have no way to know."

* * *

A GATEWAY DELIVERED Gavin to the approach toward a ruined castle in central Vushaar. To his cursory examination, nothing seemed to have changed. He walked through the gateway with its inscription in an ancient—now dead—language, crossed the courtyard, and trudged up the steps of the collapsing keep.

The moment he set foot inside the keep, Gavin called out, "Ho, Othron! Have time for a visit?"

He felt a Conjuration effect wash over him, then Othron's reply, "I always have time for friends, Kirloth. Please, join me."

Gavin crossed to the sole remaining room of the keep that had not yet surrendered to the ravages of time, just as a section of its wall pulled back and slid to one side. He made his way down the stairs and soon arrived in the cavernous space the world's oldest lich called home.

"It hasn't been *that* long since we crossed paths, my friend," Othron said as he greeted Gavin and ushered him into a plush armchair. "What brings you all this way?"

"I dispatched five Wraiths to investigate Skullkeep and provide general intelligence on the fortress and its garrison," Gavin began, "but their main objective is to locate the Necromancer's soul jar and be ready to destroy it on command. I trust he would notice its destruction?"

Othron chuckled amid a clacking of teeth and bones. "Oh, yes, my friend. He most certainly would. Now, if one of your people were a bit overzealous and destroyed it before we were ready, all is not lost. It would take him a year and a day to craft a replacement, and during that time, he would be supremely vulnerable."

Gavin nodded his understanding. "That is certainly a boon, but I've always been a 'belt and suspenders' guy."

"Belt and suspenders? I'm afraid I don't understand the reference."

"Oh, my apologies. It's a phrase from my birth world. Back home there are two methods for holding a person's pants up... belts and suspenders. Suspenders are elastic bands with clips or buttons that attach to the pants and go over the person's shoulders. If someone says they're a belt *and* suspenders person—"

"Then, they like the insurance of multiple methods," Othron concluded. "Yes, I see. Very descriptive. How can I help?"

"I would like to examine you through my *skathos* to see if I can detect the link to your soul jar. If I can, I want to examine it and see what I can learn about it. I'm not planning anything invasive that might interfere with the link, and I won't even try without your permission."

Othron sat in silence for several moments. "If it were anyone else, Kirloth, I would not respond well or kindly. As the years have passed, I have noticed myself becoming increasingly reluctant to do anything that might threaten my continued existence. It's... well... after all this time, I have no interest in learning whether an afterlife awaits me. That's the risk to existing forever, you see; after a time, ensuring your existence continues becomes the only thought in one's mind. Please, proceed."

Gavin closed his eyes and concentrated on his *skathos*. Even here, deep within the earth, he sensed the heightened level of power Drakmoor acquired through his return from what locals termed the Refugee World. At first, he didn't notice anything untoward or different. But... as he quieted his mind and damped down the radiance of his own power, he found it. A faint swirling thread that connected the skeletal form in front of him to something off in the distance. He concentrated on that link and decided the other terminus wasn't more than thirty yards away.

"Your soul jar is thirty yards or less that way," Gavin said after several moments of silence as he pointed.

Othron reacted as if slapped. "By the gods, Gavin... no one has ever discerned the link to my soul jar before. I honestly didn't think you'd do it."

Still submerged within his *skathos*, Gavin devoted his full focus to the link. He didn't touch it or attempt to manipulate it any way, but he did everything in his power to examine it otherwise.

"Huh...that's kind of weird," he said after several moments of silence.

"What?" Othron asked. "What's weird?"

"Nature's Protector basically kidnapped Lillian and Mariana when I sent them north to visit those members of the Old Alliance, and when I went to discuss the situation with him, he turned out to be a priest or something of Milthas and called forth his god to chastise me for my arrogance. Milthas animated a statue in his ruined temple, and I severed a link to that statue that was very similar to this link to your soul jar. At the time, I thought severing the link severed Milthas's connection to Lornithar, but what if it didn't? What if severing that link cut Milthas's soul off from his body and, then by destroying the statue, I killed him?"

"That is a rather scary proposition," Othron remarked. "I don't know how many dark elves there are on the far side of the Godswall Mountains, but if you did kill Milthas, I'd imagine they're a bit wroth with you. That was Lornithar's major mistake, in terms of the pantheon he raised. Unlike Valthon in the wake of the Godswar, Lornithar didn't grant those deities he raised true, independent power. They were all... well... extensions of him, for lack of a better term. That was why Valthon asked us not to kill any of them at the time; he was concerned how that would affect the unraveling of reality that created such things as arcane magic."

"Oh." Someone really should have told him that he wasn't supposed to kill any of Lornithar's pantheon... assuming that's actually what he did in his confrontation with Milthas in Arundel. "Uhm... I should probably investigate that. Consult with my boss or some such."

Othron barked a laugh. "Well, it has been long enough now that I would assume someone would've discussed the matter with you, if you did something you shouldn't. Did you get what you need?"

Gavin nodded. "Yes, I think so. I wish I could actually test whatever solution I develop, but I'm not about to risk you... and any other test would risk alerting the Necromancer to the idea. I don't know that would grant him the ability to counter it, but why help him make my life difficult? I hate to chat and run, but would you forgive me if I went back to work more on this?"

"Of course, I'll forgive you. The Necromancer is the greatest threat we shall encounter; I do not begrudge you wanting to be as prepared as possible to face him."

"Thank you, Othron. I appreciate your help today."

Othron stood with Gavin and walked with him to the staircase. "Think nothing of it. I would consider it a favor if you would ensure whatever notes or diagrams or thoughts you record do not survive this endeavor. I don't *know* that I have any enemies after all this time, but... well..."

Gavin smiled. "No one will ever know what I've discovered, Othron. I give you my word on that."

The lich clapped Gavin on his shoulder and nodded his thanks once more. Then, Gavin climbed the stairs to reach the ground floor of the ruined keep, whereupon he opened a gateway and left Othron's keep behind. He needed to collect his thoughts before visiting Kiri.

Upon arriving in the Citadel, Gavin gathered the notes and diagrams that he'd left on the table in the sitting room. A short walk delivered him to the private study that not even Hartley dared enter. There, with fresh sheets of unblemished parchment plus his stylus and inkpot, Gavin proceeded to transcribe all his observations and thoughts regarding the link he observed between Othron and his soul jar. As soon as that was complete, he wrapped those sheets in a powerful protection that would destroy them beyond any reconstruction if anyone other than he himself ever touched them. The protection further extended to encrypting the text and drawing to prevent people from reading them from afar. He valued his friendship with Othron and Othron's trust in him too much to risk those notes getting loose in the wild.

He leaned back in his seat, considering his thoughts. He still couldn't escape the desire for a test of some kind, and in truth, Xartham was available. All reports pointed toward him being a rather unsavory individual, too. But no matter how much he desired a test of his plan, he couldn't bring himself to essentially declare war on someone who had never done wrong to him or anyone he termed 'his.'

Beyond that, he had no idea where Xartham was or whether Xartham and the Necromancer kept in contact. If they communicated often, the sudden disappearance of his mentor might put the Necromancer on his guard or otherwise make their task more difficult.

No.

For now, he would continue working up his idea and doing what he could to learn and research whether his actions in Arundel had killed Milthas in truth or simply left him as a mere mortal elf as he originally surmised. Based on the surprising similarity between the two arcane threads, Gavin felt studying *that* outcome might be as fruitful as his conversation and work with Othron.

Now, he just had to determine how to research an event that happened something like two years in the past...

CHAPTER 7

The Cavaliers milling about the palace courtyard no longer gave it a second thought when Gavin appeared out of nowhere. Yes, they tensed, but as soon as they recognized him for who he was, they went back to their activities.

Gavin paid them no mind, beyond waving hello, as he crossed the courtyard and took the steps into the palace two at a time. Unlike his first visit to the palace, the halls and corridors were familiar to him now, old hat even. The large anteroom where petitioners waited for Varne to announce the King's court stood empty, and he paused a moment to consider the best option for finding his wife. Considering it was late afternoon, he didn't think they would still be holding court, but it never hurt to check.

A short walk delivered him to the doors that allowed petitioners and guests into the throne room, but only one Cavalier stood there. If court had still been in session, Varne—the Royal Herald—and at least one more Cavalier would have occupied the area.

"Looking for Her Highness, Milord?" the Cavalier asked.

Gavin nodded. "I didn't think they'd still be holding court, but if I hadn't checked, they would've been."

"Ain't that always the case," the Cavalier agreed. "No. T'weren't too many petitioners this morning, and they wrapped it up rather quick like. But since it's still some time a'fore the evening bell, yer best bet is their offices in the administration wing."

"Gotcha, thanks. Have a good day," Gavin replied.

"You as well, Milord," the Cavalier intoned as Gavin pivoted on his heel and strode back the way he came.

PAST THE DOOR where Terris held his war councils during the siege, Gavin strode deeper into that section of the palace and arrived at a door almost covered with Cavaliers. They snapped to attention at Gavin's approach, and he smiled.

"Stand easy," Gavin said. "So, I guess I've found my wife and father-in-law."

One of the Cavaliers nodded. "Ye'd be right in that, Milord, plus a gaggle of city nobles."

Just then, raised voices carried through what Gavin knew to be a *very* thick door. He held zero doubt whatsoever that Kiri could protect herself and her father after Declan's tutelage and her near-daily practice, but the thought of someone raising his voice—for the raised voice was certainly male—to her or her father sent his mind down dark paths.

"I think I'll step inside," Gavin remarked, and more than one Cavalier shuddered at the cold, merciless tone his voice now held. A tone many had come to associate with Kirloth. Forming a clear image of his intent was beyond reflex now, and he invoked a Word of Transmutation, "*Zyrhaek.*"

A faint aura of amber shimmered across the hinges and latch just before Gavin swung open the door in utter silence.

"I'm telling you now, Your Highness, that rabid fool you call a husband won't always be around to protect you and His Majesty, and while Fallon means well, he's just a mage. You'd be far better off to set both aside and choose a consort who can provide you real protection."

Gavin gestured for Kiri and Terris to remain silent and keep their seats as he entered the room behind the handful of nobles standing between their desks and the door into the office.

"Rabid fool, am I?" Gavin asked. The nobles froze, and Gavin smiled when the backs of their necks went pale. In his experience, it took a serious fright for the back of a person's neck to pale. "It has always been the thought in my mind that 'rabid' implied a certain lack of control, as if one would attack anything that moved. Now, if my understanding about the term 'rabid' is correct, your rather unkind characterization of me certainly could not be accurate, because you still live. Would you agree with my assessment?"

Gavin watched the speaker's jaw work, but he heard no sound.

Terris's expression was not kind at all. "I think this latest stratagem was ill-considered on your part, and if you leave right now, I *might* decide not to give the Archmagister your names."

The nobles turned almost as one, and Gavin took one step to the side, unblocking the door. In almost the blink of an eye, the nobles fled the office, sounding like a stampede of large animals as they put as much distance between them and Gavin in as short amount of time as possible.

"Are they any threat to either of you?" Gavin asked.

Terris chuckled. "They wish they were, but no. I have people watching them and their social circles, but so far, it's all talk and bluster."

Gavin shrugged. "As long as it remains talk and bluster, I'll leave them be."

Terris quirked one eyebrow upward. "You know, Gavin, my family survived for quite a few years before you arrived. You don't need to feel as though you have to handle every threat that arises."

Gavin smiled as Terris broke into a smile of his own, but Gavin's mind went straight to Marcus's journals and the numerous accounts of his mentor foiling plots against the Vushaari crown. The Vushaari king during the Godswar had saved Marcus's life, and the old wizard never forgot that. In the end, Gavin decided it was better to let Terris enjoy his illusions.

"Of course, Terris. I'll leave it in your capable hands."

Now, Kiri quirked an eyebrow, and Gavin knew she'd ask him about it later. Ah, well... he had no secrets from his wife, merely topics he hadn't discussed with her yet.

* * *

THE NEXT MORNING, Gavin lay awake, holding Kiri while she slept against him, and he smiled at the thought of how his fortunes had turned out. He never would have expected to be married to a princess when he woke up in that alley all those months ago, and as much as he found many of his acts since then to be darker than he would have preferred, he wasn't all that sure he would go back and change any of it if he could.

The magical 'trap' he had laid across the corridor to Kiri's suite triggered and provided him with a mental image of who triggered it. Kiri's maid en route to help Her Highness start the day.

He nudged the stunning—and still sleeping—form draped across him. "Kiri, it's time to wake up."

"No... don't wanna."

"Your maid is on the way. Do you want her to catch you draped across me like this?"

"Damn," Kiri growled and rolled to the side. "Would it kill the wench to be late once in a while? I was *sleeping*."

Gavin grinned. "Yes, you were, and you looked adorable doing it."

By the time the maid trotted through the bedroom door, they were at least decent, and Gavin was even well on his way to being dressed. He only lacked the gold robe negligently tossed across a chair. The maid clicked her tongue at the sight of the robe's state, but Gavin didn't care. If she knew half of the stress and headaches the office that robe represented gave him, she'd toss it across the back of a chair, too.

When Gavin turned to make his goodbyes, Kiri charged across the bedroom and wrapped him in a tight hug as she tiptoed to kiss him. When she broke the kiss, she looked up at him and said, "I love you, Gavin."

"I love you, too, Kiri."

It took all Gavin's willpower not to grin at the scandalized gasp the maid added when Gavin addressed the Crown Princess by name. Instead, he collected his robe of office and invoked a Word of Transmutation, "*Paedryx.*"

In the blink of an eye, he vanished from the room.

APPEARING in his personal chambers in the Citadel, Gavin glanced at the clock hanging on one wall. Then sighed. As much as a nap appealed to him, it was too far into the morning for that. Besides... the idea wasn't nearly as appealing without Kiri. He loved how she felt in his arms.

Well, first things first.

He tossed the gold robe onto the hamper and proceeded to collect a set of fresh clothes from one of his armoires. Then, he added his current attire to the pile on the hamper and went to the bathroom to wash up and prepare to face the day. As he washed, he turned over the burgeoning idea for researching his confrontation with Milthas. It seemed feasible, but he wouldn't know for sure until he tried it.

FINDING the laboratories in the Citadel required asking Hartley. Gavin stood off to one side while various specters worked through emptying the room of all its furnishings under the watchful gaze of the spectral majordomo.

"Milord, may I ask *why* you need this laboratory devoid of furnishings?"

Gavin smiled. "Of course, you may ask, Hartley." He waited just long enough to give the impression that was all he was going to say, then chuckled. "I am going to attempt an experiment, and if the attempt succeeds, having physical objects in the room will be dangerous."

"Ah," the specter remarked. "What kind of experiment would make furniture hazardous?"

"A large-scale illusion that would hide any physical objects in the room."

Hartley nodded once. "Very well, Milord. The staff and I are immune to illusions, so I shall not inquire further."

The last four specters moved the final lab table through the over-size door, and Hartley bid his farewell, closing the door behind him as he left. The space looked right to Gavin, so now, all that was left was to create his version of virtual reality.

He started with a collection of chalk. That would work for his first attempt, and if successful, he would return with a hammer and chisels to make the runes permanent. He crossed the hall to the next room and retrieved the Drakmoor equivalent to a man-lift. It was dwarven-made from mithral with large wheels. Axles connected each pair of wheels, and a driveshaft connected the two axles. The drive-shaft in turn connected to a vertical driveshaft that ran up to the plat-form, terminating in a gearbox. The platform-side of the gearbox sported a hand-crank, complete with a comfortable grip. A second hand-crank operated the mechanism that would raise and lower the platform.

The steering was a little problematic, but for something with the weight of carbon fiber and the strength of steel or better, it wasn't horrible. It took a few minutes to get it into position, and Gavin climbed up the dwarf-sized ladder two rungs at a time until he stood on the platform. It was a simple matter to work the second hand-crank to position his head near the room's ceiling, and he sketched the first glyph. Then, he moved to the next stone block and sketched the glyph again. When he reached the end of the platform, he returned to the first hand-crank and moved the platform along the wall to the next set of stone blocks.

OVER THE NEXT FEW HOURS, Gavin sketched the same glyph on every stone block along the ceiling before moving the lift to the center of the room and sketching that glyph on every stone block along the floor. Once complete, Gavin stepped back and looked over his handiwork. It looked good... for a start... but the more he thought about it, the more Gavin felt the illusion might weaken in the center of the room at the farthest points from the glyphs.

Well, nothing for it, then. Overkill was always underrated, right?

THE SUN HAD long since set by the time Gavin stood from the final glyph. *Every* stone block in *every* wall now sported it, along with *every* stone block that made up the floor. The ceiling appeared to be a single slab of stone, so Gavin didn't have the structure of stone blocks to help guide his placement, but the job wasn't too bad.

"Are you ready for dinner, Milord?" Hartley asked, fading into view not too far from Gavin's elbow.

"Huh?" Gavin turned from his examination of the room. "Oh, Hartley... I didn't see you there. What was your question?"

The spectral majordomo adopted a much-put-upon expression and answered, "I asked if Milord was ready for dinner. It is getting quite late."

Gavin nodded, his eyes returning to the glyphs all over the room. "Oh... food... right. I don't really feel hungry, Hartley, but I suppose I probably should eat something before I actually test this. I'm finally ready to do that, I think."

"I will be the first to admit that I am no master of arcane lore, not even a practitioner of apprentice quality," Hartley remarked, "but might it not be better to perform the test when you're fresh in the morning, Milord?"

"It probably would." Gavin sighed. "Especially if the test works. If it doesn't, no big deal, but if it does, I'd be all wound up to do a proper job of it. I probably should stop for the moment. Good thought, Hartley. Thanks for looking out for me."

The specter bowed. "You are quite welcome, Milord. Even if it were not my primary duty, Her Highness asked me to keep an eye on you while she was in Vushaar."

"That sounds like her," Gavin remarked, chuckling as he turned to follow Hartley out of the lab. "So, what's for dinner?"

"Whatever you desire, Milord."

* * *

GAVIN RETURNED to his project after breakfast, feeling refreshed and ready to complete the experiment. As he stood in the doorway, looking over all the glyphs repeating across every surface, he felt a measure of gratitude that Hartley had interrupted him the night before. It was extremely doubtful that he would've overextended himself, especially at his current level of mastery, but a good night's sleep never hurt anyone. And... he'd missed more than a few down through the years, so he might as well do a better job of taking care of himself.

"Okay... so how do I want to do this?" Gavin muttered to himself.

The glyph contained runes for Transmutation, Evocation, and Illusion. The Illusion component would take his memory of the confrontation with Milthas and create a three-dimensional experience of it. The Transmutation component was two-fold: the first to make the Illusion 'real' and the second to pierce the veil of Time to connect the illusion to the event and environment themselves. If he was correct, this would make the overall effect a pocket replay of those moments, wherein everything was duplicated... including his sense of the link he severed. The final component, the Evocation, would tie the effect to the ambient magic, which would act as a power-source to sustain it until such time as Gavin felt no further need of it. *That* was the easiest part of the whole thing, as he had done it many, many times.

He rolled and stretched his shoulders as he took deep breaths and closed his eyes. He put everything out of his mind, concentrating solely on the effect he desired to create. It took more effort than he was used to, but he soon had what he felt was a sufficiently accurate mental picture. All that was left was to invoke the composite effect.

"*Zikthaes-Rhyskaal-Uhnrys-Idluhn.*"

For the first time in... quite a while... the invocation staggered Gavin. The power coursing through him and into his effect felt as though he held onto a live electrical wire. Pain savaged him, every millimeter of every nerve lighting up and overloading the receptors in his brain.

After what seemed like hours of agony, it stopped... all at once and without warning. Gavin staggered to catch himself from falling as rigid muscles relaxed. He gulped in mouthfuls of air, his focus on surviving more than checking his work. Soon enough, though, he felt calm returning to his body, and he opened his eyes.

A huge smile spread across his face as he beheld a frozen moment inside the confines of the laboratory. Every detail of the confrontation with Nirrock and Milthas seemed duplicated, but his smile faltered when he reached out with his *skathos* and felt only the Illusion.

"Huh... well, damn," Gavin said, almost sighing the words. "Well, back to the design phase, I guess."

As he started the turn to leave, a new thought stuck him. He wasn't standing inside the effect; he was just outside it in the doorway. He took another deep breath, hoping he hadn't inadvertently created an actual portal to the confrontation, and stepped inside.

The sudden change was jarring. His stomach flip-flopped more than once as his *skathos* went wild. Both settled soon enough, and Gavin closed his eyes to concentrate.

Yes... it worked! Standing inside the illusion, everything felt as he remembered. He reached out through his *skathos* and touched the piece of the effect that put it in motion, reliving those moments from when Nirrock summoned Milthas to inhabit the statue all the way up to when the Guardians came to inform him of the Necromancer's invasion. Even in the recreation, everything happened so fast.

He touched the control again and attempted to convey that it should proceed at half-speed. He grinned when it did. This time, Gavin concentrated on the link that formed and animated the statue, comparing his sense of that to his sense of Othron's link to his soul jar. It wasn't totally dissimilar, but it wasn't the same, either.

After several more run-throughs, Gavin felt he had as clear a picture of Milthas's link to the statue as he'd ever get, and he *still* didn't feel he had a proper understanding of whether he'd killed

Milthas, severed his link to Lornithar's power, or simply severed his link to the statue.

While his experiment was indeed successful in one respect, it had not achieved the results he desired. Gavin felt like scowling as he stepped back outside the effect and dispelled it with a Word of Tutation. As he closed the lab's door behind him and headed in the general direction of the library, he contemplated where he would go from there.

CHAPTER 8

Gavin leaned back against his seat. He and Declan enjoyed the hospitality of the sitting room on the main floor of the Citadel, and Hartley assured them tea and snacks would arrive soon. He still worked the issue of how to further research severing the link between the Necromancer and his soul jar, but there being only three known liches in the world made determining the next steps a bit problematic.

"So, what brings you to my door?" Gavin asked.

Hartley wheeled a cart into the sitting room laden with a tea service and a selection of cookies and other baked goods.

"Refreshments are served, gentlemen," the spectral majordomo intoned before he faded out of view.

Gavin always wondered if Hartley actually left when he did that or was merely invisible. "Thank you, Hartley."

There was no response, and Gavin put the matter aside for the moment.

Declan leaned closer to the trolley, claiming a biscuit before he slathered butter over it. "All five of our Wraiths have successfully infiltrated Skullkeep. They didn't send more than the code for 'infiltration successful,' so I don't know anything else beyond that."

"I've been working on a way to sever the Necromancer's connection to his soul jar. I'd like to think I've made progress, but I won't know for certain without an actual test. Unlike the slavers, liches are in rather short supply."

"There's always Xartham," Declan remarked between bites. After the biscuit disappeared completely, he continued, "Though he's been uncharacteristically quiet of late. It almost makes me wonder if you got him when you wiped out the slavers."

Gavin shrugged. "I have really no way to know. I suppose we could always ask Othron, but I don't want to cross any lines, you know? He's a friend, and I don't want him thinking we're trying to learn more about him to end him. But... he did say it would take the Necromancer a year and a day to re-create a soul jar if we destroyed it and not him. Do you suppose that's how long it takes a lich to re-form from the soul jar if their physical form is destroyed?"

"Possibly, but it's been over a year and a day since you wiped out the slavers. It was almost a year when the Necromancer sent you off on your cross-planar jaunt. We still need to sit down sometime and discuss that. I want a record of it for the chronicle I'm writing."

Gavin nodded as he selected a cookie and munched on it, washing the crumbs down with a swallow of tea. "I know. If you can find a time when we can do it that won't sacrifice other important tasks, I'm all for it."

"Excuses, excuses..."

Gavin chuckled and shook his head. After a few moments of companionable silence, he asked, "Do you think things will calm down once we re-take Skullkeep?"

"Getting a little ahead of yourself, there, aren't you? Success is not foreordained, you know."

"If I don't believe we can do it, why make the attempt in the first place? All of these people are counting on me to lead them, and leading them into something I myself don't believe in seems like one of the grossest forms of betrayal. So, no... I don't think I'm getting ahead of myself."

"As long as you're not overconfident," Declan replied. "As for things calming down, I'd like to say 'yes,' but I can't help the feeling that this is just a beginning. The Lornithrasa are still out there and active, and yes, it's possible the only major 'thing' left is to beat them back into the shadows. But... I don't know. I was just starting my training with the Wraiths when we had the previous campaign to reduce the Lornithrasa's numbers, and this doesn't feel like I remember that time period feeling. Of course, there's all kinds of difference between the person I was then and the person I am now, so that probably plays a part in this, too. I know that's incredibly imprecise, but I wouldn't count on retiring after this."

Gavin nodded. "Maybe so, but I'm hoping I'll be able to set the gold robe aside at the end of this adventure to Skullkeep. Say, do we even know what the fortress's actual name was after all these centuries? The only name I've ever encountered is Skullkeep."

Declan took another swallow of tea and shook his head. "If it had another name or was supposed to, whatever it was has been lost to time. I've never seen any documents or records that refer to the fortress of Hope's Pass as anything other than Skullkeep. The commanding officer who oversaw the final stages of construction named it, as the opening of Hope's Pass on Tel's side was still a rather gruesome battlefield. The druids spent more time rehabilitating that area than the armies spent building the fortress."

The two friends spent another hour or so catching up before Declan needed to be on his way, and since Gavin had his own business at the College, he walked out with his old friend.

* * *

GAVIN ENTERED the office of the Chief Inquisitor, and the young mage working as Reyna's assistant jumped to his feet. He stammered a greeting, and Gavin smiled, waving him to be at ease.

"Is the Chief Inquisitor in?" Gavin asked.

"Let me announce you," the young mage answered as he nodded.

He turned and almost dashed to the door that led to Reyna's inner office, knocked twice, and opened the door just far enough to lean inside. Gavin easily heard him inform Reyna that the Archmagister was waiting, and he grinned at Reyna's almost waspish reply.

"Then, why is he *still* waiting?"

The young mage pulled back from the door and gestured toward it for Gavin. "She'll see you now."

Gavin stepped into Reyna's office, and he smiled as Mariana's friend stood and came around her desk to greet him. As she stepped back from the handshake, Reyna glanced toward the door to the outer office and rolled her eyes.

"Of course, I'll see you now," she remarked, her tone little more than an exasperated grumble, as she gestured for Gavin to take the seat of his choice. "Who in their right mind would keep the Archmagister waiting?"

"I take it he's new?" Gavin asked.

Reyna shrugged and rolled her hand back and forth in the common gesture of 'kind of.' "He is, but he isn't. He graduated while you were on the Refugee World, and he's always been rather competent and steady. Not sure what his issue is today."

Gavin plucked at the hem of his attire. "It's probably the gold robe. I've seen it reduce even the most confident and accomplished arcanist to adolescent stammering."

Reyna nodded her agreement. "So, what can I do for you, Milord?"

"You know, I'm looking forward to the day when I won't be Archmagister, just so I can get away from that 'Milord' business. I'm *Gavin*, Reyna."

Reyna replied with a soft smile and a shake of her head. "While that might be your name, it's been a long time since you've been just 'Gavin.' Being Head of one of the Great Houses confers the rank of Duke by itself, not to mention your rather impressive list of accomplishments. If getting away from 'Milord' is your sole reason to hand over your office, I'm not entirely certain you'll be successful. And then, there's the fact that you will always be the first Archmagister after the death of Bellock Vanlon and the tyranny of the Royal Family. A lot of people have commented on how Bellos chose the Head of

House Kirloth to be Archmagister, you know, and many seem to consider it a kind of renewal or rebirth for the Kingdom."

"Kirloth and the Apprentices founded the Kingdom, so only Kirloth and the Apprentices could set it right? Please, tell me you don't believe that, Reyna."

Reyna answered with a noncommittal shrug. "It doesn't matter what *I* personally believe, Gavin. I'm just one person who happens to know you and has known you for quite some time. Your changes in the short time you've been Archmagister—even counting the year or so you were gone—have done a lot to give the people of Tel hope again, and they won't forget that anytime soon. But I'm certain you didn't come here for this discussion."

Gavin chuckled and shook his head. "No. I wanted an update on your investigation into Drannos Muldannin."

"For one, he hasn't set foot on College grounds that I can prove since Alanna Veldin's case. Per your authority, I accessed the quarters assigned to him here in the Tower, and they showed no signs of occupancy or significant use in quite some time, as in decades if not centuries."

"I see," Gavin remarked. "Very well. Put the word out for all Inquisitors to be on the lookout for Magister Drannos Muldannin. If anyone sees him on College grounds, they are to notify you personally at once. Do not engage. Do not attempt to apprehend. You will contact me, and *I* will handle the matter."

"May I ask why the sudden interest in this particular magister?"

"If I tell you, you will not write it down or speak of it to anyone. Do you agree?"

Reyna replied with an immediate nod. "Yes."

Gavin took a deep breath and released as a slow sigh. "Because Othron told me that he taught Emperor Xartham how to become a lich, and Xartham in turn went through dozens of would-be apprentices until one succeeded. Xartham's sole success was a man named Drannos Muldannin, who Othron now claims is the Necromancer of Skullkeep."

Reyna collapsed heavily into her seat behind her desk. "That... I don't even know how to begin calculating how damaging that has been to the Old Alliance, Tel, or even just the Society. Drannos Muldannin has been the Magister of Thaumaturgy for... something like sixty years. Are you certain you can trust Othron in this?"

"I would trust Othron with my life or the life of my daughter," Gavin replied. "He wouldn't lie to me about this."

Reyna still looked shell-shocked. "With... with your permission, I will institute an investigation and review of all Council decisions proposed or heavily influenced by him."

"You can if you want, but you'll just be chasing your tail trying to determine which decisions he really cared about. If the Necromancer of Skullkeep is the same person as our Magister of Thaumaturgy, he's been sitting right under all our noses for many, many years. He even managed to fool my mentor, though it would be interesting to see if they ever crossed paths. I've already reviewed the College's academic policies and the Society's general policies, and I haven't found anything that truly stands out as egregious. He couldn't go too far, because the Society is based on the Arcanists' Code, and only the sitting Archmagister can modify *that*, just like Tel's Constitution."

"Yes, I suppose you're right," Reyna remarked, heaving a sigh. "It's just... I just can't believe someone could perpetrate that level of fraud successfully for *sixty years*. That's insane. Surely, he would have made mistakes."

Gavin nodded. "Oh, I'm sure he did... here and there. Maybe small ones, maybe not. Honestly, after all this time, I doubt there's any way to know for certain. And the more I think about it, I'm not all that sure it really matters in the long run. We'll settle the matter when we re-take Skullkeep."

"I wish I could be as relaxed about this as you seem to be."

Gavin grinned around a chuckle. "If it makes you feel any better, I've had some time to come to terms with the idea. I was a bit gobs-macked when Othron told me."

"I imagine you were."

"Well, unless you have anything more for me, I'll get out of your hair. Be sure to alert everyone to watch for him, but at this point, I doubt he'll turn up in Tel again. Maybe, if he thinks we haven't tripped to him, but our mobilization has not been particularly quiet. And... our target isn't exactly a secret, either. I'd say he's hunkered down at Skullkeep, preparing his forces to meet ours. I feel certain he'll stay there until the matter has been settled, one way or the other."

Reyna nodded, standing as Gavin did so. "I will keep you apprised of any developments and put the word out at once."

"Thank you, Reyna," Gavin replied and left the Chief Inquisitor to her work.

* * *

As HE WALKED the main corridor of the Tower's ground floor, Gavin considered his next steps. He wanted to check in with the Army's general staff, wanted an update on the status of their mobilization, but the regular meeting was in just two days. One of the few personality types Gavin genuinely despised was micromanagers. So—despite how much he wanted to visit the general staff—he took a deep breath, released it as a slow sigh, and counseled himself to wait for the meeting.

A bell rang throughout the city, and moments later, classroom doors all around him exploded open to permit the students' egress. The group that charged into the hallway right in front of Gavin almost skidded to a stop as they stared at him with wide eyes. More than a few jaws worked, but no one made a sound.

Gavin smiled and gestured for them to proceed, and the students dashed off, more than one casting a wary glance at him over their shoulders. The more he thought about it, the more Gavin decided it would've been the same for him if he'd attended college at an institution administered by the President of the United States. Not that such a thing would ever happen on Earth, but it was the closest parallel that came to mind.

"There's no reason you couldn't be one of the instructors now, you know," a weathered voice said from just behind Gavin's left shoulder.

He grinned and turned to see Valera standing a respectful distance away. "Yes, there is. I barely have enough time to accomplish everything I feel an Archmagister should accomplish. If I tried to add grading papers and overseeing lab time, something would have to give. So, why add that in the first place? Maybe once the Necromancer has been dealt with, we can revisit the topic, but right now, there is simply too much to do."

Valera replied with an enigmatic smile and just enough of a shrug for Gavin to notice. "From everything I've heard, you would be a superlative instructor for our wizard students. I would very much like to revisit the topic, especially if certain other rumors I've heard prove true."

Gavin wanted to ask her what rumors those were, but he suspected they involved his desire to step down from being Archmagister and saw no reason to air that particular laundry just yet. "Yes, well... I won't deny that I enjoyed teaching, the few times I was able to do it. I'm not sure there is sufficient lecture material to make an entire class out of the Words of Power, so you'd have to help me plan the class."

"Oh, I'm sure you could fill the time, Gavin. I have no doubt of that at all. Even if you spent half the term telling personal experience stories, those would carry far more educational value than a recounting of most other instructors' *lives*. You have experienced and survived a lot in the short time you've been with us."

Gavin's nod was almost rueful. "Yes... I have."

"Well, I don't mean to keep you. It seemed like a perfect moment to say hello."

"Thank you, Valera," Gavin replied. "It's always nice to speak with you."

Valera turned into her office, and Gavin resumed his walk toward the Grand Stair. Seeing no end to the horde of students filling the hallway, he instead stepped into an alcove and teleported back to the Citadel.

CHAPTER 9

Even though this was not his estate, Gavin felt a special kinship with the meeting room the Conclave of the Great Houses used at the Mivar Estate. He still remembered the blindsided expression on Lyssa's face when she had learned he was the heir to House Kirloth and Marcus's apprentice. He wasn't sure it had even been three full years since that day, but so much had happened since his first Conclave that it felt like almost a lifetime ago.

He was both looking forward to this meeting and dreading it, all at the same time. Rather than deal with the frustration of conveying the army's general staff up to the Citadel and also rather than trying to occupy a room in the Tower of the Council, the College's main building, Gavin chose to accept Torval's offer to host the meeting at the Mivar Estate, which was why people now stood in the Conclave room who had never seen it—or anything like it—before.

"I'm not entirely certain this venue is the best place to discuss sensitive military information," the ancient general nominally in charge of Tel's army growled as he peered around the room with a jaundiced eye. "There's no telling what spy holes the ceiling or these walls have."

Gavin slid into the seat for House Kirloth at the head of the table and gestured for the rest of the Conclave to assume their seats. He reflected on a report the Wraiths provided him on the army's general staff and how all indications pointed to many of the general staff being Royalists. Just how they thought to remain loyal to a family that no longer existed puzzled Gavin a bit, but the murmuring nods of agreement the other officers made to reinforce the old soldier's remark underscored the Wraiths' observations.

"General, I'm not certain you have sufficient understanding to evaluate this room's security," Gavin replied. "We planned the campaign that ended the mercenary threat to Tel Mivar in this room, and we have held wide ranging discussions on the state of Tel in this room without any of that reaching unwanted ears. Now, all that being said... if you don't feel the Mivar Estate—and this room in particular—is sufficiently secure to discuss recruitment, training, and force levels for our coming Skullkeep campaign, I am quite happy to host the meeting in the Citadel. But I'm afraid you gentlemen will have to climb the... how many flights of stairs, Lillian? Is it twelve or fourteen to that last landing in the Grand Stair?"

Lillian smiled as she almost purred her answer. "It's twenty-four flights actually, Gavin."

The old warhorse blanched. "Twenty-four flights of stairs, you say?"

"Yes, General, I believe so," Lillian replied. "I could be wrong, of course, but I promise you the number's higher if I am."

Gavin watched the general staff share a look between each other and fought the urge to grin when each of them reached for one of the empty chairs at the table.

"Well, if you say you've held sensitive discussions in this room before without that information leaking," the old warhorse said, his tone somewhat chagrined, "I am certainly willing to trust your judgment and experience."

"I appreciate your faith in me, General," Gavin remarked. "So, where do we stand?"

Over the next few hours, the general staff delivered detailed information on current force levels, the recruitment drive, and the training status of all the new solders. Gavin watched them refer to a sheaf of parchment time and again as they did so and decided they would leave those documents with him. After all, it never hurts to get a second opinion.

"AND THAT IS EVERYTHING WE HAVE," the general said at last, bringing their remarks to a close. "Do you have any questions?"

"Not at this time, thank you, General," Gavin replied, "but you will leave a copy of your notes with me, if you please. I might want to refer back to them between now and the next meeting."

The officers shared another look, and Gavin thought one of the younger ones looked a bit antsy at his decision. After several moments of silence, the general nodded his agreement and passed his collection of notes to Wynn, who then passed them on until they reached Gavin, who laid them on the table and folded his hands on them.

"Very well, General, thank you. Unless you have something else, you're dismissed."

"Thank you," the general replied and stood, his officers standing also.

They filed out of the room, and Gavin waited until the door swung shut on silent hinges and latched before he looked to his associates.

"So... comments?"

Torval shook his head. "Unless they're deliberately understating things, the force levels sound a little low to me."

"I agree," Lyssa Cothos replied, "and why is it taking so long to recruit new soldiers? Anytime the late unlamented king wanted new regiments, he just conscripted people."

Gavin winced. "I would prefer volunteers make up our forces if at all possible. I will order conscription if it's necessary, but I would much rather we have an army made up of soldiers who *chose* to join. If nothing else, I would think it raises the base morale."

Sypara Wygoth nodded. "I can see how that might be. I for one would like to see if their internal numbers match the notes he gave you. I know I saw reports sent to the crown from Wygoth Province that were not wholly accurate. By the time I got around to tracking down whether it was an attempt to undermine me by the civil governors, the royal family was dead and you the Archmagister, so the question became moot."

"Oh, I think I'll be able to lay my hands on accurate information," Gavin replied with an almost predatory smile. "I made sure he left me his notes, so we'll have something to compare. Otherwise, I imagine he'd try to play the 'we never said that' game. I don't like purges; I never have. But if the general staff is not carrying out its duties, I don't see any other choice."

"No," Carth agreed. "You need people you can trust to do what they need to do and provide accurate reports to you. Without that, the government can't function. If they're not doing their jobs, the only question to me is whether to fire them or allow them to retire and draw a pension."

"It honestly depends on what my independent audit finds. We cannot afford—and I cannot abide—gross dereliction of duty; in that case, I feel very strongly that my hands would be tied. But... if it's something like old age... as long as they haven't undermined the Kingdom or the army, I could see retirement in their near future. I hate object lessons. I hope they don't force my hand.

"But moving on. We have an Alliance Council meeting next week, where we should learn how our allies are doing with their mobilizations. It would not surprise me for the dracons to be sitting at the shore of the Vischaene River with their army wondering where the rest of us are. They can be a bit eager at times."

Braden—the one person who had as much if not more experience with the dracons than Gavin—rumbled a chuckle. "That might be understating things. Overall, they have been *very* insistent about contributing what they feel is their part, plus providing recompense for their mistake in deciding the Gods abandoned us when Bellos did not name a new Archmagister. I've tried explaining that we forgive them and understand how they could have arrived at that conclusion, but sometimes I feel like I'm talking at a stone cliff. They decide how they're going to handle things, and that's how they handle them. The only person who might be able to change their minds is you, Gavin."

"If things get too egregious, I'll have a chat with the Council of Clans," Gavin agreed. "Aside from the meeting next week, is there any new business?"

No one spoke up, so Gavin rapped his knuckles on the tabletop and stood. "Very well. Torval, thank you for hosting."

Torval smiled. "It was my pleasure, Gavin."

With that, Gavin stepped away from the table, slid his chair back in, and strode from the room. He had to visit a certain chapterhouse.

* * *

GAVIN RETURNED to the Citadel after tasking the Wraiths to investigate the true status of Tel's army. He hoped their findings mirrored what the general staff reported. Contrary to what he was sure many people believed about him, he did not enjoy upsetting everyone's apple carts. Just because he did it well didn't mean he set out to do it.

After checking in with Hartley, Gavin went to his study and eased into his favorite seat. The matter of not having a way to test whether he could sever a lich's link to its soul jar bothered him. The idea of attempting some kind of simulation occurred to him, but after thinking his way through it, he realized that he wouldn't know if the link severed because that's what he wanted to happen or because that's what would actually happen.

The matter frustrated him to the point that he actually considered asking Othron to teleport him to Xartham's palace, just to test his theory. But no matter how appealing he found that solution, he cast it aside. He didn't know how that would affect his friendship with Othron, and he valued that more than the test.

* * *

LIFE at the Necromancer's stronghold was not as difficult as Cyn feared it would be. Yes, a number of soldiers—and not all of them male—tried things, but after she knifed the guy who helped himself to a handful of her ass, matters calmed rather quickly. When her sergeant summoned her later that day, she fully expected to be ushered out of the fortress or killed and raised into the undead horde, and she almost didn't believe it when the sergeant just laughed and told her not to kill anyone else if she could keep from it. He seemed to consider it an example of her skill that she had killed the guy with one strike and so quickly after grabbing her.

No. Life at Skullkeep was not horrible at all... at least, not overall. The one thing she had not been prepared for in the least, though, was *the smell*. If she had stopped to think about it, the idea that undead would be rather foul seemed axiomatic. They were animated corpses in various stages of decay, after all. Magic animated them and kept them from falling apart, but whoever developed those spells apparently never gave any thought to blunting the putrid odor of death that surrounded them like a heavy cloak. And the presence of over ten thousand corpses in a relatively small space seemed to intensify the stench by at least an order of magnitude.

Spending as much time as possible inside the fortress seemed to help... at least those spaces two or more rooms *away* from exterior walls. What shocked her more than the smell of the undead, though, was how no one seemed to care if she explored the fortress, and aside from the Necromancer's quarters—or *the Master*, as most people referred to him there—none of the spaces seemed off-limits when not in use. She had in fact tested that her second week there by 'stumbling' into a meeting room while the Necromancer met with his lieutenants; other than the Necromancer himself rudely pointing out the room was in use, no one said anything about it.

Part of her loved exploring the fortress. It was something like six *thousand* years old. It both resembled other architectural styles she had seen... and didn't, all at the same time. Aside from the greater stability and safety re-taking the fortress would achieve, she hoped their overall objective was successful for the simple reason that she would love to spend days wandering this fortress and soaking up its history.

In the meantime, she had a job to do. As part of her general objective of collecting intelligence on the fortress and its garrison, she had already communicated back a rough count of undead and the fact that the undead generally milled about in the courtyard, left largely to themselves. It was a large space that Cyn suspected had once doubled—or perhaps, tripled?—as a parade ground, exercise yard, and inspection area. Aside from the historical accounts she had read, standing on the west wall looking east, it was obvious that the planners intended Skullkeep to serve as a customs point once the Old Alliance normalized trade and relations with the descendants of those defeated in the Godswar. The arrangement of the two gates and how the fortress itself abutted the courtyard made that obvious to Cyn.

Aside from gathering general intelligence, her *other* objective—and in her mind, the true primary—was the location of the Necromancer's soul jar. The idea that the Necromancer was a lich like Othron made enormous amounts of sense, given that there was no indication that the Necromancer who invaded Tel Mivar was a different person from the one who first conquered the fortress five hundred years or so ago, not too long after the assassination of Bellock Vanlon.

She wanted to say that the soul jar was hidden away in the Necromancer's quarters somewhere. Given its importance to his continued existence, it made perfect sense that he would want to keep it close and very well protected. But his quarters being the obvious choice made Cyn consider other alternatives. She didn't want to ignore the search for hidden rooms or spaces elsewhere in the fortress, simply because the soul jar *had to be* in his quarters. So, her plan was to rule out all the places within the fortress that it wasn't.

Cyn strolled down the hallway of the first underground floor. That level held all the storerooms for the kitchens that fed the still-living part of the garrison. She silently thanked the builders of the fortress for using sconces like those in Tel Mivar, that provided a steady flame for light without radiating heat or consuming fuel. Having grown up in Vushaar, which used the non-magical methods of lighting, the difference was both obvious and pleasant.

As she strolled along in her explorations, she added to a mental map of the fortress. When she returned to her cot, she'd add the floor to the map of the fortress she was making. No one had challenged her on it yet, but if they did, she felt that her interest in historical places was sufficiently established that it would seem normal for her to draw a map of her explorations. It made sense to her, anyway, especially since she annotated her sketches with whatever struck her as especially interesting. She used those annotations to obscure her notes of more tactical or strategic value.

"You there, stop!" a male voice almost shouted behind her.

Cyn turned and saw a man with sergeant stripes striding her way. "Yes?"

"Who are you, and what are you doing on this floor?"

"I'm Cyn. I've been here about three weeks, and I'm exploring."

The man's eyes narrowed at the word 'exploring.' "Exploring, you say? Why?"

Cyn shrugged and smiled. "I love old places. Ruins. Buildings like this. It was the main reason I applied to join; I wanted to explore the fortress. Did you know there's a ruined castle in central Vushaar that's almost as old as the kingdom itself? I haven't been there yet, but I've read about it."

The sergeant winced. "You might want to give a second thought to visiting that particular ruin. It's not uninhabited, and the resident doesn't take kindly to guests of our allegiance. We lose scouts in that region on the regular."

"Oh... well... that's unfortunate. Maybe I'll just settle for reading Declan the Dandy's account of Gavin Cross's visit there. I still have so many old places to see in the world. I'd hate to die young just because someone or something doesn't like that I work for you guys."

Eyes narrowed again. "How do you know Declan the Dandy?"

"I don't, but I'd love to. I hear he's quite the ladies' man, and he has just seen so much. Have you read his treatise on architectural styles of Kyndrath? It is the best primer on the subject that I've ever found. Everyone else just skips over all the historical significance and influences. Can you believe that?"

"Oh... you're *her*."

"Her who?" Cyn asked, smiling.

"Never mind. Just don't let your enthusiasm for exploration interfere with your duties."

"I wouldn't dream of it, Sergeant. After all, if I lose the coin from this job, how can I explore more old places?"

The sergeant shook his head and turned, walking back the way he'd come. Cyn smiled and waved, in case he happened to glance back, and then resumed her exploration of that floor.

CHAPTER 10

Gavin welcomed Declan into the sitting room, gesturing for him to take a seat. He chose the armchair on the right side of the hearth, and Gavin chose the left. Gavin regarded one of his oldest friends as the silence extended, and from what little expression leaked through Declan's fierce self-control, he knew whatever the bard brought with him was not good news.

When Declan still had not spoken beyond his greeting, Gavin said, "What is it, Declan? I can tell it's something you consider bad news, but there's no point in stewing on it."

Gavin watched him take a deep breath and release it as a heavy sigh.

After maybe one more heartbeat of silence, Declan said, "The Wraiths passed me the report on the current status of the army, and... well... it's not good. There are no signs of any recruitment drive. There are no signs of a wholesale draw-down, but none of the standing units are up to full roster. When people retire or their term ends, that slot in the unit often isn't re-filled, and it seems like the personnel people deny about one in every fifteen to twenty who tries to re-enlist."

Gavin sagged against his seat. A confusing, convoluted morass of emotion swirled through his mind, and he wasn't certain he could parse them all. Anger, sure; he tasked the leadership of Tel's army with mobilizing for the campaign against Skullkeep, and... well... they didn't do that. Disappointment, absolutely. But the single greatest emotion that assaulted him was disbelief. It was unbelievable that the army leadership would ignore or outright disobey his orders, especially given the culture and mystique and esteem that surrounded the office of the Archmagister.

It wasn't personal to Gavin. At least... he didn't take it personally. Yes, the leadership's lack of compliance could be rooted in personal grievances, but that didn't matter to Gavin. He didn't recognize those issues. The *Kingdom of Tel* needed the army mobilized. The *Kingdom of Tel* needed the threat of the Necromancer ended. None of the issues facing the world at that moment made any *personal* difference to Gavin. Like some people back on Earth would say, Gavin didn't have a dog in the fight.

It would require no effort at all—zero, none—just to tell Bellos, 'I quit,' and hop the portal back to Earth... leaving Drakmoor to fend for itself. In fact, from a purely personal point of view, that was probably the better choice; it absolutely was safest, especially if he collapsed the portal behind him.

But that's not what Gavin agreed to do when he accepted the mantle of Archmagister.

"Well, this is a mess," Gavin said, almost a mutter, when the shock of Declan's revelation ran its course at last. "So... what's my play, here? Who handles the charges of insubordination these people need to face?"

Declan blinked. "Uhm... Gavin, that's you. The army has its own internal justice system, but it's set up to bring charges before a group of higher-ranking personnel. The people responsible for this have no higher-ranking personnel. The person ultimately responsible reports to you."

Gavin shook his head. He couldn't find the words to voice the full breadth and depth of his feelings, so he just sighed and shook his head.

"Fine. I need a list of everyone complicit in this. I'll issue writs for the Wraiths to collect them and hold them until we can work through those who would take their places to make sure the problem won't continue. This is *not* what I wanted to accomplish today."

Declan pursed his lips.

"What?" Gavin asked.

"Your order is all the authority the Wraiths need, Gavin. I thought we were past that."

Gavin sighed again. "I do not like having that much authority. I never have. But fine. So be it. Round them up, and I'll be along with some people to help interview their replacements. It would help if the Wraiths also compiled a list of the successors."

"It shall be done."

Declan stood and left.

Gavin's eyes came to rest on the floor, but he wasn't looking at it. No. His mind swirled through all the headaches and challenges and... just the sheer mess of all that was his responsibility to fix.

"What ever happened to the idea that life was supposed to be fun?" he groused, pushing himself to his feet. He left the sitting room —and then the Citadel—without another word.

THE PASSAGE of a couple hours delivered Gavin, his friends known throughout the arcane world as the Apprentices, and a collection of Inquisitors capable of casting Divination of Truth to the headquarters of the Army of Tel. Gavin's first thought was to bring a contingent of Battle-mages, as he had done when he cleared out of the remnants of the Royal Guard all those months ago, but he decided instead to keep matters as non-confrontational as possible. He felt a handful of wizards and mages—with himself in the vanguard—would not be an undue provocation... especially given his status as head of government for the Kingdom Tel for as long as he held the office of Arch-magister.

Declan met him at the main entrance with a group of plain-clothed Wraiths and handed him a sheaf of parchment.

"These are the names of those personnel next-in-line to assume leadership of the army," the bard explained. "I made multiple copies, so you can divide the list however you see fit."

"Good. Thank you," Gavin replied. "I want this handled quickly."

Gavin turned and began passing parchment to the people with him, and he chose not to ask Declan the precise hows and wherefores he had made a perfect number so that each of Gavin's helpers had a copy of the list. There were some things simple men—like Gavin, in this instance—just were not meant to know.

"You all know the questions you need to ask after casting Divination of Truth?" he asked after passing out the list.

They answered with a mixture of silent nods, "Yes, sir," or "Yes, Milord."

Gavin nodded once. "Very well. I'll handle the two most-senior officers. If the aura shifts red on *any* of the questions, flag that person and make sure they are confined under guard until we have a chance to investigate further. Any questions?"

When the group remained silent for several heartbeats, Gavin gestured toward the entrance. "Proceed, then."

He watched each of the Wraiths pair off with one of the arcanists as he stood a few feet off Declan's left shoulder. When only he and the bard remained, Gavin said, "Well, old friend... let's get this done."

Declan led Gavin into the headquarters, where his people were already causing quite the stir. They walked to the office where the top officer on the list waited under guard, and Gavin enjoyed the wide eyes, slack jaw, and pale complexion that greeted him as he entered the office without warning or announcement.

Shooting out of her seat like a rocket to snap to attention, the officer in question looked to be a middle-aged woman. She wore her salt-and-pepper hair in a plain ponytail that day, and she filled out her uniform with a fit, muscular build.

"Good day, Major. I don't know that we have ever met before, but as my attire suggests, I am Gavin Cross, Head of House Kirloth and Archmagister of Tel. Do you know why we are disrupting your day?"

The major swallowed hard, then said, "I... I imagine it involves the general staff's non-compliance with the mobilization order, Milord."

Gavin smiled. "Very good. We're already off to an excellent start. Now, here's how this will go. I'm going to invoke a Divination effect that will duplicate the effects of the spell Divination of Truth. Are you familiar with it?"

"Yes, Milord," the major replied, jerking a choppy nod.

"Excellent. Once that's in place, we're going to discuss a few things, and I will evaluate your answers as well as the invocation's reaction to you. Do you have any questions before we begin?"

"No, Milord."

At this point in his mastery of the Art, Gavin required less than moment to clear his mind and establish his intent before invoking the Word of Divination, "*Klaepos.*"

The full resonance of his power slammed into the ambient magic, forcing reality to shift according to his will, as a gray aura surrounded the major.

"First off, Major, please sit and relax. There's no reason to be tense about this or fear for yourself or anyone depending on you." Gavin followed his own request and sat in one of the guest chairs facing her desk, as she complied. "Now then, are you complicit in the general staff's obstruction of my orders to prepare Tel's army for a campaign against Skullkeep?"

"No, Milord." The aura surrounding the major shifted from a foggy gray to bright, pristine white.

"Excellent," Gavin remarked. "That is my primary concern, but as long as we're here, let's discuss a few more things."

By the time Gavin left the major's office, she was the commanding general of all Tel's forces, and she held an order Gavin wrote and signed to such effect in case she needed any confirmation.

. . .

WHEN HE STEPPED THROUGH THE HEADQUARTERS' main entrance, Gavin found the rest of his team waiting on him, and everyone reported their people passed. Now, all that remained was the assembly of the headquarters staff to announce the removal of the former leadership and investiture and promotion of the new officers.

Ah, well. No time like the present...

* * *

GAVIN RETURNED to the Citadel drained. Emotionally. Mentally. But not physically so much, depriving him of the trifecta. He stood in the hallway, facing the sitting room he used for conversations with one or two people but not looking at it. With each passing day, he grew less and less enamored with holding the office of Archmagister.

Awareness of what he needed most exploded in the forefront of his mind, and he smiled at the thought.

"Hartley!"

The spectral majordomo faded into existence a few feet in front of him. "You bellowed, Milord?"

"I am taking the rest of the day... and possibly tomorrow... to rest and recharge. Please inform Nathrac that I am going to my family's estate on Earth if I am needed for any emergencies, and I will return no later than end-of-day tomorrow."

Hartley nodded once. "Very good, Milord. Do try to have fun."

"Thank you."

Hartley faded from view as Gavin went to his quarters, where he packed a duffle with a couple sets of clothes that did not relate to his office at all.

* * *

GAVIN STEPPED through the portal that connected his childhood home to the former Sivas Estate he had claimed as his own. The house where he grew up still engendered a feeling of calm that nowhere else he'd ever visited could, which made it the perfect getaway.

Beyond the relaxing effect, the air smelled different here. The easy way out was to chock it up to random post-Industrial-Era pollution in the air that Drakmoor didn't have... despite the valiant efforts of horses and their 'exhaust' everywhere. Gavin never liked to take the easy way out of anything, but at the same time, he hadn't come to Earth to perform an in-depth atmospherical analysis, either.

He saw his daughter sitting on the porch, fiddling with her phone. She still badgered him about learning one every chance she could, and Gavin privately admitted that she probably had a point. But... he didn't expect to be on Earth all that often, and smartphones and the like wouldn't work in Drakmoor. Not beyond being glorified calculators and cameras, and once the batteries ran out, there was no way to charge them that wouldn't risk overloading them.

Sure... he could devise a device that would charge a battery via lightning or even magic. Given all the ingenuity he could access, there was no doubt of that at all. But what was the cost of introducing such devices to Drakmoor? By and large, the societies there were stable. For everything they needed that simple machines couldn't do, there was magic. Introducing advanced technology would only serve to destabilize the world, and he saw no value in doing so.

"Hey, Dad," Jennifer said. "What brings you here?"

"Oh... well... I guess the easiest way to explain it was that I needed a mental health day. I just handled a nasty situation that should never have happened in the first place, and dealing with it left a bad taste in my mouth. I invited Kiri to come with me, but she's occupied with helping Terris run Vushaar right now. She sends her love."

Jennifer smiled. "Yeah... you certainly married up, Dad."

"Don't tell her," Gavin replied, adding a conspiratorial wink. "I don't think she's figured that out yet. How are you?"

"All right, I guess. Alexis canceled on me again, but I understand. I wouldn't want to suffer through the drive from D.C. to here, either."

Gavin's eyes narrowed. "Is the person in charge of the presidential detail still being a horse's ass?"

Jennifer snorted a laugh. "I'm not sure you're supposed to refer to senior Secret Service personnel as 'a horse's ass,' Dad."

"If the shoe fits..." Gavin's voice trailed off as he considered the situation. He hadn't expressly come to Earth to handle power trips, ignorance, or whatever this guy's problem was... but at the same time, he didn't appreciate anyone hamstringing an arcanist. And that's exactly what this ignoramus was doing. In the end, that settled his course of action more than any other facet of the situation, and he nodded once. "Text Alexis that we're coming to visit."

Jennifer's head shot up so she could meet her father's eyes, worry dominating her expression. "Uhm... are you sure about that? I mean... I'm pretty sure you're still *persona non grata* with France over Toussaint's villa. It might make things complicated for Chelsea if she 'receives' you at the White House."

"Do you want to help me educate the idiot that's causing problems for Alexis or not?"

Jennifer closed her eyes as she took a deep breath and slowly sighed it out. "You won't kill him, right, Dad?"

"Of course not. How's he supposed to learn anything if he's dead?"

Jennifer worked her lower lip between her teeth for a moment before she released another put-upon sigh and lifted her phone. She tapped the screen for a bit with her thumbs, and a few moments later, it chirped a tone.

"Okay," Jennifer said. "Alexis *and* her mom are expecting us. Chelsea asks that we arrive in the rose garden."

Gavin nodded. "One second. Forgot something important."

He climbed the three steps up to the porch and opened the front door of his childhood home and spoke at a louder volume than normal, "Mom, Dad... sorry to arrive and run, but I need to visit D.C. to educate an idiot. It shouldn't take long, and I came to spend a couple days before going back to Drakmoor. Be right back."

He pulled the door shut without waiting for their reply and focused on his memories of the White House's rose garden. He included his daughter in his intent and invoked a Word of Transmutation, "*Paedryx*."

The world blinked, and they now stood at the edge of the rose garden, facing the colonnade that connected the West Wing to the original mansion. Chelsea and Alexis Hall stood a stride or two off the colonnade, and Alexis's expression lit up as she ran to Jennifer and drew her friend into a hug.

"Sorry to cancel on you," Alexis said mid-hug, "but the drive to your place is a killer. Five and a half hours is no joke."

"It's okay," Jennifer replied. "Dad's a little fed up with whoever is saying you can't just gateway there, like you used to. That's honestly why we're here."

Chelsea arrived at the periphery of the hug in time to hear Jennifer's statement, and she regarded Gavin with one raised eyebrow. "He'll survive, I hope."

Gavin huffed a sigh and shook his head. "Reduce one Renaissance-era villa to molten rock, and I'm apparently some kind of murder-happy hobo. No, Chelsea... I'm not going to kill the guy. He can't learn if he's dead, and there's no guarantee that whoever replaces him won't be as big of an idiot. Who is he, anyway?"

"Nathan Victorino," Chelsea answered. "He's the division chief in charge of the dignitary protection arm of the Secret Service. For what it's worth, we've tried speaking with him about it, but he digs his heels in every time and refuses even to consider that what Alexis is saying has any validity."

Gavin's lips curled into a smile that did not touch his eyes. "Then, we'll just see how he responds to my methods."

Chelsea did not appear to be all that reassured, but she turned and led them into the White House.

"How do you want to do this?" Chelsea asked.

Gavin pursed his lips as he considered the question. "Hmmm... I think I'd like to borrow a hallway where it's unlikely we'll be interrupted."

"Upstairs in the Residence sounds best, then," Chelsea replied.

A few minutes later, they stood at one end of the hallway Gavin remembered from the visit that ended with his rescue of Alexis's brother. As the President was now in the hallway, a handful of Secret Service agents stood at strategic positions.

Chelsea produced a phone from her pocket as she said, "Would you like me to call him?"

"No," Gavin said. "Just take my hand and concentrate on thinking of him."

Chelsea frowned but did as Gavin asked. To Gavin's experienced eye, it looked like his daughter fought a grin, but that didn't surprise him. Kiri had told her the story of how Gavin teleported their travel party and something like three hundred slaves to the palace court-yard in Vushaar.

As soon as Gavin held Chelsea's hand in his, he focused all his intent on the man she knew as Nathan Victorino, then invoked a Word of Transmutation, "*Paedryx*."

In the blink of an eye, a man of Hispanic descent appeared in the hallway next to Chelsea. Fear, bewilderment, and not a little disbelief all mingled within his expression. It took him no time at all to focus on Chelsea.

"Ma - Madam President? Wha... how did I get here? And *where* is here?"

"You're in the upstairs hallway of the Residence, Nathan," Chelsea said as she indicated Gavin, "and this is Gavin Cross, Archmagister of Tel. I'm sure you've read some reports or files on him by now."

Even as wild around the eyes as he looked at suddenly standing in a hallway in the White House, Nathan's expression became even more so when he realized he stood in front of a man who was a nuclear power in his own right.

"W - why am I here?" Nathan asked.

Gavin leveled his best 'Kirloth' glare on the man as he said, "I find your continued intransigence about Alexis using gateways to be insulting, not just to her but myself and arcanists in general. I have brought you here to show you a demonstration in an attempt to cure what I hope is simple ignorance and not something else. Rest assured that you do not want me to escalate my methods. Now... stand in the middle of the hallway, and I ask the Secret Service agents on hand to stand with you."

It was a testament to how off-putting his current situation was that Nathan didn't raise any objections as he walked down the hall and stood at roughly its mid-point. When Nathan held his silence, the other agents joined him.

"Alexis, go to the far end of the hallway," Gavin instructed.

His former apprentice walked to the far end of the hallway and turned to face him.

"Mister Victorino, if I were to ask Alexis to return to us, how easy would it be for you to intercept her?" Gavin asked.

"Simple," Nathan answered. "She would walk right by us."

Gavin gave the man an almost-predatory smile. "Excellent. Let's test that. Alexis, join us over here, please."

Alexis took a breath an invoked a Word of Transmutation, "*Paedryx.*"

An archway of crackling energy colored hot pink rose out of the floor in front of both Alexis and her mom. As soon as it reached the proper dimensions for a door, it flashed, becoming a gateway between the two points. Alexis stepped through it, and the gateway vanished as soon as she stood at her mother's side.

The Secret Service agents surrounding Nathan seemed nonplussed, but Nathan himself gaped.

"You didn't intercept her, Mister Victorino," Gavin said. "Care to try again?"

"But... how..." Nathan stammered.

Gavin's expression shifted into almost a glare. "Alexis is a true arcanist, capable of reshaping reality to her will. She could travel to China just as easily as she traversed this hallway. Now... will you withdraw your silly prohibition on her using what I have taught her?"

"Sure... I guess so. It flies in the face of every security practice, but I don't see how her travel could be any more secure than that."

"Good," Gavin remarked. "Then, I have no further need of you. If you do not follow through on this, we shall speak again."

He focused his intent on returning Nathan from whence he came and invoked the Word of Transmutation once more, "*Paedryx.*"

Nathan Victorino vanished in the blink of an eye, almost as if he never was.

"I trust you returned him safe and sound, Gavin?" Chelsea asked.

Gavin scoffed. "Of course. I will consider this matter to be closed, but Alexis, you will inform Jennifer at once if this happens again. If it happens a third time, an object lesson may be in order."

Alexis grinned. "I've actually missed the tower. It's a lot more peaceful than Washington."

"You're welcome any time," Gavin replied. "Thank you for your hospitality, Chelsea. I wish you all the best."

Gavin then focused his intent on his parents' home. "*Paedryx.*"

The world blinked, and he and Jennifer once more stood on the porch of the house where he grew up.

"Now... maybe I can focus on a little relaxation," Gavin muttered as he entered his parents' house.

CHAPTER 11

The days passed, and the Wraiths reported that the Army of Tel worked not only to comply with Gavin's mobilization order but also seemingly to make up for lost time and the former leadership's dysfunction. The results pleased Gavin overall, but he regretted that the former general staff forced his hand. He never wanted to be the kind of heavy-handed authority figure he had seen so many times. While he did prefer to earn people's respect, he cared more about necessary tasks being finished in an accurate and timely manner.

In the wake of the latest update from the army and that update's confirmation by the Wraiths, Gavin decided that it was long past time to check in with Valera and make sure he wasn't ignoring any issues with the College or Society.

Sera—Valera's long-time assistant—looked up as Gavin entered the outer office of the Collegiate Justice. She no longer paled or squeaked or showed any other sign that his presence intimidated her, and he hoped he didn't, not that she had learned to hide it better. He didn't *want* to intimidate anyone, even on those rare occasions when it was necessary.

"Hello, Sera," Gavin said as he stopped a respectful distance from the desk. "Is Valera available?"

"Let me check, Milord," Sera replied and stood. She moved to the door leading to Valera's private office, knocked twice, and leaned inside. Moments later, she righted herself and pulled the door closed, then turned back to Gavin. "The Magister does indeed have time for you, Milord. Please, proceed."

Gavin smiled and thanked her as he crossed the office and entered Valera's private office. Once again, it struck him how the space never seemed to change and was a perfect extension—or perhaps, expression—of Valera.

The Magister of Divination and Collegiate Justice smiled her welcome when Gavin entered and, the moment the door latched, rose to her feet and came around the desk. She extended her hand, which he accepted, and said, "Welcome, Gavin, it has been too long. Please, sit."

Handshake over, Gavin allowed her to direct him to one of the plush armchairs she used for guests and watched as she sank into the one opposite him.

"Now... I know there have been some unforeseen challenges of late, and more than once, I've seen the weight of your office in your eyes. So, tell me true; how do you fare?"

Gavin took a deep breath and released it as a slow sigh. "I'm well enough, Valera. Although, you are correct; I am beyond tired of the responsibilities this office entails. I cannot imagine anyone pursuing it as a life appointment. If you will keep this between us, I have already secured an agreement from Bellos that I will step down from being Archmagister once Skullkeep has been dealt with. I have even argued rather strongly in favor of a person to replace me."

"That's good to hear. I miss the young man who came to me and agreed to mentor students. Have you given any thought to what you will do once you no longer wear the gold robe?"

"Not as such," Gavin answered, shaking his head. "I do know I want to spend more time with Kiri, but I can't help but feel that will be tricky. I don't want to step on Fallon's toes. He's a good man."

Valera leaned back against her seat. "I'm not worried about that. You could always have a quiet word with Terris or Kiri if they're coming to you first instead of their Court Wizard, and closer proximity would mean you could help Fallon learn more about his craft, as well. You did spend how long in the capital?"

Gavin smiled at the fond memories of the days *before* he took up the Office of Archmagister. "Oh, it was a few months at least. Speaking of your great-nephew and great-great-niece... how is that going?"

A faint blush colored Valera's cheeks. "You, sir, are an incorrigible meddler. But yes, the reconciliation is going well. Terris used the copy of the Mulan Genealogy that you gave him to restore what my father ordered destroyed, so I should thank both you and that rapscallion you called a mentor who stole the book in the first place. I am once again Princess Valera Muran, daughter of the royal family of Vushaar. Come to think of it, I'm probably Head of House Muran, too. I have no doubt it's a House of one, but I think I may alter my prayers to Bellos now that the family and I have reconciled. House Muran had a long and proud history, once upon a time, and I would not see it vanish from the world."

"I'm glad things are going well between you and your brother's descendants. Family is important, whether you love them or hate them."

"So, since you've already shared one secret by saying you're not long for the office, care to share one more and tell me who you argued for to replace you?"

Gavin chuckled. "I probably should keep things fairly close, especially since we're going into the military campaign, but I argued for Lillian to replace me."

Valera rested her head on the high back of the armchair and stared at the ceiling. After a time, she brought her eyes back to him once more and said, "She is an inspired choice, I think. Plus, you've not said anything that leads me to believe you'll disappear off the face of the world, so I suspect you will be ready if anyone chooses to challenge her overmuch."

"It is rather impossible for Kirloth to be the terror in the night if he's stuck in plain view wearing a gold robe for all to see," Gavin remarked. "I wanted out of the office as much for that as anything else."

"Yes, I see," Valera responded with an understanding nod. "If you ever have to move against... oh, say, Emperor Xartham... in your capacity as Kirloth, it could create unintended consequences for Tel if you are also Archmagister at the time."

"Exactly. So... aside from all that, is there anything regarding the College or the Society that requires my attention, or at least could benefit from it?"

Valera sat in silence for several moments before she shook her head to answer 'no' as she said, "Not that I can think of. As much as I hate to jinx us all, things seem rather quiet on this particular front at the moment. I'm sure it will blow up at the worst possible time, but apparently, we haven't reached that time yet."

Gavin chuckled. "Oh, I'm sure it'll come soon enough. Probably when the assembled armies are right on the cusp of engaging the Necromancer's forces."

"Have you given any thought to how you'll defeat the Necromancer himself? I am aware of several attempts that looked successful but ultimately failed."

He started to answer but his promise to Othron flashed through his mind. Instead, he said, "Yes, I have several irons in the fire on that front. Any one of them should see to the matter, and I would think all of them succeeding should guarantee his demise."

"It's always important to be prepared, and thinking things like that through now might save you from being caught unawares on the battlefield. Many the wizard has not survived that."

"Trust me; I have no intention of ending up as a zombie or skeleton or whatever in his undead horde." An idea popped into Gavin's mind without warning, bringing a smile with it. "Valera, please excuse me. A matter has just come to my attention, and I should probably pursue it without delay. It's one more log in what I hope will be the Necromancer's funeral pyre."

Valera pushed herself to her feet as Gavin did likewise. "Of course, Gavin. See to whatever requires you. I will alert you if anything erupts from the College or Society; have no fear or worries on that."

"Thank you, Valera, and good day."

He turned and left the office without another word. The moment he stood in the hallway, Gavin teleported straight to his laboratory in the Citadel.

He went immediately to his drafting table. It wasn't a true drafting table in the Earth-sense of the term, but it was where Gavin worked all the designs he later tested. It seemed almost axiomatic that the Necromancer would seek him out personally in any conflict, especially after his quasi-victory during the aborted invasion of Tel Mivar. So, why couldn't he employ a little misdirection? First, he set out to design as near perfect a protection as he could envision; whatever poor soul agreed to act as the decoy needed all the defense and protection Gavin could devise. Normal weapons. Magical weapons. All the elements, plus Interation, Transmutation, and Enchantment effects. By the time he stopped thinking of protections to add, he had an impressive list of runes that filled half his notepaper.

Then, he focused on the Illusion that would make the poor volunteer appear to be Gavin Cross, Head of House Kirloth and Archmagister of Tel. That wasn't as difficult as the protections, in all honesty. He could create a robe for whomever, which lessened the amount of work the Illusion had to accomplish, and he might even be able to counterfeit a wizard's medallion... as long as he didn't try to make it *functional*. If he did that, only one person could wear it, and not the decoy.

Once the Illusion met his intent and standards of quality, the next step was to anchor and power it. Gavin wanted the composite effect housed in and anchored to something easy to handle, and on the surface, it seemed the counterfeit wizard's medallion was the perfect place. But was it too obvious?

The more he thought about it, the more certain he was that the medallion *was* too obvious. He liked the idea of something wearable, but... he wasn't one for jewelry. As he considered how to anchor the effect, his eyes happened to fall on his hands, where they rested on the notepaper in front of him. He grinned like a fool when he focused on the tradition from Earth he asked to include in the wedding and his marriage... specifically, his wedding ring.

"Oh, that's priceless," he said, not expecting a response as he was alone in the laboratory. "One ring to fool them all..."

With *that* problem solved, Gavin stood and went to the terrace that overlooked the Vischaene River delta. He spent a few minutes choosing the perfect stone for what he wanted, then dashed back to his laboratory. He didn't feel like going back to Earth to see if the jeweler had an exact copy of his wedding ring, especially not when he could transmute a stone to gold and then transmute that gold into a perfect replica of his ring.

All that remained was how to power the composite effect.

The last thing he wanted was to create an item that worked every time someone slipped it on a finger. That seemed unwise, at best. No. He wanted the ring to draw power from himself and request power each time someone slipped it on a finger, giving him a sense of who would be wearing it.

This was yet another composite effect that would mimic the Speaking Stones in a slight way, while communicating information across a long distance without a relay or courier. He leaned back against his seat at the drafting table and rubbed his chin. Divination, of course; that would 'record' the sense of the person who donned the ring. Transmutation, next, to create a message portal—for lack of a better term--straight to Gavin. Last, Enchantment to deliver the conveyed information to him.

Gavin sat back and looked over the work thus far. It looked good, and it all seemed to hang together. He snorted a laugh at that thought. Famous last words, right?

Now that he had the ring sending him a sense of who donned it, he needed to create a 'channel' back to it from him that would activate the feed of power the effects needed to work. Again, Transmutation to create the link. Then, Evocation to move the energy. Yes,

Evocation sounded right. If he were touching the ring, he could push power to it by will or choice alone, but he would not be touching the ring in all probability. And it felt correct to include Tutation to stop the link and terminate it until such time as someone donned the ring once more.

At long last, Gavin set aside his stylus and leaned back against his seat, rolling his head and shoulders when he discovered stiffness from so long without moving. He looked at a graduated hourglass and scoffed, shaking his head in mild surprise. The day was gone, and the sun had quite probably set over most of Tel Mivar. It was a little different for the Citadel, due to its sheer altitude, but the fact remained that he had spent several hours on this project without realizing the passage of time. That was both good and bad.

As he considered the hourglass, Gavin also realized he felt a little disconnected from the world, and he didn't like that at all. Then, he realized how long it had been since he saw Kiri, and he liked that even less.

Right, then... it was time to visit Vushaar.

* * *

GAVIN RETURNED to the Citadel the following morning, after spending the evening and night in Vushaar. It felt good to spend time with Kiri and Terris, and he made a mental note to do more of that. It was all too easy to lose sight of what really mattered in life, and family was the very top of that list.

He returned to the laboratory and, retrieving the stone purloined from the terrace, sat at the worktable. He woke up with an excellent idea of how to imbue and test the rings, and he wanted to get started on that.

"*Rhyskaal.*" In the blink of an eye, invoking the Word of Transmutation changed the lump of rock on the worktable to a lump of pure gold.

"*Rhyskaal.*" Another invocation converted the lump of gold into a collection of rings, all an exact duplicate of each other.

His idea for testing the rings required five, but when he made the rings from the lump of gold, he didn't set a specific number. Instead, he focused his intent on creating rings that were an exact duplicate of his wedding ring, using up the entire lump of gold for however many it would make... which seemed to be eight.

The first ring he imbued would make whoever wore it look like Gavin—complete with gold wizard's medallion—without making the person *sound* like Gavin. He figured that would be simple enough; after all, he was long past the point of having problems creating a static image of a horse.

He had just finished stamping the final rune into the interior of the ring when Hartley faded into view beside the worktable, saying, "Milord, Declan has arrived and is waiting to speak with you."

Gavin smiled. "He has excellent timing. Thank you, Hartley. Is he in the sitting room?"

"He is, Milord."

He scooped up the ring he had just finished and left his lab at an energetic walk.

DECLAN STOOD when Gavin entered the sitting room, and the two quickly shook hands. Gavin had never paid any attention to it, but Declan stood about half a head shorter than he did, which was perfect for the test. But he wanted to get Declan's business out of the way, first.

"So, what brings you to the Citadel this morning?" Gavin asked, as he gestured for Declan to resume his seat.

"I just wanted to update you on the recruitment and mobilization efforts of Tel's army. They're making good progress in overcoming the shortfalls of the previous leadership, and if they maintain their rate, the army will be back to its peacetime roster inside a couple months."

"That's good. We need to have another meeting of the Old Alliance to find out where everyone else is in their preparations. I don't want to throw a horde of green recruits at Skullkeep if we can avoid it; that just seems like the ideal recipe for a high casualty count."

Declan nodded his agreement. "So far, a lot of the 'new recruits' are in fact veterans who want to re-enlist, but the staffing office denied them. They do have several training cohorts going, but the vast majority of the army—at least as it stands now—will be veterans."

"Excellent. So, I'm glad you arrived when you did," Gavin remarked. "I'd like your help with something."

Declan shrugged. "Sure, why not? What do you need?"

Gavin held out his hand toward the bard, a simple gold ring in his palm. "Put this on."

Declan took the ring from Gavin and slipped it onto a finger. It resized to fit him, and all at once, an image of Gavin replaced Declan. Looking over the illusion, Gavin broke out into a huge grin. The likeness was perfect.

"What?" Declan asked. "Was it supposed to do something?"

It took all of Gavin's willpower not to erupt in laughter. It sounded like Declan's voice came from the base of the fake Gavin's neck, all while the illusion's lips moved in sync with the bard's words. Yeah... the illusion worked.

"Take off the ring," Gavin said.

Illusory Gavin did so, and Declan was visible once more.

"So," the bard began, "care to share with the rest of the class?"

"I decided that having a decoy would be nice when we finally confront the Necromancer, since I think it's a safe bet that he'll focus on me. That ring is the first test—a proof of concept. When I'm finished with it, it will make a person look and sound like me while layering them in multiple protections. Speaking of that, I need a Wraith volunteer who could be a body double for me. And Declan, make sure whoever it is truly *volunteers*. I don't want anyone to be volun-told. The protections should hold and provide complete safety, but there's always the chance they won't."

Declan shook his head. "You don't have to worry about that. If you put out a call for a volunteer to the Wraiths, half the chapterhouse will stand up. I'll go work on the selection now and bring five or so finalists to you for selection."

"While you're out, track down Lillian. We'll ask her to pick the one closest to me in build."

"Sounds good," Declan replied, as he stood. "I'll get right on that."

CHAPTER 12

Following his meeting with Declan, Gavin decided to visit the Foundry. Several days had passed since he last visited the place, and he felt it was past time for an update. He created a gateway to the facility, choosing to arrive a couple yards south of the Tel Roshan road which put him a dozen yards or so from the Foundry's gate. As soon as he arrived, he smiled at the litany of dwarven invectives interspersed with instructions that reached his ears from inside the stone walls.

Gavin headed for the gate and smiled as a soft breeze that carried just a hint of salt caressed his face. He loved days like this. No clouds worth mentioning. Warm but not sweltering. And a pleasant breeze just strong enough to ruffle his robe. He wished every day could be like this, and he smiled at a memory of his mom telling a young Gavin that bad days help us appreciate the good days.

A chuckle escaped his lips. He wasn't so sure about that piece of motherly advice anymore, but he still carried remnants of the deep, ingrained, inherent certainty that Mom knew everything and could do no wrong.

.   .   .

He stepped through the gate and found the courtyard in a state of barely controlled chaos. There had to be at least thirty to forty dwarves clustered around half that many wagons. One dwarf stood on the top of the largest wagon, directing the rest with a calm, invective-laced aplomb that kept the horde moving like a choreographed dance. From what Gavin could make out, it seemed he arrived while the dwarves unloaded equipment, though he had no idea where they were in the process.

Gavin headed in the maestro's direction, and he made it all of about fifteen feet before the dwarf atop the wagon saw him. The dwarf waved a greeting and called another to his perch to take over directing the work before he descended Mount Wagon to meet Gavin.

"Good day to ye, Milord," the dwarf said, extending a hand in greeting. His voice hovered right around the dividing line between tenor and bass, and it was a little worn from extensive use. "Ye picked a good day to visit. We're unloading the first forges now."

As he shook hands with his greeter, Gavin spied an anvil coming off a wagon that was almost bigger than the dwarf who accepted it with a grunt. "I can see that, sir. Is there anything you need that I can provide?"

The dwarf turned an appraising eye toward the chaos behind him and regarded it in silence for several moments. Eventually, he grunted and turned back to Gavin, shaking his head. "No, Milord. Not that I ken name. That boy Braden has been all over us, making sure we have everything we need, and if there was something he couldn't handle, I imagine he could rustle ye up fast enough. Though... people seem to step rather sprightly around him as it is. As everything stands now, we should be ready to begin working on the first test blanks by next week. We'll need someone on-hand then to stamp the runes and embed the magic before we temper them."

"That's easily handled. I'll get with Braden, and we'll do our part to be ready. For the first few blanks, I imagine you'll have to suffer through having both myself and Braden on-hand. Once we're certain we have the process sorted and reliable, I'll turn it over to him, so he can begin the process of selecting arcanists to help him."

The dwarf nodded his agreement as he absently scratched at the roots of his braided beard. "Aye... that will work. Braden's a good lad with a head on his shoulders. He'll make a good point man on the project for ye. Right, then. These forges won't unload themselves. Have a look around if ye like, but be damned sure ye stay out from underfoot."

That said, he pivoted on his heel and crossed the short distance to the base of his former perch, ascending Mount Wagon once more and sending his temporary replacement off on other duties. Gavin couldn't hear what he told the replacement, but the departed dwarf stepped off rather smartly. He hung around, watching the slightly controlled chaos from a safe distance for a short time, but it was apparent that the dwarves had everything well in hand and had no need of an Archmagister lurking about. With a departing wave to the dwarf conducting the nigh-anarchic symphony, Gavin left the Foundry's courtyard and returned to Tel Mivar via gateway once he was beyond the wall.

* * *

IT WORRIED Cyn a little bit that she didn't notice the stench of all the undead pervading the fortress as much anymore. Of the things she never thought she'd get used to, the stench of a truly massive horde of undead was pretty close to the top of her list. It was a complex mixture of rotting flesh and a cornucopia of alchemical substances that she had never encountered before, and she sincerely hoped she never would again... at least after this assignment was over.

The weeks she'd spent at Skullkeep allowed her to assemble a pretty good collection of intelligence about the living contingent to the fortress's garrison, and she'd already sent that out to her contacts. The one objective that continued to thwart her was puzzling out the location of the Necromancer's soul jar. She didn't expect that he'd stash it somewhere any random person walking by would find it, but she'd searched the public areas of the fortress under the guise of her fascination with old places. After the first week or so, everyone stopped paying her any attention at all.

The only place she hadn't searched was the fortress commander's quarters, which she believed the Necromancer had claimed for his own. Which made a certain amount of sense. The more she considered it, the more sense it made for him to keep such an important item rather close, so it was logical that it would be stashed in his quarters somewhere.

Which led to her problem.

The Necromancer kept his quarters warded any time he wasn't in there. She had no magical ability whatsoever, but her Wraith tattoo had a number of protections built into it. One of them made the tattoo tingle in the presence of protective effects that weren't hers... like the wards on the door to the Necromancer's quarters. It was enough to make her growl in frustration.

But it was reaching the point that she'd have to take some risks. She wasn't sure how far along the mobilization was, but there was no chance she'd risk letting down her mentor... not to mention Gavin himself. When the assembled forces of the Old Alliance laid siege to Skullkeep, she would damn well have the location of that soul jar and be waiting for the signal to destroy it.

The wind fairly whipped across the roof of the fortress's central keep. It was bad enough that she grabbed a stray rock and used it to keep the wind from whisking her cloak off to parts unknown. She leaned as far over the battlements as she could, peering down to discern if she'd chosen the correct place—not to mention side—of the keep. If she was right, she'd drop down to the windows leading to the Necromancer's quarters. If she was wrong... well... she'd probably spy one or more of the company commanders engaged in a bit of fun.

First, she pulled on the climbing harness and tightened its straps across her torso at the shoulders and across her pelvis. Not too tight, just snug enough. She then strapped the ankle bag containing one hundred feet of silk rope to her right ankle, filled in such a way that it easily came out of the bag without snagging or kinking; more than one Wraith had eyed that particular innovation with a certain amount of suspicion when Gavin brought it back from the world he called home, but it quickly proved its utility and was now a staple of all infiltration kits. Personally, she *loved* it.

Then came the small matter of feeding the rope through the control surfaces of her climbing harness before she tied it to the eye at the end of her grappling hook. In the event of a fall, those control surfaces would tighten and save her... as long as the rope and grappling hook remained secure.

She peered over the side one more time before she put the barbs of the hook into place. She pulled against it as best she could from her poor angle, and the hook seemed to hold. One last deep breath, and Cyn clambered up onto the battlements and tugged the rope as she leaned toward the edge. The grappling hook still held, so she slipped over her side, entrusting her full weight to it. Still good, and a sigh of relief escaped her control.

A few moments later, Cyn hung even with one of the windows and smiled when she didn't recognize the room's contents. She'd already searched all the company commanders' quarters, so if she didn't recognize any furniture or possessions, she had to be looking into the Necromancer's quarters. And what's more, her tattoo didn't signal the presence of any wards. Kind of shoddy for him not to consider this approach, especially as old as he was.

She eased through the open window, paying *very* close attention to her tattoo, but it never flared or tingled. Not once. As soon as she stood inside the space, she felt like she should duck right back through the window and shimmy back up the rope. She'd proven that she could access the quarters, and since she didn't know when the Necromancer was due to return—especially since he answered to no one but himself, Cyn didn't want to risk being discovered.

But... she was here. *So close.*

Fine. There was one thing she would check. Something she *needed* to know if she were to feel safe sneaking back into the room the next time the Necromancer left the fortress. She made her way to the door that led to the rest of the fortress, and as she approached within five or so feet, her tattoo flared. She backed away, and it settled.

Good to know.

Taking care to leave no trace of her presence in the rooms, Cyn returned to the window and quickly climbed back up to the roof. Peeking over the edge revealed no one, so she clambered over the battlements and set about collecting everything and stashing it in the magical space made to look like a satchel. After all, it wouldn't do for someone to see her walking through the fortress wearing a climbing harness, now would it...

* * *

UPON RETURNING TO THE CITADEL, Gavin went straight to the laboratory he used for design work. There, he settled onto a comfortable stool in front of his drafting table and proceeded to draw a map of the composite effect he wanted embedded within each weapon. One or two were specific to the type of weapon; after all, it would be the height of folly to try to give a hammer or mace a sharper edge. But the effect that would make a blunt weapon—like a hammer or mace—hit harder would benefit a sword or arrow as well.

About a half-hour in, Gavin realized he was chasing his non-existent tail, and he ignited his jumbled notes and took a step back, deciding a better start was to list the effects he wanted overall and then mark the weapons that would be appropriate for each effect. Fortunately, the drawing paper he used at his drafting table almost filled the entire top. He soon realized he needed the space.

Gavin leaned back from the drafting table an uncounted time later and skimmed over his work thus far. The list of effects was rather impressive—even to him—and he thought he'd accounted for most of the weapons the assembled army would use. Blades, axes, hammers, maces, morningstars, staves, bows, crossbows, arrows, quarrels... and even shields. At first thought, Gavin started to place the shields with armor, since they were primarily protective or defensive in nature, but then, he remembered watching a group of Cavaliers in Vushaar as they practiced a choreographed shield bash. He didn't know how prevalent such a practice was, but he decided it wouldn't hurt to include the shields on both the weapons *and* the armor list. It might make for a bit of a balancing act—especially since most items could only hold a finite amount of power—but that's what testing was for.

The fun part was going to be protecting himself and Braden while they tested just how much power a normal shield could hold.

After a short break where he stood and walked around the room while drinking water and partaking in a quick snack, Gavin returned to the drafting table to take up the task he'd started with. Now that he had an organized list of what effects he wanted to add to which weapons, he felt the process of assembling the preliminary formula would be much easier.

THE NEXT TIME Gavin looked up from his drafting table, he saw night through the laboratory's windows. He had no idea what time it was, and he was a little surprised that Hartley hadn't interrupted him for dinner. The Citadel's spectral majordomo didn't often allow him to skip meals. He looked over his assembled notes once more and smiled at his work for the day. Despite not knowing what time it was, he had a credible start on the formula to embed his desired effects into weapons. All that remained now was to decide whether he wanted to proceed with testing that or spend the next day working on the effects for the armor.

Decisions, decisions...

Perhaps it was best to leave it until the morning when he was fully rested and fed. Yes. That sounded best. After one last moment of basking in his accomplishments, Gavin turned and left the laboratory. As he walked through the doorway, he realized he should probably catch up with Braden, too, and get his thoughts on the effects list.

CHAPTER 13

The Foundry was a symphony of hammers striking metal against a backdrop of smoke curling high into the sky. Gavin stood unnoticed in the courtyard and watched a collection of the finest smiths the world had ever known work their craft. He smiled at the semi-recent memory of the lead smith approaching him during a visit and asking if there was a way to open the work bays to allow better airflow, both for the forges—because the bellows had to draw air from *somewhere*—and for heat dissipation.

It was the work of little more than two hours to convert each forge space to what amounted to a stone pavilion and embed effects that prevented any weather beyond wind from entering them. It was an even smaller matter to tie those effects to the ambient magic to keep them stable and operative in perpetuity.

The most recent report Gavin read indicated the Foundry had produced something like six hundred weapons and sets of armor, and he was rather glad for that. None of them were prize works a wealthy patron would eagerly claim, but they were sound and functional. Which was all the rank and file wanted. It was the rare soldier who cared whether his or her weapon of choice came with filigree or a jeweled pommel.

Looking around the courtyard once more, Gavin wondered just how early he was for the appointment. He didn't see Braden anywhere, but he did see the master smith happily working a piece of hot metal. He couldn't tell what the finished product would be, given his distant vantage, but he didn't doubt its quality.

His *skathos* flared mere heartbeats before a gateway opened a few feet behind him. He turned and watched Braden step through it from somewhere. That was another thing he hoped to rectify once he set aside the gold robe. Gavin hadn't seen even half of Tel, let alone the rest of the world. In fact, he'd seen more of Vushaar simply from taking Kiri home, and Vushaar wasn't even the realm he considered 'home' in Drakmoor.

Maybe he should consider Vushaar home, given that his wife would one day rule it as queen, but what he maybe *should* do wasn't what he did. He felt a deeper connection to Tel than anywhere he could ever remember being, even the Cross Estate back on Earth.

Now... that wasn't to say he wouldn't defend Vushaar or his Earth family. At the end of the day, he was—and always would be—Kirloth, and may the Gods have mercy on whoever threatened either Vushaar or his Earth family, because he certainly wouldn't.

"Milord," Braden said, adding a nod of greeting.

Gavin bit back a sigh. "I'll give you that one since we're technically in a public setting. How are you and your mother?"

Braden smiled. "Mother's well. She's discussing some disagreements with the miners' consortium. That's why I'm a wee bit late. She wanted me in the discussion, and I lost track of time."

"Miners' consortium?" Gavin's thoughts went straight to the Wygoth Mines and Water Works that he'd essentially claimed after eliminating House Sivas all those months before. "Are any of my people giving your mother fits? I can settle *that* right now."

Braden was rather quick to respond. "No, not at all. The miners working at your holdings have been the counterpoint to all the drama. The more the other miners hew and cry, the more they stand out for their non-participation. The foreman at your holdings made a very public statement that he had no wish to get involved in that mess, because you pay them better than any miner's ever been paid in the history of Tel. He's not about to risk upsetting the apple cart."

"Good. I'll make a note to send him a bonus and 'thank you' note for standing up to whoever's organizing the mess. Would it help your mother for me to get involved at all?"

Again, Braden quickly shook his head. "No, but thank you. Buried inside all their posturing and melodrama, they do have a few valid concerns. If you show up, they'll just piss themselves and run screaming into the woods, which—while thoroughly entertaining— wouldn't solve much."

"Fair enough, but make sure your mother knows I stand ready to assist if I can do so."

"I appreciate that, Gavin, and I know Mother will, too. If it looks like it will impact our ore commitments for the general mobilization, we may ask you to 'mediate' the dispute, but it's not that dire yet."

Gavin nodded his understanding. "So, how are we going to test this? Grab one of the swords from the stockpile?"

"We should ask Torgas, since he's the master smith and all. I'm sure we could just grab something off a shelf and have at it, but it would probably be best to get his input on this. And let's face it, if we pull this off, he'll want the bragging rights of being involved... even if all he did was hold the sword for us while we embedded the effects."

Gavin chuckled as he nodded, gesturing for Braden to lead the way. "Fair point, and far be it from me to keep a dwarf from his entertainment."

He followed his former apprentice across the courtyard to where Torgas bent a piece of metal to his will. As they approached, Gavin watched the corded muscles of the dwarf's arms contract and relax with each swing, and he marveled at the amount of power the smith controlled. For all the advances Earth had made, Gavin questioned if it was truly progress... and not for the first time since regaining his memories. The medical advances were progress without a doubt, but... Gavin cut off that thought with a half-snort and a shake of his head. He had started toward the thought that wars were not as easy if all the weapons were made by hand, but the truth of it was that people in power didn't care whether their wars were difficult or easy.

The campaign to reclaim Skullkeep wasn't just his war, but he was the spearhead, the driving force behind it. The Old Alliance had sat for six hundred years and let the Necromancer run damn near rampant, and for whatever reason, no one had stood up and said, "This is important. We're going to do this."

Perhaps, the conditions weren't right. Perhaps, the walking nightmare that Tel's royal family had been kept the other Alliance members' attention. Perhaps... perhaps... perhaps.

It was one more iron in the fire Gavin labeled 'no one in their right mind would want this job.' His mother didn't understand how an entire world could depend on one person, especially when that person was the son she'd lost thirteen years before, and Gavin kind of saw her side of it. But at the end of the day, there wasn't anyone else he would trust to do it. At least, once things were stabilized and Skullkeep was back under the Old Alliance's control, he'd be able to step aside and have something closer to a normal life.

Their arrival at the master smith's anvil pulled Gavin out of his thoughts, and he smiled his greetings when Torgas realized he and Braden were there. Torgas quickly handed off his project to another smith and waved for Gavin and Braden to follow him back to the courtyard, where distance from the forges allowed them to have some semblance of a conversation.

"Today's the day, is it?" Torgas asked when he stopped and turned to them.

Gavin gave an answering nod. "Yes, I think it is. We wanted your input on something. Should we use one of the stock or something ready to temper?"

Torgas scratched at the chin hiding beneath his braided beard as he looked back to the forges. It was plain from his expression that he was deep in thought. After several moments of silence, the dwarven smith nodded once and brought his eyes back to Gavin. "We should try both to determine the best process. We have something like six hundred of both weapons and armor already finished, and we need to know whether we can use them or if they were just training pieces."

"Good idea," Gavin replied. "Where do you want to do this?"

Torgas shrugged. "No reason not to do it at the forge. We have the workbenches and tools and everything there already. I'll grab something from the stock and meet ye there. Tell those layabouts in me forge to find somewhere else to be."

"No offense, Torgas, but I'll let you do that. They don't know me from some bum off the street."

The master smith cast a skeptical eye at the gold robe Gavin wore before he snorted a laugh and headed toward the secure buildings that held the finished stock. By silent agreement, the two wizards waited for him to return, a short sword resting against shoulder, and followed him back to his forge. With a few quick words, Torgas sent the smiths using his space to another forge and placed the short sword on his anvil and turned to Gavin and Braden.

"So, how do we do this? And what do ye need from me?"

Gavin withdrew folded parchment from inside his robe and laid it out atop the sword and anvil. Braden leaned in for a better look and soon made appreciative sounds as he skimmed the design.

After a moment, he straightened and gave Gavin what might be charitably described as a skeptical expression. "You want to cram all that into a blade?"

"You're the foremost expert on imbued items that we have. If you think it won't work, tell me before we get too far into it."

Braden shook his head. "It isn't that. From what I can see, you've balanced everything very well. It's just that... well... there's an imbued sword in the family armory back in Tel Wygoth. It supposedly dates back to the Godswar, and it isn't even half as powerful as this sword will be. I know you said we'll be binding the effects to each soldier's oath, but the thought of this falling into a bandit's hands is just terrifying. I'm not sure normal armor could stop an imbued blade with these effects."

"That's why I want to bind these effects to the oath of service the soldiers will take during outfitting."

Braden nodded his acceptance and scanned the workspace before turning back to Torgas. "We'll need some way of etching or engraving runes into this blade."

"Aye, moment then." The master smith trundled off to a storage locker that bore its own collection of runes and withdrew a stoppered bottle and engraved stylus, which he brought back to the anvil. "Here. Acid for etching and an engraving pen. The pen is specially prepared to act like a quill. Just dip it into the acid and write the runes you want on the blade. The acid will do the rest. I have a rinse to remove any excess acid without damaging the blade."

Gavin picked up the parchment and stepped back from the anvil. "You have more experience with this part than I do. Tell me where you want me to hold the parchment."

"That's fine right there." Braden accepted the pen from Torgas, who then removed the stopper from the acid with care. Braden dipped the pen into the acid and began etching the first rune.

A SHORT TIME LATER, Braden finished the final rune and stepped back, nodding for Torgas to re-stopper the bottle of acid. The master smith returned the etching acid to the locker and came back with a stoppered flask. He bit the stopper out of the flask and held it with his teeth while he carried the blade to the glowing coals. Placing the tip of the blade against the stones lining the forge, he poured a liberal amount of the flask's contents on the blade just below the crossguard. As soon as most of the liquid ran its course down the blade, he carried the sword back to the anvil, then held out his hand for the engraving pen. As soon as Braden handed him the pen, Torgas pointed to a cloth on the workbench and went back to the forge to wash the pen while Gavin grabbed the cloth and wiped down the blade. Torgas returned from the forge with the flask stoppered once more and set the flask aside on the workbench before wiping down the pen with the cloth he reclaimed from Gavin.

"Right, then," Gavin said. "That was the easy part."

Without another word, Gavin produced a small knife from inside his robe. It was a tiny blade, not even large enough to be worthy of a name like dagger or dirk. He pricked his thumb and placed one drop of blood into each rune, then wrapped his thumb in a cloth he pulled out of another pocket.

"Ready, Braden?"

The giant of a man who had once been Gavin's apprentice chuckled and shrugged. "Why not? If this works, it won't be the first time I've witnessed you making history."

Gavin shook his head. "I'm not doing this to make history. I just want to give our soldiers the best weapons and protection possible. When I drop my hand, begin the composite effect."

Braden nodded as he closed his eyes and took a couple deep breaths.

Gavin made his own mental preparations, and as soon as Braden opened his eyes, Gavin lifted his hand, held it a second, and dropped it.

Braden's deep, rumbling baritone joined with Gavin's tenor to invoke a composite effect utilizing a Word of Transmutation and a Word of Evocation, *"Rhyskaal-Idluhn."*

The moment Gavin completed the invocation, he closed his eyes again and focused on his *skathos* to watch the effect take hold and settle into the blade. For the first few heartbeats, it looked perfect. Beautiful, even. But as he watched, Gavin saw the power contained within the composite effect start a cascade throughout the physical structure of the blade. It progressed almost too quickly for Gavin to process, but all at once, he realized where the cascade would end.

"Rhosed-Paedryx."

A protection effect surrounded the three of them less than a full heartbeat before the sword blinked out of existence. Both Braden and Torgas jerked back and looked all around, and Gavin waved for them to follow as he jogged outside the forge. They followed, their expressions betraying bewilderment, and Gavin silently pointed up as he himself looked that way.

They looked up just in time to see a massive explosion some five hundred feet above the Foundry, the sound eventually reaching their ears.

"What happened?" Braden asked.

"I watched the composite effect through my *skathos* and saw that it was destabilizing the physical structure of the sword. Granted, I was a bit unilateral in my decision, but I took it as a matter of faith that neither of you wanted to be face-to-face with an explosion like that, no matter how protected you were."

Torgas patted Gavin's arm. "Aye, lad... ye thought right as far as I'm concerned. What's next? Revisit the design of the power ye want to imbue in the weapons?"

"Possibly," Gavin admitted, "but I'd like to try the same process on a sword that hasn't been tempered yet. If the metal still has a certain amount of malleability, it might accept the power of the effects I want the weapons to have."

Torgas scratched at his chin again, nodding after a few moments. "Aye, it might at that. We'll just wander through the forges and find a smith who's almost finished with his current project. Out of twenty smiths, that should nae be difficult. And if the blade is still hot from the forge, it should accept the runes better."

THEY SOON ARRIVED at a forge where the smith was within moments of tempering the blade. Torgas stepped in and asked the smith to heat it back to forging temperature and then retrieved the engraving pen from that smith's locker.

Braden placed a protection against heat on himself and accepted the pen, then bent to his task of drawing out the runes on the blade's surface. That completed, he and Gavin once more invoked their composite effect.

Gavin watched the effect take hold through his *skathos*, and the result could not have been more different. Yes, the runes and their intent focused the invocation and channeled its power, but Gavin watched the blade absorb additional power direct from the ambient as the fundamental structure of the blade altered itself to accommodate the changes being wrought upon it.

In the space of a handful of heartbeats, the blade that had glowed red mere moments before now looked freshly tempered and bore the series of glowing runes that powered, focused, and maintained the effect Gavin wanted the weapons to have.

Both smiths shared a look before turning to Gavin and Braden. Torgas spoke. "Was it supposed to do that?"

Gavin and Braden shared a look themselves, and Gavin eventually shrugged as he replied, "Sure... why not? Is there any way to test the blade without trying to hack someone apart?"

Torgas nodded and waved for the two wizards and the smith to follow. He led them to an area screened from view by all the forges that was set up as a practice yard. A series of startlingly life-like dummies wearing armor decorated the yard, and the master smith patted the smith's shoulder before pointing to the nearest dummy.

The smith advanced on his victim as Torgas said, "We've done our best to ensure each of the practice dummies are as close to a living person as possible. They have analogs to blood, tissue, and muscle... all hanging on a respectable fake skeleton. A few generations back, a smith outed himself as a rather sick soul who robbed graves in the night by advocating we use actual skeletons in our test dummies."

By that point, the smith had reached his position and set himself. He drew back and put his whole body into a downward diagonal swing toward the dummy's left shoulder. If the blade was untempered or flawed in any way, it would shatter like weak pottery... but it didn't shatter. Instead, one of the runes flared bright as a noon-time sun just as it made contact with the shoulder and sheared through armor, dummy, and the pole that supported everything with no apparent resistance. The parts that were no longer attached slid off and either plopped or thunked as it struck the ground. There was so little resistance to the blade that the smith overbalanced and almost fell into the part of the dummy that still stood.

Silence reigned for several moments until Torgas cleared his throat. "Well, lads... I think yer magic works."

* * *

WITH THE PROCESS established for the weapons, Braden brought in the wizards selected to work with the smiths, asking for their oaths under Divination of Truth before allowing them anywhere near the Foundry. A few were a little shaky in their commitment to refrain from using the opportunity for personal gain, and Braden chose not to select those. Even being a few wizards short, he didn't think it was enough to affect the overall timetable. He gave the wizards they hired a week to get up to speed and set them to working with the smiths to imbue the existing stock of weapons by reheating them to forge temperatures.

The composite effect put many of the assisting wizards on their backs the first time or two they invoked it, and Braden felt he acquitted himself well in not grinning at their misfortune. The average rank-and-file were finally learning what it meant to be one of Kirloth's apprentices.

In terms of the armor, Gavin and Braden tested those effects with a breastplate fresh from a forge and witnessed similar results to that of the weapons. When it came time for testing, they found that the imbued effect provided its protections to the entire body and not just the sections protected by the armor itself. Gavin had hoped that would be the case, but it was always nice to have confirmation.

CHAPTER 14

Ever since her father returned to Earth, Jennifer's life had been something of a roller coaster. Between learning that she could re-shape reality to her will to the whole mess with the federal government and her father's resolution of the situation with Jerome Toussaint... it seemed like she spent her days dancing on a raft that floated atop quicksand.

Some days, it floated rather well. Other days... not so much.

Most people lived their lives with an illusion of control that was paper thin. Whether that paper was construction paper that had some heft to it or that translucent stuff used to print pages of the Bible, it was still paper. Jennifer's control over her life was a little more defined than paper, but calling it control still seemed a vast exaggeration.

A case in point... income.

In the modern world, income was a necessity. The days of getting by on the barter system were—for all intents and purposes —the past. Jennifer had not held a true job since before her grandparents found her in Baltimore. Yes, she was a college student. Yes, she used the college fund her father's will had created, which still felt a little odd to her given her dad's whole 'not as dead as we 'thought' situation. But that college fund only provided for tuition and books.

So, how did Jennifer get by?

For ninety-nine-point-nine percent of the world's population, the answer was getting a job. For Jennifer? When she needed money, she just picked up a rock from the backyard or the forest and transmuted it to gold. No one had yet asked the question of just *where* she was mining the gold, which she felt was rather fortunate. She even had a nice smelting system to convert the rock-shaped gold into one-pound bars. Practicing to the point that she could transmute the rock straight to a bar with a set weight was on her list, but she hadn't quite gotten around to that yet.

It was just one facet of the furball—or maybe kerfuffle—that was her life now.

She was grateful to be alive. She was grateful to have her dad back. She was grateful for her friend Alexis, whom she would never have met and built a friendship with if it hadn't been for her dad. She was grateful for a whole host of things.

She would've been very, very grateful to have even the vaguest idea of what she wanted to do with her life, but like so many people, she was a work in progress.

An obvious option was to open an arcanist school with Alexis. Especially if Alexis finished her law degree and passed the Virginia Bar exam. But ultimately, she agreed with her dad. Earth wasn't set up to have wizards wandering around the countryside. It didn't have any of the institutions or cultural awareness or understanding to keep arcane proliferation from totally destabilizing the entire world. Leaving aside the fact that she was essentially a nuclear power in her own right, she could crash commodity markets on a whim... just by transmuting a couple tons of something that was common into something else that was extremely rare. Gold, rhodium, platinum, palladium, even uranium or plutonium... just to name a few.

That was a major reason she never ventured far from Graham unless she stepped through the portal to visit her dad. If people—especially governments—ever truly understood the scope of her power, there would be a kiosk in every country of the world where a line of assassins stepped up to take their number and await their turn to try removing her and Alexis from the population.

Now serving: #1,654,297. Please ensure your affairs are in order.

As much as Jennifer wanted to snort at the thought and as much as she felt there might be a grain of truth to it, intellectually, she knew that particular fear was probably more emotional than rational. Oh, sure... there wasn't anything stopping Bubba from the wilds of Montana or Texas or wherever from buying a firearm and traveling to Virginia to take his shot at her. But that wasn't government-level work. No matter how emotionally real the fear of a global initiative to kill her might be, there was one reason she didn't grant that fear too much weight, rationally speaking: Kirloth. Specifically, Kirloth in the form of her father.

The Glyph of Kirloth still stood out like an honest person in politics when looking down on France at night. An angry, red warning to the world, the color of molten lava. All these months later—nearly a year since her father eradicated a Renaissance-era villa on France's equivalent of the register of historic places—the lava had not cooled. It defied all attempts to *make* it cool.

The most recent attempt involved a vat of liquid nitrogen carried to the site via helicopter. When the vat opened and dropped its payload, everything around the lava froze and shattered, which was mostly just grass and some gravel landscaping paths. The surface temperature of the lava dipped two degrees for five seconds.

More than one scientific commission existed to explain why the lava on the site of Toussaint's villa hadn't cooled, and so far, none of them had made it past shrugs while saying, "It's magic."

So, in that respect, Jennifer felt her fears of assassination were largely unfounded. She doubted any other country on the planet wanted their own lava bed after attempting to kill her, and heaven help them if they succeeded. A small spike of terror ran through her at the thought of her dad's response if some government actually did kill her. Kiri had told her enough stories that she—like any sapient creature with half the sense God gave a goose—feared piquing Kirloth's ire. No... not ire. Wrath.

Were twenty-something women supposed to worry about assassins and the collateral damage they might create?

Her grandpa opened the screen door and stepped onto the porch, just as she snorted and shook her head. He sat on the swing beside her and put his arm around her shoulders.

"You've been sitting out here a while. Anything an old man can help with?"

She shook her head. "I don't see how, Grandpa. I started trying to figure out what I wanted to do with my life... you know, like any other person my age... but seem to keep tripping over being able to re-shape reality on a whim. I'm sure the Feds would want a word or two if they knew I created a lump of gold every time I want some petty cash."

Her grandpa chuckled. "I can see people taking a dim view of that. Liquidating through our bank in town will work for a while, but we should probably figure out a better solution for the long-term."

"I can't believe the gossip train isn't going full-steam ahead all over town about it, but I haven't heard a peep."

"Well... you can probably thank your father for that. After he left that FBI SWAT team in the roundabout flower bed for however long, I've noticed the people of Graham don't look at us quite the same as they used to anymore. Conversations seem to cease when I walk into Martha's diner. I don't let it stop me, and Martha tells 'em off right quick... but your father changed how people see us."

She nodded. "I've seen it, too. So, with all this hanging over my head, how am I supposed to pick a path in life?"

"Well, like everything else, I'd say that you shouldn't let it define you. Seems to me that it's a tool, just like anything else, and how you use it will show the world who you are as a person. I can't say what you should do, and I wouldn't even if I could. The answers that were right for me won't be right for you, if they even apply."

"It just seemed like I was finally starting to get a handle on things, you know? Sure... the pain episodes were a problem, and I'm grateful

Dad recognized what they were. But aside from that, I felt like I was starting to get everything together, and then... well... Dad happened."

Her grandpa chuckled. "Yeah. He did. Why do I get the feeling 'Gavin happened' or 'Kirloth happened' is a viable excuse for almost anything in the other world?"

"That's another point, too, Grandpa. Given what I can do, should I even be in this world anymore? Should I just move over there?"

"If that's what you want to do, sure. You should absolutely do that. Your grandmother and I would appreciate it if you visited from time to time, but you should go where your heart takes you. Chase your dreams and your happiness, sweetheart... whatever that means and wherever it takes you."

Jennifer nodded. "I guess that means I need some dreams, then."

"Everyone has dreams, and you're in a far better position to make yours reality than most."

"I've never given dreams much thought, Grandpa. So much of my life has just been a matter of survival that the topic never really came up."

Her grandpa nodded. "I get that. So, why not go explore the world on the other side of the portal? At least there, you'll be free to be who you are. There's not really a place for wizards on Earth."

Jennifer's immediate reaction was to expound upon why that was a bad idea. But as she inhaled to do just that, she stopped and considered. Was it really such a bad idea? Aside from the brief visits right after her dad created the portal, she didn't really know anything about the world. She hadn't seen much of it at all.

"You know... that might work, and if I'm going to do it, I might as well ask Alexis if she'd like to go. Even if she doesn't, I should probably tell her I'm going, just so she won't try texting me or anything. You mind if I invite her to continue using the keep as a getaway from all the nonsense in D.C.?"

Her grandpa chuckled and shook his head. "Of course not. Your grandmother and I consider that keep yours... well, yours and your father's. Especially since I'm not sure either one of us could get there without the portal after your dad rearranged that promontory to create the keep. I might be mistaken, but I think it's almost a sheer cliff all the way around now."

Jennifer frowned as she thought about that. "I'm not sure I've ever explored the far sides of the promontory, come to think of it. I don't remember ever going farther than Kiri's training area. Thanks, Grandpa. I feel better."

He pulled her into a hug and patted her back. "That's what I'm for. Don't forget to say bye when you decide to go."

She nodded her agreement as she stood. An idea crossed her mind that brought an impish smile to her face. Both Alexis and her mother had said to visit any time, but Jennifer always did them—and especially those tasked with their protection—the courtesy of calling or texting before she simply appeared somewhere on the White House grounds. A desire to shake things up every so often probably came from her dad, but she wouldn't deny that it was a core facet of her personality. She stepped into the yard and waved at her grandpa before invoking a Word of Transmutation.

"*Paedryx.*"

The world blinked, and Jennifer now stood on the path where her father always brought them when he teleported or opened a gateway to the Rose Garden. The collection of floral scents buoyed her spirits, and she smiled at an agent no more than five feet away.

She was so close that she heard every word when he lifted his wrist to his mouth. "Be advised; Glenda is in the Rose Garden."

Jennifer was half a step into motion when she heard that and froze, turning to give the agent her full attention. "*Glenda*? Really? Do I look like a witch to you?"

The agent smirked. "Would you rather your designation was Maleficent? There aren't too many options."

"What about Young Kirloth? That's how most of Dad's world addresses me. Say... if I'm Glenda, what do you call my dad?"

Jennifer couldn't believe it when the agent paled. "Miss... I need to continue my rounds. You're cleared to proceed to the Residence."

"Fine, then. I'll just ask Alexis."

. . .

By that point in her association with Chelsea and Alexis Hall, Jennifer knew the White House rather well, possibly even as well as one of the tour guides. It took her little time to find Alexis in one of the Residence's sitting rooms, poring over her Bar Exam study guide. She knocked on the doorframe, and Alexis erupted out of her seat, almost sprinting across the room and throwing her arms wide.

"What are you doing here?" Alexis pulled her into a tight hug that threatened to compress her ribs enough to fit in a soup can. "You never said you were coming."

"I decided it was time to shake things up. Did you know your valiant protectors call me *Glenda*? What is up with that? Oh... and what do they call my dad? The guy who called me Glenda looked like he wanted to piddle down his leg when I asked."

Alexis broke the hug and stepped back just far enough to meet Jennifer's eyes. "You sure you want to know?"

"Really? It's that bad?"

Alexis shrugged. "Depends on your point of view, I guess."

Jennifer sighed and rolled her eyes. "Come on. Give."

"Apocalypse."

"You know... that's not really too far off the mark. I'm not sure Dad would approve, because I'm fairly certain he'd just as soon teach as be the big bad bogey man, but if the shoe fits..."

Alexis ushered her into the room and almost pushed her into a seat across from hers. "What brings you here? I can't believe you decided to drop by for a visit just to shake up the Secret Service."

"I've decided I want to explore the world Dad has called home for the last couple of years, and I thought I'd ask if you wanted to tag along."

Alexis shook her head, rather fervently in fact. "Even if I didn't have the Bar Exam so soon, I don't want to go back there unless I have no other choice."

"What? Why? It didn't seem like *that* bad of a place."

"For you, maybe, but Lillian Mivar and the rest of your dad's friends were ready to kill me just because of my House Glyph... remember?"

That stopped Jennifer cold. How could she have forgotten that? The meeting where her dad introduced everyone was very tense until he smoothed things over, all because Alexis was House Sivas. She still hadn't gotten the complete story on why House Sivas had such an unsavory reputation, but she had learned that it was fairly pervasive in the magical society over there. What they called the Society of the Arcane. No one had anything good to say about House Sivas; at least, they didn't admit it, if they did.

"Right. Ouch. Okay. Yeah... maybe you going along isn't such a great idea, but it would be hilarious to watch your travel party in Tel Mivar. You can't deny that."

It took a few seconds, but Alexis's serious mien finally cracked as she giggled. "Oh, goodness... that would be such a hoot. But as much as I'd enjoy that, I still think it's the wiser course for me to stay here and focus on the Bar Exam. Who knows? By the time you return, I may be a full-fledged attorney, licensed to practice and everything."

"Yeah. That will be great. You want me to hang around for moral support?"

Alexis waved that off right away. "Nah. You go visit your dad and his world. I've thought you were feeling a little directionless the last few times I visited the keep, so maybe this will help. You'll have to tell me everything, too."

"Okay. I'll do that."

Jennifer stood, which prompted Alexis to do the same before pulling her into another hug. Then, Alexis walked her out of the sitting room and stopped in the doorway. An agent stood not too far away and didn't bat an eye when Jennifer invoked a Word and vanished from the hallway.

The agent turned to Alexis "Is she gone, ma'am? I mean... has she left the premises?"

"Yes."

As Alexis returned to her studies, she heard him say, "Be advised; Glenda has left the building."

CHAPTER 15

The portal to her dad's world loomed before her. From what Jennifer could see, it was as nice of a day there as it was at home... well, her grandparents' home. She had not decided yet if she would tell her dad right away that she was there, in his world. Part of her liked the idea of getting an unbiased impression of the place. She highly doubted that she would see the 'real' world if her father—Kirloth and the Archmagister of Tel—traveled with her.

Which was why she was traveling without her medallion visible.

Yes, she would have it and would wear it, but she had no intention of revealing her identity unless it was necessary. She hadn't decided just what 'necessary' looked like, yet, but the whole idea of visiting the world was a bit of a work-in-progress.

Nothing to it but to do it. The phrase felt like a memory, but Jennifer couldn't remember where she'd read it or heard it... which didn't change its truth at all. She took a deep breath and released it as a slow sigh. Then... she walked through the portal.

The passage through tingled. Everything from her skin to her soul, but it was over mere heartbeats after she stood in the other world. The first thing she noticed was the air... or more accurately, how it smelled. It was clean and crisp and carried hints of horse manure but none of the industrial pollution that permeated even the 'cleanest' air on Earth. The dirt at her feet looked a darker, richer brown, the grass and the leaves on the trees a more vibrant green. And through it all, underpinning everything, was the sense of raw power flowing through her *skathos*.

She turned away from the yard to find an estate bustling with activity. People loaded and unloaded wagons. The workers in the stable cared for horses or led them to the nearby blacksmith's shed. She caught a faint glimpse of more buildings and some fields behind the manor house, and she smiled at how unassuming the manor looked. It was a simple, two-story house, and if she knew her dad, the master suite was on the ground floor with guest rooms on the second. She surmised a good portion of the ground floor served as the office for overseeing the manor and her dad's holdings throughout the world.

"Excuse me, miss. How did you get through the gate?"

Jennifer turned toward the gruff, weathered voice and found herself facing a man somewhere between her dad and her grandpa in age. He wore basic armor, but her *skathos* told her it wasn't as ineffective as it appeared.

She gave the man her best winsome smile. "I didn't come through the gate, sir."

The man eyed her with a speculative expression for a heartbeat or three before his gaze flicked to the portal and back. "And just who are you that you could use that?"

"Jennifer Cross. Gavin Cross is my dad."

"Young lady, there are very, very few who would have the nerve to claim that if it wasn't true, but I would not be doing my job if I did not ask you for some form of proof."

Jennifer grinned as she hooked her thumb and finger around the chain of her medallion and lifted it into view. The man took one look at it as it rose above the neck of her top and blanched.

"F-forgive me, milady. I... I—"

"No forgiveness necessary, good sir. Dad would rather you ask me for proof of my identity than let someone you didn't know wander around the estate. You did the right thing, and Dad wouldn't say different."

The footman jerked a nod, but his expression—his whole demeanor—suggested he still felt more than a little fear.

Jennifer didn't like that the man's first and fundamental reaction toward her family was one of fear... or at least powerful unease. She gave the man her best smile and made to leave when a thought struck her.

"Sir, is it possible for me to borrow a horse?"

The footman nodded. "Have you ridden a horse before?"

"Some, but not a whole lot. Dad told me about Jasmine."

"Ah, yes. Your father and that mare have a very unique relationship. I've never seen the like of it. Come, milady. The stables are this way."

The footman turned and headed for the large building Jennifer had already decided was the stables. As they approached, her escort waved to a young man who set aside his bucket and walked to meet them.

"Yes, Garn?" the young man asked.

"This is the master's daughter," the footman said. "She has need of a horse but hasn't spent much time in the saddle. Help her pick a mount that will treat her well."

The young man nodded once. "Of course. I'm happy to help."

Without another word, the footman left Jennifer to the young stablehand's care.

"So, you're Kirloth's daughter?"

Jennifer nodded as she looked over the stables. "Yes. I know we look about the same age, but there are some irregularities there."

The stablehand chuckled. "Milady, it's magic, and it's Kirloth. I don't see how there wouldn't be irregularities. Until Marcus the Black Robe recognized your father as his heir, the whole world believed House Kirloth had died out. I've heard some rumors that your father is from the Refugee World."

"Yes, and so am I. I grew up thinking magic and dragons and all this were just stories."

The stablehand stopped and turned to her. "Really?"

Jennifer replied with a single nod.

"That... that's a lot to have hit you at once. Can't imagine it was easy."

Her mind went back to the early days of her father returning. How it felt like the world had disappeared out from under her and left her totally ungrounded all over again. In many ways, she still grappled with those feelings of not knowing where she fit in anymore and what the world meant to her and... it was a huge jumbled furball that she didn't know how to face, let alone process.

She realized the stablehand stood in silence, looking to her for a response, and she sighed. "You have no idea."

THE STABLES HOUSED and provided for twenty mount-worthy horses, and the stablehand walked her through her choices. All of them seemed very well cared for—from what little Jennifer knew—but only one seemed to connect with her. Colored like a blue roan, he stood just a shade taller than she did at the shoulder.

When she started to approach him, the stablehand tensed and lifted a hand as if to stop or caution her, but he just gaped when the massive horse trotted over to her and dropped his head low enough for her to reach. She smiled and rubbed his neck as they had something of a moment. She wasn't sure quite how long they stood like that, but the moment broke when the horse snuffled and nudged her shoulder with his nose.

She grinned but didn't stop rubbing his neck. "What... are you hungry?"

He nudged her shoulder again, and it gave Jennifer a very playful vibe.

"Okay. Let me see if I can get you something." Jennifer turned to ask the stablehand about some apples or a sugar cube and found him staring at them with wide eyes. "What?"

Her question seemed to knock the stablehand out of his reverie, and he shook himself like a wet dog. "That was amazing. He's never responded to anyone like that. He doesn't seem to like anyone touching or petting him, and we've pretty much left him to himself because he gave us no other choice. He almost killed one of the new hands a few weeks ago."

"Well, that won't be a problem anymore, will it?" Jennifer turned to the horse who had followed Jennifer out of his stall and stopped at her side, almost like a puppy. "You'll let these good people help me take care of you, won't you?"

The horse eyed her in silence for a moment, but after a handful of heartbeats, he snuffled again and seemed to give a single nod.

"I'll take that as a provisional yes. Now, how about a treat for my new friend?"

The stablehand turned and hurried over to a bucket, withdrawing a couple apples. He made quick work of cutting them into quarters and moved to hand them to Jennifer. The horse, however, had other ideas and stepped forward to intercept him.

"Here, now." Jennifer hurried forward and put herself between the horse and the apples. "We're friends, so you're supposed to let me give you treats."

The horse stopped and eyed her again, as if trying to decide whether she made any sense. After another long moment, he snuffled again and seemed to relax.

Jennifer grinned and rubbed his muzzle as she accepted an apple quarter and held it out for him, her hand as flat as she could manage it. "Thank you."

The horse accepted her offering and made quick work of it before nudging her shoulder again.

"Oh... want some more?" She smiled and offered him another apple quarter which disappeared just as quickly.

By the time she fed him two apples in quarters, she felt they had established a rapport, and turned to the stablehand. "So, what do I need to take my new friend for a ride?"

.   .   .

SHE FELT like a couple hours had passed when she finally left the estate. Learning how to care for a horse on the trail with the stable-hand took up most of it. As they trotted down the road that connected the estate to the Tel Roshan highway, she decided that she'd call him Ajax. No one at the stables knew if he had a name, since he'd been at the estate since before the change-over to Kirloth's ownership, and the horse seemed to respond to it.

The Tel Roshan highway lived up to its name. It was a wide thoroughfare with plenty of room for large freight wagons to pass side by side. A small raised ridge ran along the center and the sides, just enough to alert teamsters that they might want to pay more attention. Unreadable script decorated a signpost at the edge of the highway, with arrows pointing to her left and right. The same characters started both sets of script, and she assumed it was how the people of the area wrote 'Tel Mivar' and 'Tel Roshan.'

She focused her mind on an idea and invoked a Word of Enchantment, "*Zaenos.*"

The script on the signpost swirled and wiggled until it shifted into English, and she saw she was right. The top line of script with it associated right-pointing arrow read 'Tel Roshan," and the other script with its left-pointing arrow read 'Tel Mivar.'

Which didn't help her all that much in deciding where to go. Oh, sure... she had told everyone that she was coming to visit her dad, and while that wasn't a lie, it wasn't the whole truth, either. What she wanted more than anything else was to explore the world that had turned Gavin Cross into Kirloth and see if it helped her develop any insights into her own path.

A solitary rider in armor with a surcoat bearing heraldry she knew nothing about stopped in front of her and offered a pleasant smile. "If you don't mind me saying so, you look a bit lost."

Jennifer chuckled, settling on a smile. "I'm pretty sure that's a metaphor for my whole life, recently."

The man replied with an understanding nod. "Well, I dislike leaving someone lost along the road, but I have business in Tel Roshan."

She looked left, back the way he came and toward Tel Mivar. Toward her father and everything it meant to be a daughter of House Kirloth. Then, she pulled her attention back to him. "I haven't seen Tel Roshan. Do you mind if I travel with you?"

His smile widened. "Not at all."

Jennifer nudged Ajax into motion, and after a glance over his shoulder, the man moved deeper into the highway to give her room. After a short time, he glanced her way before returning his eyes to the road. "So, what has you on the road today, if you don't mind me asking?"

"Do you prefer honesty or just conversation?"

"My mother always told me honesty was the best policy."

She smiled. Then, her smile faded, and she shrugged. "I... don't know, really. I've felt lost for the last little while, and I felt like I need to get out and explore the world a bit. I'm hoping that seeing new places will help me sort out my place in life."

He nodded his understanding. "I can see that. I can't say I've ever experienced something similar. I grew up knowing my path."

"Oh, really? May I ask what that is?"

"It's nothing glamorous, I assure you. I'm a mid-level administrator for Mivar Province. I'm going to Tel Roshan to assist with some issues that have arisen regarding the new tax code the Archmagister established shortly after he took office."

Jennifer pursed her lips to bite back her immediate thought. Unfortunately, he caught her at it.

"It's fine." He made a dismissive wave with his hand. "Most people find what I do boring drudgery. I'm used to that."

"I really shouldn't have reacted that way. I..." She felt a blush heat her cheeks, betraying her slight embarrassment as her voice trailed off. She didn't know what to say.

He shook his head. "No... seriously, it's fine. If I was the type to be sensitive about my job, I would've sought out something that let me boast of derring-do, carving my way through ne'er-do-wells as I swung from a chandelier... or some such nonsense. By and large, my job has me home in time for dinner without any major travel or danger. The missus likes that, and it lets me watch my children grow up. Soon enough, we'll face a list of brave lads and lasses who will never come home again, what with the upcoming campaign."

Jennifer frowned. "Upcoming campaign? I'm not sure I've heard anything about that."

He turned his head to look at her askance. "Seriously? You've not heard of the campaign that's mobilizing? Have you been hiding under a rock... or maybe chained up in a basement or something?"

"I don't get out as much as I should, but I haven't noticed any chains or rocks overhead. Mind bringing a girl up-to-date on current events?"

He looked her over once again, and it was clear from his expression that it was an appraising look that had nothing do with her attractiveness. After a few moments, he sighed and shook his head. "Well... it's not like anyone who can see lightning and hear thunder couldn't find out about it within moments of sunrise. See, the Archmagister is mobilizing the Old Alliance to re-take Skullkeep and put paid to the Necromancer for good. I don't know any specifics, but the army fort outside of Tel Mivar has exploded with all kinds of activity."

Jennifer wasn't sure whether she should affect indifference or heightened interest. The last thing she wanted was for this nice fellow to think of her as spy for Skullkeep. She thought she remembered her dad mentioning it at some point, but it was such a vague thought that she couldn't tease it into full recollection. She settled for another question.

"Have you heard anyone talking about what the Archmagister's chances of victory are?"

Her traveling companion shrugged. "Who knows? The Archmagister has accomplished quite a bit that no one ever expected. It stands to reason that he would have a better chance than most. But who knows if he'll even be among the troops?"

Yeah... Jennifer couldn't see her dad sitting in a plush study somewhere while countless people risked their lives for his goals. "From what little I know of him, I don't see him sitting somewhere behind the lines. He'll be as close to the action as possible. After all, doesn't he have to confront the Necromancer?"

"You'd think, but that didn't work out so well last time. No one's really sure what happened, but he and the Vushaari princess vanished for something like a year when the Necromancer tried raiding Tel Mivar. But everyone also says that the Archmagister went into that fight at far less than his best. So, who can say?"

It took all her willpower for Jennifer not to correct the guy on his understanding. After all, she'd heard the whole story from Kiri. Thinking of her dad's wife, she bit back a snort. It wasn't all that uncommon back home for someone to suddenly have a stepparent younger than they were, but she couldn't think of anyone else whose stepmom could sink a throwing knife into a dummy's eye from fifty feet away. Every time she thought of Kiri, the predominant thought on her mind was how she dealt with those bank robbers back home; Alexis's travel party hadn't even really had time to react, let alone act. But she didn't think she should mention how the Archmagister's chances might increase if he brought his wife along; Jennifer wasn't sure that information was for public consumption.

"You know... it just occurred to me I hadn't introduced myself. My name is Jennifer."

"It's a pleasure to make your acquaintance, Jennifer. I am Arne."

Jennifer replied with a smile and a nod as they continued on their way to Tel Roshan. Arne looked toward the road, and she allowed her gaze to wander over him. Perhaps, it wasn't such a bad idea to travel incognito after all.

CHAPTER 16

The new day dawned clear and bright, and Jennifer couldn't believe how rested she felt for having slept on a bedroll under a travel tent. Their camp was in the center of a copse of conifers, something Arne called a traveler's waystation. A prepared fire pit—complete with ceramic pipes to duct air to the base of the fire—made the center of the camp, and felled logs laid around it served as seating. The stream that burbled nearby was a bit on the cool side for bathing, but a whispered Word of Evocation handled that.

A fresh set of clothes were a bit more challenging, especially since she hadn't packed a bag or anything, but she teleported back to her dad's estate and stepped through the portal for a change of clothes... all under the guise of a nice long bath. She didn't want to risk too much of Arne's credulity, so she stuffed some folded clothes in a canvas satchel and brought it back with her. When she returned from her 'bath,' Arne regarded her new satchel with a slightly skeptical eye but said nothing. After a quick breakfast of trail rations, they saddled their mounts and set off once more.

They rode in silence for a few moments after leaving the copse of trees before Arne spoke. "I should warn you. There's a forest coming up that straddles the border between Mivar and Roshan Provinces, and the highway winds through it. For the most part, it's a safe stretch of road... but... every so often, a group of people who believe themselves marginalized decide to take up banditry. If there's a lot of traffic on the highway, they usually keep their heads down, but if there's only a wagon or two or just us, they might put in an appearance. You any good in a fight?"

Jennifer fought the urge to smirk... and mostly succeeded. "That depends on what you call a fight."

Arne barked a laugh and nodded. "Fair point. The more 'professional' outfits have both archers and footmen. If there's more than six in the overall group, we might want to avoid a confrontation. Do you have any coin you can afford to sacrifice if it comes to that?"

"Oh, I'm sure I'll make do."

Arne cast her a side-eyed glance. "You sure are an odd one, Jennifer."

"Are you sure your marker for odd isn't skewed? I think I'm fairly normal."

Her traveling companion chose to yield on that one, and they moved on to other topics, the clip-clopping of the horses' hooves serving as a backdrop to their conversation.

A FEW HOURS LATER, noise that sounded almost like a pitched battle reached their ears, and they rounded a curve in the road to find a three-wagon caravan beset on all sides by bandits. Canvas stretched across ribs covered the wagons, which radiated a low level of Tutation to Jennifer's *skathos*. She wondered if it was a protection from elements or something else.

But that was a matter for another time.

"There's no way to know who's on which side." Arne scowled as they took in the melee. "I see a couple people cowering in the wagons, so they're probably non-combatants, but otherwise, this looks like a free-for-all."

Jennifer gave Arne her own sideways glance. "We have to stop this, just to sort out who's who. I'll handle it."

"How will you—"

Before Arne could finish his question, Jennifer focused on a clear image of her intent in her mind, then invoked a Word of Enchantment. "*Thymnos.*"

She didn't do anything to constrain her power at all, and it slammed into the ambient magic like the detonation of a stick of dynamite tossed into a tranquil lake. Pain savaged her guts as the invocation took hold, and Arne gasped and clutched at his left wrist as every armed person collapsed to the ground.

One tear escaped each eye as Arne held his wrist, and his voice was a little strained. "Are they…"

"Just asleep. Those people hiding in the wagons shouldn't be affected. I focused on putting the armed people to sleep."

She wasn't sure how to interpret the look Arne gave her before he nudged his horse up to a slow walk. As he neared the first wagon, Jennifer just barely heard a terrified voice.

"Please, don't hurt us! We surrender!"

"You're safe." Arne waved in a 'come out' gesture. "Come out and help us sort out these people. They're just sleeping."

Jennifer nudged Ajax up to a slow walk and joined Arne just as a young woman peeked her head out of the covered wagon. Stringy hair the color of hay framed a face masked with anxiety and a small thread of terror.

"They're just sleeping? You're sure?"

"Yes, I'm sure." Arne gave his best attempt at a reassuring nod. "My friend is an arcanist; she did it so that we could sort out the good people from the bandits without harming anyone."

She came the rest of the way out of the wagon, revealing that she held the hand of a smaller child who seemed very intent on sucking his (or her) thumb. The child was young enough that it wasn't easy for Jennifer to determine gender, and she didn't know enough about the differences between boys' and girls' clothing in this world to hazard a guess.

The young woman cast a nervous—almost fearful—glance over the sleeping fighters, and she worked her lower lip between her teeth. "How long will they be asleep?"

"I can wake them up one by one, once we secure the bandits," Jennifer replied. "Do you mind helping us figure out which is which?"

The young woman gave a choppy nod, still pressing her lip between her teeth.

A couple more people emerged from the other wagons by then, all casting their own fearful glances at the mass of sleeping fighters. Arne nudged his horse forward and introduced himself and Jennifer twice more, once for each wagon. Jennifer watched someone in the very last wagon look her over before directing an urgent whisper to Arne. He then turned around in his saddle, allowing himself a grimace as he too looked her over once more. He nodded and turned his horse to come back to Jennifer.

"I don't suppose you happen to have any proof that you're one of the good arcanists, do you?" he asked when he arrived once more at Jennifer's side. "That lady back there didn't see a wizard's medallion, and we all know that the arcanists who follow Milthas or are allied with Skullkeep don't wear them."

She tried. Jennifer really tried to maintain her nonchalance, but a heaving sigh escaped her control. "I was hoping to keep this part of my identity a secret. Do you promise me that you won't spread this around?"

Arne chuckled. "I'm not promising anything until I know what we're discussing."

In reply, Jennifer used her thumb and finger to grasp the silver chain that hung around her neck and lifted her medallion into view. Arne's eyes shot wide—almost wider than Ajax's hooves—as some color drained from his cheeks and neck the moment the Glyph of Kirloth on her medallion came into full view.

"How... who..." Arne's voice came out strangled, as if he had to voice air to move so he could speak.

"The Archmagister is my father. It's complicated. He trained me in the Art while he was away; that's part of why it's complicated."

Arne nodded and took a couple slow, deep breaths. Then, he nodded one more time before turning his horse around and riding him back to the woman who'd raised the concern. Jennifer could see a visible change in the woman's demeanor during that exchange; the woman was much more relaxed, seeing Jennifer's medallion glinting in the patchy sun that broke through the arboreal canopy overhead.

After a few more moments, Arne turned his horse and once again rode back to Jennifer. "So... how long will they be asleep?"

"Uhm... until I wake them... maybe? I wasn't too precise on duration when I invoked the effect. I just wanted to put every armed person in the melee asleep."

Arne puffed out a breath. "Right, then. It sounds like we have some time. Can you tell if there are more bandits anywhere close?"

Jennifer frowned as she considered the question. She *should* be able to invoke a Word of Divination and reveal any bandits who hadn't joined the fight but still remained close. She rubbed her chin as she considered the question further, trying to decide what form she wanted the divination's answer to take. She suspected her dad would use something he called a scrying sphere, but she didn't have much experience with those. Or maybe the sphere was how the invocation manifested naturally?

She bit back a growl and shook her head. She was taking too much time thinking about it. She formed her intent in her mind and focused her full concentration on that mental image. All that remained was to invoke the Word of Divination.

"*Klaepos.*"

Once again, her power struck the ambient magic completely unchecked. It was a steam-driven battering ram hitting a thousand-year-old castle wall that had never been repaired. Arne gasped again and clutched at his left wrist.

"Dammit, woman, don't you know how to trickle your power?" His question came out strained. "Every wizard for who knows how far will know you're here with a resonance like that."

It was time to confirm her suspicions. She kept her head down just a little bit and facing straight ahead while she peeked at him from under her eyebrows, all while giving him a playful half-smile. "And just what would you know about how much power I'm throwing around? I don't see a medallion around your neck."

Arne's expression as he met her eyes wasn't *quite* a glare, but it would do until the real thing came along. The glare faded as he pinched the bridge of his nose and sighed. Then, he glanced behind him over his right shoulder; no one was close enough to see. He held out his left arm just enough to give her a good—though clandestine—view and pulled back his sleeve... revealing the tattoo of a Wraith.

Jennifer didn't quite gloat, but she did grin. "Thought so."

"So, your father told you about us?"

Now, she couldn't keep from beaming a huge smile. "Told me about you? Arne, I've met Declan and watched him spar with Kiri."

He gave a slow nod. "Yeah... that would do it. Very well. It's good we know where we stand with each other, and yes, I will keep your secret if that is what you wish. Let's get these people sorted."

BEFORE LONG, the caravan's people were awake and checking over their wagons for damage, while the would-be bandits were standing with their hands tied together and tied to each other. Tel Roshan was far closer than Tel Mivar, at least according to Arne, and Jennifer agreed with him that they should take the bandits with them, rather than burden the caravan. After several rounds of gushing thanks for saving them, the caravan went on its way, leaving her and Arne with their prisoners.

A SHORT TIME passed in relative silence as they rode toward Tel Roshan before Arne turned to her. "So, any particular reason you didn't fully introduce yourself when we met?"

"I wanted to get a feel for this place without being under my dad's shadow."

"Yeah... good point. Kirloth—whether your dad or his mentor—casts a pretty long shadow in this world. I can't really blame you for wanting to see people's honest reactions without it looming over you."

"Did you know Dad's mentor? The man he called Marcus?"

Arne nodded. "Oh, yes. Everyone in our organization knew him. He was a fairly major force of nature in his own right, but then again, you'd have to be if you personally dueled a god... and won. He had very defined views and opinions on what was right and wrong, and he didn't mind going a little dark if it served the greater good. Sure... it's easy to say that going dark for the greater good is an oxymoron, that no good can come from going dark. But I'm not so sure of that. He did an awful lot to safeguard this world during the centuries everyone else thought him dead, and our organization served as his eyes and ears throughout the world."

Jennifer nodded. Both her dad and Kiri had talked about what it meant to be Kirloth, and there was a chance—very slim, but still a chance—that she herself would be Kirloth one day. She wasn't sure how she felt about that. Wasn't sure she was up to the... responsibility. But she wouldn't know if she didn't learn more about the world and the role Kirloth served in it. She probably wouldn't truly know if she was up to the task until it came to her, but that was a matter for the future. Hopefully, the far future.

* * *

ARNE RODE along at Jennifer's side in silence. He wasn't quite sure what to make of her revelation that she was Kirloth's daughter. Probably Young Kirloth, in fact... given that she was an adult and fully trained arcanist.

He fought the urge to shake his head in dismay... and mostly succeeded. It was his kind of luck that he'd fallen in with the one person who could more easily ruin his plans than any other soul walking the world.

Young Kirloth... damn and blast.

Could he afford to keep her with him? Could he afford not to?

One thing was certain. He couldn't let her follow him around like a puppy once they reached Tel Roshan. That would end any hope of achieving his objectives.

The Wraiths paid well enough, but he wasn't getting any younger. And the Necromancer had offered him immortality. Sure... it would probably end up being some form of undeath, but he didn't want to die. He didn't want to just... stop.

That thought scared him more than anything else in his life. That, one day, he'd simply end. That there wouldn't be anything left of him, beyond a moldering corpse planted in a stretch of ground somewhere.

No. If he could find a way to cheat that outcome, he'd do so without a second thought.

Who cared if the price was going against everything he'd held dear his entire life? He certainly didn't.

A stray thought crossed his mind, and he paused to consider it. Should he try capturing Jennifer and taking her to the Necromancer *with* the information he—or maybe it—wanted him to steal? That would surely guarantee his success, right?

He risked a glance toward his traveling companion. Nothing too obvious, just a slight turn of the head to facilitate more than his peripheral vision.

She was powerful. Very powerful. He wasn't sure he'd ever known any arcanist as powerful as she was, and that was including her father. Of course... he'd never been around the Archmagister when he was wielding the Art, but he still remembered what it had felt like when the man ended slavery. He wasn't sure he'd ever forget that pain from his tattoo.

That—more than anything else—convinced him he had no business trying to capture Jennifer for presentation to the Necromancer. It wasn't the kind of thing to fail at on the first try... and what was worse, he might just succeed.

He had no idea what 'Dear Old Dad' might do if someone

abducted his daughter, but he was damn certain he never wanted to find out.

He wanted to sigh, but kept it in. No... the only thing to do was keep her with him for a time and then tell her he had some business or something to do that wouldn't work if she was with him. He could part company with her and deliver the information to Skullkeep with her none the wiser.

It wasn't an ideal plan. It wasn't even all that good of a plan. But it was the best plan he had at the moment. Such was the nature of life at times.

* * *

JENNIFER WASN'T sure what to make of Tel Roshan. It looked just enough like Tel Mivar—at least inside the walls—that there was an almost eerie, 'deja vu but not quite' feeling as she followed Arne down the main thoroughfare to the nearest guard post. She hoped they'd be able to hand off their prisoners without much fanfare, and she really hoped Arne would be able to keep her out of it as much as possible. She didn't like revealing her identity in a formal report. Showing Arne her medallion was one thing, but a formal report might make its way to her dad before she was ready for him to know she was here.

"This street looks so much like the one I saw in Tel Mivar that it's eerie."

Arne snorted a laugh. "Yeah... all the province capitals are like this to a degree. Kirloth—your father's mentor—and his apprentices raised these cities from the very bones of the earth. I don't know if they didn't realize how similar they made the cities, or if it was a conscious choice, but I've experienced the same thing in all of them except for Tel Cothos. They raised that city on an island in the middle of the lake that feeds the Vischaene and a couple other rivers; that alone makes for quite a different ambiance."

The thought of a city sitting atop an island in the center of a lake brought a smile to her face. "I'd like to see that."

"No reason you can't. Here... we can hand off our associates at this guard post."

"Keep me out of it as much as you can, please?"

Arne glanced her way over his shoulder, a half-smile curling one side of his mouth. "I will."

IT WASN'T long before Arne returned, the would-be bandits now in the custody of the Tel Roshan guard. He swung up into the saddle without a word and nudged his horse up to a slow walk. Jennifer nudged Ajax to follow. Once they were well out of earshot of the guard post, he broke the silence.

"If anyone should ask—which they shouldn't—the caravaners and I were able to subdue the bandits."

"Got it." Jennifer nodded. "What if the bandits start talking about the wizard who put them to sleep?"

He scoffed. "Guards aren't in the business of putting a lot of stock in what criminals say, especially if they're repeat offenders, and a few of the ones we turned in carry the brand. They'll say anything to escape the noose, but it won't save them."

"Wow... you execute bandits here?"

"No." Arne shook his head. "We remove criminals who refuse to change their ways from society, and before you get heated over hanging innocents, we only hang people with two brands after they've committed another crime. Has your father shown you Divination of Truth yet? It lets us be absolutely sure there are no mistakes."

Okay. That did make a certain amount of sense, especially since the divination didn't hurt the target. She almost wished she could find a way to introduce it to the justice system back home, but that would mean bringing magic into more of society, which was not a path she wanted to walk. The societies of Earth just weren't set up for it.

"So... where to now?" she asked, still mulling over what she'd learned.

Arne sighed. "I should probably drop you off at a tavern or inn while I handle my business."

"Ashamed to be seen with me so soon? Why... we just met."

He snorted another laugh. "No; it isn't that at all. I'll be meeting with Carth Roshan's deputy, and there's always the chance he'll peek in. I have no problem taking you with me if that's really what you want."

Oh. Yeah. She had met Carth Roshan, both when her dad first returned to this world and later at his wedding.

"You say there's a nice tavern close?"

Arne didn't even crack a grin as he pointed to it less than half a block ahead of them.

CHAPTER 17

Jennifer wasn't sure what to expect from a tavern named The Boar's Rest, so she approached it with more than a little trepidation in her heart. The building itself looked no different than any other building inside Tel Roshan's walls. Much like the buildings of Tel Mivar, this too was made of an off-white stone with faint striations of black and gray. There were no seams in the stone. The tavern's door appeared to be a block of solid wood without any apparent seams or fastenings, and when she operated the latch and pushed, it swung open easily and silently, ringing a bell mounted over it.

Jennifer stepped inside and found herself alone, except for a tall and muscled man in an apron. He stood behind the bar, wiping down thick glass mugs with a cloth. He nodded a greeting to her without slowing his work. Pleasant smells wafted out of the kitchen behind him and prompted her stomach to growl. Her stomach growling embarrassed her, and she hoped he didn't hear that; she hadn't realized it had been so long since breakfast.

It felt a little eerie standing in a tavern that had no other customers, so she sauntered up to the bar and gave the man her best friendly smile.

"Are you open for customers?"

He nodded. "Pick your seat, and one of the girls will be right with you."

"My thanks."

Jennifer turned and looked over the room. Her choices were tables for the most part, but booths ran along the wall, with one of the booth's benches built onto—or maybe into—the wall itself. There was a little mini wall that separated the tavern's foyer from the dining area, and she smiled as her gaze landed on the corner booth. That suited her right down to the ground.

She wasn't even fully comfortable in her seat when a young brunette—no older than fourteen—stood at the edge of her table. "Good day to you, mistress. We have a haunch of beef on the spit, fresh bread baked just this morning, and your choice of ale, mead, or wine."

"Any fruit or vegetables to go with the beef?"

The young brunette bobbed her head. "Why, yes, mistress. If you like, we can whip you up a fine salad to go with the beef."

"That sounds good, and what do you recommend for the drink?"

The young brunette darted a cautious look over her shoulder, but the man at the bar was nowhere in sight. "Uhm, I'm supposed to say the ale is the house speciality, but it always leaves me with a sour stomach. I personally think our mead is the best we have."

Jennifer winked at her and smiled. "I think I'll have the mead, then."

A SHORT TIME LATER, Jennifer was wiping the last handful of bread across the plate when the tavern's door slammed open on the other side of the wall next to her. The man behind the bar looked up and immediately frowned as a thick-bodied, barrel-chested man covered in furs stomped up to the bar. He held a chain in one hand, and Jennifer glared at the sight of a woman wearing a collar attached to the other end of the chain. The poor soul looked filthy, and the rags she wore barely held together.

"Hanskarr, I've told you before... slavery's illegal now. Take that collar off her before I have to report you."

The fur-clad man just chuckled. "Ganj, yer not man enough to report me. Now, gimme an ale a'fore I crack that worthless skull o' yers."

Jennifer barely heard the soft voice, almost a whimper. "Please, sir, I'm hungry. May I eat?"

The fur-clad man—Hanskarr, apparently—looked over his shoulder and sneered. "You haven't earned any food yet."

He drew his hand back to strike the woman, and Jennifer had seen enough. She stood and stepped around her table. "I think that's just about enough out of you."

Hanskarr looked up, laying eyes on Jennifer for the first time, and his sneer only intensified. "You think you have the stones to stop me, you worthless wench? Come on, then. I have another collar that would look very pretty around your neck."

Jennifer leaned far enough to one side to make eye contact with the tavern keeper. "What's the penalty for keeping a slave, now that it's illegal?"

The man scratched his chin and shrugged. "Not sure, really. I haven't heard of anyone actually doing it after the Archmagister wiped out all the slavers and anyone who'd ever used a slave brand. That's a fair bit of deterrence, you know."

Jennifer fought to keep her non-expression steady, but on the inside, she was a little impressed. Despite everything she'd seen her father do, the idea that he wiped out all the slavers and anyone who had ever used a slave brand just felt significant.

"Well, it seems the Archmagister has already established a precedent, then." Jennifer focused her full attention on the man as she invoked a Word of Interation. "*Thraxys*."

Hanskarr made a dreadful racket when he hit the floor. Well... his *corpse* did. The chain rattled and clinked as it fell free, and the woman screamed and jumped back when she realized he was dead.

Jennifer focused on the chain *and* the collar and invoked a Word of Transmutation. "*Rhyskaal*."

The woman screamed again as the chain and collar made a pile of iron dust on the floor.

"Might I borrow a broom?" Jennifer asked. "It seems I made a mess on your floor."

The man Hanskarr called Ganj leaned forward just far enough to look over the bar at the corpse that now decorated his establishment. "Is he dead?"

"Very."

"Then, I'd say you made a little more than a mess. I'm afraid I have to call the town guard and report this."

Jennifer grimaced and sighed. "Yes, fine. Do what you have to do. Can we get his victim some food and better clothing first, though? I'm happy to pay for both."

Ganj looked a little wild around the eyes for a second. "You're just going to stand there and accept that I'm calling the guard? I... I'm not sure what to make of that."

"I never wanted to create trouble for you. My friend just asked me to wait in your tavern while he met with some people."

About that time, an older woman and three young women—one of whom was the brunette who brought Jennifer her food—stepped out of the back. They stopped when Ganj held up his hand, but that didn't keep the woman from speaking.

"Ganj, what happened? We heard a noise and screaming."

Ganj grimaced. "Hanskarr came in and finally offended someone he couldn't intimidate or kill, and she made *very* short work of him."

The older woman gasped and rounded the bar, all while gesturing for the younger ladies to stay where they were. Her eyes shot wide at the sight of Hanskarr's corpse, and she jerked her attention up to Jennifer.

Jennifer reached into her pocket and withdrew a one-ounce gold coin, flipping toward the bar. "Will that cover my food, her food, and some clothes for her?"

Both Ganj and the older woman gaped at the coin. The woman was quick to say, "It'll cover that and more. That's far too much, mistress."

"No, it's not, especially if you consider the mess I've caused. I'd take it as a kindness if she could get some food and if someone could dash out to a shop nearby for some better clothing than the rags she's wearing."

Ganj picked up the coin and frowned as he turned it over in his hands. "There's no mint stamp on this. Where did it come from?"

Aw, shit. Jennifer really should've thought of that. "So, yeah... I'm not exactly from around here. I've never seen any of your coinage, but I figured gold always spends no matter what it looks like. That's a one-ounce coin, pure gold."

Heavy footfalls entered the tavern, accompanied by an odd jingling. Four people in a mix of chain and scale mail stepped into view, and Jennifer understood the odd jingling.

"Various people reported hearing..." The armored woman's voice trailed off when she saw the corpse on the floor. "What happened here?"

Jennifer stepped forward. "It's my fault. The dead guy came into the tavern with this young woman in a collar attached to a chain that he held, and when I confronted him about his poor behavior, he decided to present a credible threat to my life. I defended myself and removed the collar from the young woman."

"Where is it?" the armored woman asked.

"Right there." Jennifer pointed to the pile of rust-colored particles on the tavern floor. "You're members of the town guard, right?"

"Yes, that's correct. I'm Sergeant Brenna," the armored woman replied, "and how is that the collar?"

Jennifer scoffed. "Well, I didn't have the key, and I certainly wasn't going to go pawing a corpse to see if he did. So, I transmuted it."

One or two of the people behind Brenna took a half-step backward.

Brenna looked down at the pile of rust for a heartbeat before returning her focus to Jennifer. "You transmuted it, you say. You don't look like a mage."

Jennifer fought the urge to heave a sigh. She really didn't want to announce herself, but she didn't see any way around it. Besides, her anonymity was a small price to pay if it meant the young woman could go about making a better life for herself. She lifted one hand and used its thumb and forefinger to grasp the chain hanging around her neck and slowly brought her medallion into view.

The moment the Glyph cleared the neckline of her top, *everyone* in the room paled. More than one pair of eyes went wide, and the woman she had freed passed out as if someone had flipped an 'off' switch.

"I... I see, milady," Brenna said. "I... please forgive me for intruding upon your day, and we will see to the corpse at once."

"And no part of this will come back on them?" Jennifer asked, indicating Ganj and who she assumed to be his family.

Brenna was very quick to shake her head in a fervent 'no.' "Not at all, milady. They had no part in this."

Just then, more footfalls entered the tavern, and a group of men and women in black robes trimmed in crimson led Carth Roshan and his son Wynn into the tavern.

"There was a power flare near here," the lead man in a crimson-trimmed black robe said, "and we are searching for the source."

Brenna looked like she wanted to hide under a rock. "Ah... Lord Inquisitor... uhm..."

Carth Roshan stepped forward. He glanced at Brenna's shoulder where her rank insignia rested and made his best attempt at a comforting smile. "Sergeant, please... be at ease. We merely seek the source of the flare. We need to make sure that whoever it was presents no threat to the city at large."

"You're looking for me, Carth," Jennifer said, drawing the new arrivals' attention for the first time.

Wynn snorted and shook his head. "I *knew* that resonance felt like Gavin but wasn't. What are you doing here, Jennifer?"

"You know her, milord?" the man in the crimson-trimmed robe asked.

Both Carth and Wynn nodded. Carth said, "She's the Archmagister's daughter."

Wynn turned back to Jennifer. "Mind telling us what happened?"

Jennifer sighed and took them through it all, including how she wanted to explore Drakmoor without anyone knowing she was here... especially her father... and ending when she killed Hanskarr.

Wynn turned to the woman she'd saved, who was now sitting on a nearby chair. "Will you consent to a Divination of Truth to confirm what she said?"

The woman still looked a little wild around the eyes, but she hesitantly nodded. Wynn invoked a Word of Divination, and a gray aura faded into existence around her. Over the next few moments, she confirmed the events that led to Hanskarr's death, including his treatment of her.

Carth turned to the town guard and the Inquisitors. "It is my determination that there is no crime here, beyond Hanskarr's treatment of the woman. Do you agree?"

Sergeant Brenna and the lead inquisitor both agreed and led their respective groups back out of the tavern, the town guard promising to return with a cart for Hanskarr's corpse.

"Did Arne ever meet with you, Carth?" Jennifer asked, breaking the ensuing silence.

Carth turned to her, giving her a frown of confusion. "Arne? Who is that?"

"He's someone I met on the highway. He said he had a meeting with one of your people, and there was a chance you'd crash the meeting. That's why I said I'd wait for him here."

Carth's frown deepened. "I honestly don't know of any meeting like that, but that doesn't necessarily mean anything."

Jennifer started to say more, giving him the story Arne gave her, but she thought better of it. What if that story was the cover to hide his true purpose? She didn't want to expose him, especially if he was on Wraith business to Tel Roshan. That wouldn't be good for her, him, *or* Carth.

"Don't worry about it." She gave a dismissive wave and turned to Ganj. "Am I still welcome to wait for my traveling companion here?"

For a moment, she thought Ganj's eyes were about to erupt out of his skull before he said, "Are you serious? Of course, you're welcome.

We've never hosted a wizard of House Kirloth before... nor House Roshan, Your Graces."

Carth chuckled. "Be at ease, goodman. Wynn and I will take our leave and allow your day to start wandering back in the direction of normal."

Jennifer bid them good day and watched them leave, only to fight another grimace as everyone else in the tavern turned awed expressions her way. She lifted her medallion and hid it inside her clothes once more, then asked, "I don't suppose there's any way for us to go back to how we were before Hanskarr?"

Ganj snorted and shook his head. "Milady... no offense... but you're daft if you think we'll just forget you're the Archmagister's daughter."

Jennifer heaved a sigh and sagged into a handy chair. "I was afraid of that."

It wasn't long before the older woman brought a fresh platter that looked just like what Jennifer had eaten. She laid it on the table in front of the woman Hanskarr had enslaved and laid utensils beside the platter before she retreated. The woman looked to Jennifer, her expression little more than that of a whipped dog.

Jennifer nodded. "That's your food. Don't gorge yourself, but eat your fill. If that means more than you have right now, we'll buy more. Deal?"

The woman looked at Jennifer in silence for several heartbeats before she tore into the food without a word. Jennifer hid a smile at seeing her eat, and she leaned back against her chair and tried to figure out just how much she had screwed herself over by saving this unnamed woman.

In all honesty... saving someone was never screwing herself over. It couldn't be. But at the same time, she pretty much destroyed her anonymity, so it was only a matter of time before her father knew she was here... if Arne hadn't sent that message already. There was just no way to know, but she hoped Carth and Wynn would keep her presence to themselves.

No matter how hard she tried to be upset with herself over it, she knew she would never have just walked away and allowed this woman to continue suffering. So, she might as well own it. The thought of what Alexis would think almost made her snort a laugh, but that would require far too much explanation for that moment in time, and she was glad she stifled the snort.

It wasn't long until the woman cleaned her plate, just as Jennifer had done, and it was then time to track down better clothes. She stood and looked to Ganj. "If a man answering to the name of Arne comes looking for me, tell him I'll be right back as soon as I see to her clothes."

Ganj looked like he wanted to say one of his people could handle that, but something stopped him. He simply nodded and went back to wiping mugs.

CHAPTER 18

When Jennifer brought the woman back to the Boar's Rest, Arne sat in the corner booth where she had eaten earlier that day. He scowled at the tabletop before he noticed her, and once he did notice her... well... his disposition did not appear to improve.

"Would you care to explain to me just what in Lornithar's Abyss you were thinking?"

Jennifer simply stopped and crossed her arms across her midriff while she lifted one eyebrow. "Excuse me?"

"There's no excuse for you! I only asked one thing of you... one thing! You were supposed to sit in a tavern—preferably this one— and *do nothing* until I came for you. What in all creation do you call mobilizing half the city's Inquisitors and drawing out the Duke and his son? Because it sure as shit wasn't *nothing*."

"Somewhere along the way, you must've developed the mistaken impression that I somehow work for you. I saved this woman from a horrible life."

Arne scoffed. "What... you think *she* matters? She's just some guttershite. She's nothing spec—"

"*Zaenos*." His voice cut off with an *urrk* as Jennifer's invocation of a

Word of Enchantment caused his neck muscles to spasm. She had never felt such rage swell within her, threatening to take control. It took all her willpower not to render Arne down to his component elements. "You need a time-out, you bastard."

Then, she did the one thing she swore she'd never do. She invoked the Word of Transmutation her dad used on the FBI SWAT team. "*Uhnrys.*"

Arne froze, and Jennifer bit her lip to keep from laughing. Her invocation caught him with his neck mid-spasm. Then, she turned to the woman at her side. "Don't you believe one word of what he said. Do you understand?"

The woman stared at the floor, as she had since Arne started talking. She didn't respond or react to Jennifer's words. Jennifer had seen girls like her back on Earth. While she wasn't sure the same methods she had used to draw them out of their fear would work on Drakmoor, she didn't have anything else to try. The downside was they took some time.

"Do you mind going to that table over there and having a seat? I need to call a friend to figure out what to do with this guy."

The woman gave the barest hint of a nod before she trudged over to the indicated table and sat with her back to the corner booth.

Jennifer kept from sighing, but only just. She didn't like her choices at this point, and she'd made such a resonance in the ambient magic already that her dad probably knew precisely where she was and what she was doing. No help for it, then. Besides, she always preferred to do something right the first time.

She formed a clear picture of her intent in her mind, focusing all her will on it, then invoked a Word of Divination. "*Klaepos.*"

A scrying sphere faded into existence in front of her and revealed that Declan was about to get involved in some activities he would prefer she didn't interrupt. And that was fine. He hadn't done anything yet, beyond help the nice blond-haired lady out of her dress, so it wasn't like Jennifer would be interrupting... much.

"*Paedryx-Thyphos.*" Her invocation of a composite effect—her first, in fact—savaged her with a vicious pain, and it took all her willpower to keep from crying out. As the effect took hold, Declan vanished from the room with the blonde—appearing at her side—while a message wrote itself in cloudy white letters in the space he had just occupied:

Please, be patient. He'll be right back. I only need to borrow him for a moment.

Declan sputtered his shock, until he focused on Jennifer. Then, he sighed and shook his head. "I should have known. Not even your father would have pulled something like that."

Jennifer gave him her best insouciant smile. "Hi, Declan. I need your help."

"Most people contact me by letter. They don't abduct me."

"A letter would've taken too long, and besides, I only have another two minutes or so."

Declan frowned. "What? Why?"

Jennifer pointed at the frozen Arne. "I locked him into a frozen moment for about five minutes, give or take. I didn't know what to do."

Declan didn't quite grimace at the sight of Arne, but she suspected it was a near thing. "How did you get mixed up with him of all people?"

"It's a bit of a long story." Relaying the tale took the most of her remaining time on the frozen moment, so she repeated the invocation to add another ten minutes or so.

A startled gasp escaped Declan's control. "You really shouldn't throw that Word around like it's confetti. Your father said his mentor wrote in his journals that it was pretty much forbidden back before the Godswar."

"Oh." Jennifer's expression fell, then turned inquisitive. "Did Marcus write why?"

"Not that your father ever told me, so you should take it up with him. Either way, how do you know you didn't kill him?"

"Honestly... I don't. And right this second, I'm not too worried about that. He turned into an ass all of a sudden, and I don't understand why."

Declan chuckled. "Well, I do. He went rogue. I don't know what he was doing here, but I promise you it wasn't..." He cast a furtive glance around before continuing. "...my associates' business. No one has heard from him in something like half a year."

"Shit. Maybe I should've killed him."

"Oh, no. It's very difficult to get information out of a corpse, and only a wizard could interrogate his spirit. Well... a wizard or an extremely proficient mage. I saw your father do it once."

"So... what do we do with him?"

Declan sighed. "Well, I need to go break a very nice young lady's heart—"

Jennifer snorted. "I'm sure it wasn't her heart that you thought was nice. I used a scrying sphere to find you."

"—and I would ask that you put him to sleep. We have items that can break a sleep effect, and I need to take him to a chapterhouse for a discussion." If Declan worried over Jennifer seeing him and his friend through the scrying sphere, he certainly didn't show it.

Jennifer formed her intention in her mind once more and focused her full will on it as she invoked another composite effect. "*Rhosed-Thymnos.*"

Arne snapped out of the frozen moment, and his head thunked against the tabletop as he fell forward... already in a deep sleep.

"That should do it, I'd say. Now, if you don't mind sending me back? On second thought, I can arrange for the local chapterhouse to collect him, and I won't need to disappoint Rose after all."

Jennifer shook her head and invoked the Word of Transmutation once more. "*Paedryx.*"

Declan vanished as quickly as he'd appeared, reappearing back in the room with the blonde whose name was apparently Rose.

She pushed Arne out of her mind and walked over to the table where the woman sat with her shoulders slumped. She pulled out the chair opposite the woman and sat, crossing her legs under the table and leaning back against the chair. The key, she knew, was to get the woman to speak first. If the woman spoke first, it almost guaranteed at least *some* level of interaction, and Jennifer could work with that.

After several moments, the woman lifted her head fractionally and almost whispered, "What's to become of me?"

Jennifer maintained her pose as she replied, "What do you want to become of you?"

"I... I don't know. This is the first time since I was little that someone didn't own me. Would you like to own me? I... I'm not sure what I'm supposed to do without that."

Jennifer's heart went out to the woman. She should've learned some life skills, but washing clothes and cleaning would only take someone so far. And she was pretty enough that Jennifer would fear for the woman's safety even if she managed to place her with a house that needed someone to handle the laundry or cleaning.

"What about when Dad... I mean, my father... ended slavery? Didn't that free you?"

"It should have, I guess. Hanskarr didn't brand me, or he would've died. But that didn't stop him from grabbing me, tying me to the bed until he could have the blacksmith make the collar and chain, and then lock me in it. Does that sound free to you?"

Good. She was starting to get some fire back. Some spine in her spirit. Maybe that vile so-and-so hadn't broken her completely.

"Which brings us back to my original question. What do you want to happen next for you? For that matter, how old are you?"

The woman squared her shoulders, and she gave Jennifer an almost-challenging look. "I'm seventeen. Why? Is there a problem with that?"

Woman? Ha... more like child, but Jennifer wasn't about to say anything of the sort. Okay. Maybe people matured faster in this world than Earth. Maybe they had to. But that didn't change the fact that this girl was young and very obvious bait for predators.

"No. No problem. I'm just trying to understand where you should be in life versus where you are. It might help me help you. Do you have any skills or education?"

The girl's fire vanished, and she shook her head as she broke eye contact. "No. Momma taught me a few sums before we were branded, but she never taught me any writing. Then, once I started filling out, it didn't matter anymore."

Well, damn.

"So, what's your name?"

"Kellea. If I have a family name, I don't know it."

"Right, then, Kellea. What would you say to being my guide? I'm from the Refugee World, and I came here to explore a little bit of the world my dad... er, father... now calls home. The last person who I thought might grow into the job proved a total disappointment, and I could really use some local talent. I'll pay you a silver a day and provide all meals and clothes and needed equipment. What do you say?"

"Mistress, you... you can't. A whole silver? Each day? It's too much. I'm not worth—"

"Stop right there. Yes, you *are* worth it. You have knowledge I need. I'll be utterly lost without a guide."

Kellea sat in silence for several heartbeats before she jerked a choppy nod. "Yes, Mistress. I'll be your guide."

"Excellent. Now, I need to find a moneychanger or a bank. I only have gold coins, and they weren't minted in Tel."

THE BANK OF TEL was only too happy to help Jennifer with her coinage problem. It took some fast talking on Jennifer's part as to why she didn't want to draw on the family's accounts, but the manager let her leave after changing her gold coins for a selection of gold, silver, and copper coins minted in Tel. Now that she had an example to work from, she could make more of the coins at need. Sure... someone would probably argue doing that devalued the existing coinage, but it wasn't like she was making the coins out of substandard materials. If anything, her coins would be more pure than what Tel minted. A tiny, persistent doubt in the back of her mind kept whispering that the authorities wouldn't see it that way, so Jennifer resolved never to mention it to anyone.

After all, that was the simplest solution... right?

THEY STAYED in Tel Roshan one more day, so Jennifer could be certain Kellea had everything she would need for the trail. Since the Wraiths who came to collect Arne didn't say or do anything about the horse Arne had been riding, Jennifer saw no reason not to gift it to Kellea. Especially given how Arne had treated her. Kellea sputtered and stammered over the gift, but Jennifer ran roughshod over the young woman's protests. After all, she would need a quality horse if she was to be Jennifer's guide... was that not so? And wasn't Arne's horse a quality mount? Well, then... a perfect match!

In the end, Jennifer decided to stay in Tel Roshan yet another night, just because the bulk of their preparations took most of the second day, and she didn't like the idea of leaving the comfort of their inn, only to make camp not even half a day outside the city. That made no sense at all, and what's more, the inn had heated baths.

* * *

THE MORNING SUN warmed the right side of Jennifer's face as she and Kellea rode out of Tel Roshan the next morning. If the gate guards knew who she was, they also had strict instructions to keep it to themselves, because they didn't treat her any differently than they did the other travelers ahead of them. Jennifer hoped Carth kept his promise about keeping her presence to himself, but there was no way to know. After all, Wynn and her dad were good friends, and she couldn't see one of *her* good friends keeping something like this from her. So, yeah... it was only a matter of time until her dad knew she was here.

"Where are we headed, Mistress?" Kellea asked once they'd put Tel Roshan behind them.

Jennifer frowned. "You know, I'm not really sure. Are you from this region of Tel?"

"No, Mistress. When I was little, Momma and I lived in Cothos Province. I know my way around the rest of the kingdom, but none of it is truly home. Not like my memories of Momma are."

"Would you like for me to try to find her?"

Kellea shook her head. "No, but thank you. I know where she is. If we keep going this way, we'll ride by her grave in about two days."

Yep. The taste of her foot hadn't changed all that much since the last time Jennifer put it in her mouth.

"I'm sorry, Kellea. I didn't know."

"No way for you to know, Mistress. They killed Momma shortly after... well... it was years ago. Way before your father made himself known in the world, even."

Jennifer nodded her understanding, but she still felt rather awful. She knew what it was like to lose a parent, especially at a young age. The deep sense of loss and uncertainty. The hollow pit in the heart that will never be filled again. Oh, yes. She knew *that* feeling very well, and she wished she hadn't brought it back to Kellea.

"Did anyone ever find..."

Now, Kellea broke into a smile. But it wasn't a happy smile. It was a vicious, almost savage thing. "Oh, yes, Mistress. Even if they didn't run afoul of someone worse than they were, there's no telling how many people they branded for their own betterment. When your father ended slavery, they would've died screaming in the worst agony they'd ever known."

Well, all right then. Maybe she needed to ask her dad just what he'd done to end slavery.

CHAPTER 19

Clouds darkened the sky to the west, threatening to bring in a storm from the sea. Kellea kept casting fearful glances that way, but the prospect didn't bother Jennifer at all. Her dad had told her about making the camp wards on their way to Vushaar that first time, and she already had a set of wardstones in her saddlebag from the trip to Tel Roshan with Arne.

As he crossed her mind once again, she fought the urge to scoff and shake her head. The Wraiths really needed a system to recall their tattoos when someone goes rogue, but maybe it was a rare enough occurrence that no one cared. Or... Declan had lied to her, in that the Wraiths knew exactly where Arne was and waited to catch him in the act of advancing his plans. Either was possible, she supposed, and she wasn't sure she cared enough to work through which option was the most probable.

On top of that, she still wrestled with the question of what to do with her life. She didn't feel that her explorations thus far had granted her any meaningful insight, but was that because it wouldn't or because she just hadn't given it enough time? Yet again, the thought crossed her mind how much easier life would be if it came with a guide or instruction manual. The whole 'make it up as she went along' idea just wasn't working.

But what was she supposed to do? With a Word, she could re-make reality to her will. After that, where could she find a mean-ingful challenge? She wasn't sure she liked her dad's choices. This world seemed nice enough, but she was still on the fence about whether it was nice enough to devote her life to shepherding. Admit-tedly, that wasn't her dad's choice... *yet*... but he certainly spent more time in this world than back home.

Before she thought to stop it, she exhaled her current breath as a heavy sigh.

"Something the matter, Mistress?"

Yes, but should she even discuss all this with Kellea? Would she have any insights, let alone meaningful insights?

"Sorry, Kellea. I'm just working through some thoughts in my head. I'm not sure my trip here will help me the way I wanted it to help me."

"I understand that, Mistress, but are you sure you're here for the reasons you think you're here?"

Jennifer blinked. "Care to explain your thought there?"

"On the one side, it's completely selfish. If you were not the person you are and if you had not been in that tavern when you were, you wouldn't have been able to impact my life the way you have. From another side, Bellos chose your father to be Archmagister of Tel; is it really so difficult to believe that one or more gods might be nudging you as well?"

Whoa. That thought set Jennifer back a bit. Because... no... the thought had never once entered her mind that someone—or some extra-dimensional entity—might be affecting her thoughts or feel-ings. If that really was the case, was her trip to Drakmoor really her idea? How was she supposed to know?

"Well, shit..." Jennifer's tone was... disgruntled... at best. "Do these gods of yours really do stuff like that?"

"I... I really don't know, but if one god chooses who rules Tel, why can't that same god or another nudge other people toward the paths they want?"

"That doesn't help at all, Kellea. Dammit... I refuse to be led around like a dog on a leash. I lost too many years dancing to someone else's tune, and I'm not about to go back to that. Not at all."

Jennifer was not so wrapped up in her own situation that she failed to see Kellea's flinch when she really kicked her unhappy tirade into high gear. Seeing the woman she'd saved from one of the worst situations imaginable flinch as if fearing that Jennifer herself would beat her or worse... well... that took the wind right out of Jennifer's sails.

"Damn. I'm sorry, Kellea. I'm not going to hurt you, and I didn't mean to scare you. Please, forgive me."

They rounded a curve in the road that followed a valley through the rolling hills that seemed to make up that area of Roshan Province before Kellea could respond. A man sat astride a tan horse with black between its knees and hooves. He and his mount occupied the very center of the road. He was handsome enough with sandy hair and a Van Dyke beard, and he wore a brown robe over whatever other clothes he had.

As Jennifer and Kellea neared him, he lifted his hand in a wave of greetings as he smiled. "Good day to you, ladies. Would you mind an additional traveling companion? I'm on my way to visit family in Wygoth Province, and I find journeys always go better with pleasant company and conversation."

Jennifer couldn't keep her eyes from narrowing just a bit at the man's words. From what she knew, Wygoth Province was north of Roshan, so why was he facing *south*? She glanced at the ground between them and around his horse, taking in as much of the road's condition as she could. The dirt was largely undisturbed; it didn't look like there was recent travel anywhere near his horse's hooves.

Jennifer took a deep breath and released it as a heavy sigh. "Look, whoever you are, I don't mean to come across as unwelcoming, but I've already had one traveling companion go bad on me. If you're going to Wygoth, why aren't you facing north? And why are there no signs of hoof prints in the dirt around you? Whatever your deal is, just come clean, and we'll work it out. I've already killed one man this week, and I'd really like to avoid accumulating my father's body count. I've seen how it weighs on him."

By the time Jennifer ended her speech, Kellea stared at her with wide eyes. But Jennifer didn't care. Sure… it was borderline rude, but so was playing whatever game he wanted to play and later forcing her to kill him in defense of herself or Kellea. She already had enough skeletons in her closet and ghosts in her past. She didn't need any more.

The man surprised her by breaking into a huge grin. "Your dad busted me when I made a point of introducing myself, too."

Jennifer frowned at the use of a word and phrasing from Earth. How did this guy know that? Who was he? "Fair enough. If you know my dad, then you know he doesn't take surprises well. So, stop with the games and introduce yourself like a respectable person."

"Are you sure you want to know?"

Jennifer was getting really tired of all the games. "I'm pretty sure I wouldn't have said it if I didn't really mean it. I'm not one of *those* types of women."

He responded with a shrug that oozed indifference. "So be it. Just remember you asked for it."

The tan slowly drained out of the robe he wore, leaving gold, as a gold dragon-head medallion faded into view. Black runes circled the cuffs of his sleeves, and the next thing Jennifer knew, Kellea was off her horse and on the ground in a full kowtow.

Jennifer leaned over and regarded her local guide for a moment before returning to sit upright in her saddle and brought her focus back to the man. "I'm guessing she recognizes you, and based on her behavior, I'm guessing you're one of those gods she mentioned. So… Bellos?"

He broke into a smile and nodded once. "At your service, Miss Jennifer. You seemed to be having some concerns, and I thought I would visit to give you the chance to discuss anything that might weigh upon you. Please, Kellea, stand up and return to your mount; none of us have ever expected such obeisance."

Kellea's hands shook as she stood and remounted her horse, and to Jennifer's estimation, she looked more than a little wild around the eyes.

Bellos nudged his horse with his heels and guided her over to Jennifer's right. "So, what's on your mind?"

"There's no way you have time for *that* list, but the most immediate concern is whether someone messed with my head to get me to come here."

Jennifer nudged her horse's flanks with her ankles, setting off on a slow walk again. Kellea and Bellos both moved to keep up with her.

Bellos chuckled but ultimately shook his head. "No one 'messed with your head,' as you put it. All the thoughts and feelings and unease that led you to visit this world were your own and no one else's. The old man has been known to meddle a bit, but the rest of us are not so heavy-handed."

"The old man? Who's the old man?"

"Valthon."

Jennifer heard what suspiciously sounded like a terrified squeak escape Kellea's lips. So, was this Valthon—whoever he is/was/whatever—so fearsome that calling him 'old man' invited reprisals? There was just too much she didn't know.

"Okay, then. If I really am here of my own choice, do you have any advice on what I should do with my life?"

Bellos chuckled. "I'm not sure I'm the one to ask that. Have you discussed your situation with your father?"

Jennifer shook her head. "He has too much going on right now. I don't want to bother him. Besides, even as grateful as I am that he's back in my life, I spent many years making my own way. Yes... I didn't always make good decisions, but I'm perfectly capable of charting my life."

"I have not said or thought anything to the contrary. But I do know that your father went through a crisis of conscience and purpose as well, and his choices set him on the path to become the man he is today. Beyond that, it is very much your family's legacy that those of House Kirloth make the hard choices so no one else has to."

Jennifer scowled before she pushed the expression away. "That's all well and good, but what if I want to do something different? What if I don't want people to be afraid at the mere mention of me? And don't tell me that's not what happens with Dad. I've *seen* it. When I saved Kellea in Tel Roshan, the sight of my House Glyph scared a family half to death."

Bellos nodded as he sighed. It was a heavy sigh, laden with regret and remorse. "Jennifer... the reputation of House Kirloth rests squarely on the shoulders of the man who trained both me and your father in the Art. And that reputation is very much what he explicitly desired to create. I'm not sure we have the time or you have the interest right now in the full whys and wherefores of how 'Kirloth' became the most feared House in the Society of the Arcane, but talk to your dad sometime. He's read many of our mentor's journals. All I ask is that you not walk away from your heritage. You are too powerful and too important."

"And just what is *that* supposed to mean?" Jennifer turned to look at Bellos, giving him her best stink eye.

"The first time I spoke with your father, he too asked me questions I was not prepared to answer at that time. Unless I'm wrong... if I gave you a full and honest answer to your question, I fear you would wish I hadn't."

Jennifer took a deep breath and blew it out in one explosive puff. "Yeah... that isn't going to come back to bite my ass. Not at all. So, let's circle back to my original question, then. What am I supposed to do now? I fit in on Earth even less than I did before, and I don't feel like I fit in here, either. I am totally serious, here. What is my place in life? What am I supposed to do with all this power I have?"

"The simple answer is 'whatever you want.'"

"Shit, man... that is such a cop out."

Bellos turned a laugh into a snort. "Yeah. You can get away with those fairly easily when you're a god. But I gave you an honest answer. Just don't forget that everything a person does has consequences, so a wise course might be to determine what consequences you prefer and then figure out how to make them happen."

"Yeah... you're no help."

Now, Bellos did laugh. "Not once did I ever promise to help. I just said we could discuss your concerns."

"I'm not even sure I know enough to figure out what all the consequences will be."

"If it makes you feel any better, few people do."

Bellos lifted his head and looked off to his right. Jennifer did, too, but all she saw was grassy, rolling hills.

"Please, forgive me, Jennifer. I'm afraid I've run out of time for the moment. If I can manage it, I shall return to continue our conversation later."

"Awesome." Jennifer gave him a thumbs-up. "More non-answer answers. I'll look forward to it."

Bellos laughed as he and his horse faded away.

Jennifer and Kellea rode in silence for a few minutes before Jennifer turned to her fellow traveler. "Did that really happen? Did the god of magic really spend some time riding with us and chatting?"

Kellea's only reply was a slight squeak and a nod that carried undertones of both terror and anxiety.

Since it seemed Kellea needed some time to regain her composure, Jennifer turned her thoughts inward, replaying the discourse with Bellos and trying to determine if it helped her at all. On the one side, she should probably be happy—or at least relieved—that no one was messing with her. That her desire to travel Drakmoor was her own choice. But that still didn't put her any closer to deciding what she should do with her life. Alexis had mentioned that they should go into private investigations or something like that, but that didn't appeal to Jennifer. Not a whole lot, anyway. She didn't even own a fedora.

* * *

THE BOOK that lay on the desk in front of Gavin was a four-hundred-year-old treatise on combating undead. It was far more verbose than it had any right to be, and the author had zero concept of how to tell a story. The thin pages felt incredibly fragile to his touch, and he was amazed the cover and spine still supported the massive tome's weight.

Not for the first time since cracking the volume, Gavin leaned back in his seat and allowed himself to sag against it. He sighed as he rubbed his eyes and questioned yet again his determination to see if any value existed in what many modern scholars referred to as 'the definitive guide to undead.' He was only about a quarter into it, and unless it improved substantially very soon, the modern scholars who hailed it were liars.

A soft footfall drew Gavin's attention, and he opened his eyes to find Declan crossing the distance from the library's door. Arriving at the table, he lifted the tome with great care—just enough to see the title—and snorted his derision before settling into an armchair at Gavin's right.

"Why in all the world are you slogging through that monstrosity?"

Gavin shrugged. "I'm trying to prepare for Skullkeep. Everyone says that this is the so-called 'definitive text on undead,' but I'm really starting to think they lied."

"Trust me. They did. The man who wrote that was an insufferable boor and pedant, and everyone wanted him out of the academic world. But he refused to go until he penned something the scholarly community hailed as a masterwork. I read the journal entry of a fellow who called a closed-door secret meeting where there was an almost unanimous vote to praise the idiot far and wide as soon as he slapped his name on something, regardless of its quality... just to get him to retire."

Gavin turned to look his friend square in the eye, then slowly raised one eyebrow. "Are you serious? You're not messing with me?"

"I swear, Gavin, I'm honest. In public, every scholar will tell you that book is the greatest work on undead in the last thousand years, but in private, they wouldn't even tear out the pages to use as toilet paper. It's not even worth the effort it'd take to burn it."

Gavin grimaced as he reached forward and almost slapped the book closed. "Well, shit... that's frustrating. I think I've spent about an hour on it already."

"Undead really aren't that complicated, until you start getting into the sapient versions. The magic that animates skeletons pools in the skull, so crush that or decapitate the skeleton, and it becomes a stack of bones on the ground. Zombies are pretty much the same, just with more rotting meat. Ghouls... well, there are different types of ghouls, and a couple of the types have things you need to watch out for, like poisoned claws or a necrotic aura. But by and large, the Necromancer uses skeletons and zombies for the rank-and-file of his garrison. Ghouls are like the sergeants, and there are living soldiers either mixed in among the undead or forming their own units. None of the Wraiths have reported seeing any activity or presence from the people across the Godswall Mountains, but the Necromancer does have a handful of apprentices... or at least he did at the last report. Sometimes, he goes through them a bit quickly if they fail to impress him."

"Well, that's cheery. Nothing brings down morale like fearing for your life if you have a bad day at school."

Declan snorted. "No doubt about that, but I'm sure people who seek out the Necromancer for training aren't incredibly upstanding citizens in the first place."

"Anything else going on worth noting?"

"Yeah... about that... Jennifer is in Drakmoor."

Gavin blinked. "Say what?"

Declan just nodded. "She pulled me over to Tel Roshan to get my advice on dealing with a Wraith... except he was on our rogue list and she didn't have a way to know that."

"Is she okay? Did he hurt her?"

"Whoa... slow down there. She's just fine. She didn't want you to know she was in the world... or however you should say that when you're talking about crossing dimensions like walking from room to room. I gathered she has some thoughts and feelings to work through, but she didn't exactly confide in me. I've arranged for her to have a couple Wraiths covering her, but they're under strict orders to only show themselves if Jennifer's life is in imminent peril."

Gavin leaned back in his chair and rubbed his hand down over his face. "That's probably best. I... well... Jennifer and I are in a good place now, I think, but she took my death very hard. She made some choices that had the potential to impact the rest of her life."

"Hate to tell you, Gavin, but all of our choices impact the rest of our lives... even the innocuous stuff. But as far as Skullkeep goes, stop stressing about it. You were not on top of your skills when you faced the Necromancer before, and that's not the case this time. Gather the army—which you're already doing through the Old Alliance—and arm them and train them. Yes, there will be casualties. But I truly believe we'll come out the other end of this in good shape."

Gavin nodded. "Thanks, Declan. I was just about to get some food. Care to join me?"

Declan smiled. "I'll never turn down food."

They stood and left the library, the old tome forgotten as they discussed other matters.

CHAPTER 20

It was a mostly pleasant day for Jennifer. The slight overcast provided a buffer against the hot sun, and Tel—at least the sections she had ridden through—didn't seem to have the pervasive summer humidity that was a fact of life back in Graham. The breeze blowing in from the sea to the west brought hints of salty sea air.

Kellea wasn't bad company, either. She was a good conversationalist, and despite her lack of education, she was certainly intelligent and—like so many people from Jennifer's own background—was very world-wise. She knew how the world worked from the bottom up... because she'd had to live through it. Jennifer didn't think she'd ever faced the same challenges Jennifer had faced (and failed), but that was largely a good thing.

No matter what path she ended up choosing for herself, Jennifer intended for it to be something that would keep her as far away from the public view as possible. She didn't have skeletons in her closet. She had whole cemeteries.

And looking back over the second half of her life, Jennifer couldn't help but be glad that—no matter how much she'd suffered —Kellea had never *actively chosen* to ruin other people's lives.

Jennifer had, and she felt certain the weight of it would be with her the rest of her life.

She just hoped that all the trouble her dad had made to secure her freedom from her past would allow her to find some small way of atoning for all those young women she'd recruited for Toussaint. In her heart of hearts and late at night when she was so sleepy that the walls she kept up throughout the day just to function began to slip, she wasn't sure she could ever fully atone for it all.

Jennifer shook her head and made an explicit effort to pull herself out of those thoughts. She had no idea what Kellea had been saying for the past several moments, and as much as it might prefer otherwise, it probably showed in her whole demeanor.

And Kellea proved that beyond any doubt when she asked, "Are you well? You've seemed very far away for a little bit now."

Jennifer held her silence for a few moments but ultimately shrugged. "'Well' is very relative, I'd say. Yes, for the most part, I'm well enough. I just have some things in my past that weigh me down. Choices I made that I should've been stronger and avoided. I was admittedly in a very bad place mentally when I made those choices, but that doesn't excuse them. It doesn't make it okay that I made the choices I did."

"Would you like to talk about it? I can't promise you any great insights, but I can promise a sympathetic ear."

"Thank you," Jennifer replied, allowing a small smile. "I... well... I'm honestly afraid to tell you the full story. I'm afraid of what you would think of me if you knew."

They were riding close enough that Kellea could reach across and lay a comforting hand on Jennifer's upper arm. "I'm not sure you see it the same way that I do. You saved my life, Jennifer, and you *chose* to do that. Yes... maybe you made the choice that you did because you're running from the ghosts of your past that haunt you. Or... maybe you chose to act because you're simply a good person. I have to admit that —as the person on the receiving end of the choice—the precise *why* doesn't really matter all that much when compared to the *what*. And the *what* is that you stepped up when you didn't have to and not only saved my life but fundamentally changed it for the better. Even those who have the power to act rarely do so. Your father is another good example of that. He chooses every day to try to make our lives better than the day before... or the week before... or the month before. If you extend that to years, even a corpse would see that our lives are so, so much better for him agreeing to become the Archmagister. Does it matter to us *why* he made that choice? No... not really. Just that he did. Everyone makes mistakes, Jennifer... *everyone*. And it takes real courage to judge people for who they are and what they do now... instead of who they were and what they did. So, if fears over what I'll think of you are all that's keeping from lightening the load you carry even a little bit, put them aside and talk about whatever you need to talk about."

Jennifer sighed. It was so hard. Especially in light of how much shame she felt over her past.

"So, I don't know how much Dad has publicly discussed how he came to be here. I don't know if it has ever come up, but the truth is that he was born in what you know as the Refugee World... and he died right before I turned thirteen."

Kellea gasped, her hand flying to cover her mouth. But Jennifer didn't stop. She proceeded to tell her story to this woman she hardly knew. She didn't hold anything back and talked for what seemed like hours. Just as it was reaching that time of day where they should be looking to make camp for the night, she reached the point in her story where she decided to explore Tel on her own in hopes it would help her sort out what she wanted to do with her life.

Kellea held her silence as they moved off the road to a clearing. She didn't say anything even while they unsaddled their horses and brushed them down. As soon as they finished with their horses but before they set into the business of actually making camp, she walked straight to Jennifer and tip-toed to pull her into a tight hug.

"I am so sorry you had to survive that," Kellea whispered into Jennifer's ear while she maintained the hug. "Your choice to help me means all the more to me now. I feel very confident that a lot of people would not have come out the other side of that recognizing their actions and choices as mistakes and something that should be atoned for."

Kellea broke the hug just before it would have become awkward and stepped back, looking Jennifer right in the eye. "I'm very proud of you, Jennifer... and not because you chose to help me. It takes courage to try to be better, and in my experience, most people are cowards."

Jennifer fought to control the tears that wanted to fall. Looking back on it, she wasn't sure she'd been wholly honest with herself about how much she feared Kellea would reject her, and Kellea's response demolished that weight.

"I don't know if the guilt you feel will ever truly go away," Kellea continued. "Honestly, I kind of hope it doesn't. It's also been my experience that the people who don't feel guilt are the worst people in society, so the fact that you do feel it—and feel so much of it—speaks very well about you... at least to me."

Jennifer didn't have the words. 'Thank you' seemed utterly insufficient for the sliver of peace Kellea gave her. But she felt she had to say *something*. "Thank you. I really appreciate that."

Kellea beamed a smile. "You're welcome. Now... I'm hungry. Let's see about camp."

They set about the business of making camp and cooking their evening meal. As they sat on a felled log and chatted while they ate, Jennifer made a mental note to take Kellea back to Earth and show her what people called camping there.

A stream burbled nearby, and after eating, they washed their cookware, flatware, and utensils and left them to dry while they washed themselves. When she returned to camp in a set of fresh clothes, Jennifer smiled at how good it felt to be clean. She liked Ajax, and she felt Ajax might like her... or at least appreciate her.

But that didn't mean she wanted to smell like him.

As she laid out her bedroll in the small tent she carried with her since her father's estate, Jennifer realized that maybe—just *maybe*—deciding to visit and explore Tel was the right decision after all. She truly had not expected to find any answers there. But she just might find what she needed.

* * *

THE NEXT MORNING, they made a quick breakfast of trail rations and hot tea. Yes, it wasn't the most appetizing fare Jennifer had ever enjoyed, but it was filling. She knew without a doubt that it would carry her through to the midday meal.

From there, breaking camp was simple and old hat to her at this point. They each took care of securing their bedrolls and collapsing their respective tents before saddling their horses. Ajax nickered when she greeted him and brushed his nose against her shoulder. She'd never had the kind of bond with anyone that she had with Ajax, and she was at a little bit of a loss to describe it. Still, she wasn't about to knock it. Ajax felt like a best friend across many years to her, even though they'd just met not even three weeks ago.

She wondered if that's how her dad felt about Jasmine.

The very last thing they did was to smother the coals of their fire, first in water and then dirt. After that, it was very unlikely they would flare back to life and cause an unwanted fire. Jennifer didn't know how common wildfires were here, but back home, it seemed like a day didn't go by without a news headline discussing some section of the West Coast that was burning.

That thought brought her back to how she'd always wanted to see the great sequoias in California, and she resolved to make the trip when she went home, rather than risk waiting too long and watching a news story about a forest fire consuming them.

She and Kellea both made one final walkthrough of their former camp to ensure they weren't leaving anything or that they hadn't missed something. Everything seemed to be good, so they led their horses back to the road and mounted up.

· · ·

IT WAS AROUND MID-MORNING—A few hours later—when they rounded a curve in the road and found the remains of a caravan alongside the road. Three wagons sat empty in the shade of the trees that lined the road. Two of them had broken wheels, and the third's rear axle looked like it had splintered in the middle.

The area around them seemed unnaturally calm. No birds. No chirping insects. Just the clopping of their horses' hooves. It put Jennifer on edge.

If the wagons hadn't been moved from their direction of travel, they pointed toward Tel Roshan. They bore no markings or any indications whatsoever of who owned them, and there wasn't any sign of what they'd been carrying.

Several dark patches dotted the road around the wagon, and Kellea nimbly slipped off her horse and knelt at one. She swiped her finger through it and rubbed her now-red fingertip against her thumb. The dirty liquid spread easily.

"This isn't very old." She looked up at Jennifer, frowning. "The blood hasn't had a chance to congeal yet."

Jennifer gnawed at her lower lip as she scanned the trees around them. There was no sign anyone watched them, and while she wanted to be sure, she was also afraid of scaring them off if she invoked a Word. No footpad in their right mind challenged a true wizard in full command of her power. Well... no one who wasn't suicidal, anyway.

In the end, she decided to risk it. She made short work of clearing her mind, focusing only on her intent, as she invoked a Word of Divination, "*Klaepos.*"

An aura of faint light fell over her eyes, and she took her time looking all around them. In her vision that was now slightly hazy, she saw outlines of critters everywhere and even a few larger animals—perhaps deer or their equivalent—but no outlines of people. When she invoked the Word, she'd focused on seeing all mammalian life within two hundred yards, and she now felt a lot safer. The anxiety of being exposed faded along with the effect as she released the power fueling it.

"What was that?" Kellea asked.

"I wanted to be sure we weren't being watched."

The silence extended for several moments until Kellea said, "Well? Are we?"

Jennifer pointed off to her right toward a cluster of trees. "There are a few curious squirrels over that way and what I think is a family of deer farther on... but no people within two hundred yards."

Kellea gave her a flat look. "You are such a brat sometimes."

"Who normally patrols the roads?"

Kellea grabbed a handful of dirt and used it to clean the blood off her finger and thumb. Then, she stood as she brushed off her hands. "There are guards in each province whose sole job is patrolling the roads. Whichever detachment patrols this road either just passed through or is on the way here. They don't publish their schedules, so there's no way to know precisely where they are in their patrol route."

"I don't see any sign of bodies. Do you?"

Her associate gave the area a good look-over, slowly turning in place as she did so. "No, but that doesn't mean much. The people who did this could've carried them just far enough into the trees that they'd be difficult to spot."

She really didn't like walking—or riding, as the case may be—away from something like this. It galled her that the filth responsible might never be caught. That thought sounded a little ironic, given her past, but it didn't change anything.

"I don't suppose you have any experience at tracking, do you?"

Kellea looked up at her as if she'd suddenly sprouted a second head. "What makes you think I know anything about that?"

Jennifer shrugged. "It didn't hurt to ask, did it?"

"Well, no..."

Jennifer allowed a slight smile to curl one side of her mouth. "But you also didn't answer the question, either."

Kellea sighed. "Fine. I picked up a little bit of tracking while that brute dragged me around at the end of a chain. It's not something I ever thought I'd use, you know?"

"I get that. So... do you think you can figure out where the people who did this went?"

Kellea blinked, then gaped at her. "What? You want to find these people? What about the province guards?"

Jennifer just shrugged. "We're here, and they're not. If we knew where they were or if they'd arrive soon, it might be different, but the more time passes, the better the odds are that the people responsible will vanish into the wind."

Kellea looked up at her in silence, her expression suggesting that she wanted to scowl but couldn't quite bring herself to it. "Okay. Fine. I'll have a look around. As dense as the forest is, though, we'll probably have to lead our horses or tie them off somewhere to graze."

"We'll chase that cat when we get to it. Do your thing."

When it seemed obvious that leaving horses wasn't going to dissuade Jennifer, Kellea heaved a sigh and started working her way around the scene in an ever-widening spiral. Jennifer watched in silence, wondering if it was something she could learn or even wanted to learn. She loved learning new things, but it was always a trade-off of value and utility versus time. Sure... she could totally learn underwater basket weaving, but was there sufficient value in it to justify the time? After all, time was the ultimate non-renewable resource, and she had too much to atone for to waste time on frivolities.

After a little bit, Kellea returned to where Jennifer waited astride Ajax. She pointed a thumb over her shoulder. "They came out of the forest over here and escaped back the way they came. I think they took the people who were using the wagons with them."

"Okay. Let's see where the trail leads."

Jennifer dismounted and led Ajax by the reins as Kellea did the same. Just as the forest started to thicken to the point that the horses would have rough going, the trail led by a small clearing. It looked like it would serve as a suitable pasture for the horses.

Jennifer pointed to a spot where the clearing seemed to make a point. "Take my tent and bedroll over there and lay out the bedroll to cover the ground and then the tent to cover the bedroll. We'll put the saddles and horse blankets on the bedroll under the tent."

"And just what will you be doing while I handle the grunt work?" Kellea asked over a smirk.

"Warding the clearing to be sure no one steals or harms our horses until we get back."

That drained the playfulness right out of Kellea's demeanor. "Oh. Probably a good idea."

While Kellea handled her part, Jennifer went around the clearing selecting stones that were just large enough for her to etch a rune or two into the surface. From what her dad had said when he taught her about wards, they were both similar and unlike composite effects. While it was relatively easy to invoke a short-term multi-faceted ward, if the wizard wanted it to last for any significant length of time, she needed to anchor the ward to something and provide a power source. In this case, Jennifer was going to anchor the ward to stones around the periphery of the clearing, and the ambient magic itself would provide the power source. As she worked her way around the clearing, she couldn't help but wonder how much more difficult this would've been before her dad forged the link back from Earth to Drakmoor and equalized the ambient magic levels.

She remembered him telling her how the link Nesta forged during the Godswar seemed to have acted as a funnel that gradually 'drained' the ambient magic in Drakmoor to Earth. As far as she knew, he still wasn't certain why the power hadn't reached a certain saturation level and pushed back against the drain... but it hadn't. She still remembered how the rush of the power equalizing itself through her dad's permanent portal had put him on his ass faster than a finger-snap. If it put her dad on his ass—the guy who the people of Drakmoor recognized as *Kirloth* and possibly the most powerful wizard walking the world—she wanted absolutely no part of that whatsoever.

She felt like the power of her birthright was coming to her more easily than it had when she first started studying it, but she still didn't feel like she was anywhere close to the level of mastery her dad casually displayed every day in off-the-cuff invocations. If he wasn't her dad, she'd probably be **terrified** of him and what he could do. It certainly seemed like the Feds were, seeing as how the Secret Service gave him the callsign 'Apocalypse.'

Those thoughts carried her through finishing her circuit of the clearing, and there was now a small stone every three feet or so all the way around the clearing. When she straightened from placing the final stone, she saw Kellea was waiting for her, and the horses were calmly grazing wearing only their bridles and the associated reins.

Jennifer roved her eyes over the clearing, turning everything over in her mind to see if she'd missed anything. She didn't **think** she had, and all that remained was invoking the ward. She'd be lying if she said she wasn't a little nervous about that, but they needed to get a move on if they were going to catch up to whoever attacked the caravan.

She closed her eyes and took slow, deep breaths as she cleared everything from her mind but the intent she desired to achieve. It took a little more effort than she was used to, most of the reason being her nerves at such a complex working of the Art, but she chided herself on her mind wandering and re-focused on the image of the ward.

Once she felt like her intent was firm and clear in her mind, she took one last deep breath and invoked Words of Tutation and Evocation to create the composite effect, "*Sykhurhos-Idluhn.*"

The resonance of her power struck the ambient magic like a two-ton boulder hitting a kiddie pool. As she felt it lash the very fabric of reality in waves, Jennifer wouldn't have been surprised if Wynn and Carth felt that invocation all the way back in Tel Roshan.

All around the clearing, points of light corresponding to the stones bearing the runes she etched began to glow. They increased in radiance, pulsing ever brighter, until they seemed to reach a critical mass where they glowed a solid bright light. Spires of pure power that as thick as Jennifer's wrist exploded out of each stone, cycling through every color of the rainbow and then some while curving up to meet over the very center of the clearing, and the confluence formed a large orb that was easily the size of a basketball back on Earth. The Glyph of Kirloth faded into view directly above the orb and quickly shone brighter than the sun overhead. And just as soon as the Glyph solidified, a column of power thicker than the breadth of Jennifer's shoulders Shot down from the orb, spearing into the earth as if it were a harpoon.

Lines of power soon faded into view from the point where the central column met the grassy dirt and flowed out to each stone. It wasn't long until both Jennifer and Kellea watched waves of power pulse through the arcing spires to the orb, down the central column, and then back along the ground lines to the wardstones.

The flow of power ran for several minutes before the ward's manifestation gradually faded from view. The Glyph of Kirloth was the final piece to fade, and it remained in sight almost twice as long as the rest of the ward.

As soon as the Glyph winked out, though, Jennifer felt her strength wane as if someone had removed her battery, and she only vaguely processed her butt hitting the grass as she fought to remain conscious.

CHAPTER 21

In the wake of warding the clearing for their horses, Jennifer had little choice but to take a couple moments. The first time she tried to stand, her legs wobbled, and her knees refused to consider the matter further. Kellea retrieved a bedroll from the tent and brought it over, so they'd at least be sitting on something that wasn't just bare grass.

They sat in silence while Jennifer munched on some jerky, and after a few moments, Kellea turned to her.

"I've never seen anything like that before, Mistress."

Jennifer gave her a flat look. "Not 'Mistress,' Kellea. *Jennifer*. My friends actually call me Jen more often than not, but I think that might end up being a bridge too far. I'll consider 'Jennifer' a win."

Kellea looked down at the bedroll where they sat. Jennifer could see a blush coloring her cheeks and neck, as an embarrassed smile tried to curl her lips. "I... I don't know if I can. Folk such as me shouldn't ever put on airs with folk such as you."

Jennifer fought the urge to growl. She knew what this was... and... even understood it to a certain degree. In a society where people could re-arrange local geography on a whim, it was simple self-preservation to bow and scrape to *everyone* who might be more powerful. The problem... from what she could see... was that too many people *liked* it and felt it was their just due.

And in that moment, sitting on a bedroll in the midst of a forest in the middle of nowhere, a sudden spark of understanding flared in her mind. This—*this right here*—was part of what her dad meant when he made some vague, random statement about what it means to be Kirloth.

Sure... some random little lordling might have power enough to force obeisance from the average populace, but if that same lordling tried abusing his or her power with her dad—at least back before he wore the gold robe—there was no doubt in her mind that the little lordling would only do so *once*.

And given how she'd seen her dad react to abuses of power, she gave even odds at best for the little lordling's *survival*.

That was a part of what it meant to be Kirloth. Protect those who could not protect themselves. Protect those who the law should see and safeguard but didn't... for whatever reason.

"Kellea, I'm going to let you in on a little secret. Folk like you and folk like me? We're the same folks. I am no better than you. I am not worth more than you. Every single person is valuable, Kellea. Every person has something they can be proud of. They just have to find it. Those sad sacks who get off on abusing their power? They've never found it... if they've even searched for it. That's not me. It never will be."

"That's awfully easy to say when you're the one who can kill whole groups of people in one go."

Jennifer sighed. She understood. She really did. She wasn't sure about the best way to go about proving the reality of what she said... especially when she sat in a world with centuries of evidence to the contrary. It was a mixed-up situation and probably one she should discuss with her dad. In the end, the only thing she knew to do was nod in acknowledgement of Kellea's statement and finish her jerky.

She'd just have to keep chipping away at it.

* * *

SOON ENOUGH, Jennifer was back on her feet. Kellea returned the bedroll to the tent, and they resumed their journey once more. Kellea led, being the tracker, and as time passed, she noted that it seemed like they were catching up to the group that had fled the three wagons.

Just as Kellea waved Jennifer close and whispered that they were probably within earshot, four people stepped silently into view. They all wore leather armor that was mottled in leaf and grass greens, bark browns, and bark grays. Their leather jerkins had hoods that all four laid back as part of the movement of revealing themselves. What worried Jennifer most was that they moved with total silence under the trees. No snaps of twigs. No rustle of leaves or branches. She hadn't even thought she and Kellea were being watched.

Kellea fought her instinctive reaction to drop to her knees and curl in on herself. Jennifer saw her abject fear.

But that wasn't Jennifer's way. Not at all.

She took the necessary steps to stand between the four and Kellea, and she used her thumb and forefinger to lift the silver chain around her neck and bring her wizard's medallion into view. She dropped the chain to let the medallion settled against her sternum and squared her shoulders as she readied herself.

The four stopped no more than eight feet away, and as one, they dropped to one knee.

One of the center two spoke just loud enough for Jennifer and Kellea to hear. "Milady, we exist to serve. Your father sent us to watch over you at a distance, being very clear that we were not to interfere with your travels unless your life faced a dire threat. If you continue on this path, such a threat is less than two hundred yards farther on."

"How do I know you are who you say you are? I've already had one rogue slip into my good graces."

All four stood, and they seemed almost to smirk as the spokesperson continued. "Ah, yes... Arne. He has come to... regret... involving you in his plans. He begs for your forgiveness almost daily now."

Well, that wasn't chilling at all...

One of the ones who had thus far remained silent took a half-step forward. "Milady, Declan himself selected us for this posting. I give you my word... each of us will lay dead before harm comes to you."

Jennifer wasn't sure she approved of such devotion, but these people seemed far more like the other Wraiths she had encountered and didn't give off that worrisome vibe Arne had from time to time... before he finally flipped out.

"Very well. Thank you, and I accept your service. What is so dire about the threat ahead?"

"It is an encampment of several dozen men and women, all experienced at killing. The only methods available to you for dealing with them would also rob you of those you wish to save. Eliminating the threat they pose and securing the survivors of the small caravan is a task best left to us."

Jennifer almost scoffed at the thought that four people could handle themselves against several dozen, but then, she remembered watching Kiri work through her forms back before her dad figured out how to get them back to Drakmoor. And according to Kiri, she wasn't even that good.

It didn't sit right with Jennifer for someone else to fight her battles, but at the same time, she had no choice but to agree that she wasn't built for a precision engagement. Yes... she absolutely could wade into that camp and eliminate them all with no threat to her, but like these Wraiths said, it was almost guaranteed that she'd eliminate the caravan survivors as well.

She rolled her shoulders as she sighed. "What would you have us do?"

"Return to the clearing you warded for the horses and wait. We have already dealt with the sentries that would have spotted you both. Come nightfall, we will finish this and bring those you wish rescued to you by morning."

"Okay then. You do you. We'll be at the clearing. If you can identify any individuals with rank, you might want to capture them for questioning if at all possible, instead of simply killing them. But I don't want any of you risking your lives to take a prisoner when dead works just as well."

"Thank you, Milady, for allowing us to safeguard your life."

Jennifer watched them pull their hood back up over their heads and melt back into the forest. *That* really shook her up. She was watching them... staring at them, almost... and they still somehow vanished into the trees like they'd never been there.

Heaving one last sigh, Jennifer turned back the way they'd come. "Come on. We might as well have a warm camp waiting for them when they arrive."

* * *

THEY MADE the return trip to the clearing much faster than their journey away from it. Several times, Kellea tried to ask who those people were that they would so nonchalantly attack several dozen experienced fighters. Even at night with some—or even most—of them asleep, that still seemed like too much for Kellea to accept.

And Jennifer *wanted* to tell her. She really did. She didn't like keeping secrets from those closest to her, and that sudden realization —that Kellea was now part of her closest circle of people without her even realizing it—put her off her stride for a moment. Regardless, she knew the Wraiths' secret was inviolate. Her dad hadn't even told his closest friends... Lillian, Braden, Wynn, and Mariana. From what he'd told her back on Earth, it was *Lillian* who connected the dots and identified Declan as a Wraith.

In the end, she told Kellea that she would have to bring the matter before her father, before she could tell her anything about those four. That Kellea herself would probably have to go before her dad was obvious to the woman at that point, and her new expression suggested she regretted even thinking about asking.

The sound of semi-raised voices reached them before they reached the clearing. They were still too far to piece together what the voices were saying, but the simple fact that they heard voices at all prompted them to take on a more stealthy approach.

They crept forward with an abundance of caution, crouching as they moved from tree to tree. It helped that this forest seemed to be all ancient growth, with the thinnest tree Jennifer had seen so far being twice the size of her thigh. Trees like that hid people very well.

Soon enough, the clearing came into view... along with a collection of unexpected guests. They wore a mixture of leather, chainmail, and scalemail with all-metal helms that had a solid nose guard. There were eight of them, and one stood right at the edge of the ward... close enough to pound his fist on it. Every time he struck what should've been open air, the impact produced a solid **thunk**, and small waves of power rippled outward a short distance from the point of impact.

The horses seemed to ignore the people—if they were even aware of them—as they grazed unperturbed.

"I've never seen anything like this, Sarge... have you?" the guy pounding the ward said.

A woman at the center of the group shook her head. "No. I can't say as I have. It galls me to return to Tel Roshan for a spell-breaker, especially since we have no way to know whether those horses or that tent are even connected to the people responsible for attacking those wagons."

Jennifer dropped her medallion back inside her clothing and stepped out from behind the tree that sheltered her. She made it halfway to the group before they noticed her, taking care to stand in a shaft of sunlight that broke through an opening in the leafy canopy high above.

"The spell-breaker you speak of," she said. "Is that person a mage or a wizard?"

The woman—the group's sergeant apparently—eyed Jennifer with an appraising expression. "Not that it's any of your business, but he's a mage. What few wizards we have already went west as part of the mobilization."

"Ah. Well, in that case, you'd be better off just saying 'pretty please.' I laid that ward, and I'd be impressed if a mage could break it."

The sergeant's gaze went from Jennifer to the clearing and back again. Her skeptical expression made it plain that she didn't believe a word Jennifer said.

Her dad's friends had told her about times like this, and she'd always thought she'd never do it... but the temptation was just too strong. She brought her thumb and forefinger up to her neck and gathered the chain between them. As she lifted the chain but before the medallion came into view, she said, "Oh... forgive me. Allow me to introduce myself."

She felt and heard the medallion hit her chest after she released the chain, and she enjoyed the temptation to smirk as— one by one—each of the eight saw the Glyph of Kirloth in the center of her medallion that now gleamed in the sun... then promptly paled. All of them—even the sergeant—very obviously moved their hands away from their weapons... whether hilts or bows or crossbows... and they took a half-step back almost in unison.

"Milady, please forgive us," the sergeant said. "We are the patrol for the road just behind us, and we started searching the area when we discovered the damaged wagons."

Jennifer smiled. "Please, stand easy. No one who respects and follows the law has any reason to fear me... or my father."

If they had been pale before, the knowledge that they faced the Archmagister's daughter looked to have them two steps shy of sheer, unmitigated terror.

Jennifer continued, "My people and I tracked those responsible for the wagons to a sizable encampment deep in the forest, and they are moving to secure it and any survivors from those wagons as we speak. If you like, you are welcome to share our camp while we wait for the report."

The sergeant swallowed hard, and Jennifer saw how she fought to maintain eye contact and project some semblance of authority and calm. Sadly, she wasn't wholly successful. "If the camp is even close to as large as you say, we should return to Tel Roshan and arrange for prisoner transport."

"Oh, sure... you can do that if you want, but if you bring transport for more than a handful, I suspect you'll be wasting your time."

The guards had already started moving away but froze as Jennifer completed her statement. The sergeant glanced from Jennifer to her people and back again before asking, "May I ask why, Milady?"

"When faced with a threat, my people don't allow half-measures. If they can capture the leadership of the camp, they will, but their natural response to any threat is to kill it."

The sergeant swallowed hard again, and she glanced at the trees around them as best she could without moving her head. It was clear she wondered if any of those people were nearby, not that she seriously contemplated threatening Jennifer. After all... no one in their right mind threatened anyone from House Kirloth. And even if someone was suicidal enough to attack Jennifer and succeed, their life (or lives) would be measured in hours if they didn't kill the Archmagister along with her. The far more terrifying thought was that maybe—just *maybe*—anyone who harmed this woman might measure their life in years... or even *decades*.

The sergeant nodded a few times, but slowly. "I understand, Milady. In that case, would you forgive us if we resume our patrol? We can send a message to Tel Roshan for one wagon to retrieve anyone you choose to hand over."

In that moment, another realization struck Jennifer. In this world, *she* was no different than the 'big names' back on Earth. She was one of the backroom power brokers, and she wasn't in the mid-level, either. Or even on the fringe. Oh, no. She and her father were the top of the pyramid. If she presented herself to 'society' here, she'd have people hanging off of her, desperate for any scraps that might—even provisionally—increase their status.

She'd flipped her social position upside down, simply by walking through a door.

Okay... the trans-dimensional portal wasn't *quite* a door, but she felt the metaphor held.

So, what should she do? Her recent years—those years after her grandparents came to Baltimore for her—told her that she should rail against her status. That she should fight to establish a more equal distribution of power among the people.

But how was she supposed to do that?

She was a nuclear power... simply because of a genetic inheritance from her father. And she wasn't alone in that. Her dad's closest friends were almost on the same level. Maybe not quite as big a nuke as her dad, but each and every one of them could use his knowledge to produce the exact same result as what he'd done in the Middle East when he went to rescue Alexis's brother.

How was she supposed to distribute power like *that*?

Maybe the short answer was that she wasn't supposed to. Maybe the longer answer was that she shouldn't try to distribute that power, but instead encourage people to use it well and for the right reasons. What was that saying back on Earth? Be the change you want to see in the world?

As the province guards disappeared into the trees, Jennifer waved for Kellea to join her. Kellea did so without hesitation, and she would've done so if Jennifer had waved while speaking with the guards. Jennifer appreciated, respected, and valued that trust.

People like Kellea should never have to live in fear of their neighbors... simply because those neighbors were born with power like Jennifer felt pulsing within her every moment she was awake. Her dad described the ambient magic as a vast sea just waiting to be tapped, and she agreed. It was always right there... at the edge of her conscious thought or awareness... and it almost hungered to be used.

It didn't feel sapient. It didn't feel aware, not really. But that didn't keep Jennifer from having the feeling that the power wizards held used them as much as they used it. That was a very sobering thought, and it was one more brick in the path that Jennifer sought to chart with this journey.

* * *

THE FOUR WRAITHS returned to the camp using the utmost stealth. They spared no effort to ensure that none of the camp's inhabitants had even an inkling that they were near. Along one side of the camp, a large tree that was easily two feet thick served as a vantage point for clandestine observation. Two of their four disappeared into the foliage surrounding the camp to seek out sentries.

Not even a handful of heartbeats later, a flaming boulder roared into the camp at a high overhead angle. It struck the center of the camp and threw up a massive dust and debris cloud... including some pieces of people. When the camp erupted in chaos, the Wraiths saw no reason to wait and set out on their task.

CHAPTER 22

The next morning, Jennifer rolled out of her tent and stretched. She froze mid-yawn at seeing a Wraith standing at the edge of the ward. As soon as she realized she stood there with her mouth open, she closed it and set off across the clearing.

She stopped at the edge of the ward, and the Wraith—one of the women—made a partial bow. "Milady, we have secured the five highest-ranking people at the camp. There are documents you should see."

"All right. Let me collect Kellea, and we'll set off."

The Wraith nodded once.

It was a simple matter to 'collect' Kellea. The Wraith advised them that the encampment was close to another road, and they might want to bring their horses... as the Wraiths had already collected their horses during the night. At a shrug from Kellea, Jennifer agreed, and once they were packed up, she dispelled the ward on the clearing.

The Wraith led them back along the trail they'd scouted the day before, and it wasn't more than mid-morning when they entered another much-larger clearing that served as the home to the encampment. Almost all of the tents were collapsed and secured, with only a handful—including a rather large pavilion—remaining.

The Wraith directed Jennifer to the pavilion, and at Jennifer's nod, Kellea followed along. As she entered it, she saw the pavilion was separated into two 'rooms.' The larger and front area seemed to act as a combination office, meeting room, and dining room. The smaller area at the rear of the pavilion seemed configured for sleeping quarters. An older man sat trussed to a chair, and he snarled at Jennifer when she entered.

"Who do you think you are? You have no right to attack us. Do you even know who I am?"

On any other day, Jennifer might have been in the mood to play games with the guy, but ever since the Wraith had informed her there were documents she needed to see, she'd had a bad feeling about the whole situation that had only gotten worse. Without saying a word, she withdrew her medallion from inside her clothes and let it fall to her chest.

"I haven't the foggiest idea who you are, and I'm honestly on the fence about whether I care. Do you know who *I* am?"

From how pale his complexion became and the beads of sweat that erupted on his forehead, Jennifer suspected he had a very good idea of her identity... if he didn't know precisely who she was. He shook his head slowly side to side, and his voice sounded like he was trying to convince himself as much as inform her.

"I'll never talk. Not one word."

"We'll get back to that, I'm sure." Jennifer turned to the Wraith. "You mentioned documents?"

The Wraith collected a stack of parchment from a side table and placed it on the table in front of Jennifer. The trussed-up guy's breathing went into overdrive at the sight of them, and he found his bonds as if to get free.

"Those are private papers! You have no right!"

Jennifer shrugged. "The way you're acting, there's obviously something here you don't want me to see. So, let's just find out what that is, shall we?"

She pulled the chair out from the table and sat, then began to examine the papers. The one on top was innocuous enough; it looked like a supply manifest, delineating food and equipment for a couple thousand people if she interpreted it correctly. The next document appeared to be a multi-page report on the weaknesses of Tel Mivar, specifically if one wanted to claim the city from inside the walls. The next few documents covered the other province capitals: Tel Roshan, Tel Cothos, and Tel Wygoth. Beneath those, Jennifer found a multi-page timetable that started from the day Tel's army moved out to lead the forces of the Old Alliance in assaulting Skullkeep.

Not good. Not good at all.

Jennifer looked up to the Wraith where she waited, asking, "Is all this credible? Not just someone's sick fantasy?"

"It appears credible enough. There's a map on that desk over there that seems to have the locations of all the staging camps—like this one. The only way to know for certain is to investigate further. Honestly, Milady... we should inform your father."

Jennifer shook her head. "No. No, we shouldn't. If there is a credible threat... yes, of course. He needs to know. But we won't know that until we investigate further. Is it within my authority to draw on your organization's resources and personnel?"

A small smile quirked the woman's lips. "Yes. Your father was very clear that—should you care to exercise it—your authority over us is second only to his."

"Can we pull more people to work with us on investigating these sites without hampering other operations?"

The woman nodded. "It should be possible."

"Good. If it is within our power and authority to handle this, I'd rather do that without bothering Dad. He has enough going on right now that he doesn't need this on his mind, too."

The woman nodded, more like a half bow. "Very well, Milady. I shall request another eleven of us under your name. If the other camps are like this one, fifteen should be more than sufficient."

Jennifer flipped through the documents again until she found the food and equipment manifest. She tapped it as she shifted her attention to their captive. "What I don't understand, though, is the attack on the three wagons. If this *is* a manifest and if it's accurate, you have all the food and equipment you need, from the looks of it."

The man grimaced, settling into a scowl. "Giltan is such a damned fool. He spent his whole life as a bandit, and he'd been going on and on about what a sweet score a good caravan is. I thought we had him under control, but he apparently slipped the leash and took a few people with him two days ago. That was not authorized. It should never have happened."

Jennifer shook her head as she fought the urge to laugh. "You're not kidding. If Kellea and I hadn't happened upon those wagons, we never would've investigated and found your camp."

The man's scowl hardened into a glare. "If I thought for a moment that idiot still lived, I'd beg you to let me kill him. Stupid!"

"Well... in this instance, your bad luck is our good. Yes, it's unfortunate he attacked those wagons, but if it was going to happen anyway, I'm glad it did at a time and place where we'd discover them." Jennifer turned to the Wraith. "So, what do we do with him?"

"You have three options... hold him, kill him, or turn him over to the authorities. Turning him over to the authorities might precipitate your father learning of this situation. If you hold him, you have the option of interrogating him at your leisure."

Jennifer's mind went back to watching the recording of her father 'interviewing' the guy who tried to shoot him back in Graham, and she grinned at the thought of this guy spilling everything he knew.

"Do we have a way of transcribing what he says?"

The Wraith simply nodded. "We have already requested it. I expect it to arrive here by the end of tomorrow."

"Fair enough. We'll wait till we have it, then. Make sure he has food and water. I'm tempted to say cut off his pants and the seat and just let him use a chamber pot, rather than risk untying him enough to walk to the latrine."

The Wraith seemed to appreciate that thought. "You would have fit in well with us, Milady. It shall be done."

Jennifer stood and headed out of the pavilion. She stopped at the entrance and turned her head just enough to speak over her shoulder. "Don't injure him too much when you cut off his pants and the chair's seat."

When Jennifer left the pavilion, the prisoner looked far more terrified than he had when she entered.

* * *

THE NEXT MORNING, Jennifer exited her tent and found eleven more Wraiths than there had been, and the woman who'd been working closely with Jennifer held up a crystal. Jennifer eyed the crystal in silence for a moment, raising a single eyebrow.

"I take it that's the recording device?"

The woman angled her head very slightly to the side as if to communicate 'sort of.' "It is the crystal that will store the image and sound around it. None of us can use it. I'm told only an arcanist can activate it. Once it has stored images and sounds, however, a simple command word will retrieve them."

"Well, that's lovely. I don't suppose you have the information I need to have it record?"

The woman's expression mimicked the satisfaction of a cat who didn't just get the cream but ate the canary, too. "Of course, Milady."

She withdrew a piece of parchment and handed it to Jennifer. The parchment held written instructions in what she thought was a woman's hand, but she'd never seen the handwriting of anyone close to her dad to know if it came from one of them.

Regardless, the instructions were fairly straightforward. Simply invoke a composite effect of Illusion and Transmutation to imprint the image and sounds of the crystal's surroundings. The embedded effects already present in the crystal would handle presenting the recording in the future.

"Huh... seems simple enough. Are we ready to do this?"

The woman's expression became a grim smile. "Our captive in the pavilion had a bad enough night that I think he'd share what he knows for the promise of a walk. It would be an embarrassing walk, though. His male pride isn't nearly as impressive as I'm sure he'd like to think it is."

Jennifer snorted a laugh. "Well, hopefully... I don't obtain direct evidence of that. I'm happy to take your word for it. All right. Let's go."

The woman led Jennifer into the pavilion, and Jennifer had to admit the poor sod looked rather awful. Even if the Wraith hadn't front-loaded her expectations, there's no way she could've missed the fact he was not in a good place mentally.

"Oh... thank the gods. Please... please... tell me what you want to know. I don't care. I'll say whatever you want if you'll just let me walk to the latrine." He actually broke down into sobs then. "Last night... last night was horrid. Please... tell me what you want to know."

While Jennifer didn't exactly have a deep wellspring of compassion for the guy, she also wasn't one for gratuitous torture. She touched the woman's arm and led her back outside the pavilion. Drawing the Wraith close, Jennifer whispered, "You guys didn't torture him, did you? He seems pretty broken already."

A smirk fought to escape the woman's iron self-control. "I wouldn't call it 'torture,' Milady."

"Well, what would you call it, then? No... never mind. Just tell me what happened."

"The other woman of our original four came to us from a... well... an abusive background. She has improved significantly since she joined our ranks, but she still rather strongly dislikes the males of the species. After the second time he pissed on her while trying to use the chamber pot, she... well... came rather close to gelding him. Admittedly, he only pissed on her shoes. Still, though... I'm honestly surprised his screams and begging didn't wake you; they were rather horrific."

Jennifer shuddered. "I'm kinda sorry I asked. Okay. Let's get back in there."

When she stepped back inside the pavilion, the captive's expression lit up like a child faced with a mountain of presents at Christmas. "Oh, thank the gods. I was afraid you'd left completely. Please... please, you have to save me."

Jennifer read over the instructions on the parchment again and took a deep breath, letting it out slowly as she focused her intent. Then, she invoked a composite effect of Illusion and Transmutation, *"Zikthaes-Rhyskaal."*

The resonance of her power slammed into the ambient like a pneumatic battering ram striking a weak clay wall. If there had been any fellow wizards present, they would've fallen to their knees, gasping at the savage violence of it. The crystal she held began to glow and lifted from her hand to hover in the air directly in front of the captive and over the center of the table.

"Now then... it's not that I don't trust you," Jennifer said as she regarded the captive, "but... well... I don't trust you. *Zaenos.*"

The man's expression blanked and became one of vapid adoration as he gazed lovingly at Jennifer. "Oh, please, Mistress... I only want to please you. Tell me what will please you."

"Tell me what this camp is. Why are you here? What's the purpose of all this?"

"Oh, yes, Mistress. I can certainly do that. This is one of several staging camps around Tel. We are preparing to reclaim the Kingdom when the usurper takes the armies of the Old Alliance to assault Skullkeep. Then... when they're too battered and weakened to matter, they'll come home to find they've been ousted... just as he ousted all of us. It's beautiful, really."

Jennifer glanced at the Wraiths surrounding the table, trying to make sense of it. She *thought* she remembered her dad talking about how the royal family had ruled Tel during the centuries between Bellock Vanlon and Bellos naming him as Archmagister. "So... you and yours are royalists, then?"

"Oh, yes, Mistress... well... I was. Now, I care only for you. Please, Mistress, there must be more I can tell you. Or if you'd only untie me, I can serve you further. Do laundry, wash your feet, care for your horses... I care not, as long as it pleases you."

"And what was your position in the grand scheme of this?" Jennifer asked.

"I commanded this camp, and I am one tier below those in charge of our mission."

Jennifer gnawed at the inside of her cheek, not enough to harm tissue, but it was an unconscious habit from her childhood that she'd never fully broken. It tended to surface when she was deep in thought.

She turned to the Wraith who'd become something of her liaison. "Get him pen, ink, and parchment. Free his hands. He will write down the name of everyone he knows who is his level or higher in this conspiracy."

"Oh, yes, Mistress. I shall happily do so."

Writing implements quickly arrived, and the captive set to naming his co-conspirators in writing. Soon enough, he'd filled a sheet front and back with names and looked up at her like an expectant puppy waiting on its treat.

Jennifer turned to her Wraith liaison. "Does he hold any further value to us?"

"I don't believe so, no."

Jennifer invoked a Word of Tutation, "*Rhosed.*"

The expression of vapid adoration left the man's face, and the crystal dimmed and slowly descended to lay on the tabletop.

"What should we do with him?" the Wraith liaison asked. "Before you get too far down one train of thought, you should know that we finally found the people taken from those wagons. There was one family per wagon, and those they didn't kill in the initial attack died when the idiot brought them back to camp... children, too."

Jennifer clenched her jaw, and it felt like she might draw blood from her palms with her own fingernails. "He ordered the death of children?"

The Wraith liaison merely nodded.

"I was tempted to offer him mercy."

"And now?"

Jennifer turned to regard the former leader of the camp. Given his sudden change of expression, she suspected he saw his death in her eyes. "Give him to your man-hater friend. Tell her I said to have fun."

CHAPTER 23

L ater that day, Jennifer returned to the pavilion. The camp leader was nowhere in sight, not that she expected to see him. Not anymore. She went straight to the map of Tel. She knew roughly where she was, because someone had drawn an X through one of the red dots. She tapped each remaining dot as she counted. Twenty-four. Twenty-five with this camp they'd just cleared. That seemed... a little low for taking over a country.

Movement pulled her attention away from the map, and she smiled at seeing the liaison enter the pavilion.

"How many people were at this camp? You said several dozen the other day, but do you have a better count now?"

"Seventy," the liaison replied as she crossed the intervening distance and stopped at Jennifer's side. "Why?"

"So... there were twenty-five camps total, and we just cleared this one. That's something like seventeen hundred people. Isn't that a little low to take over a country?"

The liaison shrugged. "Maybe. Maybe not. The average army is only ten to fifteen thousand. I don't know about the other province capitals, but Tel Mivar's city guard only numbers around fifteen hundred. If you already had people inside the walls and complete surprise, you could probably capture even a province capital with less than five hundred people, especially if you know the city's weaknesses."

Jennifer nodded. She didn't like that information. That made it all too easy... all too probable... for them to succeed. But wasn't there something about a garrison her dad told her?

"Hang on... does the city guard include the garrison?"

The liaison froze. She slowly turned away from the map on the table to face Jennifer. "Where did you hear about the garrison?"

"Dad told me. At least... I think he did. Something about activation sigils scattered throughout Tel Mivar. Does every province capital have them?"

The liaison took a break, holding her silence as she slowly exhaled, then nodded. "It was a pact offered by the soldiers of the Army of Valthon just after the Godswar ended. When they died, they would move on to their afterlife... but in times of grave threat, they could be called back—reactivated as it were—to defend the province capitals. Each and every one of them offered it willingly."

"Damn... talk about the ultimate inactive reserve force. Okay, so how do we activate them?"

The liaison shrugged. "No one knows. Obviously, your father does. He activated Tel Mivar's garrison. Unsettled quite a few people doing it, too. But that's kind of expected when blue-tinged phantoms start rising out of the ground and taking up positions throughout the city. You could always ask him."

Jennifer gave her a flat look. "I'm trying to help Dad by not adding to his plate. Besides, I feel like this is something I need to do."

"Yes... we understand that, but Tel is your father's responsibility. The Kingdom of Tel as a whole. He deserves to know what's happening, even if he entrusts you with the responsibility of handling it. Informing him but also telling him you want to resolve the issue shows that you respect his responsibility and authority enough to tell him what's happening, and telling him you want to handle it for him communicates that you want to help him, too. Far too many people would run straight to him with this and dump it at his feet."

Jennifer sighed. "Yes... okay... I see your point. I'll visit Dad. Want to tag along?"

For a split second, the liaison's non-expression slipped, and Jennifer thought she saw a bit of fear at the thought of meeting her dad. She didn't say anything, though, and waited in silence.

After a few moments, the liaison shook her head. "I... do not believe my presence would add anything to the discussion."

Jennifer really wanted to call her on it, but that was a good save at the very least. "Well then, you can help my find my way back, then."

Without waiting for a response, Jennifer stood and walked outside the pavilion, scanning the ground for what she sought. It took a few minutes... mainly because no one likes to camp on a rock... but she returned to the pavilion holding a small stone just big enough to cover the cup of her hand.

"Dad told me how Lillian and Mariana used a teleport beacon during their diplomatic mission to the northern members of the Old Alliance." She rummaged through the pavilion until she found what she felt was a suitable implement and set to scratching out runes on the stone's surface. "Yes... it eventually got them into trouble, but no one can deny the handiness of it."

As soon as Jennifer felt the runes were ready, she pricked her thumb and swabbed some blood onto the surface of the stone as she invoked a Word of Transmutation, "*Rhyskaal.*"

They both watched the blood vanish into the stone as the runes became crisper and more defined. Within a couple heartbeats, they began to glow with a soft radiance. Jennifer held the stone for a few moments more, concentrating on it until she felt the power of her intent fade, then held it out to the liaison. The liaison accepted it with just a hint of wariness, and Jennifer fought the urge to smile.

Then, Jennifer frowned. "You know... I feel kinda bad. I've been thinking of you as 'the liaison' all this time. I'm sorry. I should've asked your name when we first met."

The liaison offered Jennifer a soft smile. "Shara, Milady. Once upon a time, I was a miller's daughter."

Jennifer smiled. "Thank you, Shara. Now... well... I should probably visit Dad. Sure you don't want to tag along?"

"Erm... no. I think my time will be better served here."

Jennifer didn't say a word, despite how much she wanted to tease Shara, as she rolled up the map. "Well, I'm going to offer Kellea the same option, though I suspect her answer will be much the same as yours. Keep an eye on her for me, please?"

Shara nodded once. "We shall all lay dead before harm comes to her."

If these fifteen Wraiths were even half as good as Kiri, it would take some serious harm to get through all of them. She nodded her thanks and left the pavilion, intent on seeking out Kellea.

* * *

THE COURTYARD of the College of the Arcane hadn't changed much since the last time Jennifer had visited. Her gateway opened on the smooth stone path that connected the gate to the steps of the ancient keep that had come to be known as the Tower of the Council. She saw the stables off to her right and thought one of the horses milling about the paddock might be Jasmine... but she wasn't sure.

"What brings you to the College?" a voice asked, pulling her attention away from the stables. She turned and found a man who looked about her age. He wore a red robe with silver runes on the cuffs of the sleeve, and his expression seemed to hover on the edge of a sneer.

"Oh... I'm just here to visit my dad. I have something to show him."

"Aren't you a little old to be running your newest handpainting to your father?"

For the briefest moment, anger tried to spike within her. For the briefest moment, she *longed* to put this arrogant prig in his place. But that would not serve her greater intent. He wasn't wearing a medallion, so it wasn't like he posed much threat—if any—to her. So, she decided to take a different tack.

"Oh, you know us Daddy's girls. We're never too old to make papa smile. Have a good day now." Jennifer skipped into motion after giving him a finger wave. She didn't look back as she headed for the Tower, but it was impossible not to hear him sputtering behind her.

Whether he was some sort of self-styled ladies' man or merely the College greeter, Jennifer had no interest in further interaction with him. He gave her a smarmy vibe, and she had plenty of those from visiting used car lots back on Earth.

"Here, now! You can't just..."

Jennifer didn't stop or slow. If he wanted to accost her, he could bloody well catch up to her. She was up the steps and inside the Tower before she felt a hand close on her elbow, and *that* shredded whatever frivolity remained. She turned only her head to face him, and her expression showed none of her earlier playfulness.

"If you enjoy having the use of that hand, I strongly suggest you remove it at once."

Now, the man's sneer did break free. "And just what is a commoner going to do about it? You're already deep inside College grounds, and I don't see your daddy anywhere."

Jennifer regarded him in silence for a moment. Sure... she could whip out her medallion and scare the piss out of him, but she couldn't shake the feeling this wasn't the first time he'd accosted a woman. She didn't like the idea of leaving him free to re-establish his dominance on someone else after she made him piss himself in fear. That never ended well with people like him.

Before Jennifer could settle on what to do, a woman's voice pulled her attention away from him. "Jennifer? What brings you to the College? It's been simply ages, dear."

Jennifer turned and smiled when she saw an elderly woman in a white robe standing at the intersection a few feet away. "Valera, it's so good to see you, too. I think you have another predator lurking in your midst. This fellow seems to think he has the right to grab whatever woman he chooses—especially if they're commoners—and we have no recourse."

Valera's expression settled into an unreadable mask as she eyed the mage holding Jennifer's elbow. "Is that so?"

"Magister, I found this one inside the gate, halfway to the Tower. She refused to identify herself or give any reason why she should be on College grounds."

"You don't say." Valera's expression was still unreadable.

Just then, another woman—closer to Jennifer's age—stepped into view from the other side of the intersection. She wore a black robe trimmed in crimson. "Ah, good. I've been looking for you, Valera."

At the sight of the new arrival, Jennifer felt the man holding her elbow jerk in surprise. His grip slackened, and as she glanced his way, she saw he looked like nothing more than cornered prey.

"Reyna," Valera said, "has anyone ever told you what excellent timing you have?"

"Timing? Uhm... er... no. What makes you say that?"

Valera smiled now and nodded her head toward Jennifer. "I do believe our guest has caught the mage who's been preying on commoners. If you're feeling particularly merciful, you can take him into custody."

The woman Valera called Reyna still hadn't looked in Jennifer's direction. "And if I'm not feeling merciful?"

Now, Valera's expression turned absolutely evil as she pointed toward Jennifer. "Tell her father."

"What? Why would that..." Reyna's voice trailed off as she turned to see where Valera pointed. It was apparent she understood when her confused expression vanished. "Oh. You know... I think maybe you're right. I think we *should* tell her father."

A rustle of fabric heralded the arrival of a tall, broad-shouldered man in a gold robe. He wasn't paying attention to his surroundings as he looked at papers—well, probably parchment—in his hands. "Tell whose father what, Reyna?"

Jennifer felt like an absolute, mischievous brat as she grinned and said, "Hi, Dad."

"Jennifer?" Gavin's head turned her way, and he took in the situation just as quickly as Reyna. His eyes narrowed at what Jennifer suspected was the hand still clutching her elbow, though now it felt more like a vise... as if she were the only life preserver in sight of a man overboard at sea.

Reyna stepped back as Gavin stepped forward, and he crossed the distance between Jennifer and the mage almost in the blink of an eye. His expression was eerily calm. "Young man, I don't know who you are or who you *think* you are, but when you tell me why you have violated my daughter's personal space—not to mention her person— I assure you with all that I am that your reason had better be *exemplary*."

When no response seemed to be forthcoming, Jennifer filled the void. "Valera thinks I found the mage Reyna has been searching for, something about preying on commoners. And I have to say, Dad, she might be right. When he approached me outside, he gave off a very unsafe vibe. I probably would've been afraid of him if not for... well... being your daughter and all."

Jennifer gave the arm the mage held a jerk, and he was smart enough to let her pull away. She stepped off to the side and waited. The silence extended for several moments, before Gavin broke it.

"Reyna, take this one into custody and investigate the truth of Valera's guess. If he proves uncooperative, inform me at once."

The mage broke free of his terror paralysis and pivoted on his heel. He took one step toward the doors, winding up to a good sprint, when Gavin invoked a Word of Enchantment, "*Thymnos*."

Jennifer expected to feel the resonance of her dad's power concuss the ambient like something just a few steps shy of a nuclear blast, but strangely, what she felt was little more than a whisper.

But it was an effective whisper.

Every scrap of tension left the mage's body the instant Gavin made his invocation, and he plowed head—well, *nose*-first—into the stone floor. There was a ghastly *crack* that made Jennifer wince and shudder. Reyna hurried forward and rolled the mage onto his side, revealing a river of blood cascading out of his askew nose. She cast a questioning expression toward Gavin.

He nodded overtop a sigh. "Yes, fine... call in a healer from the temple."

Without another word, her dad turned and headed toward the large staircase across the intersection from the entryway. As he moved, he nodded his head for Jennifer to follow. She hurried to join him. Her dad maintained his silence all the way up the staircase until they stood at the final landing before roof access. There was an archway built into the wall, and Jennifer almost leaped out of her skin when a blue, translucent phantasm stepped out of the solid stone wall.

"Yes, Milord?"

"Access to the Citadel, if you please," her dad replied, as if he conversed with blue phantasms every day of the week and twice on Sunday.

The specter nodded once and inserted his left hand into the wall, just beside the archway. Jennifer felt—as much as heard—what sounded like a massive latch releasing, and the stone inside the archway began swirling like a whirlpool. As soon as it reached a speed where the individual stones in the wall were no longer visible for the swirling, there was muted flash, and the archway became a door to another place.

Through the archway, Jennifer saw what looked like fine carpet lining a stone hallway, and an arch lined the intersection where the short hallway met another. In the center of the arch, the keystone sported the Glyph of Kirloth that glowed faintly.

Her dad stepped through without any reservation, and she hurried to keep up, slightly afraid that the portal would close without her.

This was the Citadel of the Archmagister, the equivalent to the White House back on Earth, and she'd only been there one other time... when her dad brought her, Alexis, and her grandparents there immediately after creating the portal. It didn't look like much, just a well-furnished castle really, but there was a subtle ambiance to the place that Jennifer didn't quite understand. In many ways, it felt like she was coming home.

Her dad lifted a hand and made a swirling motion with a finger, gesturing to the structure as a whole. "This was the original Kirloth estate. Unfortunately, he never recorded that anywhere, and the Archmagisters after him used it as their residence and refuge. I can prove our family's claim to it nine ways from Sunday, but I can't help but feel doing so would tiptoe around the edges of dirty pool, especially since I claimed all of House Sivas's property in the wake of that fiasco. If you feel like you just came home, that's why."

Her dad turned right at the intersection and led her easily fifty feet down the hallway before stopping at a door on his right. He opened it and gestured for her to enter. As she did so, she saw it was the conference room where she'd met his friends from this world for the first time.

He closed the door behind him as he followed her inside and went straight to a chair, into which he unceremoniously flopped. Jennifer followed suit without his bidding, and he seemed to appreciate that.

"So... I don't want to sound like I'm not happy to see you, but Declan intimated that you were doing some soul searching. I figured you'd come say hi when you were ready, but this doesn't feel like that kind of visit."

Jennifer chuckled. "I should've realized he'd tell you I was here. And you're right... this isn't that visit. I stumbled onto something that I feel I can resolve on my own, but one of the Wraiths convinced me it was the respectful thing to do to make you aware of the situation."

She watched a perplexed frown overtake her dad's expression, and he leaned forward, gesturing at the rolled up document in her hand. "And I take it that whatever you're carrying relates to that?"

Jennifer nodded as she stood and unrolled the map. "I don't know how much Declan told you, and honestly, I can't remember what all I told him. So, the short of this is that I came over here to explore and learn about this world a little bit. While I was on the way north from Tel Roshan, I came across three wagons all having some level of damage that made them inoperable. There was blood on the ground, and I was worried for whoever had those wagons, so I tried my hand at a little tracking."

If her dad didn't completely believe her about being alone, he didn't show it.

"The Wraiths you put on me—I'm guessing after my run-in with Declan—melted out of the forest around me and said I was about to stumble onto a camp that was beyond me if I wanted any survivors. So, I waited and let them handle it. They captured the five highest-ranking people in the camp, and over the course of interrogations, they revealed they're part of a plot to capture the province capitals while you're away with the army at Skullkeep. That map was in the command tent, and I'm guessing it shows the locations of all the other encampments. I requisitioned another eleven Wraiths—bringing the count up to fifteen—and... well... I want to handle this. The Wraith who had been interacting with me the most convinced me you should be aware of this, even if you agree to let me handle it. I was just going to handle it and tell you later."

She returned to her seat and tried not to look too eager for any sign of her dad's approval. She'd never tell him, but she'd come to realize that she wanted so very much for him to be proud of her.

Her dad sat in silence for several moments, his eyes roaming over the map. She longed for some sign of his thoughts, but he was better than a professional poker player at non-expressions.

"Jennifer, even after all these months, there are still times when it doesn't seem possible that you are all grown up. I hope you never understand what it feels like to miss so much of your child's life. My immediate gut reaction is to get you as far away from this as possible, but that's the reaction of a dad with a little girl who's just starting her teens. Not only would I be doing you a disservice to allow that to be my reaction, it would also be disrespectful. But... no matter how much I know I need to turn you loose, I hope you'll forgive me for feeling a little protective, which will take the form of detailing an additional fifteen Wraiths to your command for this. If four Wraiths can see to one of these camps, I see no reason thirty would fail, and

I'll even restrain my urge to have them keep you as far away from it as possible."

Jennifer felt a little excess moisture in her eyes as she smiled. "Thanks, Dad. That... well... it means a lot. I know you're busy, so I don't want to keep you."

Her dad stood when she did, and before she could move to roll up the map again, he pulled her into a tight hug. He held her for several heartbeats without saying a word, but when he broke the embrace and stepped back, he looked her square in the eyes.

"Jennifer, you don't ever have to feel like you need to earn my acceptance or my pride. You have been and will always be the best part of my life. Kiri can tell you that finding my daughter—even though I had no idea who she was for most of my time here—was never far from my thoughts once I realized I had a daughter. I don't care whether you earn a tenure in the White House or work as a cashier at the grocery store in Graham. I will *always* be proud of you. I love you, Jennifer."

Jennifer couldn't stop herself from swallowing as she nodded. "I love you, too, Dad."

He stepped back and allowed her to collect the map and then walked her back to the archway. They chatted about her grandparents back on Earth, mostly, and how well she was keeping in touch with Alexis. He touched a stone that didn't look different from any others in the wall, but the archway quickly became a portal back to the Tower of the Council.

"Be as careful as you need to be out there, Jenny. The extra Wraiths will arrive within a day."

"Bye, Dad. You be careful, too."

Her dad just grinned. "Me? I'm always careful."

She couldn't resist giving him a look that expressed just what she thought of *that* statement and stepped through the portal. She waved to him one last time as the portal closed and then headed down the stairs to the Tower's entrance, eager to return to her mission.

CHAPTER 24

The arboreal canopy high overhead shrouded the terrain beneath it in a kind of dusky twilight. It was cooler in the forest... much more pleasant than the hot sun that had pressed down upon Jennifer in Tel Mivar. She had never considered herself much of a technology junky, but she'd come to realize that she missed air conditioning... among several other 'comforts of home.'

She, Kellea, and the first fifteen Wraiths waited for the other fifteen her father ordered to join them. He'd said they'd be waiting on her when she returned, but maybe he didn't expect her to teleport straight back?

Either way, they sat around the mostly torn down camp and chatted or played card games or practiced and trained. It also gave Jennifer plenty of time to think about her status in the group and its operations. On the one side, she appreciated that her dad wanted to keep her safe. It meant a lot to her that he still cared about her like a dad... even though it was understandable, as his memories of her as a little girl were so recent for him.

Having reached a decision, she waved Shara over to a chat. The Wraith Jennifer thought of as her liaison to the rest excused herself from the conversation around her and made her way over to the felled log where Jennifer sat. It didn't escape Jennifer's notice that Kellea was the only one out of the other people in the former camp who came very close to her at all, but their insistence to treat her differently than even Kellea finally wore down all her resistance. She no longer cared.

"Yes, Milady?" Shara asked when she arrived.

Jennifer pointed to another felled log off her right side—at about two o'clock—and gestured for Shara to sit. "I've been thinking about my role in all of this. I don't like that I'm treated as some kind of fragile doll that must be protected."

Shara's lips quirked, and Jennifer immediately grinned. "Okay, yes... from your perspective, I probably *am* a fragile doll that must be protected... but I'm not. Not really. Yes... I know very little of how to win a close-up, face-to-face fight. I'll give you that. But what I *can* do is put the entire camp to sleep. I should've thought of that for here, instead of letting you four go through the camp all by yourselves during the night subduing it. Unless you can talk me out of it right now, I want that to be our operating procedure from here on out. You and yours can then secure the camp without the same level of risk. And... well... it lets me be useful. Besides, we may come across a camp that has an arcanist, and it would be better to have me close than even a moderate distance away at that point."

Shara listened to Jennifer in silence, maintaining eye contact while doing so. When Jennifer wound down, she replied, "You make excellent points, and I understand where you're coming from. I see no reason we can't move forward using that as our standard. Honestly, if we do that, we don't even *need* the additional fifteen Wraiths, but your father wanted you to have them, so we're almost stuck here waiting for them. We could move out to another camp, but why make it more difficult for them to find us? No one wants that."

"All right. Let me know as soon as they arrive, and we'll head out to the next camp. Oh... have we made any provisions for one or more people from other camps arriving here as message couriers? I'd hate for us to be discovered, all because someone showed up here after we left and only found a clearing. I don't want these people to go to ground on us."

"That is a very valid concern," Shara said. "I think we should leave five Wraiths here to guard against that, and as we clear out all the camps closest to this one, we pull everyone back together and move on to a new region."

Jennifer nodded as she pulled out the map and unfolded it, waving Shara over to her. "I like that. Here... if these camp locations are accurate, we can clear all the camps in western Roshan and Wygoth provinces and still have Wraiths left over. Then, we start moving east, and once we get a couple days ahead of the farthest east camps that we've cleared, the Wraiths at the farthest east camps move forward to re-join us."

"That sounds good, but how will they know when to move?"

A memory of a story her dad told her popped into her mind, and she smiled. "That might not be too difficult. Can you have someone gather thirty stones—preferably smooth—that can fit in the cup of a person's hand?"

Shara nodded once. "I'll see to it now."

Jennifer re-folded the map and went inside the pavilion that had once served as the camp leader's home away from home. Most of the furniture and accoutrements remained, and she went to the chest she knew held writing implements. She carried a stylus, bottle of ink, and a stack of parchment over to the table and sat to sketch out a design for an imbued item... well... *thirty* imbued items.

* * *

UPON LEAVING Young Kirloth in the pavilion, Shara went straight to the stream that ran close by the camp and provided its water. Yes... she absolutely could've farmed out her request, but Shara didn't like that. *She* understood what Young Kirloth wanted and why. That almost certainly wouldn't be the case with anyone else.

Yes... she could take the time to explain the situation, but why should she bother when she herself could handle the request easily enough?

She enjoyed working with Young Kirloth. The young woman seemed to have a decent head on her shoulders and wasn't full of herself at all. Shara had developed the impression that the young woman had some darkness in her past, but these days, who didn't?

Still, though... Young Kirloth seemed especially sensitive to it. That conclusion didn't come from anything she said or did. It was more a sense that Shara had from the young woman's priorities and worldview.

In all truth, she *liked* that about Young Kirloth. She liked working for someone with a conscience... even if it seemed a bit overactive at times. Far too many people in the world cared naught for how their actions or priorities or views affected others. Shara didn't believe people should live their lives for others, but at the same time, she appreciated people who tried to make the world a little better for their travels through it.

She chuckled as she collected her fourth stone. There were probably people who would look at her askance for those thoughts, given what she did for a living. She was *essentially* an assassin. She made no effort to hide it, either. She knew there was something broken inside her... or at least, something that everyone else would say was broken.

Shara took pride in her mastery of her chosen craft. When she was assigned a challenging task—even if said task was the elimination of one, specific person—and when she completed that task flawlessly without leaving any evidence that she had ever been there? That was a matter of pride to her.

Almost everyone else in the world—aside from her colleagues—would be appalled that she took pride in something like a well-executed murder or infiltration for information. She didn't just know that; she *understood* it. And the Wraiths valued her anyway. In fact, they had recruited her out of the Tel Wygoth dungeon, where she awaited execution for a host of actions that the province and kingdom as a whole deemed criminal. She understood those actions had been illegal, but she still felt they were appropriate to the circumstances and would do the same things all over again if given the chance.

Shara stopped and considered the belt pouch that was moderately full of palm-sized rocks now. Dammit all... she'd lost count. She moved over to a rather large stone and leaned against it as she withdrew all the rocks from the pouch and re-counted them. When she moved the final rock from her hand to the pouch, the count was twenty-two. She repeated 'eight' to herself a few times, hoping she wouldn't lose count again as she went back to her task.

It took little time at all to collect the remaining stones Young Kirloth requested, and she secured the flap of the pouch to make sure they didn't bounce out as she returned to camp. After all, there was no reason not to do a little agility practice.

That was the major reason she felt so many other Wraiths were lacking. They didn't display the same commitment to their craft that she felt they should. *She* turned a simple walk to return to camp into a series of cartwheels, shoulder rolls, and handstands. Most of her associates probably would have just trudged back through the underbrush.

When she broke through the brush that lined the camp, she saw that the fifteen extra Wraiths had arrived, and she forced herself not to react when she caught sight of the leader of the group. Bertram. A self-serving, egotistical nightmare. She despised even the thought of working in the same organization as him, let alone the same unit or assignment. Even though her demeanor and expression betrayed no hint of her internal thoughts and feelings, she braced herself for what she knew was an imminent power struggle over who would have and control access to Young Kirloth.

It wasn't that she sought to raise her status through proximity to House Kirloth. No... not at all. She merely **liked** Young Kirloth. She enjoyed working and talking with her. Shara felt she was a kindred spirit in a lot of ways and found that... comforting.

By that point, she approached the cluster of Wraiths surrounding Bertram, and the ass himself had noticed her. As the cluster of people around him opened to admit her, she put every effort into keeping her expression and demeanor void of any reaction.

"Hello, Bertram."

* * *

MOVEMENT in her peripheral vision pulled Jennifer's attention away from her sketches and thoughts. She looked up and saw some guy she didn't know standing almost at her elbow. He wore Wraith leathers and held a collection of stones in his cupped hands.

"Hello. I don't believe we've met. I'm Jennifer."

"Yes, Young Kirloth, it is an honor to meet and work with you. I am Bertram, and as I am now the senior Wraith, I have taken over all of Shara's duties in regard to liaising with you and overseeing this operation."

Jennifer fought the urge to frown. There was... something... about this guy that she wasn't sure she liked.

"So, Shara was the senior Wraith among the fifteen that were already here?"

"Ah... no. Not quite. But it isn't my fault that they failed to exercise proper protocol."

Now, Jennifer *knew* something wasn't right. No one had ever mentioned anything about protocol to her, and as far as she understood, the only person who could supersede her with the Wraiths was her dad.

From the man's expression, some of her skepticism must've slipped into her expression or demeanor. Not that she really cared at this point. "Are those the stones I requested?"

"Oh... uhm... yes?"

Jennifer raised one eyebrow. "Don't you know? Or did Shara tell you she was delivering something to me, and you demanded to be the one to deliver it yourself? If you don't know what Shara was doing for me, how can you be sure she hasn't made a fool out of you?"

Bertram's expression darkened just a hint at that thought, but before he could speak, Jennifer invoked a Word of Divination, "*Klaepos*."

A circular area about six inches above the table's surface began shimmering and rippling like a still pond into which a stone is thrown. Within a handful of heartbeats, that area became a scrying sphere focused on Declan. Jennifer smiled at seeing him alone and in what looked like an office or a study.

She squared her shoulders and once more invoked a Word of Divination, "*Klaepos*."

This time, however, the scrying sphere appeared in front of Declan and displayed Jennifer, Bertram, and the fringe of her scrying sphere.

"Hi, Declan."

Declan apparently was so deep in concentration that he failed to notice the appearance of the scrying sphere, and he started, one hand going to a dagger hilt as he scanned the area around him and finally settled on the scrying sphere.

He closed his eyes and rubbed his forehead with the hand that had reached for a dagger just a moment before. "Jennifer, has anyone ever told you that you can be a very trying individual?"

"Oh, I'm sure dozens of people have, Declan. You're just one of the lucky ones to see me more than most."

He gave her a flat look. "I'm not sure 'lucky' means what you think it means. How can I help you?"

"I wanted to ask a question about Wraith seniority and proper protocol."

All of a sudden, Bertram started fidgeting at her side. "Uhm... if you will excuse me, Young Kirloth..."

Jennifer speared him with an expression that was nowhere close to kind. "Oh, no, Bertram... you've made your bed. Now, you get to lay in it. If you take even one step, I'll freeze you in place."

Sweat broke out on the man's forehead, and both his expression and demeanor suggested very strongly that he wanted nothing more than to bolt.

Declan regarded them both in silence for a few moments before his expression turned wry. "If you're asking about Wraith seniority and proper protocol, I'm betting Betram there has tried singing his old song and dance to elevate himself by getting closer to you. I don't know what you're doing precisely, but at the conclusion of it, Bertram will most likely do everything he can to use his association with you —however brief—to advance himself."

"So... from what you're implying, there isn't such a thing as Wraith seniority or proper protocol?"

Declan snorted a laugh. "The only proper protocol we have is basic civility... which I argue should be a given throughout every intelligent race. And no, we don't use seniority like armies use date of rank or anything like that." Declan's eyes flicked to Bertram for a moment. "Some few of us have tried to implement such a thing from time to time, but it never gains any support among the Wraiths as a whole."

"Is it within my authority to expel someone from the Wraiths?" Jennifer enjoyed the sudden gasp she heard a short distance to her right.

"Oh, I wouldn't go that far, Jennifer. He honestly does have his uses."

Jennifer let her true feelings about how Bertram had conducted himself flow into her expression and demeanor. "Then, we need to trade him out for someone else. I do not appreciate liars or ass-kissers, and Dad wanted me to have thirty Wraiths with me. This idiot's lips are so brown all the soap in Tel wouldn't clean them. If I'm stuck with him, there is every chance that I'll return only twenty-nine Wraiths when I'm finished, and I have the feeling none of the other people with me would miss him overmuch."

Declan regarded them both in silence for several moments before he nodded once. "I'll arrange for another Wraith to meet you forthwith, and Bertram? If whatever you're clutching is important to Jennifer, kindly hand it to her before you make yourself scarce. I'll notify the local chapterhouse to expect your arrival. Don't dawdle, either."

Bertram laid the thirty stones on the table a few inches from

Jennifer's right elbow and scurried out of the pavilion like the rat she was sure he was.

Jennifer beamed. "Thank you, Declan." Then, her grin turned utterly evil. "You should send him to work directly with Dad for a while."

For several moments, Declan made no reply, verbal or otherwise. Finally, he slowly shook his head side to side. "No... I don't really think that idea is very wise."

"Oh, come on... it would be very fun to watch."

His expression suggested she didn't sway him in the slightest. "Jennifer... just because a given course of action would be fun to watch does not preclude it from being unwise. Not to mention detrimental to the poor man's life expectancy."

"Ha! So, you know how Dad would react to him, too!"

Declan sighed. "Jennifer, I know your father rather well at this point, and I hold an enormous amount of respect for you. You literally cannot fathom the sheer weight of even his simple day-to-day decisions. Yes... Bertram has a reputation for being a boot-licking fop, and neither you nor I are the only people who believe that reputation is well-earned. But that doesn't preclude him from being a valued Wraith; it simply means that we are very careful about what assignments we give him."

"I trust you will make certain the appropriate people know I am less than pleased with his time with me. I am happy to speak to anyone you like if it will help drive the point home."

Declan gave her a rather rueful smile. "Young lady, I give you my word that *no one* will be surprised he survived only because you called me first. I wouldn't be surprised but what calling me stymied someone's plan to remove him from the organization, but that's a question for me to look into. I'll have a replacement for dear Bertram at your location by tomorrow morning. Will there be anything else?"

Jennifer beamed again. "No... thank you, Declan."

"Thank you, Jennifer."

Jennifer invoked a Word of Tutation, "*Rhosed*," to cancel both scrying spheres.

Almost the exact same moment her scrying sphere vanished, Shara stepped up to the entrance to the pavilion. Jennifer smiled and waved for her to enter.

As she did so, Shara made a point of obviously looking all around. "I don't see your new liaison anywhere. Did you give him a job so soon?"

Jennifer snorted a derision-laded laugh. "I had a quick word with Declan via scrying spheres, and we reached the conclusion that if the Wraiths wanted to continue to enjoy whatever expertise Bertram brings to the organization, he should stay as far away from me and Dad as possible. For some reason, Declan thought sending Bertram to work directly with Dad might have a detrimental effect on the man's life expectancy."

"I sneaked a glance inside before you created the scrying spheres, and I daresay his life hung by a thread with you, too."

Jennifer curled her fingers to mimic claws. "I *despise* ass-kissers, Shara. I don't have the words for how much I don't like them. Why did you let him take over for you?"

Shara regarded her in silence for several moments, then asked, "Honestly?"

"Well, yeah. Of course, honestly."

"One of the others had started a betting pool over how long he'd survive before you killed him, and I wanted in on it."

Jennifer sat in silence for several moments as she considered that. Finally, she shrugged. "As good a reason as any, I suppose."

CHAPTER 25

With Bertram handled, Jennifer turned her attention back to her sketches. She *thought* her design should work, but it might require a bit of trial and error before it did. After all, she'd never had the opportunity to hold one of the Speaking Stones, which meant in turn that she had no way to judge the effect imbued in them.

That was something else her dad had casually mentioned that blew her mind. Apparently, wizards could use their *skathos* to almost 'read' items imbued with power and get a sense of how to duplicate them. These knock-off Speaking Stones would be her first attempt at that.

She didn't doubt that she'd succeed. How many attempts she'd need *before* she succeeded was the question.

Her dad also told her that the Speaking Stones were crystals. Did they need to be crystals to do what they did? Her instinct said 'no.' But if that was true, why did they look like crystals then? Was it merely aesthetics?

"I'm sure they're sorry for doing whatever those drawings did to provoke such a frown."

Shara's remark pulled Jennifer out of her thoughts, and a small smile curled her lips as she shifted her attention to the Wraith. "Oh, you are, are you?"

"Undoubtedly. If a wizard of House Kirloth frowned at me like you were just frowning at those sketches, I'd be on my knees, begging for forgiveness, faster than you could blink."

Though Shara delivered her words with an open, unfettered smile, all Jennifer heard was the implied threat that she and her father posed to anyone around her. Jennifer's smile died a sudden and not-quite-painless death.

Shara moved to sit in the chair at Jennifer's elbow. "Please, tell me what I said that ruined your smile. I was trying for a joke, and I thought I'd succeeded."

Jennifer pursed her lips and turned to look at the tabletop a few moments before she sighed, then turned back to Shara. "I don't like how everyone's immediate, gut reaction around me and my dad is fear. In some cases, abject terror. I never wanted people to be afraid of me."

Shara offered her a soft, consoling smile. "I understand, and your father openly said the same thing... at first. I suspect he simply stopped saying it instead of no longer feeling that way. The unfortunate situation is that there's nothing you can do about your House's reputation. It might as well be carved in stone that's protected from weathering and damage. Your father's mentor built it in the blood and bone and flesh of many, many foes."

"He did?"

"Oh, yes. When people speak of Kirloth in terrified whispers... more often than not... they mean your father's mentor. *He* was the most fearsome, implacable force in the world for over six thousand years, and he did it all outside the public view. Your father has... carried on the legacy, if not the extreme ruthlessness. When your father ended slavery, something on the order of three thousand people fell over dead, branded as if they themselves had tried branding your father."

Jennifer frowned. "He never told me about that. What happened?"

"Well... would you believe that your father's mentor originated the brands?" Jennifer gasped as her eyes shot wide, and Shara nodded as she continued. "I don't have all the particulars, but I do know that the slave brands did not work until the man your father knew as Marcus provided the answer. Based on a few things your father has said, it sounds as though Marcus managed to ritualize a composite effect."

Shara paused and waited for Jennifer's reaction... which never came. "I... well, frankly, I expected more of a reaction."

Jennifer looked away as she blushed. "I'm not all that advanced in my studies yet. I know the basics, and Dad says I know enough about what to do versus what *not* to do to study on my own, but that didn't really mean much to me."

"I... see. So, you are aware of and understand composite effects, yes?"

"Oh, sure. Dad taught me about them. Using two or more Words of Power to accomplish something a single Word couldn't."

Shara smiled. "Yes, that's exactly right. Which means that the person doing it *must* be a wizard... or a true arcanist, as the ancient histories call them."

"Oh, yeah... of course."

"Anyone can perform a ritual and bring about its intended result. After returning from the Refugee World, your father has been over-heard to call them the vending machines of magic."

And Marcus ritualized... all at once, the sheer scope of the man's mastery flared bright in Jennifer's mind.

"Ah, yes... now, you understand."

"How did he do it? Does Dad know?"

Shara shrugged. "If he does, he hasn't shared that knowledge. Of course... if he does, I can't exactly blame him for keeping it close. I can think of all manner of nefarious uses such knowledge could have, especially if the process is relatively simple. Fortunately, magic has been waning for so long in this world that most modern wizards are little more than empowered mages. They don't understand the Words of Power... if they even know them. Any one of your father's closest friends—the Apprentices, as they're called even yet—could obliterate whole tens of other wizards."

"I didn't think Lillian or Mariana or Wynn or Braden felt that powerful when I've met them."

"Raw power is only *part* of the equation," Shara countered. "The crucial difference is that *they*—those four the world calls the Apprentices—received training from one trained in the Words of Power. Master-level knowledge will go a long way to equalizing a power imbalance... but... it also helps that wizards of the Great Houses of Tel have traditionally been more powerful than most."

Jennifer smiled. "Oh... I'm sure that absolutely does help. But I see what you mean. Marcus trained Dad, and he in turn trained Lillian and the others. From a few things Dad said while he was back home, he thought Wynn really came into his own with the second group of apprentices."

"I don't know anything about that, I'm afraid. It has not been part of the documents we have. Declan might know."

"I've bothered him enough lately. He probably feels frustrated simply thinking about me."

Shara merely shrugged.

The conversation didn't seem to have anywhere else to go for the moment, so Jennifer worked to bring her mind back around to what she wanted to achieve with the stones. Shara seemed to understand the change in her focus, and she moved to stand.

"You don't need to leave or even stand... unless you just want to," Jennifer countered.

"I am supposed to be your guard, Milady. Guards do not sit."

Jennifer turned back to look Shara squarely in her eyes. "My name, Shara, is Jennifer."

"Yes, Milady, and it's a pretty name." Shara's expression most resembled what her dad could've called a shit-eating grin.

Jennifer gave her a resigned sigh and turned back to the papers, not saying a word when Shara moved to stand about six feet away from her right side. The design looked ready and one-hundred-percent workable, but there was really only one way to find out.

"You ready to duck if this goes bad?" Jennifer asked, not even looking toward Shara.

"Of course, Milady." Jennifer didn't **need** to look to know the imp grinned over her continued refusal to use Jennifer's name. Ah, well... at least it was better than Bertram. A stray thought still argued that she should have given him some kind of reminder that he'd earned her displeasure.

Resisting the urge to growl, Jennifer closed her eyes and marshaled her thoughts. Clear mind. Certain, unwavering intent. A couple deep, relaxing breaths... and she retrieved one of the stones from the tabletop.

One last calming breath, and she invoked her composite effect, using Words of Transmutation, Divination, and Conjuration, "*Rhyskaal-Klaepos-Gozdrahk.*"

Her power slammed into the ambient, creating the most vicious and potent resonance she'd felt thus far. At almost the exact same time, a bright, kaleidoscopic radiance shrouded the stone she held, and she *felt* it change according to her will.

A deep sense of awe and wonder filled her soul. No matter how many times she used the power that was her birthright, each and every time still felt as joyous as the first. Did her dad feel like that? She'd have to ask him sometime.

The bright light around her hand faded, revealing a cylindrical and clear crystal that looked like someone had joined two pyramids based on isosceles triangles by pressing their bases together. The crystal held uneven lines in its imperfect pyramids, making it look more naturally formed than shaped by hand. Her *skathos* informed her that the crystal held not just power but also her desired effects that would use said power. She rolled it around in her hand for a moment, then absently tossed it toward Shara.

"What do you think?" she asked as her Wraith scrambled to catch the crystal before it struck the ground.

"I think you should not so casually throw around priceless artifacts."

Jennifer snorted a laugh. "It's not old enough to be an artifact...

234 ROBERT M. KERNS

but otherwise... what do you think?"

"Without another, it's impossible to gauge how successful you were beyond creating a pretty prismatic crystal."

"Excellent point, my shadow. One moment..."

Another invocation later—this one sapping her resilience and leaving her a tad winded—she held another crystal. She concentrated on the crystal and felt that Shara held another one.

"Well... I can tell you hold that one. Jog to the other side of the camp, and let's see if we can talk."

Without a word, Shara set out. As she left the pavilion, she snapped her fingers, and two of the original four Wraiths moved to occupy either corner behind Jennifer.

So much for having a few moments alone...

It wasn't long at all until the crystal in Jennifer's hand warmed to a pleasant temperature, and Shara's voice filled the pavilion, "Milady, can you hear me?"

Jennifer grinned and focused on the crystal in her hand as she said, "Ain't any nobility here, lady. This is just plain ol' Jennifer."

"Hmmm... perhaps I have the wrong crystal. Or perhaps you're the maid?"

It took all of her willpower to keep from blowing a raspberry and hoping the crystal communicated it. "I'd say the crystals work. Come on back. Only twenty-eight more to go."

* * *

THE PASSAGE OF THREE WEEKS—PLUS or minus a day or three—found Gavin at his desk in his office in the Citadel. All manner of documents littered the desktop, and he leaned back in his seat and rubbed his eyes. It seemed like he'd been staring at reports and readiness numbers for all of his life... even though he'd only received the current stack that morning. He was tired. No... exhausted. The past several weeks had been an exercise in herding cats to keep all the members of the Old Alliance pulling together to be ready somewhen *close* to that mythical standard called 'on time.'

One of the preparations over the last few weeks he was exceedingly proud of was invoking a region-wide block on scrying. It was the better part of two thousand square miles in area, and it was positioned so that the edge of it was no more than a hundred feet or so away from Skullkeep. He left an opening in the block for the College grounds, since the instructors used the College as the target for the students' early attempts at scrying, but the only reason he knew to do that was a conversation with Valera that sprung up from a stray comment he made about the scrying block.

The colder temperatures were coming, and it was futile to resist the turning of the seasons. And winter only favored their opponent, because the bulk of Skullkeep's forces were largely indifferent to the environment... at least in terms of weather and such. It didn't matter to a zombie, animated skeleton, ghoul, or flesh golem what the weather was like. Cold. Raining. Hot. None of that affected them. Now... the far extremes? Absolutely. Zombies, Ghouls, flesh golems—well, anything except skeletons, pretty much—would burn just as well as anything else. Surrounding any undead in ice would affect its mobility but wouldn't really harm it much... if at all. Acid would affect them... but it would also hamper the Old Alliance's forces, too.

The absolute best way to counteract undead was through clerics, especially an order like the Warpriests of Tel, and Gavin was very grateful that his friend Ovir had placed the full resources of the Church of Valthon behind Gavin's effort to reclaim Skullkeep.

If he was being totally honest with himself, Gavin wanted no part of another military campaign. The closest to such a thing he'd ever come was way back when he first woke up in Drakmoor. He and his friends had basically swiped several units from the Army of Tel to defeat a plot to destabilize and 'conquer' the Society of the Arcane. Oh, sure... 'swiping' those Army units had been totally legal and aboveboard, because the Great Houses of Tel were so intertwined with the civil government of the Kingdom, but he still hadn't enjoyed having to do it.

Ideally, Gavin could just travel to Skullkeep and have a talk with the Necromancer, find out what motivated him and what he really wanted, and establish some kind of working agreement. The huge, huge problem with that was Gavin wasn't sure he could trust the ancient lich. He had fully vetted proof that the Necromancer had suborned the royal family of Tel. He had vetted proof that the Necromancer was behind the attempted civil war in Vushaar. There was no way to know what kind of schemes and plans and who knew what else the bag of bones actively pursued... or had already completed or achieved.

If it was something so simple as a desire for power driving him, then... sure... use whatever force was necessary to secure the Old Alliance. But what if it wasn't? What if all of the Necromancer's machinations didn't aim for making him The Great and Powerful Ruler of All He Surveyed?

That line of thought—more than anything else—had kept Gavin up at night.

And he couldn't forget that Lornithar and his Lornithrasa were still out there doing... well... whatever it was they were doing. The Void Scar on his forearm had shrunk down to a line no thicker than fine thread while he was on Earth, and ever since he'd created a channel for the ambient power to basically equalize itself between Earth and Drakmoor, it hadn't really given him much trouble at all.

He still fought back a shudder as he remembered what it had felt like to push through it just for his day-to-day living, not to mention anything more. Checking it every morning within minutes of waking up had become a habit at this point... and a habit that Kiri did *not* appreciate. Maybe one day, he'd be able to put it out of his mind, but every so often, it was almost like he sensed a connection to something *through* the Void Scar.

He had never spoken of that to anyone... not even Kiri. Maybe he should have. No. He probably should have. But he just couldn't bring himself to do it. Once he was free of the responsibilities of the Archmagister, he could turn his attention to researching the Void Scars... and everything else on his list of projects.

He heaved a sigh as he closed his eyes and rubbed his face. The fact that he was woolgathering so much showed how mentally fatigued he was. Maybe a break from all this was in order.

"Hartley!"

The Citadel's spectral majordomo faded into existence at the side of Gavin's desk. "You bellowed, Milord?"

Gavin gave the ghost a flat look atop silence for a moment, but it was all part of the game they had evolved between them. "I think I need to take a break for an hour or three. I'm going to visit the Foundry for a little bit, and then, I think I'll go to Vushaar to see Kiri. Don't wait up. Worst case, I'll be back in the morning."

"Very good, Milord. You've looked a little wan, the last few days. Some sun—or at least heat from a smith's forge—will do you good."

If he could've managed it without Hartley knowing in advance what he was doing, Gavin totally would've invoked an effect that let him pat the spectre on his head. It would've been an escalation of their game, but Hartley's expression the first time he did it would've been worth the majordomo's eventual response.

"Right, then... you know how to find me if something arises that absolutely, positively cannot wait until tomorrow. Otherwise, don't have too raucous a party while I'm gone."

Hartley replied with a wry expression. "As if we'd ever let you know how raucous our parties are..."

Gavin laughed. "Good one! I'm going to nip up to my room and pack a small satchel, then I'll head out. You need anything from me before I go?"

"No, Milord. It's good that you're taking the time. A number of us in the staff have been... well, not worried. Perhaps concerned?'

"Thanks, Hartley. You know you're always welcome to address these things with me, right?"

The ghost gave a single, certain nod. It was almost a mini-bow. "Of course, Milord. Earlier today, I promised the staff to mention it tomorrow, but you have removed the need for such. Safe and happy travels, Milord!"

Gavin thanked him again and left his study to pack an overnight bag.

CHAPTER 26

Gavin stepped through his gateway, entering the Foundry's courtyard. All three blacksmith workshops seemed to be working full-bore... at least based on how much smoke fled the chimneys. Moments later, the sounds of steady hammering reached his ears, and he smiled when he saw Braden and Torgas—the Foundry's master smith—exit one of the forge buildings.

They met each other about halfway between where Gavin's gateway had delivered him and the forge building, and Braden was quick to offer a handshake underneath a big smile. Of course... with Braden's stature, nothing he did was 'small.'

"Braden... good to see you." Gavin turned to Torgas. "Good to see you as well, sir."

"Come to check up on us, have ye?" the master smith growled, though the twinkle in his eyes belied his gruff tone.

"Oh, good sir... I would never presume to check up on you. Check *down*, maybe, but never *up*."

The master smith's expression did not look kind... not at all... but once again, his amusement shone in his eyes. He pivoted on his heel and stomped back to the first forge building, muttering something about bastard arcanists having no respect for craftsmen.

Braden and Gavin both shared a laugh as they fell in behind Torgas. Gavin glanced to him as they walked, "So... how is everything going?"

"It's going well, Milord." Gavin tried not to wince at 'Milord.' "We will start cycling soldiers through for their equipment... well... I think sometime this week. Based on the numbers we've received from all the alliance members, we have fifty percent over the number we'd need. Master Torgas said we should plan for a certain amount of breakage, especially in the arrows and quarrels, but I personally disagree with him. I think the effects we're imbuing into the gear will only improve the durability. At least, I hope so. As a 'just in case,' like you enjoy saying, we rigged up a lesser-quality sword that I imbued and then broke the blade. We did it out in the field, a solid hundred yards or more beyond the Foundry's wall. When we executed the test, the explosion resulting from breaking the blade was... a bit impressive."

A frown took over his expression as Gavin stopped and turned to Braden. "Just how big a rock did you have to use to break one of the imbued blades?"

"A big one. We should probably call it a boulder instead of a rock, honestly. It was closer to a box shape than a sphere and about eight feet square. We don't know what happened to the rock. The explosion either vaporized it or threw it gods know where. It certainly didn't come down anywhere within five miles of the Foundry. I gave up scrying at that point."

Gavin considered the matter for a moment and ultimately shrugged. "Fair enough, and I agree with you. I personally don't expect we'll have to worry about breakage, but maybe we should adjust the imbued effects to account for it... just in case."

Braden closed his eyes and groaned. "Do you have any idea how much imbued equipment we have? That would definitely push the timetable back several days... if not *weeks*. Maybe even months."

"Ouch. I love that you've put all this time to good use, but damn. Okay. Keep on keeping on as you are. I'll discuss the matter with Kiri and Terris after I leave here. See what they think about how we should handle it." Gavin stopped and turned to face the closed gate as if he could look through the solid stone to see their testing site. "Damn, Braden... you don't do things halfway, do you?"

The first true Artificer in over a thousand years replied with a huge grin. "Nope! But then again, I learned from the best."

* * *

AFTER ALLOWING Torgas to conduct him on a brief tour of the Foundry—including the strong-houses that stored the imbued equipment—Gavin congratulated them on jobs well done and bade them farewell. Returning to an area just inside the Foundry's wall and outside the traffic pattern, he invoked a Word of Transmutation, "*Paedryx*," opening a gateway to the palace courtyard in Vushaar.

He stepped through the gateway and smiled at seeing the Cavaliers around the courtyard relax. It wasn't the first time he'd arrived in the palace complex this way, but he couldn't fault their professionalism. While odds highly favored a sudden gateway heralded his return to visit Kiri and Terris, such was not guaranteed, and a heightened level of awareness and readiness was appropriate. He made a mental note to have a word with the commander overseeing palace security, because so few people ever said 'thanks' or 'good job.'

The Vushaari palace was old hat by now, and he knew his way around the structure that served as both the Royal Residence as well as the kingdom's primary administration center far better than he once did. Still... given the hour, his wife and Terris could be in any one of a half-dozen places. Depending on their agenda, the list possibilities could be as long as a dozen.

Fortunately, he encountered Varne—the Royal Herald—in the Grand Salon as he went to check the throne room first.

"Ah, Milord Archmagister," Varne greeted him, bowing deeply at the waist. "It is a great pleasure to have you with us again."

Gavin smiled as he responded to the bow with a nod. "It's good to see you, too, Varne. And nice to know you're still adept at slinging the bull."

Varne grinned. "Oh, dear me, Milord. I would never..."

Gavin and Varne both knew very well just how far the herald went in his efforts to safeguard the fragile egos of the Vushaari nobility, but Gavin simply smiled and held his silence... on that topic, anyway. "So, Varne... if I were of a mind to say hello to my wife, where would you suggest I go?"

At that question, Varne's expression became slightly circumspect. The herald pursed his lips and looked away. Gavin did not like that reaction *at all*.

"All right, Varne. Out with it. What's going on?"

"Ah... uhm... well, I'm not sure I should say, Milord. I know how much you respect your allies' autonomy and never want to interfere in messy, internal matters."

It took all Gavin's willpower to keep from rolling his eyes. "Oh, come on, Varne. Now, I know you're slinging the bull, because I clearly remember standing on the northern ramparts of the city's wall and electrocuting a rather large number of the soldiers besieging the city a couple years back. If I truly didn't 'want to interfere in messy, internal matters'—as you put it—why didn't I just drop off Kiri and teleport my people straight back to Tel Mivar? Have an answer for that one, hmmm?"

Varne's shoulders slumped as he winced. "Yes... right... not the best evasion there, was it? So, there's a bit of a flap involving a few middle-tier noble families. They feel as though Fallon went outside his authority when he not only refused to accept their children as apprentices but went on to send letters to the nearest Arcane Academies—as well as the College of the Arcane—that they were unsuitable candidates. His Majesty and Her Highness are currently hearing the matter in the throne room."

"I wonder why Fallon didn't contact me about this. It clearly touches on the purview of the Society of the Arcane. Well... I was already heading to the throne room, anyway."

Varne valiantly endeavored to hide a wince as Gavin clapped him on the shoulder and set off down the corridor.

· · ·

WHEN GAVIN APPROACHED the closed doors that led to the throne room, the Cavaliers posted to either side of the doors as well as across the hallway from the doors snapped to attention. He smiled in greeting to them and pointed at the doors.

"I hear my wife is inside. Any issue if I pop in to say hi?"

The Cavaliers all shared a look, and the senior-most—an older man of moderate years with weathered skin and collection of scars—snorted a laugh. "Not at all, Milord... and a damn shame it is that we can't follow you in to watch."

Without another word, the grizzled veteran heaved his door open, and Gavin didn't miss a step as he angled to it and walked right in.

The throne room of the Vushaari royal family hadn't changed much since he'd seen it last, but then again, it had only been a couple months. He still smiled at seeing the Mivar Crest worked into the floor as a mosaic of covered tiles, but while it was true artistry, what honestly provoked the warm regard was seeing the Glyph of House Muran almost hidden in the mosaic's design.

A cluster of people stood not too far from the raised dais where Kiri and her father sat. Fallon stood just off the dais at the King's left hand, and the Royal Scribe who recorded all matters of the court sat at a small table with stacks of blank parchment, several quills and pots of ink, and a shorter stack of parchment that held writing. Four Cavaliers stood against the wall on either side of the raised dais. Gavin saw Kiri's and Terris's expressions brighten at the sight of him walking through the door, and even Fallon himself let slip a tiny, fleeting smile.

The gallery section of the throne room that provided seating petitioners and anyone else who chose to visit the Royal Court was empty. It didn't even have any empty chairs. Huh... he didn't realize that the palace staff trotted out the seating for the days Terris held court and squirreled it away somewhere for the rest of the time. On one hand, it kinda made sense, but on the other, it seemed inefficient.

"Good day to you, Milord," Terris said, as Gavin neared the dais. "It is a pleasure to have you with Us... as always."

"It's always a pleasure to be here, Terris. Hi, sweetheart. You two seem a bit busy. I could amuse myself in your Archives until you and Kiri finish this."

Kiri gave him a small smile in recognition. Given the gravitas of the situation, he figured that was the best he could hope for. After all, she'd probably have an unkind word or two for him if he swept her off what was once her mother's throne and dipped her with a long, slow kiss.

Terris didn't even bat an eye at Gavin's use of his first name, even though a couple members of the group before the dais seemed a tad scandalized. "Milord, We would never presume to tell the last of the Divine Emissaries how they should spend their time, but it just so happens that the matter before Us touches upon your authority as head of the Society of the Arcane. Might We impose upon you to hear the matter with Us and advise on its dispensation?"

"Of course, Terris. I'm always happy to help." Gavin snapped his fingers as he invoked a Word of Conjuration, "*Thyphos.*"

If any wizards had been present, the raw, savage force of Gavin's power striking the ambient would've driven them to their knees. A padded chair that appeared to be made of mahogany winked into existence between Fallon and the Royal Scribe. Gavin approached it and sat. He looked all around as he asked, "So... what have I missed?"

"The matter before Us is the assertion by these nobles that the Court Wizard's response to their request to take their children as apprentices and subsequent conduct constituted gross insult to their noble lines. They are—frankly—demanding We strip the Court Wizard of his position and imprison him for a period of time."

"Well, now... that's rather serious." Gavin frowned and turned to regard the Court Wizard. "Fallon, what's your side of all this?"

The man in question moved so that Kiri and Terris could see him as he responded to Gavin's question. "Their children are unsuitable for admission into the Society of the Arcane, Milord. When the families said they'd go 'above me' to have their children admitted to the College in Tel Mivar, I made the point of penning a missive to the Admissions office there, detailing my objections to them."

Now, *that* jogged Gavin's memory. "Hang on... I remember seeing something cross my desk from the Admissions office. They kicked the can up to Valera, and she felt—due to the political nature of it—that she should pass it up to me." He smiled when he finally recalled his response.

One of the parents apparently didn't appreciate being kept waiting. He was a bull of a man, barrel-chested with fiery red hair and beard. "Well? If it crossed your desk, then surely you approved it. Why haven't we been informed?"

Gavin's smile grew to a chuckle, and Fallon, Kiri, and Terris *all* recognized that chuckle. It wasn't due to mirth or commiseration. Not at all. "I was very clear in my response that I trust Fallon's judgment and offered to burn the documents for the Admissions office if they were low on lamp oil."

He thought he heard the delicate sound his wife made when she tried to contain sudden amusement. It sounded like a mix of a cough and a snort that was muffled by a heavy curtain.

For himself, Gavin leaned back against his seat and regarded the man with an insouciant expression while he awaited a response. Some might have thought that he specifically phrased his answer the way he did to get a rise out of the nobles in front of him, and they'd be well within their rights to do so... especially if they had any experience with Gavin whatsoever.

But the simple fact was that such was not the case. Those documents arrived on his desk while he was working on the preparations for the Skullkeep campaign, and quite frankly, he felt they were not of sufficient importance to warrant diverting his attention. *That* was why he responded to those documents in the way he did. Curiously enough, the Admissions office didn't take him up on his offer to burn them, though.

"You dare insult us to our faces?" the nobleman veritably roared. "I demand—"

Gavin invoked a Word of Transmutation, "*Rhyskaal*," and the man silenced. Funnily enough, he kept right on talking for a heartbeat or two before he realized that he wasn't making any sound.

"Don't worry," Gavin said. "I altered the air around you for a short time—until I change it back, really—so that it doesn't transmit sound. See... I think you're operating under at least one fairly major misunderstanding, and before we can move forward, I think we need to clear it up. The God of Magic *asked* me to take up the mantle of Archmagister, and part of me really wants to know what gives you the right or authority to demand *anything* from me. But really... at the end of the day, I just don't give a damn.

"I don't even remember the full content of those documents regarding your children. Not to put too fine a point on it... but there was absolutely no reason the matter should have ever come to my attention. A member in good standing filed documentation that he believes your children are unsuitable for the Society, and given the sheer number of papers involved, I feel he included more than sufficient justification for his statement.

"But! I value Tel's alliance with Vushaar. I value people in general. And I'm always open to the possibility that I might be wrong. Fallon, are you willing to swear to me on your life that I will agree with and support your conduct in this matter?"

Fallon lowered his eyes to floor and held his silence for several heartbeats before making eye contact with Gavin once more. "Yes, Milord, I am."

Gavin turned back to the nobility. "Well, you just heard how certain he is of his conclusion. Tell you what... I'll make you this offer. I am willing to conduct my own investigation into the matter right now. If I find that Fallon acted precipitously and sullied the honor of the Society, he will not leave this throne room alive. *However*... if I uphold his conclusion that your children are unfit, I will forever ban your entire *families* from ever joining the Society, because—in that case—you've wasted our time with a load of utter horseshit. I can't say that I appreciate that. So... speak."

Gavin snapped his fingers once more as he reached out with his *skathos* to sever the tiny tendril of power fueling the Transmutation of the air around the nobleman.

The incensed nobleman opened his mouth and took a deep breath to speak, but one of the other noblemen grabbed his arm. The new fellow was shorter and wiry; he reminded Gavin of Wynn Roshan in a lot of ways, except he didn't seem to have Wynn's boundless energy.

"Stop," the man said as he grabbed the fiery nobleman's elbow, then looked to us. "Milord, Your Majesty, Your Highness... may we discuss this unexpected offer before we respond?"

Both Kiri and Terris looked to Gavin, clearly suggesting he should answer.

Gavin shrugged. "I have no problem with that, but be aware that this is not a piecemeal endeavor. Whatever you decide, it will affect *all* of you."

A couple of the noblewomen didn't seem to like that thought *at all*, and they led the group to the far side of the throne room where they conversed in hushed tones. Gavin leaned back against his seat, casually draping his right leg over the right armrest of the chair while he waited. He wanted to ask Fallon how he'd been and see if he was enjoying his latest round of apprentices, but even though he himself didn't really care, he didn't want an appearance of favoritism on his part to adversely affect Terris and Kiri in the future with these people.

But then again... if they were the types to try this kind of chicanery, they would probably cause Terris and Kiri issues regardless. So, he raised his finger to get Fallon's attention and then motioned for him to step closer. The Vushaari Court Wizard did so, leaning close.

"Yes, Milord?" his voice was little more than a whisper.

"So, I didn't read the papers at the time, and honestly, it's not like I don't have other things on my mind. Give me the skinny on the situation. What's the deal?"

Fallon smirked. "I could give you any number of reasons that would make you loathe the thought of *any* members of those families *ever* joining the Society, but this one tops them all. The children only want to become mages to gain more power... to better control and exploit their families' holdings."

"You don't say..." Gavin remarked, as his expression became somewhat stony.

"Oh, but I do say, Milord."

"Thanks. If they're dumb enough to accept my offer, at least I know where to dig to end this farce quickly."

Fallon nodded and returned to his previous place.

It wasn't too much longer before the families returned. Gavin noticed that the women—presumably the mothers—didn't seem all that happy, and he wondered what was about to happen.

"Milord," the wiry nobleman said, "we have decided that we accept your offer. We feel confident you will see our side of things if you take but a few moments to investigate for yourself."

Idiots. It took all Gavin's willpower to keep from laughing out loud. Yeah... this wasn't going to go how they expected or wanted.

"Alrighty, then," Gavin said. "Let's move this right along. Parents, I want you to step off to one side and give your children some space. I will question them directly."

The fiery nobleman was quick to interrupt. "Now, see here! We are their—"

Gavin eyed the man with a glare. "You can be silent, or I will silence you. Either way, you *will* comply. You've accepted my offer. At that point, your part in this ended."

The wiry guy saved his fellow nobleman by taking his elbow again and pulling him off to the side as everyone else complied with Gavin's instructions. As soon as there was a good ten feet between the noble children—well, teenagers, really—and their parents, Gavin invoked a Word of Divination, "*Klaepos.*"

Each child acquired their own gray aura.

"All right, kids. I've invoked an effect that will duplicate the spell Divination of Truth. That's the gray aura you all have now. When you tell the truth, the aura will become bright, pure white... but if you lie, the aura will become an angry, malicious red. So... one of you step forward, so we can begin."

The four children all looked to one another, and it was clear that none of them wanted to step forward. In an excellent display of what Gavin had come to expect from Drakmoor's noble classes, three of the four simply took a step back... throwing their associate under the bus, so to speak.

"Don't think that nominating your friend—or perhaps *former* friend—will get you out of this," Gavin remarked and then focused on the young man now closest to him. "So, young man... why do you want to become a mage?"

"I've always loved the Art, and I would love nothing more than to study it the rest of my life." The gray aura around him shifted to an angry, malevolent red.

"Uh oh... you just lied to me. Not exactly a good start. Let's try this again. Is a desire for power the greatest reason you want to become a mage?"

"No, I—" His aura became an even angrier red. Frankly, that surprised Gavin a bit.

"Whoops... another lie. Let's speed this up a bit." Gavin pointed to each of the remaining children in turn and asked them the same question. The sole daughter surprised him by answering truthfully with a 'yes.'

Gavin motioned for the daughter to step closer and asked, "And just how would you use the power once you're a mage?"

"I'd defend my parents from all the ungrateful malcontents who think we owe them something. Our lands are just that... ours. If they don't like our terms for working our lands, they can leave, and I'd be happy to send them on their way."

Again, the spell's aura around her was a bright, pure white.

Gavin sighed and turned to the waiting parents. "It is my judgment that you will submit the names of your families and your families' heraldry so that I may include them in the registry of those lines banned from the Society's ranks for all time. The Art—what most people call magic—is a tool, yes. It is neither good nor evil. But at the same time, I certainly don't ever want to see it used to oppress those who cannot defend against it."

The families tried to wind up for protests or maybe rants, but Gavin didn't care. Whoever said discretion was the better part of valor didn't know the half of it. He felt a rather strong urge to go all 'Kirloth' on these people, but he didn't want to make a mess in Terris's throne room. Besides, if he killed them here, it would be more difficult for the Wraiths to investigate them and their associates.

He stood and dispelled the conjured chair, going to each family present and getting their respective names and heraldry, which he copied onto conjured parchment. He'd copy it from the conjured parchment to real parchment before the conjuring dissipated.

Once he had the information he needed, he turned to his father-in-law and gestured to the families, saying, "Terris, they're all yours."

Terris didn't seem overly comforted by that.

CHAPTER 27

Gavin sighed as he exited the throne room. He really should be used to people trying to use the Art as a fast path to power... even though the mage path wasn't all that fast from what little he'd learned wearing the gold robe. The whole business left a sour taste in his mouth, and he didn't understand why Terris still "went to work" each day.

No... that wasn't true or fair. Thinking over his tenure as Archmagister, he knew *exactly* why Terris did what he did. He was probably afraid of what the family who came after his would do. And it wasn't that Gavin thought the Muran line was some kind of family of saints, either. One of Marcus's journals—one that he would never allow Kiri to read—described in exacting (almost gratuitous) detail about a Muran king somewhen around the third century post-Godswar that he'd had the Wraiths kill... simply because he was *that* bad for the kingdom. The daughter who took throne upon her father's 'most unfortunate and untimely' death, though, was exceptionally competent by all accounts, and Vushaar entered something of a golden age that lasted at least two monarchs past her death.

He sighed again and opened his eyes, only to find the Cavaliers warily eyeing him. He couldn't resist a chuckle.

"Sorry, folks... that was some nasty business in there. I'll just be going now and wait for my wife in the residence."

Gavin was about ten steps down the hall when he heard a voice behind him ask, "Should we alert anyone for clean-up, Milord?"

Gavin wasn't sure whether to sigh or grin. He turned back to the Cavaliers and shook his head. "No need. They'll leave under their own power."

With that, he turned and headed off in search of one of the Wraiths who worked a servant job in the palace. He wasn't *quite* sure which job, but he figured it couldn't be *that* hard to find them.

IN THE END, Gavin resorted to a divination that provided the location of all the Wraiths in the palace, and the actual number of them actually surprised him. He hadn't realized they had so many people in the palace. He chose the closest one and went there, asking her to alert the local network to their new tasking. He almost instructed them to send the report to both him *and* Kiri, but he wanted to see what they turned up first... if anything. He didn't want to prejudice Kiri and her father against those families from the standpoint that he'd felt they required investigating if the only thing the Wraiths uncovered was that they were rich, snobbish, and self-absorbed... which was pretty much the norm for most nobles from what he'd seen. Terris struck him as a rarity in that he truly *cared* about doing the best job he could for all the people of Vushaar.

* * *

GAVIN SAT in the family room of the palace's residence. It was more of a parlor or sitting room with a plush area rug covering most of the stone floor and several pieces of furniture. A fireplace occupied one wall, and the exquisitely crafted armchairs and sofas all angled to face it. Several open windows allowed the air to circulate through the room, and he had to admit that they kept the room a mostly comfortable temperature.

Or maybe he was just accustomed to the lack of air conditioning after the all the time he'd spent in Drakmoor...

He wasn't sure which, and beyond that, he honestly wasn't sure it mattered all that much. He wasn't sure how long he'd be waiting for Kiri and her father to arrive, but they knew he was here, so he suspected Kiri would marshal things along in a bit of a hurry. They hadn't seen much of each other since the preparations for the Skull-keep campaign really ramped up.

Gavin gave the inactive fireplace a thousand-yard stare as he considered that the end of his tenure as Archmagister was within reach, figuratively speaking. Like his mentor before him, he would step down and pass the gold robe to someone else. Someone—in this case—more suited to building a stable society. Someone more suited to the polite give and take of political discourse.

He'd read the reports of how Lillian had really stepped up during his unintended sojourn to Earth, and he'd also spoken with Nathrac about her as well. Both the reports and the conversations all pointed to Lillian Mivar being the Archmagister that Tel and the Old Alliance truly needed, now that the royal family was dealt with, Tel's Constitution amended, and the Necromancer soon to be just a footnote in history.

He chuckled at that thought. His mother would chastise him for counting his chickens before they hatched and—perhaps—rightly so. But he couldn't shake the feeling that this campaign to reclaim Skull-keep was part of why Valthon and Bellos had wanted or needed a wizard of House Kirloth who was 'available,' as the Old Man put it.

It wasn't the *whole* reason. Nowhere close. But it was certainly *a* reason.

Part of him wondered about the rest of the reason, and part of him... well... didn't care all that much. He was alive when he otherwise would've been dead. He had friends and family across two worlds. He had a daughter anyone would be proud to claim, and he had a wife he loved who loved him in return. Never mind that she was fiercely intelligent and would have any runway model on Earth gnashing her teeth in envy.

The door opening pulled Gavin from his thoughts, and he smiled as Kiri led her father into the room. They had taken the time to divest themselves of the suffocating court clothes, and Gavin fought valiantly to keep from grinning at the sight of Kiri in a t-shirt, denim jeans, and sneakers. It seemed his birth world had irrevocably corrupted her.

Kiri walked straight to him and settled into his lap, snuggling close and resting her head on his shoulder as she pressed her forehead against his neck.

"I've missed you so much." Her voice was little more than a whisper... just loud enough for him to hear, really.

"I know. I've missed you, too."

Terris looked on in silence. His eyes seemed to take on a bit of extra moisture, and he turned away to gaze out the window. Gavin started to wonder what the man was thinking, but a sudden suspicion dawned in his mind. The man wished his wife could've lived to see their daughter grow into the wonderful and formidable woman she was. Gavin wasn't certain his mother-in-law would wholly approve of him, but he also doubted she'd fault his ability to protect Kiri.

After all, anyone trying to harm her should pray to whatever god they worshipped that the Cavaliers reached them before Gavin did. He might be giving up the gold robe, but he'd be Kirloth for the rest of his days.

Kiri shifted, and he shifted his attention to find her looking up at him. She seemed curious more than concerned as she asked, "What's on your mind?"

Gavin leaned forward and kissed her forehead before he answered, "Nothing much. Just thinking about how my life has turned out."

"Oh? Decide anything?"

He smiled. "If I had it to do all over again... I wouldn't change a thing, especially anything involving you."

Kiri snuggled closer to him. It almost seemed like she wanted to be physically a part of him. "I don't like you leading the armies to Skullkeep, Gavin. I... I'm afraid for you. I want to be there with you, watch your back, but I can't. I have to be the Crown Princess of Vushaar, and I don't like being pulled in two different directions."

Gavin kissed her forehead as he hugged her close. "It will be okay, Kiri. I promise you that. And yes... preparations are moving into the final stages, but we still have a week or so before we have to leave. Everyone in Tel Mivar knows how to reach me, and there's no reason I can't spend the intervening time with you."

"I'd like that, Gavin. I'd like that very much."

Terris turned back from the window and regarded them, a faint smile curling one side of his mouth. His expression carried all manner of warm undertones, and after another heartbeat or two, he left the family room.

Gavin figured Terris would join them for dinner—or vice versa—and discuss anything that may have been on his mind. If Kiri was aware of her father leaving the family room, she didn't show it.

* * *

ALL TOO SOON, it felt like it was time for Gavin to return to Tel. He didn't want to go. Not really. He'd enjoyed the time he'd spent with Kiri and Terris—*especially* Kiri—and if he didn't have the deep threads of responsibility that pulled him back to Tel Mivar, he probably would've stayed longer. Heh... threads of responsibility... more like *chains*.

But... he already had his transition away from the gold robe worked out with Bellos *and* Lillian. He hoped she hadn't accepted because she felt like she should. He hoped she accepted because it was a challenge she genuinely wanted. He might discuss that concern with Bellos upon his return to Tel Mivar. He didn't want Lillian accepting this albatross solely because he asked her if she wanted it. He could easily see her feeling like she was volun-told instead being presented with a true choice.

As he finished dressing after the bath he assumed Kiri had asked someone to draw for him, Gavin realized it had been a little while since he'd heard from Jennifer about that project she wanted to take off his hands. He knew beyond any doubt that the Wraiths would've informed him if there was a problem. And he also knew beyond any doubt that it would take something fairly significant to be a problem for **thirty** Wraiths. Still... he would've liked to hear from her once in a while. If nothing else, he was still her dad.

That last thought made him chuckle as he pulled on the gold robe that was both an honor **and** an anchor. He hadn't done the best job keeping in touch with **his** parents, so he wasn't exactly in the best position to throw stones at Jennifer.

But soon...

There was so much he was looking forward to doing once he had the free time no longer being Archmagister would allow. At a minimum, he wanted to take Kiri to Earth to visit his folks at least once a month. That would also give him an opportunity to visit with Jennifer... at least assuming she stayed on Earth. He wasn't sure what he thought of the possibility she might want to move to Drakmoor full time. She could certainly make her way in this world, though... no doubt about that. She was more than capable of achieving whatever she decided she truly wanted.

A moderately heavy sigh ended his ruminations, and he glanced at the clock. As long as it was **mostly** accurate, he still had time to say his goodbyes to Kiri and Terris before he'd be interrupting the daily session of court.

* * *

JENNIFER SAT at a small table in what she had come to think of as the command pavilion for the latest camp. The map they had found in the very first camp lay spread out in front of her, and she had to admit feeling a sense of accomplishment at the number of dots she'd crossed off over the past weeks.

They were on the home stretch now. Only camps in eastern Mivar and Cothos provinces remained.

The word among the Wraiths was that the armies of the Old Alliance would soon be moving against Skullkeep, and Jennifer wanted to have as many of these camps cleared as possible before word spread of the victory over the Necromancer.

Yes... some would probably say she was counting her chickens before they hatched, or possibly even tempting fate. But... she just couldn't entertain the possibility her dad might not succeed and come home. She just... couldn't. Horrific nightmares plagued her the one night she'd allowed herself to consider the possibility that the Old Alliance forces might lose, and she came far, far too close to a dark place that she thought she'd put behind her.

Regardless of what she decided about where her future was—whether Earth or Drakmoor—she realized those nightmares represented something buried deep within her that needed to be addressed. Once this business of the camps and Skullkeep and the Necromancer was over, she intended to track down a *very* reputable person in the mental health field and ask if she or he would accept her as a patient.

The clinical psychologist her grandparents had hired to help her when they first brought her home might be a good place to start.

Movement drew her attention, and she looked up to see Shara enter the pavilion. Jennifer smiled her welcome as the woman who'd become a close friend over the past few weeks approached and sat at the corner of the table off her right elbow.

Doing her best to keep her expression warm and welcoming, Jennifer marveled at the change in Shara's demeanor. When they'd first started interacting, she had maintained a ready stance at all times she was around Jennifer. Never once allowed herself to leave the mindset of a professional looking for threats to her charge. But now? She and Jennifer had worked together long enough that Shara knew Jennifer could easily protect the both of them... as long as Shara alerted her to a threat.

All of which meant that Shara now allowed herself to relax in Jennifer's presence... while keeping a wary eye on their surroundings.

The moment Shara relaxed into her seat, she said, "We have received word from the organization."

Jennifer nodded. "Good news, bad news, or no news?"

"The armies have mobilized to re-take Skullkeep. Since we've been expecting that, I'm not sure it qualifies as news, but I thought you'd like to know."

"Yeah, I do. Thanks. Any word on how soon they'll reach Skullkeep?"

Shara shrugged. "Our information is that they opened massive teleportation gateways for each contingent. Everyone arrived at the mouth of Hope's Pass almost instantaneously from wherever their starting points were."

"Good grief! How do they coordinate something like that?"

Now, Shara grinned. "Do you seriously have to ask?"

Duh... of course. Dad and his friends. Or... as the world knew them... Kirloth and the Apprentices.

"Okay, so Dad and the others saw to that. Hang on... let me do some mental math here. Tel and the Warpriests of Valthon, that's one. The elves from the High Forest, that's two. Vushaar makes three. The dracons make four. The giants make five, and the dwarves make six. Where'd they get the sixth wizard?"

"The dispatch indicated that the dwarves and giants traveled together."

Jennifer clapped her hands together once and pointed at Shara. "Okay, right. That makes sense. I think I remember Dad saying something once about the dwarves and giants almost sharing territory, since the giants live among the mountains and the dwarves under or within. Yeah... now that I think about it, it makes perfect sense they'd mobilize together."

"Just so, Young Kirloth."

"You haven't called me that in... in... I don't know how long. What's up?"

Shara made an exaggerated point of looking up at the pavilion's ceiling. "Nothing that I can see, beyond the support poles and lines securing the pavilion to them."

Jennifer gave her a flat look. "Okay, Miss Smarty-pants. I know I've used that Earth idiom with you before, but I'll play along. *Ahem.*

Allow me to rephrase: why did you address me as Young Kirloth when you haven't done so in quite some time?"

"I'd love to say that I did it just to get a rise out of you, but the truth of the matter is that two of those on perimeter scout duty captured a courier. I think you'll want to see the materials he carried."

Something about the way Shara said that struck a nerve deep in the recesses of Jennifer's mind that had not evolved past thinking fire was the bleeding edge of technology. She didn't know *what*. She didn't know *how* she knew. But she was utterly certain something was *very* wrong.

"Tell me. Don't make me wait."

Shara took a deep breath and let it out as a slow sigh. "The documents contained payment orders for two assassins the people behind these camps have embedded within the forces Tel contributed to the attack on Skullkeep. Their target is your father."

For a split second, Jennifer wasn't sure what she felt. Either icy claws grasped at her heart, or a very unhappy mule kicked her in the gut. Either one was bad enough. Together, they seemed to join forces and make the whole far greater than the sum of its parts.

"I can't lose Daddy again. I can't. I just can't." It took several moments before Jennifer realized she was babbling like the thirteen-years-old girl who'd watched her father die.

Then... she realized Shara held her.

She snapped out of... whatever *that* was... and patted Shara's arm. "It's okay, Shara. I'm okay now. Thank you."

Shara returned to her seat and regarded Jennifer for a couple heartbeats before she spoke. "I am not sure I understood any of that."

"Oh, that's okay. I barely understood any of it, either." Jennifer heaved a heavy sigh. "Okay. I don't know how much Dad has shared with the Wraiths, but when I was thirteen, Dad died in a car wreck. I ended up in a very, *very* dark place—mentally speaking—and did a lot of things I do not have the words for how much I regret. From what I understand, the fact that he was already dead made Dad 'available' to be put here in Drakmoor... by a certain individual Dad calls 'the old man.'"

When Jennifer brought her eyes up to look at Shara, she almost let her poker face slip. She had *never* seen her unflappable Wraith friend so pale and with such a shocked expression before.

"You… you mean…"

Jennifer simply nodded. "Dad has it on very good authority that Valthon 'meddled.' His words, not mine. I don't know the full circumstances or anything, but Dad suspects that Valthon wasn't the only one to meddle, either."

"So, can the assault on Skullkeep even fail? If… if the gods have taken such a direct hand—"

"Whoa, there! The assault on Skullkeep can easily fail, because I don't think they're meddling anymore. Like I said, I don't *know* anything for certain, but a few things that Dad has said plus a conversation I had while riding north from Tel Roshan lead me to believe they've meddled as much as they're going to. It's all on us from here on out. I think they just set the stage to give us the best chance for success we could have."

Shara seemed to shake herself… not unlike a wet dog. "That is a very… alarming, I think… yes. That is a very alarming thought."

"I agree. Which is why we need to hurry up and finish clearing these camps so that I can join the assault on Skullkeep and make sure no one kills my dad. I just got him back. I'm not ready to lose him again."

CHAPTER 28

Gavin stood at the periphery of the camp the armies constructed at the mouth of Hope's Pass. Where he stood was still a vibrant landscape. Green grass reaching for the sun high in the sky. Beautiful wildflowers scattered hither and yon, many behind him trampled by the troops and tents and horses.

But just a hundred yards away—two hundred at the most—the ancient pass became a lifeless desolation. What grasses remained were brown, desiccated husks. The dirt itself a worn brown, almost like the tan of drought-ridden plains, and certainly not rich, black soil capable of supporting life.

Barren and bare rock rose high on either side of the pass. Past the hemispherical mouth of the pass, it narrowed to little more than fifty yards wide. Twenty-five in some places.

It would be a hard, brutal slog. Tense, even. They didn't know what awaited them. Not really. The reports from the Wraiths sent to infiltrate the stronghold had been sparse. Not more than a handful between all five of them over the previous months. Gavin hoped they were well and just unable to send messages. He knew it was part of being Archmagister—not to mention Kirloth—but he didn't relish sending people to their deaths.

The Necromancer had been an open threat to the world for too long, and the time had come to see to that.

He was as prepared as he could be for the coming confrontation. But he didn't feel like he was prepared **enough**. The one time they'd confronted each other had not gone so well for him... unless you counted the trip home to reconnect with family... but he wasn't too sure that had been the Necromancer's intent.

Last night—when he'd finished what little work the others had allowed him to do on his own tent—he set in his comfy camp chair and performed a divination focused on his first confrontation with the Necromancer all those months ago.

What he discovered surprised him.

The divination carried an echo of his *skathos*—faint though it was —and the sense it gave him of the Necromancer's invocation was an Interation-laced Transmutation. Almost like a disintegration effect with an overlay of death for good measure.

Which only created more questions.

How had he and Kiri ended up on Earth? That combination should have killed them both. Why didn't it? Did Bellos—or someone else—meddle yet again? Was that it? His *skathos* in the divination didn't give him that feeling... but there's a reason the scientists back on Earth liked to point out that 'absence of evidence is not evidence of absence.'

Not to mention how it was impossible to prove a negative.

No... he needed to put all this out of his mind for the next day or so. He needed to focus on defeating the Necromancer or Drannos or whatever he preferred to call himself. Then and only then would he give himself permission to delve into all the mysteries surrounding him.

It was far past time he had some concrete answers.

Gavin allowed himself a heavy sigh, then squared his shoulders and focused on his purpose for coming outside the camp. He closed his eyes and cleared his mind of all distractions, making his intent the paramount thought in his mind. Then, he took a breath and invoked a Word of Divination.

"Klaepos."

The resonance of his power slammed into the ambient, and he thought he heard a faint scream or two from the camp about twenty-five yards behind him. As the scrying sphere began to form, he couldn't help but smile at his success.

Soon enough, he looked down on the ancient fortress this world had called Skullkeep for thousands of years. He watched the mass of undead mill about the courtyard. Noted how the walls looks poorly maintained. But poorly maintained didn't necessarily mean ineffective.

He didn't see much sign of the living inhabitants, and he couldn't decide if that was good or not. Such a large number of undead had to fill the area with a rather... **strong**... bouquet, especially since they were within a few weeks of high summer.

The courtyard was a rectangle with rounded corners, more or less, and Gavin scratched at his chin as he considered an idea. The crux of the issue was that he didn't know enough about undead. He wanted to lay down an anti-magic field around the courtyard—much like the dueling ring far beneath the College of the Arcane. But would that reduce the undead to rotting corpses and skeletons? Or would it just remove the control the Necromancer had over them, basically turning them feral?

Maybe Ovir would know... or... maybe he could convince Valthon to give him the answer.

It would be ideal if the anti-magic field just turned them off... but Gavin didn't think he was that lucky.

He canceled the scrying sphere, but just as he was about to turn back to camp, he noticed a faint resonance in his *skathos*. It was small —no larger than a person or two—and moving slowly. A walking pace at best. He readied the first Word he ever knew but waited to see what physical form the odd resonance took.

And... he was glad he did.

Not even a full heartbeat after he became aware of a faint shimmering that moved out from behind a clutch of saplings, the shimmering faded, revealing none other than the Wraith he'd met as Cyn.

She paced her steps carefully as she approached him, and when she reached a comfortable distance, she took and knee and bowed her head.

"Milord, I have come to report."

Gavin nodded, even though she stared at the ground. "Rise and stand easy. What have you to report?"

"Your scry block has frustrated the Necromancer and his students to great degree. They have massed their mercenaries to await your assault, an event they have been certain will happen 'any day now' since not long after you enacted the block. Tempers have well and truly frayed among the intelligent members of the fortress's garrison, and I myself have had to knife three people who felt a lone woman was fair game to relieve their stress."

Gavin scowled. "It's unfortunate and unconscionable that they would treat you such, but I'm glad you've protected yourself. If anyone among the Wraiths gives you any flack over it, send them straight to me without a second thought. Do you understand?"

"Yes, Milord." Cyn gave a quick, assured nod. "I believe I have also located the Necromancer's soul jar. He has a cubby hidden in one wall of his quarters that is highly warded. *Very* highly warded. Were it not for the awareness of embedded magic the Wraith tattoo gives us, I doubt I would even have found it. There was a powerful Enchantment effect that tried to nudge me away from even noticing it."

"If it is that highly warded, there's no telling what will happen if someone other than Drannos disturbs the wards. I do not want you to sacrifice yourself for this, Cyn. You may consider that an order if needed."

Cyn replied with a smile that was absolutely predatory. "Oh, Milord... you have no reason to worry. One of the fellows who met the business end of my dagger survived, and he knows beyond any doubt that he owes me his life... which I plan to claim when you assault the fortress. I will take him to the Necromancer's chambers and use him to activate the wards. If he survives, I will ask that you spare him and set him up somewhere to enjoy whatever remains of his life."

"Sounds fair," Gavin replied with a one-shoulder shrug.

"You should also know that the undead in the courtyard constitute the bulk of the defensive force. The mercenaries have been quietly slipping away ever since you laid down the scrying block. Given that the Necromancer and his students are not silent at all about how it persists despite their best efforts to dispel it, many of them have come to believe that shows you are the more powerful with your victory assured."

"Well... when we faced each other in Tel Mivar the first time, I wasn't exactly at my best. I've been hoping this second meeting would resolve much more in my favor."

Cyn beamed. "I do not think you have much to fear on that score, Milord. While I would caution you against overconfidence, morale is not high at all within Skullkeep... and... I have taken it upon myself to plant rumors and suggestions where I can to keep it low, if not drive it lower."

"Good for you. Do you have anything else to report?"

"Nothing substantive, Milord."

"Very well." Gavin nodded once. "You deliver excellent work. Be careful slipping back into the fortress."

"Of course, Milord. When you begin your assault, my minion and I will destroy the soul jar."

Without another word, Cyn slipped back into the forest and vanished from sight.

* * *

SEVERAL PEOPLE TURNED to face him as they stood when Gavin entered the pavilion that would serve as their command center. They watched him in silence as he made his way around to the only open spot at the round table that dominated the space. He pulled his chair back from the table and sat, gesturing for them to return to their seats.

"Well?" Dagrond Axesplitter demanded. "Did ye see anything?"

More than one person around the table smiled at the dwarven general's impatience.

Gavin merely leaned back against his seat. "It won't be easy, but we all knew that. The entire courtyard is a milling mass of undead. I identified skeletons, zombies, and ghouls. There did not seem to be many people manning the walls or the main fortress's battlements. A few weeks ago, I took the opportunity to block scrying for two thousand square miles, and I put the center-point far enough west that it ends about a hundred feet or so shy of Skullkeep's walls. It covers large sections of Mivar and Cothos provinces. Sure... they may know we're here, but they only way they'll see what we're doing is the ole Mark I eyeball."

Those not familiar with Gavin's odd phrases—which were all but five of the attendees—glanced at each other around the table.

After several moments, Dagrond ventured a question, "Is there a Mark II eyeball?"

Gavin fought the urge to sigh... and largely succeeded. "It's just an expression from where I was born. It means the naked eye."

Nods of understanding circled the table.

"So... how long should we rest before making the march to the fortress?" Gavin asked.

Roth Thatcherson answered, "With the bulk of our forces being veterans, I see no reason we couldn't march on Skullkeep as soon as the day after tomorrow. Using the gateways prevented us from having our support train stretched halfway back to Tel Mivar, so in full truth, there is probably little reason we couldn't march tomorrow."

Gavin scanned the expressions looking back at him around the table. No one seemed to disagree with Roth's statement. Which was both good and bad in his mind. "I'd like to at least hold here until the day after tomorrow. That will give us the opportunity to plan the assault and give us a night to see if we thought of anything we missed during the primary planning. Thoughts?"

More nods circled the table. Telanna spoke, "I agree. I believe that to be the wisest course. We can establish a perimeter of scouts to ensure that no scouts from Skullkeep reach us, and my fellow druids and I have already called the local birds to our cause. In addition to whatever scouts and sentries the generals wish to deploy, we shall also have coverage from the air."

"That's excellent, Telanna," Gavin replied, adding a smile. "I'll scry the fortress again in the morning and record the visuals to a crystal that will provide us an illusory playback at will. That way, we'll have a current reference during our planning. Does anyone have anything else at this time?"

No one spoke up, so Gavin dismissed the conference.

He watched them leave and, once they were gone, allowed himself a heavy sigh. He already knew his part in the upcoming assault. He hoped they would be able to get close enough to the fortress that he could wipe out the wall and gate blocking their approach before he had to shift to defending his forces from the Necromancer and whatever arcanists he'd recruited to his cause.

A dark and mirthless chuckle—even almost evil—escaped his control as he remembered the last arcanists from Skullkeep he had faced. They had managed to disintegrate a thirty-foot section of the Vushaari capital city's wall, which Gavin's friends—the Apprentices —reconstituted within a matter of minutes.

No... he wasn't worried about whatever arcanists the Necromancer had at his side. His only concern was the Necromancer himself. He wasn't the same wizard he'd been when they first confronted each other, and he wouldn't be walking into this fight barely standing from defeating the manifestation of Milthas. Cyn was right. He shouldn't allow himself to get cocky or overconfident, but at the same time, he couldn't help but feel this meeting would go *very* differently.

If it went even slightly close to plan, that would be nice.

CHAPTER 29

Cyn slipped back inside the fortress without notice or challenge. Even though her seniority among the Wraiths was... not great... she counted her mentor among the very best. And so, under his tutelage and wise guidance, she had developed a skillset that rivaled veterans. She had overheard Declan talking to a group of senior—*very* senior—Wraiths not too long before departing on the Skullkeep mission where he said he suspected she would be one of those rare few that set the standard for the new generation... much as he had once upon a time.

That... even the mere memory of hearing his voice say those words filled her with a fire and conviction to not let him down. It was because of him that she was anything other than a street waif who grew into a common thief or a pleasure girl working the docks of her hometown. She'd made the mistake of trying to cut his purse, and after a flurry of movement too fast for her to follow that ended with a needle pricking her neck, she'd woken up on the bed of a room far more upscale than anything she'd ever dreamed possible. He sat in a plush armchair across the room from her, honing the edge of a dagger, as he offered her the chance at a better—but far more dangerous—life.

Weeks later—after she'd passed her first assessment with the top marks in her group—she'd asked him why he'd given her that chance. She still remembered his response clear as day, "Because... once upon a time, I cut the wrong purse, too."

Cyn slipped into her room in the fortress barracks and checked all the telltales she'd left, finding them undisturbed until her return. She shouldn't have allowed her memories to overtake her so... not while on an assignment. But she also recognized that she wasn't perfect—no one was—and resolved to do better tomorrow. For now, she had work to do.

* * *

CEDRIC LOOKED up when movement darkened the doorway to his space, and he fought the urge to cringe when he saw the woman standing there. He didn't know who she was. The name she'd given the recruiting sergeant was obviously a fake, and her skills and uncaring ruthlessness—even on the practice field—terrified him straight down to his bones. More than anything else in his life, he wished he'd never even learned she existed, let alone agreed with Marc to try having a little fun with her. Now, Marc and his other friends were dead, and he was left with... her.

She stalked into his cubby, not unlike an apex predator, and closed the door behind her. She withdrew what looked like a small, stone pyramid from a belt pouch and placed it on his desk. It was covered in runes unlike anything he'd ever seen... not that he'd know anything at all about runes. She pressed the palm of her hand against one side, and all the runes lit up. Not even a heartbeat later, the room seemed to fill with some kind of pressure that made his ears feel the need to pop.

"There," she said. "Now, we can talk without risk of anyone over-hearing us."

He eyed her warily, he knew. He didn't like that... but... neither could he shake the feeling of being prey trapped with a predator.

"Not everyone here would use their ears to spy on us."

One corner of her mouth quirked in what might have become a smile in another life. "It will take care of *that*, too."

Shit... just who was she? That kind of magic wasn't exactly plentiful, not to mention the pyramid had the look of an artifact. Those weren't common, either.

"Who are you?"

She lifted one eyebrow to add emphasis to her reply, "Does it matter?"

"I... I don't know. Are you going to kill me?"

A one-shoulder shrug. "Maybe... but not deliberately. If you survive what I have planned for you, I'll see you have enough coin to start a new life somewhere no one will ask you which side you fought for when the Old Alliance reclaimed Skullkeep."

Oh... shit. What did she know? Yes... it wasn't much a secret that morale among the living garrison wasn't all that high. It also wasn't a secret that said garrison had been slowly and quietly dwindling ever since word spread that there was a scrying block over eastern Tel that made the Godswall Mountains seem tiny and incomplete. It didn't take a tactical or strategic genius to figure out the Old Alliance was coming for them—probably *soon*—and when the Necromancer couldn't break through the scrying block... well... that seemed to say everything that needed to be said about how the imminent conflict would end.

It didn't exactly help that any scouts sent into Tel never returned, either.

Yes, of course... nothing was certain in battle. Something that would have been a minor mistake elsewhere could change the fate of an entire force. But... Cedric wasn't the only one who felt the Necromancer was outmatched.

Rumors had spread throughout the fortress that the confrontation with the Archmagister happened *after* the Archmagister had already faced an avatar of Milthas... and survived. More than one person asked themselves if they'd even be employed right now if the Archmagister had faced the Necromancer fresh and untried that day.

This woman seemed to think like many of those who had quietly disappeared into the night. The Necromancer's days were ending, maybe even sooner than he realized.

"What... what do you have planned?"

She gave a minute shake of her head. "You don't need to know that just yet. I'll tell you the moment you need to know it. Just remember and focus on one thing. If the fortress is attacked, forget your assigned position and find me. I don't care who yells at you. I don't care what threats they give you. You. Find. Me." A slight pause. "Do you understand?"

He jerked a choppy nod. "I understand."

She smiled then. A full smile, before she stepped close enough to pat him on the head like he was some kind of child. "Good. Have a nice night."

She swept the pyramid back into its pouch and disappeared out the door almost faster than she had arrived, leaving him with nothing but questions and more than a little fear. It was one thing to know he'd die defending the fortress. Death by sword or axe or hammer. Maybe fast, maybe not. Or maybe by magic of some kind. Memories of those thoughts were almost pleasant compared to the unknown swirling around this woman. Saying it left him on tenterhooks did not do it justice.

Not for the first time, he wished he'd never run away from the family farm.

* * *

CYN SECURED the door to her space and flopped on the cot. Calling it a bed would've been gross exaggeration. The feather tick mattress should've been replaced long ago... but it wasn't the worst place she'd ever slept. Not by a long chalk.

Not for the first time, she was beyond grateful for the mental protections built into the imbued effects of the Wraith tattoo. Without them, her mind would be wide open for anyone capable of casting any of the mind-altering or mind-reading spells. If the tattoo had been designed by a lesser wizard, she would fear the Necromancer and his students using Words of Power to uncover the truth about her... but it was designed by the Kirloth of old, the founder of Tel.

Not even the current grandmasters of the order knew the full extent the tattoo did... or so they said anyway. Cyn wasn't too sure she believed that, but the wise person picked her battles.

Even though she had complete trust in the protections afforded by her tattoo, she was still glad the Archmagister hadn't shared any information about the upcoming assault with her. That was more than she needed to know. When the wall sentries sounded the alarms, she'd grab her guy and head toward the top of the fortress's keep... where they'd rappel down to the Necromancer's quarters. With any luck, the poor sod would even survive breaking the wards on the hidden storage space.

A part of her argued that whatever fate claimed him was more than justified, given the circumstances of their meeting. But at the same time, he had stepped up and tried to dissuade the lead idiot, so maybe he wasn't *so* bad. Maybe there was still something in there worth a chance at redemption. That speculation was the only reason she asked the Archmagister for permission to set up him with a new life if he survived. She felt she owed him that much, at least, if he made it through breaking the wards.

Once again, she felt so close to the completion of her assignment that she couldn't help but wonder what her next task would be. There was no way to know. The Wraiths had far too many organizations and governments infiltrated to even hazard a guess about where they might send her next. It could be anything from an office worker in a warehouse of some trading hub or a scullery maid on a dairy farm. Almost **anything** was fair game.

And the rumors of a big change following in the wake of this campaign didn't help, either. She hadn't heard any specifics, just a few whispered rumors of a major shake-up on the horizon. There wasn't even any guarantee those rumors related to the Wraiths themselves.

Not the for the first time, she was fizzing and popping with all kinds of ideas and thoughts, and her mind cared not at all that she just wanted to sleep. In the end, she had to work through the mental exercises she'd learned as part of her Wraith training to settle her mind. As she drifted off to sleep, one of her fading thoughts was a question about what the coming days would bring.

CHAPTER 30

The passage of three days with no assault only served to ratchet up the tension among the sapient defenders of Skullkeep to a near-fever pitch. The rank-and-file mercenaries were snappish with everyone except those they truly feared, so not even their immediate superiors were safe. The necromancer visibly stopped himself from eradicating a handful of people, because of the simple fact there was no time to replace them.

Fun times were not had... not at all.

The fourth morning, Cyn took care of her morning routine and started to perform her morning walk-around... except... she had the eeriest feeling when the thought of walking the west wall's parapet crossed her mind. There was no obvious reason... no obvious threat... but something at the back of her brain almost screamed that she had no business being on the wall that day. None whatsoever.

Those moments of hesitation saved her life.

* * *

THE FIRST RAYS of true dawn were just touching the parapet of Skullkeep's east wall when Gavin motioned for a halt. His friends—

Lillian, Mariana, Wynn, Braden, Xythe, Declan, and Ovir—gathered around him. In truth, Xythe was a bit untried—at least in magic—to have accompanied them on this journey, but Lillian and Wynn ganged up on Gavin and talked and talked and talked until he accepted her as his close-protection specialist. In short... she was his bodyguard.

Gavin felt certain that several Wraiths floated around the periphery of his location, but he couldn't exactly tell them that... not if the Wraiths were to remain the long-kept secret they were. And besides, he didn't *know* for certain there were Wraiths nearby—beyond Declan—so it didn't hurt to have a dracon with over twenty years' experience in blade-work at his side.

He scanned the faces of those the world had come to call the Apprentices, gauging their readiness for himself in silence. If they suspected his silent appraisal, they made no mention of it. After a few moments, he nodded once.

"Everyone ready for this?"

Each replied with a single nod.

"Remember. Focus on the western wall. We want the eastern wall to remain standing and serve as a backstop to keep them from retreating. We'll have to put down all the undead regardless, but while I'd rather anyone supporting the Necromancer to surrender, I do not feel it's wise to leave them free to roam the countryside."

Again, nods answered him. If anyone didn't like his stance, they knew it was long past time to debate it with him. Back in the command tent, with the staff officers to advise on military matters? Sure. He valued debate and discussion. Here? In the moment? It was time for command authority and to follow the plan.

Gavin held out his hands, and the Apprentices gathered around him, forming a line with the ladies to his left and the gentlemen to his right. They each held the hands of the person next to them.

"On three," Gavin said as he cleared his mind of everything but his intent. "One... two... three."

Five voices broke the morning's silence in a combined invocation of a Word of Evocation, "*Idluhn.*"

The resonance of Gavin's power slamming into the ambient vastly overshadowed that of his friends, but to anyone with a fine-tuned *skathos*, they were still noticeable to a degree. In the end, though, most people didn't care **what** the magical resonance felt like; they were too busy staring as the entire western wall of Skullkeep—the wall that faced the Kingdom of Tel plus its gatehouse and portcullis —disintegrated into powder and iron filings.

"Suppressive anti-magic field now," Gavin said as he cleared his mind once more.

"*Rhosed*," the five once more invoked in unison after Gavin's count.

A sphere centered on the courtyard and sized to encompass the entire courtyard coalesced into being. It was invisible, but its sole purpose was to push ambient magic away. To create a dead zone where no magic would function within its volume.

It was a matter of some debate whether the mindless undead would just collapse into corpses and skeletons or if it would just break whatever control the Necromancer had over them. The answer appeared to be... both.

Some of the undead collapsed to the ground inert. By Gavin's rough estimation, over half of the horde in the courtyard was affected in that way. But the rest? They turned rabid, attacking anything and everything within reach.

Ovir rolled his shoulders as he hefted his shield and mace. "Our turn now, I think."

* * *

CYN GAPED, her mind seemingly unable to process the sight before her. The western wall of the fortress was just... gone. She stood no more than ten feet away from where the wall had connected to the main keep, and she stared—almost in shock—at the open-air space that had been her intended path not even five heartbeats ago.

It was starting. The assault to reclaim Skullkeep was finally starting!

She pivoted on her heel and dashed back into the keep, intent on returning to her space first and foremost and then finding her pet mercenary.

Before too long at all, the battle would be joined, and with any luck, the Necromancer would rush outside to confront the Archmagister himself. She didn't know how long she had, but she knew it wasn't *too* long.

She followed the twists and turns through the keep almost on autopilot as she ran through the list of everything she needed to do in her mind. As soon as she entered her quarters, she closed the door and drew her dagger. A quick pry job later, and she retrieved two small sacks. One held the collection of coins she had... *found*... around the keep, and the other contained her stash of notes from locating the warded storage cubby in the Necromancer's quarters. She squirreled both away in belt pouches, then pivoted on her heel and left her quarters for (hopefully) the last time.

Now... she just needed to find her pet. She hoped he hadn't strayed too far.

* * *

CYN RUSHED through the corridors of the fortress. Her pet wasn't in his quarters, and he wasn't on a direct path between her quarters and his. So she had to look for him. She wasn't happy. As she approached the doorway of one of the watch commanders, Cyn heard a voice she recognized, and what it said put a scowl on her expression.

"Captain, please... I'm telling you that history girl is a spy. How many times do I have to go over this? When my buddies decided to have a little fun with her, they made the mistake of forcing the issue, and she let me live. In exchange, she made me promise to help her with something. She hasn't said anything yet—"

His voice cut off as Cyn slammed into his back, forcing him face-first into the watch commander's desk. The captain jerked back in surprise, but it wasn't far or fast enough.

Cyn rolled over her pet's back as she slashed out with one of her daggers. The tip of the blade opened the side of the captain's neck, and arterial spray painted the stone wall and floor. The captain clutched at his wound, his eyes wide as his knees buckled, and Cyn closed in to finish the job with several quick strikes... one to the armpit of the hand clutching the first wound, a second lower on his torso that punctured his right lung at a minimum, and the third finally finished the man when she drove her blade into his heart.

When she turned, her pet was upright once again, and he stared at the dying watch commander with wide eyes.

"Oh... that wasn't smart, pet," Cyn said, her tone admonishing as she shook her finger. "Do you prefer to die at the end of this? Is that it?"

The color left the man's face and neck at the same time the crotch of his trousers darkened with dampness. "I... uhm... I..."

"We'll discuss this later, pet. You know... forcing me to kill the watch commander might turn out to be a blessing in disguise. I'll make certain my master is aware that you didn't do so out of a helpful mindset, but he may still decide to reward you for it... assuming of course no further such incidents occur. Now, come with me. We have work to prepare."

Cyn thought she heard a faint whimper escape the man's lips as she gestured for him to turn and lead the way with her still-bloody dagger. She watched just long enough to ensure he was moving before she glanced away long enough to wipe both sides of the blade on the corpse behind her.

In truth, she regretted killing the man. He was one of the nicer souls she'd met in this place, and it was... unfortunate... the pet had forced her hand. Perhaps, she should've been less hasty and offered the watch commander something to change sides, but if a man can be bought once, he can be bought *more than* once.

Her pet stood dutifully at the door, acting for all the world like a beaten-down puppy. Which was fair enough, she supposed. She'd still be wary for any sudden upswells of defiance or threat, but his conduct to date suggested he was a physical coward.

"We're going to the keep's roof, pet. Start walking."

His shoulders slumped even more than they had been as he

turned right out of the doorway. It wasn't very far to the stairwell that allowed access to the keep's roof, and as they neared the final flight of stairs, she shushed him and listened. From the faint sounds, it seemed like those assigned to the roof were on the ball and already worked to set up the artillery. That... was a complication but nothing she hadn't accounted for.

She leaned close to her pet and whispered, "Be silent and wait for my return. Do not make me search for you again."

The pet jerked his head in two quick nods as she brushed past him. She climbed enough stairs to peek out of the stairwell and saw fifteen people in three groups of five setting up the ballistae mounted on the roof.

Not the easiest arrangement, but not impossible.

She wasn't sure how long she'd maintain surprise, but definitely not past the first group. She withdrew a vial from one of her belt pouches and a clutch of throwing knives with blades sized to fit into the vial. She dipped all five into the liquid in the vial and hoped it was as fast-acting as her instructors claimed. She'd never used this particular neurotoxin before.

As she climbed out of the stairwell and ran to the second group, she threw the knives in quick succession at the first group. She had trained extensively just for such a situation, and she'd always scored high on running marksmanship.

The sound of her running footfalls drew attention, but not quickly enough. Her thrown knives found their marks, and the five people around the first ballista clutched at their necks where the poisoned knives had struck. They collapsed within ten heartbeats.

The people around the other two ballistae now jerked in surprise at the sight of Cyn attacking them. After all, they'd seen her around the fortress for weeks, and she had even helped them from time to time with their duties. That surprise locked their reactions for just long enough that Cyn went through over half of the second group with kidney stabs and slices to their throats before any of them moved to respond.

Those remaining in the second group—even though they tried to react—were still too slow, and they fell, clutching their throats or their sides or their armpits.

The leader of the final group was a woman Cyn had spent a decent amount of time with, and even as she drew her sword, she shook her head and asked, "Why?"

"Because it's my job," Cyn replied.

The woman glanced at the four people standing behind her, weapons drawn but not really ready. Not after the sheer viciousness of Cyn's assault on the second group. "Do you accept surrenders? Are you *allowed* to accept surrenders?"

Cyn slowed her approach, considering. She wasn't told *not* to accept surrenders. It's just that her training concentrated on leaving no one alive behind her. She knew what her mentor would do... or at least... she thought she did. But what would the Archmagister do? She'd seen him show mercy at the oddest times, and she wondered if now would be one of those were he in her place.

"My orders make no mention of surrenders, either for or against," Cyn answered at last. "Make a pile of your weapons and gather at the opposite side of the roof from the stairwell. Pet! Get up here!"

The third ballista team frowned at her shout, but at their leader's nod, they complied with Cyn's directives. If they were surprised to see the man who joined them, they didn't show it.

Cyn herself didn't care beyond making sure they did as she said and that her pet arrived. She focused instead on examining the battlement's crenellations, looking for the faint scratch she'd made when she located the windows to the Necromancer's quarters. It didn't take her long to find it, and she started securing her rope to the nearby ballista.

The ballistae weren't fully anchored to the keep's roof, but she believed it would hold the weight of her and her pet long enough. As soon as she had the rope secured, she laid the coil by the battlements and settled into a comfortable crouch overlooking the field below them.

"Okay, then. Now we wait."

No one seemed all that interested in asking what she waited *for*.

CHAPTER 31

Ovir tapped out a staccato sequence on his shield, and the Warpriests of Tel separated from the mass of troops as he led them forward. They were an impressive sight with the morning's sun reflecting off their burnished plate armor while their gold-trimmed, silver cloaks flapped in the breeze.

They approached the slight berm that had one been the western wall, and the ravenous mass of undead that remained turned almost as one to face them. Gavin suspected the Warpriests' aura drew the undead much like bait drew predators. For any other force at arms, those undead might pose something of a problem. But for the Warpriests? If the confrontation lasted long enough, watching it might be amusing.

Ovir lifted his mace-wielding hand, and the mass of Warpriests stopped almost as one. He called out something Gavin didn't quite hear, and the entire unit bowed their heads and began what sounded like a chanting prayer... even as the undead charged at them.

When there were at most fifty feet separating them, the chanting reached a crescendo. A bright flash of light erupted among the Warpriests and settled onto them as an aura that was almost a palpable presence—a weighted blanket enshrouding the area as far as he could sense—and it was a presence he recognized.

The warm, kindly regard of a loving grandfather.

The last time he'd felt that, he been freshly awoken in a grimy alley of Tel Mivar, wearing only homespun pants. He'd been bewildered and lost, and the warm regard of a kindly—though a tad crazy —old man had been a balm against the confusion.

But now? The presence carried an edge to it. A strength and toughness that felt protective. He suspected the Old Man wouldn't directly meddle at this juncture, but Gavin couldn't help but smile at how the Warpriests' prayers manifested.

The vanguard of the undead reached Ovir's lines, and a corpse that looked slightly more aware than a zombie drew back a clawed hand and swiped at the Royal Priest of Tel. Gavin heard the creature's pained shriek from where he stood, as the undead tried to recoil almost as one.

But the press of those behind them did not permit retreat.

What would have been a pitched battle for any other force quickly became an outright slaughter. The Warpriests waded into the mass of undead, swinging their weapons and bashing with their shields, and their foes fell by tens and dozens.

It wasn't long at all until Ovir's people mopped up the last of the undead, and everyone realized that the battle had not otherwise been joined. Where were the living defenders? For that matter, where was the Necromancer?

Gavin risked closing his eyes to focus wholly on his *skathos*. Reaching out to try to get a sense of the fortress. A strong ward radiated Tutation high up in the keep. A swirling, seething mass of Interation moved at what felt like a walking pace about halfway between the ward and the main gates of the keep. There were a few weak Tutation effects in the keep's basement, but otherwise, the fortress was devoid of arcane power.

That... didn't seem right somehow.

Was the big bad Necromancer of Skullkeep a paper tiger? Where were all the mercenaries he had recruited to his banner?

Sure... Cyn had told him that they were slipping out of the fortress in rather large numbers. After all, mercenaries care more for pay than giving their lives to their employer's cause. But he would've thought some diehards would still remain. After all, it wasn't every day that you had the opportunity to face a combined force of the Old Alliance led by the Archmagister himself, right?

Gavin relaxed the focus on *skathos* and opened his eyes. He saw what looked like a balcony just above the keep's entrance, and he suspected the Necromancer would soon make an appearance.

He wasn't wrong.

The double doors that led to the balcony opened to the accompaniment of squealing hinges, and a black-robed figure ambled into view. Gavin focused his intent long enough to invoke a Word of Transmutation that would ensure his voice carried.

"Good day to you, Drannos. You've been absent from the Council meetings of late, and I decided it was time to check on you. I hope your absence isn't due to something I said."

A faint resonance of Transmutation suggested the Necromancer invoked a similar effect. "Why, no, Milord. I merely had several projects that required my attention. I must confess that I wasn't too surprised to see the Warpriests handle the chattel with little effort. But then again, I didn't put a lot of effort into them. Here... let me show you what I *have* put effort into."

The Necromancer invoked another Word of Transmutation that opened a gateway near the center of what had been the fortress's courtyard. It started at about the perfect size for a man to walk through but rapidly grew to better than fifteen feet in height at its apex and about five feet at its greatest width. Gavin couldn't see much of what was on the other side, because it was very dark, but he thought he saw masonry walls in the distance. A quick check of his *skathos* confirmed that it opened to a section of the deeper levels of the keep's basement.

Not even a heartbeat after the gateway reached its full size, a massive bipedal form lumbered through it to the courtyard. The first thing Gavin noticed—almost impossible to miss, really—was its sheer size. Easily twelve to fifteen feet tall with a stout frame to support it. The way it moved, it was difficult to tell whether it was large and ungainly or large and dextrous, and Gavin suspected they would soon find out the hard way.

Faint lines circled the base of its neck and its shoulders, and Gavin suspected similar lines encircled its thighs where they connected to its hips. They had the look of old scars... well healed and mere memories of the procedure that assembled the creature. A faint aura of Interation radiated from it, though Gavin doubted any wizard beyond himself and maybe Lillian and the others could sense it.

It was clearly a flesh golem, and it gave Gavin a vibe of strength and an almost-cunning intelligence. It took one look at the assembled Warpriests, and its expression broke into a macabre smile.

* * *

WHEN SHE HEARD the Necromancer's voice resonate throughout the fortress, Cyn jumped to her feet and leaned out to look down over the keep. Far below, she saw the black-robed figure standing on the keep's sole balcony, and she knew the time had come.

She tossed the rope over the side, making sure that it would only reach as far as the windows to the Necromancer's quarters, and she gestured to it while looking at her pet.

"All right... now's the time to earn your keep. Over the side and into the room below through the windows."

Her pet walked to the battlements and leaned over, gauging the length of the rope. When he finally processed just which room he'd be entering, the color fled his complexion at speed.

"Are you serious? Do you have any idea what will happen if we're caught?"

Cyn fingered the hilt of a dagger. "Do you have any idea how long it will take you to die if you don't start moving?"

She watched him swallow hard and glance over the side once more. He heaved a couple heavy breaths and then did as he was bidden, swinging over the battlements' crenellations to descend slowly toward their destination.

Her pet had just reached the windows when her tattoo flared, and she spun to the courtyard. She saw the massive gateway open and deliver a necromantic abomination. She almost couldn't believe her eyes. It was *huge*, even from as far away as her vantage point. She had no doubt the Archmagister's forces—especially the Warpriests— would defeat it, but she also didn't doubt that it would be one of the toughest fights they'd ever faced.

A conclusion borne out by the opening of even more gateways that allowed all the remaining mercenaries to stream into the courtyard and begin dressing their lines for an attack.

Her pet tugged on the rope twice, and she suspected he was trying to urge her to hurry. But she had other things on her mind, just then. She spun to face the sole remaining ballista team.

"You have surrendered, and I have accepted that. However, if you would prefer to start your lives after this battle with a clean slate and possibly a nest egg to help you rebuild, use this ballista to attack that abomination in the courtyard whenever you have a safe shot."

That said, Cyn checked her gloves and backflipped over the side, grasping the rope as she did so and sliding down to join her pet.

The Necromancer's sparse quarters hadn't changed since she'd scouted the space, and she took only as much time as necessary to verify there were no new traps or wards or active magical effects. There were not... at least as far as her tattoo would allow her to detect.

She pointed to a section of the interior wall. "Right then, pet... it's time to earn your fresh start. That section of the wall directly across from these windows. It looks like a plain stone wall, but that is actually an illusion with rather strong wards. From what I can tell, the only way to deactivate those wards—aside from unweaving them—is to break the illusion. So, have it."

"What... will the wards kill me?"

Cyn shrugged. "No idea, pet. I'm not an arcanist, so I can't read them. I only know they're there. They could be a simple alarm... or...

they could be a death trap the likes of which the world has never seen. We won't know until you break that illusion, so chop chop."

His expression told Cyn in no uncertain terms just what he thought of his price for a new life. For what felt like the longest time, he just stood there, staring at her. It reached the point that she started to think she'd have to kill him and trip the illusion herself.

In the end, though, he heaved another deep breath and walked straight to the wall. He started well to the right of the section, probably because he couldn't see the warded illusion like she could, thanks to the abilities provided by her tattoo. Each time he threw his open hand forward, it slapped against solid stone until he moved in front of the warded illusion. When he moved to slap that section, his arm sank into the 'wall' up to his elbow. He jerked back half a step, surprise evident in his posture, but he took another deep breath and pushed on through.

In the flash of light and crackle of static electricity, the illusion shattered. Surprisingly, her pet still stood... alive and hale.

"All right," she said. "You've done your part. Back out of there and go stand by the window."

He jerked a nod and hastened across the room. At this point, she didn't care if he fled or fell to his death or tried to strand her here by scurrying up the rope and pulling it up after him. The door into the quarters wasn't warded, so she'd happily leave that way if necessary. Assuming he did live through all of this, though, she fully intended to make good on her promise of a new life. She wasn't sure what she'd have to trade the Archmagister to make that happen, but that was the deal she struck with her pet, and she wasn't about to go back on her word... not even with someone like him.

The revealed room appeared to have once been these quarters' garderobe. As the occupant was a lich whose physical form was long-dead and desiccated, it made perfect sense that he'd use this space for his hidden vault. Three chests lined the walls of the space, and she had every intention of examining those in greater detail. But the centerpiece of the room held her complete focus.

The Necromancer had laid a stone slab across the seat with the open hole, and atop that slab rested a ceramic cylindrical jar about six inches tall and four inches in diameter. It looked like a simple container one might find in a kitchen to hold spices or cookies or some other useful item, but the runes etched into its surface that pulsed a glowing radiance revealed its true function... at least to Cyn.

She felt confident that her pet would have no idea what it was.

She stepped forward, claimed the jar in her hands, and took half a step back. When nothing immediately happened, she backed out of the former garderobe completely and turned to show her prize to her pet.

"Yeah... I saw that in there. What is it? I'm guessing it's valuable."

Cyn chuckled. "Oh, you have no idea, pet. This? It's the Necromancer's soul jar. It's what allows him to reform after a period of time if his physical form is destroyed. It's a little bit of a letdown that it was so easy to locate and acquire."

"So... uhm... what are you going to do with it?"

Cyn pulled her focus away from the soul jar and gave her pet the best evil smile she could muster. Then, she lifted the jar high overhead and threw it at the stone floor with every scrap of strength she had.

* * *

THE NECROMANCER'S massive gateway must've doubled as a signal, because a host of smaller normal-people-sized gateways soon appeared and disgorged enough mercenaries to fill the courtyard. They formed up behind the abomination, dressing their lines for an attack, and Gavin was pleased to hear his commanders order their troops to do the same.

Movement off to his left drew his attention, and he saw the Necromancer pivot and look up at the top of the keep. He did likewise and saw a single rope hanging down to a set of windows closest the battlements.

The Necromancer must've forgotten his voice amplification,

because Gavin—and everyone else—heard his snarling growl as he took a step toward the doors that had closed behind him.

Gavin focused on those doors and invoked a Word of Transmutation, "*Rhyskaal,*" that turned the entire doorway—wooden doors and all—to solid, unbroken stone.

"Oh, now now, Drannos! There's no reason to leave your party so early. Such a horrid thing for a host to do!"

The Necromancer spun to face Gavin once more, gripped the balcony's railing, and leaped over it to land in the courtyard. "I will deal with whatever interlopers have invaded my space after I see to you once and for all. I still don't know how you survived that disintegration effect, but now, it largely doesn't matter. I will enjoy animating your corpse!"

A cluster of black-robed individuals formed up behind the Necromancer, and to Gavin's *skathos*, their resonance suggested they were wizards. As a whole, the cluster had a resonance slightly more than equal to one of the Apprentices, which meant they would stand no chance in a one-on-one confrontation against even Xythe. But they were unlikely to present themselves one-on-one.

Gavin reached out through his *skathos* and severed the thread of power keeping his voice amplification active and said, "Here it comes. Our role in this is to keep their magic from harming our forces. Ovir and the Warpriests will handle Tiny over there, and the rest of our forces will deal with the mercenaries. As long as we keep our heads, this should fall together by the numbers."

Lillian and the others vocalized their agreement just as Gavin's *skathos* flared. He didn't even wait to see what effect would form; he concentrated on that resonance and spat a Word of Tutation, "*Rhosed!*"

One of the wizards on the front line, right behind the Necromancer, clutched at his head as he staggered and cried out in pain. Even with all his explorations of the Art, Gavin had never realized that spell—or in this case, invocation—backlash was a thing, but apparently, it was... if one caught the invocation before it was fully formed.

Part of him wondered what he'd done wrong with his suppressive anti-magic field earlier. He would've thought it would have prevented Drannos or his wizards from wielding the Art, but he quickly schooled his thoughts. The battle was joined, which was no time for thoughtful deliberations.

The behemoth shook itself like a wet dog, took a half step forward as it threw its arms wide, and filled the courtyard with a roar that made Gavin's ears ring. It took another half step... and then another... building up to a charge toward the front of the Warpriests' line. If the beast's roar affected Ovir and his people, they didn't show it, but Gavin felt a pang of sympathy for what they were about to face.

He couldn't help them. He had to concentrate on negating the magic of Drannos and his followers. *That* was his role for this conflict.

Another resonance in his *skathos*, and Gavin whipped out another invocation of Tutation. A painful cry. But Gavin didn't care. He focused on Drannos, waiting for the Necromancer to make his move as the battle swelled around him.

CHAPTER 32

I t... bounced?

Cyn wasn't sure what to think as she stared at the soul jar that now rolled across the floor. She dashed to catch it and did a quick examination. Huh... no sign that she'd thrown it to the floor. No chips. No dents. Nothing.

She turned back to look at the spot where it struck. There was no obvious damage to the stone floor, but she wasn't really looking up close. Still, though... the soul jar was a piece of pottery. A ceramic clay jar. It should've shattered into dozens and dozens of pieces.

A roar echoed into the room through the windows, and she took the steps necessary to look. The massive flesh golem looked to be charging the Warpriests, and she honestly wasn't sure who had the best odds in that fight. That golem was massive... and stout.

But it wasn't her problem at the moment.

Heh... it wouldn't have been her problem if she was down in the courtyard. She wasn't a frontline fighter. None of the Wraiths were. No... she needed to shatter this soul jar so that the Archmagister could kill the Necromancer and have him actually stay dead.

Except she didn't seem to be strong enough to do it.

She turned to her pet and strode over to him. "Take this and throw it against the far wall as hard as you can."

He glanced at the soul jar for a moment. "Uhm... are you sure? Wouldn't that be... I don't know... kinda bad?"

Cyn felt her neutral expression shift toward a glare. "Do you want your new life or not?"

He heaved another sigh. "Fine. Give it here."

She handed it to him, and he drew back his arm... then put his whole body into the throw. The soul jar flew across the room... struck the far wall... and fell to the floor. This time, there was a noticeable chip in the stone that made up the wall.

Cyn scowled. "By Lornithar's Abyss! What does it take to shatter that damned thing? Go get the stone slab out of the garderobe. The one it was sitting on."

Her pet moved across the room and collected the stone slab. Then, without prompting, he crossed to where the soul jar lay on the floor. He lifted the slab above his head and threw it down on the offending object.

The stone slab cracked down the center and split in two across the soul jar.

Cyn growled her frustration as she stalked out of the Necromancer's quarters. She startled a guard at the end of the hall, but she was too fast for him. She used both daggers this time—one to the left side of his neck and the other to his right kidney—and left the corpse where it fell. She didn't know whether to feel lucky or tortured that the guy carried a one-handed hammer... exactly what she left the room to find.

She hefted the blunt weapon and lugged it back to the room. Her pet was quick to jump aside when he saw what she carried. She lifted it over heard head as she bent low enough to strike the soul jar and put everything she had into her swing.

Nothing.

It didn't even look like her strike chipped it.

Another growl as she wound up to swing again. "Why..." *strike* "... won't..." *strike* "...you..." *strike* "...just..." *strike* "...shatter!"

The only result from her efforts was a handful of stone chips that went flying... either from the hammer striking the floor or the soul jar acting as an anvil.

Cyn let the hammer fall to the floor and leaned against the wall. This wasn't working. How was she supposed to fulfill her end of the deal if she couldn't shatter a simple clay jar? Yes, yes... it wasn't *just* a clay jar. It was a clay jar that contained all manner of imbued effects to prepare it to store a living soul, so that probably had something to do with her lack of success.

The damned glow from the runes hadn't even dimmed once that she'd seen.

A memory floated to the forefront of her mind and dashed away any feelings of frustrations, leaving unmitigated gratitude in its wake. Early in her training, her mentor had discussed breaking magical items that were not designed to break, and he specifically warned her about the *effects* such actions often produced.

Effects like... explosions.

More than one unwary soul horribly injured themselves—if not outright committed suicide—by breaking a magical object close to them. So... it probably wasn't such a bad thing that they hadn't been able to shatter it yet, but that raised the question of just where—not to mention *how*—she should shatter it.

Another roar from the behemoth in the courtyard made her smile. It just so happened that she had a rather nice collection of enemies at the moment to test her theory, and she suspected the perfect delivery mechanism was just a short rope climb away.

* * *

IF IT WASN'T for the fact that he stood on a literal battlefield, Gavin would've just closed his eyes and focused on his *skathos*. The flesh golem behemoth was less than fifty feet from the Warpriests' lines, and he felt fairly certain that was going to be a battle for the ages. The mass of mercenaries began moving forward, and Gavin heard the army commanders behind him giving orders to meet them.

Another flare in his *skathos*. Larger than any that came before, but still not even half of what one of his friends could produce. His invocation was almost bored. "*Rhosed.*"

About ten of the Necromancer's arcanists cried out and held their heads as they collapsed to their knees.

"You know..." Mariana's voice was almost a growl "...you could save some for the rest of us."

Gavin diverted his focus just long enough to give her a smirk. "You mean you're not capable of finding your own ways to be useful?"

She gave him a flat look, and he felt the resonance of her power as she invoked a Word of Transmutation, "*Rhyskaal.*"

An earthen wall rose up to shin height on the flesh golem just as it was about to take a step. The existence of the berm was so sudden and so unexpected, the behemoth face-planted in the courtyard. Gavin thought he felt the ground shake a little bit.

Roth Thatcherson, commander of the Vushaari contribution to the ground forces, approached them. "We're moving to meet the mercenaries' charge, Milord, but we're going to leave a contingent around you and the arcanists for perimeter security."

It sounded so odd to hear Roth address him as 'Milord.' Yes... he was the Archmagister, and... yes... this was kind of an 'official' occasion. But most times he ran into Ovir's brother in Vushaar? The man addressed him by name... as he preferred.

Ah, well... that would be all cleared up as soon as things settled down from reclaiming Skullkeep.

"Very good, Roth. Thank you. We'll do our best to keep the Necromancer and his arcanists off your backs."

Roth grinned. "Oh, trust me, sir... we appreciate that."

The press of bodies moved Roth away from them, and Gavin spared a moment to check on the Warpriests. They swarmed the flesh golem that was now on its hands and knees in the process of standing up from tripping over Mariana's berm. A quick swing of its arm sent some of Ovir's people flying.

A flare in his *skathos* prompted a quick, "*Rhosed,*" before he decided to give the Warpriests some help. He focused on his intent and invoked a Word of Enchantment, "*Zaenos.*"

Gavin felt the resonance of his invocation and allowed himself the time to watch it paralyze the flesh golem... except... it didn't. Through his *skathos*, it was like the flesh golem didn't exist. The magic—at least *arcane* magic—just slid right off of it.

"Ovir! It's immune to arcane magic!"

His older friend waved his shield to show he'd heard Gavin as he charged back into the fray.

Gavin didn't like that the Necromancer had somehow made his behemoth immune to magic. That wasn't good at all, but he wasn't sure he could afford taking his focus off the Necromancer and his arcanists long enough to break through that protection and eradicate it.

His friends—the four known throughout the world now as the Apprentices—had picked up his slack for the very short time his focus was elsewhere. He brought his attention back to the enemy arcanists and smiled at a thought. His friends were holding their own in keeping them from using magic against the Old Alliance forces; maybe it was time for him to go on the offensive.

A memory of a book he'd read before his death came to the fore-front of his mind, and Gavin smiled. If anyone who didn't know him saw that smile, it probably would've terrified them a bit. He formed a clear picture of his intent in his mind and pushed away all other thoughts or worries. He took a deep breath and invoked a composite effect using a Word of Transmutation and a Word of Evocation.

"*Rhyskaal-Idluhn!*"

He held nothing back from that invocation. Maybe he should have, but he wanted to ensure that no one would counter his invoca-tion as he had countered theirs. The resonance of his full, unbridled power struck the ambient like the detonation of a nuclear bomb. Every arcanist for *miles* felt that invocation, and of those in Skullkeep, only Gavin himself and the Necromancer didn't collapse to their knees from the sheer shock and pain of it.

But Gavin had accounted for that.

The ground under the right flank of the mercenaries erupted out from under them in a shower of rocky shards that quickly took on a red glow. Those mercenaries in and around the gaping maw disappeared as they fell screaming into the chasm.

Meanwhile, those glowing rocky shards shredded almost half of the Necromancer's arcanists, who collapsed the rest of the way to the ground. Those that didn't die outright were not long for the world as the not-quite-molten shards of granite flash heated their insides to just shy of boiling.

* * *

CYN LOOKED OVER THEIR CRAFTSMANSHIP. They had 'secured' the soul jar to the pointed steel tip of a ballista bolt with some magical adhesive putty and several leather cords. She hoped it was stable enough to keep the jar centered on the tip of the spear after they launched it at that monstrosity of a flesh golem.

Now, all they had to do was—

She gasped and collapsed to her knees as her tattoo flared an angry blood red and lit her entire arm on fire. At least... that's how it felt. In all the time since earning the tattoo, she'd never experienced it reacting to magic in such a way.

She pulled herself to her feet and looked over the edge just in time to see dozens of red-hot stone shards erupt out of the ground beneath the flank of the mercenary formation and shred many of the Necromancer's arcanists.

Damn... that had to come from the Archmagister. She couldn't imagine all of the Apprentices combined—no matter how strong they were—producing *that* much power in a single invocation. But it also meant that this was a perfect opening while *everyone* was a little shell-shocked, even the golem.

She pushed herself to stand. "Hurry, hurry! Get it loaded. We only have one shot at this."

She turned and watched the courtyard below and every few heartbeats risked a glance back to see how they were with loading the ballista. The forces down below still hadn't sorted themselves out yet when the crew chief called, "Ready!"

"Aim for the flesh golem's back, and fire!"

Part of the crew turned the ballista to the right as the other part spun the screw crank that raised or lowered the ballista's elevation. It seemed to Cyn that it took them far too long to get it aimed, but the flesh golem was only just starting to stand up when the crew chief pulled the lever that acted as a trigger.

The deep *THRUMM* of the ballista firing filled Cyn's ears, and she watched the bolt fly through the air toward the flesh golem. It all happened so fast that she almost missed how the soul jar's runes noticeably dimmed mere heartbeats before the steel point shattered it against the flesh golem.

Before the flesh golem could react to the bolt that now impaled its torso, the power magic bound into the soul jar exploded.

CHAPTER 33

Gavin watched the flesh golem push itself into a standing position despite the best efforts of Ovir's Warpriests. Now that the Necromancer's arcanists were halved at a minimum, he felt he could devote his full attention to the golem and reducing its effectiveness enough that the Warpriests could take it down.

Just as he drew breath to invoke another Word of Power, motion caught his eye. A ballista bolt flew down from the keep's roof, and it looked like it headed straight for the golem. For some reason the tip of the bolt glowed, though, and mere heartbeats before it reached its mark—just as the suppressive field dimmed the soul jar's runes and protections—Gavin realized what he saw.

In the split-second he had to react, the only thing on his mind was protecting his people from the *very* imminent blast. The suppressive field might mitigate it—at least a little bit—but he wasn't about to trust that to save his people... especially the Warpriests within melee range of the golem.

He put all his power into the thought of protecting his people as he shouted, "*Rhosed*," at the top of his lungs.

Back in high school, he'd chosen the Manhattan Project as the topic for the research paper his Junior year of high school, and as he researched and read about the incredible destructive power of even those early tests—not to mention the two devices the United States used to end World War II in the Pacific theater—he always wondered what it had been like in the final seconds at Ground Zero for the people of Hiroshima and Nagasaki. What was it like to witness those atomic blasts?

As Gavin pushed himself to stand from where the soul jar's explosion had knocked everyone flat, he thought that maybe—just maybe—he had an appreciation for perhaps a twentieth of those people's final moments.

Heat. Light bright enough to blind. A shockwave that would've reduced the forces of the Old Alliance to paste.

As he shook off the mind fog that claimed him during the explosion of power that had been bound and concentrated across hundreds—more likely *thousands*—of years, Gavin quickly scanned the area to take stock of his people.

Those among the Old Alliance forces who were not already dead on the ground still moved. Much like Gavin, they were in various stages of picking themselves up and figuring out what the hell just happened... because Gavin hadn't had time to actually *warn* anyone. He had no doubt there were a whole host of injuries that the clerics and priests and priestesses would soon be treating, but if they were still alive at the moment the soul jar shattered, the resulting armageddon didn't kill them.

The flesh golem? Gone. It was just... gone. There might have been a piece or two lying about that was large enough to identify as having come from the behemoth. But if there were, Gavin couldn't immediately pinpoint them.

The mercenaries? From what little Gavin could see, he suspected no more than half those remaining before the soul jar shattered still lived. The far side of the courtyard was a writhing mass of pained screams and agony, and picking out specific survivors at this distance was an exercise in futility.

Those arcanists of the Necromancer who hadn't died in the eruption of Gavin's magma shotgun did so when the shockwave of the soul jar's explosion turned them into red splotches of semi-liquid goo across the front of the keep... looking much like a cafeteria ketchup packet dropped on the floor and then stomped.

Somehow, the Necromancer himself survived the blast. He stood and weaved on his feet, looking for all the world like he was about to collapse once more, but he was still... well... not alive, but in existence.

Just as Gavin gathered his wits to invoke a disintegration effect against the Necromancer (poetic justice, that), a commotion erupted right behind him.

He spun just in time to see Declan grab someone he didn't recognize who was mere inches away from driving a blade into his back.

"Now, now," the bard said. "We'll be having none of that. None of that at all."

The man Declan physically restrained wore the uniform of the Army of Tel, and it bore sergeant stripes. The circumstances took Gavin by such surprise that he was just slow enough in processing what he sensed through his *skathos*.

A gateway erupted from the ground right beside him, and Jennifer charged through it with thirty Wraiths at her back. She took one look at Declan with his restrained prisoner and gave the man a nod as she half-smiled. Then, she looked past her father toward the keep itself, and her eyes shot wide.

She snarled, "*Rhosed-Rhyskaal*," and the resonance of *her* power slammed into the ambient like an avalanche. Gavin spun—again—in time to see the Necromancer cry out and clutch his head just before two stone slabs folded upward out of the ground on either side of him like two hands clapping. The slabs came together in a vicious *CRUNCH*.

When those conjured stones collapsed back into the ground of the courtyard, the crushed remains of the Necromancer's desiccated body collected in a pile of bonemeal in, around, and beneath his tattered black robe.

. . .

AN ALMOST-EERIE SILENCE settled on and around the courtyard in the wake of that world-changing 'crunch.'

Roth and Ovir soon arrived at Gavin's side. The Vushaari Cavalier pointed to the bonemeal remains, saying, "So... does that mean we've won?"

Gavin nodded as he fought to contain how proud he was of his daughter in that moment. Oh, there was no doubt in his mind that he would tell his daughter she made him proud yet again, but that was for a time in the not-too-distant future. A time when the armies of the Old Alliance were back in their respective homelands. A time after the memorials for all those they'd lost. He didn't think the casualties were as high as he feared they would be when they first set out for Skullkeep, but even with all his power, he couldn't save everyone.

But he could ensure that their families were taken care of.

He turned back to Declan and the bard's prisoner. "Keep a good hand on your man, there, Declan. I suspect Jennifer will soon tell us that he works for the operation she has been handling these past few weeks. We'll want to be sure we get them all."

Declan nodded once and stepped far enough out of the way for a soldier to bind the would-be assassin's hands behind his back. "Oh... don't you be worrying at about this here popinjay, Milord. My associates and I will see to the matter. Though... from the looks of it, maybe we should recruit your daughter. She seems to have a knack with this kind of work."

Gavin chuckled and took the few steps necessary to pull Jennifer into a one-armed hug. "If that is the path she wants, I will cheer her on. But for right now, we have some clean-up to do."

CHAPTER 34

Cyn's pet received his new life, and the ballista crew that surrendered and then delivered the decisive blow that changed the course of the battle did as well.

The representatives of the Old Alliance left a token force to act as both a garrison and a search force to see just what all the Necromancer had done to the fortress during his stewardship. Based on a few things Cyn told him, Gavin suspected they'd find more than a few ghastly surprises in the deeper basements. But the discussion of what to do with the ancient fortress across the long term would wait.

Everyone was quick to congratulate Declan on his apprehension of the assassin... until Jennifer mentioned her paperwork indicated there were two. After a little bit of... persuasion... the would-be assassin in Declan's care pointed to a corpse, naming it his associate. A casting of Divination of Truth and asking the question again prompted a bit more persuasion, but the assassin eventually agreed to give up his friend. That individual had been trapped in the rear echelons and hadn't been able to reach the arcanist contingent at all, let alone Gavin.

All in all, it took three weeks for things to settle.

* * *

GAVIN STOOD at the battlements atop the Tower of the Council, looking out over the College and Tel Mivar. He didn't know for certain if he'd achieved all that Valthon and Bellos desired when they went looking for a true-born child of House Kirloth, but he felt it was time and past time to transition to the next stage of his life.

It was time to set aside the gold robe and the office it represented, just as Marcus did before him.

Part of him felt that he should regret his decision. It would be easy to make the case that he still had so much he could do. But the honest truth was that he never truly **wanted** to be Archmagister. He merely accepted the role, because... well... he felt he needed to.

The mid-morning bell chimed throughout the city, and with one last deep breath, Gavin turned and walked through the doorway that led to the Grand Stair.

It took him no time at all to reach the main floor, and he strode to the room known as the Chambers of the Council. Upon entering, he recognized everyone who waited for him. Lillian. Mariana. Wynn. Braden. Torval Mivar. Lyssa Cothos. Carth Roshan. Sypara Wygoth. Ovir. Valera. Kantar. Declan. Even Kiri, Terris, and Roth had asked to attend this occasion whose like had only happened once before in the history of the world.

As Gavin walked down the slight incline that led to the recessed center of the space, the statue of Bellos on the far side flared in bright gold light. When the light faded, the pedestal held no statue, and Bellos—the God of Magic—stood among them once more.

As with all the other times Gavin had seen him, he looked to be a man in his early to mid-thirties with light brown hair and a Van Dyke beard. Like Gavin (for the moment), he wore a gold robe. His wizard medallion was likewise gold, except it bore the shape of a dragon's head. If one looked close enough, one of the scales on the dragon's forehead bore the Glyph of Wygoth, the House Bellos had been born into all those millennia ago.

A startled gasp led to everyone starting to kneel, but Bellos waved that way. "Peace. Remain standing, please. I am not the only person here who's far too old to kneel."

More than one person fought to hold back a grin at that comment.

Bellos turned to Gavin as the Archmagister arrived at the group. He regarded Gavin in silence for several heartbeats, finally saying, "You have done well. I don't think I could be more proud of your achievements or your conduct. You pulled the Kingdom of Tel back from the precipice on which it teetered, and in many ways, you have restored the honor of the Society of the Arcane. Are you certain you wish to proceed?"

"Oh, yes. My tenure as the Archmagister is over. I'd like to get back to being just Gavin again."

Bellos's expression seemed tinged with sorrow for just a moment. "My dear friend, I'm afraid you'll never be 'just Gavin' ever again, but I understand what you mean. Very well. I hereby acknowledge and grant your resignation from the office of Archmagister of Tel. Know that you have earned this many times over in my eyes, and those who come after you will have quite the legacy to carry on." Bellos lifted his hand and placed it on Gavin's shoulder. "I thank thee for thy service."

A flare of gold light filled the area, and when it faded, Gavin no longer wore a gold robe. His robe was now black as night... but... the runes that ringed the cuffs of the robe's sleeves and proclaimed him to be *Magus* within the Society of the Arcane glowed gold. Just like those of Marcus before him.

Before anyone could truly react, Bellos pivoted to regard Lillian. "Lillian Mivar, Kirloth recommended you succeed him as Archmagister of Tel and did so with the highest praise. I find his evaluation warranted, and I hereby offer you the lifetime appointment. What say you?"

Bellos's offer surprised no one.

Lillian took a breath and released it slowly in a quiet sigh as she looked at the floor. After a heartbeat or two, she lifted her head to meet Bellos's eyes. "I accept."

CHAPTER 35

Gavin stood on the shore of the Inner Sea. A breeze carried the salty sea air to him, ruffling his black robe as he gazed across the rolling waves. It was a cool, sunny afternoon, and Gavin thought he could pick up the faintest echo of hammers striking metal. The Foundry was not more than three hundred yards over his left shoulder.

His new status as 'just Gavin' was not even a week old, but it was still a great relief. He felt like Bellos took a vast weight off his shoulders when the God of Magic granted his request to step down. Had Marcus felt the same when *he* stepped down? There was no way to know now, he supposed.

As far as he could tell, he stood within feet of where Kiri washed ashore all those years ago. No sign or trace remained of the driftwood that carried a soaked and half-drowned princess to this shore, but he didn't really expect that, either. He'd never tell Kiri he was here, but at the same time, he needed to see it for himself.

He became aware of a presence to his right, and he turned to see an old man with wildly unkempt snow-white hair and a bushy beard that was long, long past any hope of control. He wore a gray robe that was tattered along its hem and carried a gnarled balsa-wood staff, planting its base in the sand and leaning against it as he regarded Gavin.

"You've come a long way from that alley where we met, lad, and it's been quite the adventure."

Gavin chuckled despite himself. "Yes... I'd say it has. At least, now, it's over for the most part."

"Over?" Astonishment and disbelief warred for dominance across the old man's demeanor. "Lad, it's *never* over. You've just earned yourself a brief respite. A chance to lean back and rest on your laurels for a time."

Gavin regarded his conversation partner in bemused silence for several heartbeats. "Yeah... I suppose I should've seen that coming. I don't suppose you'd offer any hints for what's around the corner?"

The old man outright laughed at that. "You should know better than that, but you've done well enough so far that I have faith you'll carry on in kind."

"Well, then... I have another question."

The old man shrugged. "Ask. I'll answer if I can."

"How did Kiri and I end up on Earth? Based on everything I've been able to discern, I'm pretty sure the Necromancer invoked a disintegration effect on me during our conversation in Tel Mivar."

The jovial old grandfather vanished in the blink of an eye. "I put far too much work into you to allow a sack of canine chew toys to ruin it. *I* changed that disintegration effect into a transdimensional teleport and shunted it down the link to the Refugee World that Nesta forged during the Godswar." Now, the incorrigible rapscallion returned. "And I figured I might as well unblock your memories at the same time. It seems to have worked out rather well overall."

Once again, Gavin chuckled despite himself. "I'd say so, yes."

"Any other questions? My time here is drawing short."

Gavin lifted the forearm that bore the Void-scar. At the moment, it was barely larger than three pieces of thread. "This hasn't bothered me nearly as much since my sojourn to Earth as it did prior to that. I hardly ever notice it now."

"I didn't hear a question in there, lad." A mischievous grin curled the old man's lips... at least as much as Gavin could tell through the bushy, unkempt beard and mustache. "The energy or power that is elemental magic—what makes a wizard a wizard—is anathema to Lornithar's void blades. That magic was very weak here before you went to Earth, because the link Nesta forged had been slowly siphoning it off to Earth over these last six thousand years. When you forged a link back by creating that first transdimensional gateway, you created a mechanism through which it could equalize between this dimension and Earth's."

The old man turned and looked over his shoulder as if he heard something before he turned back to Gavin. "Well, lad... that's all the time I have for now. Enjoy this respite while you can. I'll do my best to see you get your just due, but despite what Ovir and his clergy and all those who came before them insist, I am *not* a god. I'm just... a caretaker."

Faster than a finger-snap, the old man vanished as if he was never there. There wasn't even a divot in the sand from the tip of his staff.

* * *

JENNIFER STOOD JUST a few feet from the portal connecting her grandparents' home to her father's estate in Mivar Province. An entire world that would accept her for who and what she was lay through the portal behind her.

In many ways, it wasn't all that different from Earth, especially the section she called home. But that wasn't to say differences didn't exist. The technology gap was huge for her, but she still couldn't believe how different—how much cleaner—the air smelled in Drakmoor... even downwind from a collection of stables. Everything seemed so pure there, so natural and unmodified.

But for all her adventures and explorations, she never stopped thinking of Earth—and her grandparents' place in particular—as home.

She still wasn't sure what the future held for her, but she knew—beyond any doubt now—that her future was on Earth. Oh, sure...

she'd visit Drakmoor from time to time, especially since her dad was there. But it wasn't home. She didn't see how it could ever be home, either.

Her sojourn to the other world had settled her mind, though. She now felt like she truly belonged on Earth, no matter what niche she carved for herself. And she had another friend to carve it with her.

She glanced to her right and saw Kellea staring up at the sky... which kind of surprised her. The sky wasn't *that* different here, was it?

She looked up and immediately realized what held her friend's attention. A plane crossed overhead, far above. She smiled.

"Yeah... this world will take a bit of acclimation, but I have it on good authority that we have better shoes."

* * *

GAVIN LEANED against the door frame to his wife's office and smiled as he watched her work. He had no idea at all what information the sheets of parchment she held contained, but he enjoyed the moment that let him appreciate her unawares and all by himself. Not for the first time, he wondered what he did to deserve having such a person in his life, and he made a silent promise to himself that he would never take her or their time together for granted.

Kiri turned to claim another piece of parchment from a stack on the corner of her desk, and seeing Gavin, she smiled. "How long have you been standing there?"

"Who knows?"

Gavin crossed the room and wrapped his arms around her when Kiri stood to meet him. He gave her a long, deep kiss that she returned in kind, and when they finally broke it, he leaned close and whispered, "I love you," in her ear.

He saw only love for him in her eyes when he righted himself from the lean, and she replied, "I love you, too, Gavin."

She took the opportunity of his silent regard to pull him over to the loveseat against a nearby wall and led him to sit with her. "So, tell me how you've spent your day so far. You were already gone when I woke."

"Oh... nothing really significant. I did a little sightseeing and ended up chatting with Valthon for a little bit."

Kiri's eyes shot wide. "Ended up chatting... how is chatting with Valthon 'nothing really significant?"

"Well, it's certainly not like it was my first time. He was the old guy who woke me up in the alley not too long before we met."

"Well... what did he have to say?"

Gavin shrugged. "Not much. He explained how we ended up on Earth instead of becoming a pile of powder when the Necromancer tried to disintegrate me, and he explained why the void-scar hasn't been bothering me like it used to."

"Oh, is that all?" Kiri tried to affect an air of nonchalance... but didn't quite manage it. "And just what does have in store for you next?"

"Didn't say. Honestly, he probably didn't want to spoil the surprise."

Kiri gave him an appraising expression, as if she was trying to determine whether he was trying to feed her a line. In the end, her demeanor softened. "Well, if he doesn't have anything immediate for you, what are your ideas for what's next?"

Gavin allowed himself a sly grin as he pulled her onto his lap. "Well... you know... your dad did mention something about grand-children the other day."

WHAT'S NEXT?

This concludes the Histories of Drakmoor, but Gavin and his friends will return.

* * *

Want to keep up-to-date on my projects and receive exclusive content?

Sign-up for my newsletter:
http://kfplink.com/g8i

ACKNOWLEDGMENTS

There's an old saying: it takes a village to raise a child. I don't know if that's true or not, but it certainly seems true where publishing a story is concerned. You would not be reading this were it not for contributions from several people.

Did you like the cover? The background image was created by Jakub Skop (https://www.behance.net/JakubSkop).

I want to thank T. F. Poist and David Emenheiser for their time and expertise in making this novel the best it could possibly be.

I'm sure there are many who will see this next paragraph and think, "Goodness, he's acknowledging his parents and grandparents *again*?" My greatest regret is that I cannot hand my grandfather, Bob Miller, a paperback copy of my novels. So, yes... the Acknowledgements page of *every* story I publish will have the paragraph that follows. Consider yourselves forewarned.

Without my grandparents, Bob & Janice Miller, I honestly don't know where I'd be today; my grandfather taught me to read and love reading, and my grandmother taught me to develop and exercise my imagination. This story (not to mention my life in general) certainly would not have happened without my parents, Vernon & Judy Kerns.

THE WORLDS OF ROBERT M. KERNS

For a complete and accurate listing of all publications, both currently available and forthcoming, please visit Knightsfall Press.

Knightsfall Press - Books

https://knightsfall.press/books

SO... WHO'S THE AUTHOR?

Robert M. Kerns (or Rob if you ever meet him in person) is a geek, and he claims that label proudly. Most of his geekiness revolves around Information Technology (IT), having over fifteen years in the industry; within IT, he especially prefers Servers and Networks, and he often makes the claim that his residence has a better data infrastructure than some businesses.

Beyond IT, Rob enjoys Science Fiction and Fantasy of (almost) all stripes. He is a voracious reader, with his favorite books too numerous to list.

Rob has been writing for over 20 years, published his first novel in 2018, and has no plans to stop any time soon.

Connect with Rob at robertmkerns.com.

f facebook.com/RobertMKerns
a amazon.com/author/robertmkerns
BB bookbub.com/authors/robert-m-kerns

www.ingramcontent.com/pod-product-compliance
Lightning Source LLC
Chambersburg PA
CBHW050015120726
47903CB00006B/1784